# THE UNEXPECTED: TALES OF LUST, LOVE & LONGING . . .

R. R. Ennis

Cover Design by Renee Barratt, TheCoverCounts.com

Published by G Publishing LLC

Library of Congress Control Number: 2017911062

ISBN: 978-0-9985990-3-8

Printed in the United States of America

# ACKNOWLEDGMENTS

My heartfelt thanks to my team of editors—Anthony Ambrogio, Kathryn J. Burgess, Kathleen Comiskey, and John Hook—who patiently read several drafts of each story in this book, offering many helpful suggestions, until I was able to present them as a collection of polished work. Many more thanks to the dedicated members of Metro Detroit Creative Writers—Larry Clos, Keith Gaston, and Cecelia Salamone—who critiqued my early writing and gave valuable advice, guiding me along the path toward becoming an engaging storyteller. I am deeply indebted to all of you.

"Sometimes people surprise us. People we believe we know."

— Joyce Carol Oates, *The Falls*

# TABLE OF CONTENTS

# FAIRWAY TO LOVE

On a sunny spring day, my husband, Calvin, literally dances through the living-room doorway, exclaiming, "You won't believe what I did this morning!"

I put down the paperback novel I have been reading next to me on the sofa. Quickly, I position my left thigh in such a way that it hides the book cover of a half-naked man embracing a woman whose big boobs are about to spill out of her low-cut evening dress. Calvin often reprimands me when he finds me with what he calls a "trashy" book.

Would he rather I become self-absorbed in self-help books instead? Hasn't he complained countless times that, whenever he picks up his buddy Ted for a golf tournament, Ted's wife answers the door with her face buried in her iPad, reading some e-book about how to conquer your greatest fears or how to build self-confidence by becoming your own biggest fan? Always early for an event, Calvin grumbles that while he's waiting in the living room for Ted to finish getting ready, Angela doesn't even bother to put away her tablet and strike up a polite conversation. *He* has to initiate the talking by asking questions about what she's reading. After she abruptly responds with some nonsense about how she's following the latest "scholarly" opinion for maximizing her potential, she goes right back to reading, without even asking if he wants a glass of water or the TV turned on so he can catch the news. My romance books are fiction, a pleasant escape from the dull routines of the real world, not intended to be taken seriously. These novels don't prevent me from paying attention to Calvin: I can set them aside at any moment.

Nevertheless, my husband has warned: "I know reading's your hobby, Marie, but I'm worried you'll end up like Angela. I like that, even after all these years together, we can still sit down at the dinner table and have things to talk about during our meal, or relax afterward in the living room and just say what's on our minds. Ted doesn't have that flexibility with Angela. Her iPad has turned their relationship into a one-sided affair, rendering her incapable of talking about anything other than what's in her books."

Yes, it's true that, despite all these years together, we haven't lost the art of conversation. Like a form of regenerating fuel, our family members supply us with continual topics for discussion. Examples: our love-struck son and his demanding girlfriend; my ailing parents; Calvin's lottery-winning, spendthrift sister.

Insert a deep sigh here.

Forgive me for sounding trite, but our marriage has become too much about *talking* and not enough about *action*. In other words, there hasn't been much bedroom activity in quite some time. I may be in my early fifties and perhaps not as captivating as I was twenty-one years ago, when we got married, yet I'm still in good shape and receive compliments from time to time about my lovely blue eyes and about the way my dark-blonde bobbed hair attractively frames my heart-shaped face. When I go for a neighborhood walk or jog in the summer, my long legs (noticeable in my tight nylon shorts) and firm breasts (jutting out from a clinging tank top) still have power to turn a few older male heads. For that reason, I'm looking forward to the start of summer, just a few weeks from now. The promise of consistently warmer weather means the return of my outdoor exercise routine— and, hopefully, my comeback as an object of desire for at least one male neighbor's lustful gaze!

Clearly, you can see I'm frustrated. Calvin's idea of an exciting Friday night is taking me out to a coffee shop and trying out their latest espresso. Despite the caffeine jolt, he wants to go to bed as soon as we get home—to *sleep*. I don't understand why he hasn't initiated love-making in so long, why he foils my efforts to seduce him. Whenever I ask him what the problem is, he makes excuses, claiming he's stressed out from work or feels he has a cold coming on.

What irks the most is when he complains about *money*. A real turn-off for me. Case in point: Two weeks ago, I wore a new lace baby-doll to bed, bought when Victoria's Secret ran an online special. The nightie accentuated my cleavage and curves, in my opinion, in all the right spots. As I showed it off, he rolled his eyes, groaning, "Honey, I thought we agreed: no unnecessary purchases for a while." Pissed off— too humiliated to argue—I gave him a nasty look, then slid over to the edge of our king-size bed, without even replying to his "Good night."  But if he had uttered another word, I would've reminded him gruffly that I shut my trap when he went out and got a new golf shirt and putting iron, neither listed on our spreadsheet of consensual monthly expenses.

My good friend Elaine (from whom I borrow the novels) says his lack of interest sounds like he's seeing another woman. I'd agree if I could figure out how he would manage an affair. Except for his twice-a-week golf outings, he stays home after work, preferring to spend his free time using the treadmill and elliptical machines in the basement, attempting (without success) to reduce the spare tire around his stomach. The only other woman he sees often is his rotund, white-haired secretary at the insurance company. With her wrinkled-as-a-bulldog's face and assortment of plaid caftans, she's not much competition. Unless, he's lying about his golf—

I lose my train of thought as Calvin, now standing before me, snaps his fingers to get my attention. "Earth to Marie," he says with a serious face. "Are you there? Did you hear what I said?"

Leaning forward, I move over a little to reposition my backside on the microfiber cushion so that I'm sitting on (and completely hiding) the book. "Where've you been?" I ask with raised eyebrows, hoping to show some natural concern about him. "When you left this morning, you said something about running some errands and that you'd be back in an hour or so." My eyes dart to the multicolored clock adorning our plain beige walls. "But you've been gone for over three hours," I add with a slight frown, though I really haven't minded. I was able to get through more than half my book today.

Sitting down beside me, Calvin smiles and pats my knee. Because I'm wearing thick jeans, it feels as though he's drumming my knee with a straw. I gaze at his face, my puckered forehead indicating my curiosity: why is there a certain sparkle in his brown eyes—and warmth radiating from his unshaven face? I haven't seen him glowing like this in quite a while: not since our son got accepted two years ago by the University of Michigan in Ann Arbor, where Matt now lives and attends school.

"I was in our old neighborhood," he finally explains, with a slow, almost cautious smile. "In fact, I did a walk-through of our old house."

"You what?" I say in surprise, my eyebrows almost reaching up to my hairline. "You were out in Ferndale this morning! Why did you drive all the way out there?"

"Honey, Ferndale is only about thirty minutes from Shelby. You act as though I went to the other side of the state." Staring straight ahead at the wall, he lets out several nervous laughs.

Because his gaze stays fixed on the plain wall, I also stare straight ahead, wondering what he can possibly be seeing. As with the den and family room, there's little in here to be of much interest to anyone. Our house may be spacious and worth about a quarter of a million dollars, but we've done little decorating. Our furnishings are quite sparse. The only adornments on any of the walls are a collection of framed family photos hanging in the upstairs hallway. For years, we've lived modestly and carefully, so that we can afford to live in this affluent subdivision while stashing away a lot of money for Matt's college expenses.

"Calvin? What are you looking at? Is there some crack in the wall?"

He turns toward me, making partial eye contact. "Sorry. I was thinking about Ferndale—the memories." Though my husband is almost bald, keeping what he has on the sides and back of his head cut very short, he combs his hair with his fingers in a meticulous way, as if he has a lot to work with. Calvin only does this when he's withholding details, not telling me the full story.

"So how did you end up there? When you left this morning, you said you were going to the drug store and then to Target—"

Calvin interrupts me. "For some reason today, I felt like going on a drive. I was in a sentimental mood and wanted to check out the old neighborhood. . . ."

This time, I pat Calvin's knee, enjoying the softness of his cotton chino pants. "What brought this on?"

"Let me finish." Pausing briefly, my husband sighs with annoyance. "As I said, I decided to go on drive and check out our old homestead." He places his hand on mine and rubs it gently. "When I approached Gardendale, I couldn't believe my luck:  on the corner was an OPEN HOUSE sign with our former address listed under it. Of course I wanted to check it out. So I turned onto our old street, drove up about a block, and pulled up in the widened driveway. And there it was—the charming little bungalow we once owned!"

Naturally a little curious, I ask, "Is the siding still gray with white trim?"

He shakes his head, his eyes lit with zeal. "Actually, it's now a pleasant yellow, like the color of creamy butter, with reddish-brown shutters, roof, and trim. Once inside, I was amazed by all the wonderful updates. Both the kitchen and bathroom have been remodeled. I love the deep Jacuzzi tub, and also the dishwasher with the hidden controls and the built-in microwave above the flat-top stove. You wouldn't believe it's the same place. I could elaborate even more about the improvements, but I'd rather have you see it for yourself."

Even though I already know the answer, I ask, "What exactly are you suggesting?"

"Let's take a ride this afternoon and see our former abode. Afterwards, we can walk around downtown Ferndale and browse in some of the stores. We can have an early dinner at one of the restaurants there. How about it? Why stay indoors reading a book when you can be out doing something?"

I suppress a laugh. So he knows I've been reading. From under my behind, I pull out the book. There's no reason to hide it now.

"Very well," I decide to say. "Just give me a few minutes to freshen up before we go." I'm going along with this plan because I can tell Calvin is up to something—I'm not quite sure what this *something* is. I have my suspicions, though.

\* \* \*

Dressed casually, we set out for Ferndale shortly before two-thirty o'clock, planning to view the house at three and then grab an early dinner somewhere afterward, thus missing any crowds. We encounter an accident and traffic jam on I-75, so almost an hour passes before we finally arrive. After we drive through the small yet bustling downtown area, we travel along several residential streets. My eyes widen in delight as we take in the surroundings. Although many of the homes here were built in the 1930s and '40s, they do not show their age. From the outside, most of them appear beautifully maintained with perennial gardens and newer siding and windows.

After making a few turns, we are now riding along the street where we once lived. Despite the passing of so many years, I can recall many of our former neighbors. There was friendly Brad, a Ferndale Schools custodian, and happy-go-lucky Tabby, his wife, who lived in the blue bungalow (not the original color) with the addition in the back. A few doors down from them lived an elderly couple (I'd be shocked if they're still with us) in the plain white ranch with the gigantic maple tree in the backyard. The poor tree has seen better days: only clusters of greenish-brown leaves remain on its thick branches. I shudder to think how much it would cost to have a tree service cut that thing down.

Thus distracted, I nearly fail to notice Calvin pulling into our old driveway. But, once he says, "Here we are," the house suddenly jumps at me like a picture out of a pop-up book. A wide smile spreads across my face. I have to admit my husband is right; the place *does* look attractive. Whoever owns it did a great job in selecting the perfect yellow-and-brown color scheme. What I admire the best are the symmetrical healthy beds of rosebushes and hostas on either side of the narrow cement porch. The bungalow has definite curb appeal.

Despite the house's mesmerizing effect, I approach the porch slowly, as if just noticing a CAUTION sign posted by the steps. I'm not sure if I'm ready to relive the past—or to confront the future. During the drive, I couldn't bring myself to ask Calvin the *real* reason he insisted on coming here, not caring to hear about my dirty mind. I convinced myself that my misgivings about my husband were just the result of an active imagination. But now, with butterflies filling my stomach, I'm unable to dismiss my concerns. Can it be? Is my former rival still next door? My gaze remains focused on the empty living room visible through the screen door. I simply don't have the guts to turn my head to the left and see whether anything next door will confirm my fears.

Before entering, I signal with a nod for Calvin to knock at the vinyl screen door and call out: "Hello?" Even though it's Open House, I feel awkward about walking right in.

Wearing a navy-blue pants suit, a woman with blonde hair suddenly appears in the living room. "Hello there. Come on in," she says, her voice a flawless pitch of enthusiasm. Her thick hair comes almost to her shoulder and is curled under in a perfect pageboy. There's something about her hair that seems artificial—is she wearing a wig? Conscious of how our hair styles are similar, I find myself running my fingers through my bangs, trying to make mine look more natural and tousled, not sewn onto a forehead like hers.

In the middle of the room, she hands my husband her business card, saying with a toothy smile: "Glad you brought your wife for another look. It's Calvin, right?" He nods and tells her my name. Daintily shaking my hand, she introduces herself: "Nice to meet you, Marie. I'm Christine." She then hands me a sheet of paper describing the home's many features, such as hardwood floors throughout, central air conditioning, and a stamped concrete patio. She adds, motioning with the animation of a game show host, "This is a wonderful *three*-bedroom bungalow. Let me give you a tour, Marie. The owners have done all kinds of improvements."

I hold up a hand. "No, thanks. We'll be all right." To my knowledge, Calvin has not divulged to Christine that this was once our home, and I don't plan to either. She seems so nice and friendly, and hungry for a sale, that I'd hate to break it to her that we're only here to check out the scenery, not hunt for a house.

"If you have any questions, please ask," she says, stepping off toward the corner of the room to discreetly view something on her cell phone.

As we meander around, Calvin remarks how being here evokes certain memories from the past. We talk about that day in late February, twenty years ago, when I found out I was pregnant. Taking the next several days off from work, my husband painted all the rooms at a feverish pace, changing the color from dingy pale green to bright white.

Rubbing his lower back as we stand in the spare bedroom downstairs, which became Matt's room, my husband says, "It's amazing I was able to do all that painting—the ceilings, the walls, the trim—in less than week. Just thinking about it sends pains down my spine." He falls silent for a moment. "Now it would take me a good month or two to get all that done."

I nod thoughtfully, reflecting on our early struggles. During our first year on Gardendale, Calvin kept promising to paint the interior. As with making love to me these days, he was full of excuses as to why he kept procrastinating. I was about to give up on him and start the project myself. But once I told him I was expecting, he wouldn't let me do anything strenuous, including painting. He also went back to being as attentive as he'd been when we were dating, bringing home carry-out food so I wouldn't have to cook over a hot stove, preparing my bubble baths, doing most of the housework.

Though I never revealed my feelings, I was most pleased about another change my pregnancy brought about: sensitive to my mood swings, he appeared to stop lusting after the woman next door, no longer watching her come and go with leering eyes or striking up unnecessary conversations whenever they happened to be outside at the same time doing yard work. He limited his interactions with S_____ to polite hellos. (I can't bring myself to say her name. Perhaps if I don't say it, my worries will turn out to be trivial.)

Much to my happiness, shortly after Matt's first birthday, Calvin suggested we move into "something bigger." And we did just that. First, about five miles north into the all-brick spacious Royal Oak ranch the following spring. Then, when Matt entered kindergarten, into what I jokingly call our "sprawling estate," the four-bedroom Shelby colonial with a massive backyard, believing we were providing our son with better schools and education in a quiet, safe community.

Looking back, I question if relocating to Shelby was the best decision. Matt, shy and inclined to being a loner, didn't come out of his shell until he was halfway through high school, when he joined the Video Gaming Club and was elected Treasurer. Prior to that, his father and I spent a lot of effort and money enrolling him in various snobbish social clubs, sports team, and summer camps, hoping to turn him into our vision of a "well-adjusted" kid, but meeting with constant frustration when he failed to show any interest in the local activities.

My life in Shelby hasn't been the most pleasant, either. Buying that colonial ultimately denied Calvin and me many opportunities. Unlike our neighbors, we cannot boast of lavish tropical island vacations, display clothes from shopping trips to the upscale Somerset Mall, or recommend any entrées at pricey restaurants. If we'd stayed in Royal Oak, weekly fine dining and monthly jaunts to Somerset could've been part of our lives. And perhaps if we hadn't left Ferndale, where the house payment was even lower, we might've afforded those exciting romantic getaways to exotic places; and Calvin's enchantment over S_____ would've faded like the fragrance of a wilting rose.

*Would've . . . Should've . . . Could've. . . .* Regrets consume me until we enter the small sunlit eating area at one end of the galley-style kitchen. Was I kidding myself or what? Standing in front of the side window, I catch sight of S_____ in her backyard. The butterflies in my stomach reappear, whirling around as if they want to burst free. Feeling dizzy, I grip either end of the window sill to steady myself. I'm so shocked by what I see—despite halfway expecting it! I just didn't expect it to this extent. So this is why we're really here? Did he think I would've forgotten her? Is Calvin really such a thoughtless asshole? What a son of a bitch!

Dazed and lightheaded, I don't sense Calvin guiding me outside until we're back on the porch. With our arms linked, we head back to car, both quiet; then, on the sidewalk, Calvin stops me and, pulling away, drops a bombshell. Gazing back at the house, he says, matter-of-factly, "You know, I've been thinking . . . the house we have in Shelby is getting too big for us now that Matt's gone. In fact, he spent little time with us last summer—too busy hanging out with either his gaming buddy or his girlfriend. We've talked a few times about selling the colonial and downsizing to a condo, but we're not quite ready for that. We both enjoy having a yard and gardening in the summer—only it'd be nice to have less to take care of. I bet this sounds crazy, but maybe we should buy this place. The street is as quaint and tidy as it was many years ago. For us now, our old abode might be just the ticket: it has all the room we really need."

By this time, my dizziness has passed; my mind, though, is taking longer to process everything. "Calvin, are you out of your mind?" I motion toward the house. "How can you say something so ridiculous?"—I pause, trying to meet his gaze.

It is wasted effort because his eyes keep shifting between our old place and S_____'s. My head now clear, I add, "Let's get to the *real* reason why you want to move back here."

Calvin swallows hard and begins to rake his fingers through his hair. "What—what do you mean?" he stammers as I point to the house next door.

"When we were in the kitchen, I saw you-know-who still living next door," I explain, with my hands posed defensively on my hips. "From the side window, I saw her putting golf balls in the backyard."

He shakes his head, saying nothing.

His silence sparks my exasperation. I groan: "Your interest in returning here must have to do with her. Granted, I didn't see her that closely—but, from what I observed, she looks years younger than me. Not even a couple of lines, fine or otherwise, across her milky forehead. Just as tall, slender, and big-breasted as ever! And that red hair of hers—still flowing down her back in fiery waves. Too much competition."

Both of us become silent. Calvin stares down at the ground. I fold my arms protectively across my chest—my lips pursed pensively together, eyes riveted on the house next door, oddly wanting to take another look at S_____, while past images of her swirl about in my mixture of memories.

A more detailed explanation for our *trip down memory lane* today suddenly jumps out, hitting me square in the face like a spring-loaded boxing glove. I gather how it all unfolded. During our last summer in Ferndale, S_____ started dating this bearded Greek guy, an avid golfer. Many times, from the kitchen window, I watched them leave S_____'s house in his jeep with two sets of golf clubs in the back. That relationship ended, though her interest in golf remains.

Through the years, she has played at many southeastern Michigan courses, including the one at Stony Creek close to Shelby. It is quite possible that she and Calvin could have run into each other last spring on the fairway. At the end of the game, Calvin could've invited her to take a look at his fairly new Dodge Durango (a discounted lease, not purchased), quite a step up from those days on Gardendale when he drove around in a rusting Chevy Cavalier. As they sat together on the smooth leather seats, Calvin paid little attention to S_____'s chatter about some superficial topic, too captivated by her loveliness. Becoming emboldened, he rested his hand on hers. His heartbeat and breathing accelerated, so excited to be touching, finally, the true keeper of his heart. She smiled, then slowly licked her luscious lips, encouraging him to make another move. Interlocking his fingers with hers, he kissed her on the cheek or gently on the chin, not wanting to seem too forward and perhaps scare her away. His worry proved groundless, as she reciprocated with a very passionate smooch full on his lips. Acting on impulse, he brought his hands up to her breasts; her soft moans beckoned his fingertips to massage them. Obliging, he caressed her supple bosom. Satisfying her needs naturally intensified his own. To show her that, he tore one of his hands from her chest, freeing it to guide her palm down to his lap, so she could feel the bulging mass between his legs . . .

Trying to break the silence, my husband says, "Oh, Marie, honey, you're being absurd . . ."

But I don't respond. I'm still fixated on the house next door, and my mind hasn't finished imagining the sequence of events that brought me back to Ferndale. Pondering what developed after Calvin and S_____'s initial erotic grope fest, I come up with what seems most logical. Not too far from the golf course, on a highway road well-traveled by truckers, is a rent-by-the-hour motel, where Calvin proposed they could explore the chemistry between them in a more private setting. In a musty room, under a chintzy bedspread, their bodies at last intertwined . . . and they discovered there was enough chemistry to burn, reaching multiple climaxes before check-out time. So began their tawdry affair. And during a recent motel assignation, S_____ informed him that our old house was up for sale. This bulletin turned larger wheels of deception in Calvin's mind. If his wife was living in a cheaper place and his mistress right next door,  then he could afford and arrange more opportunities for "golf" outings. How cozy and convenient for him—and her.

At this point, I bet you're ready to say: "Enough, Marie. Stop getting carried away by your imagination." While I pride myself on having a fairly accurate intuition, I will confess something: if this scenario of my husband's infidelity were expanded with juicier scenes into novel, I would be tempted to read it. Aptly titled, *Fairway to Love*.

I let out what sounds like a snort of bewilderment, not so much directed at my husband, but more at my own conflicting morals. On the one hand, it angers me to imagine him being intimate with another woman; yet it's crazy how, on the other hand, some of my favorite stories contain graphic details of adulterous trysts. The more risks the characters take to carry on with their sleazy rendezvous, the faster I devour the book's pages.

Calvin clears his throat repeatedly. My gaze returns to him. Trying to mollify me (or mask his deceit), Calvin folds his hand in front of his belly, saying softly, calmly, "Marie, honey . . . I had no idea she's still next door." He narrows his eyes, shakes his head again. "To be honest, I haven't thought about her in years. I could care less about her."

His lined face expresses worry, genuine concern that makes me pause. Am *I* really the absurd one? Is my jealousy misguided? Maybe I have *overreacted*. If only Calvin would show me more attention, behave like a lover, then I wouldn't feel deprived, in need of answers.

Since the sun now shines intensely above S_____'s roof, I turn my head and shield my eyes, whose direction wanders down the tree-lined street. Only a few blocks ahead, across Eight Mile Road, is the city of Detroit. Although the Detroit homes in that area look similar to Ferndale's, the businesses do not. The Eight Mile side of Detroit might have a solution to our problem. If Calvin can suggest something "spontaneous" and expect me to go along with it, why can't I do the same?

One our way home, after convincing my husband to take a different route to the expressway, I will sweet talk him into stopping at a certain Detroit bookstore—Adult Delights— that houses all kinds of DVDs, magazines, and books designed to help couples "delight in new sensual experiences"—or so their *Metro Times* ad claims. The plan: he and I will each pick out a video or magazine or book illustrating ways to improve love-making. ("Think of it, Calvin, as gathering the first material for our own special adult education/enrichment class," I will say, lightly stroking his hand and forearm, to appeal to his practical side and also put him at ease about doing something risqué.) My heartbeat quickens with excitement as I anticipate the new under-the-sheets techniques we will test out tonight. Enjoying the experimentation, Calvin will forget all about S_____ and his off-the-wall proposal.

But, within seconds, the internal motor driving my enthusiasm starts losing power. Surfacing doubts are riddling that motor with holes, draining the oil. Because of Calvin's conservative upbringing and aversion to "trashy" books—not to mention his usual penny-pinching when it comes to anything I want—porn or other visual stimulants (that Victoria's Secret negligee) probably won't do the trick. Most likely, they will increase our estrangement in the sex department.

Then comes another reality check—which rings with even greater truth. No denying that my sexual experiences with Calvin, or the couple of guys before, have never equaled the titillating, and often addictive, scenes of hot passion in romance novels—scenes in which the male characters are so broad-shouldered and muscular and well-... (You get my drift—no need for me to get explicit again.) Even if my husband went back to being an assertive lover, I question if I could be truly satisfied. He could never come up to the ideal I've created in my imagination.

Annoyingly, Calvin snaps his fingers close to my face. "Marie, what are you seeing over there? What are you thinking? Care to share?"

I hesitate to respond, still staring off at the cement street, uncertain about the best direction to take. . . for myself . . . my marriage.  I bite my lower lip, speculating about an appropriate resolution for *Fairway to Love*. The notion of *honesty is the best policy* seemed to resolve the conflicts in the folktales I enjoyed as a child; however, that philosophy would hinder the plots of the books I relish now, bringing the storylines to boring conclusions.

With those facts in mind, I quickly arrive at an answer. My self-searching has triggered a spare generator somewhere inside me, lifting my emotions out of the doldrums and sparking interest in Calvin's idea. Facing him, I say with a changed tune, "You're right, dear. I don't know why I said what I did. I suppose when I see another woman around my age with a better figure, I get a little jealous." With a reassuring smile, I take hold of his hand. "And you have a point about the house: it could suit us. Let's go back inside and talk to the realtor—find out what's an acceptable offer."

"Great!"

Letting go of him, I lead the way as we retrace our steps to the front door. What's driving me to act this way has only partly to do with suspicions about him and the auburn-haired siren Selena. The major motivation: more free time for reading. When one story or chapter ends, another awaits to begin.

# VICTORY HOUSE

Despite the cool wind whipping against the back of his thin sweater, Roger paused at the start of the front walk to Victory House, reluctant to take another step. Though it now boasted an uplifting name, the facility's past could make one's heart sink in sadness. Built in the style of a square prison, with narrow slits for windows overlooking a desolate dirt road, the two-story brick building had previously served as a poorhouse and institution for the mentally ill in the 1930s through the '50s, and then as a state school for emotionally handicapped children until the mid-'70s, when public outcry over cases of abuse had forced its closure. It lay vacant for years before a nonprofit organization reopened the place in the late '80s as a long-term treatment center for alcoholics and drug addicts.

It wasn't the building's ugly appearance or depressing history that kept Roger from ringing the doorbell—but, rather, his own anxiety. Putting his cold hands in his pants pockets, he wondered what would be awaiting him inside: a foul-mouthed Ashley with wild frizzy chestnut hair and disheveled clothes, or a calm and well-groomed Ashley whose soft smile and gentle touch would put him at ease and offer hope of reconciliation. Or maybe, as a result of the intensive counseling and support, his wife would behave in a way that fit neither scenario, and how would he respond? The unknown had always intimidated him.

. . .Well, it used to, anyway. His recent struggles had forced him to deal with an uncertain future time and time again. During the five months of marital separation, he had lost a great deal—his job reporting for a major newspaper, the large two-bedroom apartment he had called home for the past fifteen years, and most of his collection of French antique marble clocks and rare Swiss pocket watches—and yet, unlike Ashley, he hadn't collapsed and ended up in a "special" place. When necessary, he could somehow summon courage from somewhere—barging, with portfolio in hand, into one editor-in-chief's office after another until he landed a new job, negotiating an affordable rent with the gruff landlord of a one-bedroom flat close to work, and demanding more money from the auctioneer of his precious antiques.

What was he so worried about, then? Since he possessed more confidence, he should have little trouble facing Ashley, even in one of her more hostile moods, and calmly tell her about the changes in his life . . . their lives. Although he was making less money at a small-circulation paper, he could still afford to keep a roof over their heads and give her the opportunity to pursue her singing career. And if she believed he was failure because they'd be living in less lavish circumstances, then so be it. He had endured her disappointment many times in the past. And if she threatened divorce, he would . . . maybe agree to it. He wouldn't want to hold her back.

Despite the inward pep talk, he moved very slowly along the shrub-lined path, as if heading down a very long gangplank, stalling the inevitable. Old insecurities, going back to when they first met, were suddenly resurfacing. On assignment, he had interviewed Ashley and her soft rock group, Satin & Suede, after a performance. (True to their name, the band members wore outfits of satin and suede.) Taken with Ashley's sweet voice, pretty face, and shapely body, he had worked up the nerve to ask her out, though he was considerably older, more than a decade, than she was. (And he looked it, too—hair with far more salt than pepper, deep furrows across his forehead like ruts in a road, sunken eyes with dark circles underneath.) Yet she had accepted and after a few more dates, his infatuation quickly had transformed into love. She had made him feel happy, complete, desired, *loved* . . . until she revealed, shortly after their wedding, that she only had married him in the hope that he'd be able to provide more media coverage for the band.

The disclosure had come one evening during a heated argument about money. Using his credit card, Ashley had charged a bunch of new clothes. He had agreed to her getting a couple of outfits, but *not* an entire new wardrobe. Waving the bill in her face, he had cried, "You must think I'm made of money." Holding a vodka tonic in one hand, she had grabbed the statement with the other, crumpling it and fuming, "And here I thought marrying a fucking reporter would further my career. What a mistake! I should've realized you guys make shit for cash." Enraged, he had grabbed her wrist quite forcefully. In her struggle to break free, her drink had flown across the living room, and they had fallen down together, with him landing on top. With her long hair splayed across the carpet, she had cried into his shoulder. Worried she had been in pain, he had tried getting off her—but she had tightened her grip on his shoulders, refusing to let him move away. Seemingly remorseful, she had then initiated a night of intense lovemaking. And thereby introducing a pattern continuing throughout their two-year marriage: fierce quarreling followed by hot sex.

Shameful as it was for Roger to admit it, he had found himself provoking her whenever he felt the need for a sexual release. Frowning, he shook his head, thinking, *What a deplorable person I can be!* He promised himself that if he and Ashley indeed reconciled, he would be a better husband and not do that anymore.

His hands now warm, he took them out of his pockets and, pausing, gazed up at the early May afternoon sky. He noticed how bright and clear it had suddenly become. *A sign of better things to come*, his grandmother would've claimed.

But Roger didn't believe in such farfetched connections between the working of the weather and foretelling the future. Explanations for the weather belonged in the scientific realm, not the spiritual or mystical.

When he finally reached the steps of the sinking brick stoop, the great metal door opened and out stepped an elderly man holding a dust rag. "Good afternoon," the man said. "Can I help you with something?" His creased brow seemed to express a mixture of caution and concern. Most likely, the man was a custodian and, from one of the windows, had observed Roger drag his feet toward the building.

To show the man nothing was wrong, Roger bounded up the steps two at a time. Facing the bearded man with a wave and smile, he said, "Hi, I'm Roger Grahame. I have a meeting with the Director—Mrs. Hubbert." To cue the man to stop blocking the door, he added, "Please excuse me."

Moving aside, the man said, "Sure thing." He pointed behind his shoulder. "Go in and head straight down the main hall. Her office is at the end."

Roger gave a nod of thanks. Not wanting to appear timid to anyone else, he didn't linger in the vestibule or study the black-and-white photos on the oak-paneled walls; he went without delay to the wooden door with the sign OFFICE on it. He knocked gently at first. When no one responded, he knocked a little louder. Finding it difficult to keep his anxiety in check, he felt himself start to perspire under the arms of his beige sweater. "Yes? Come in!" called the young-sounding female voice from the other side.

Opening the door, he was surprised to find the voice belonged to a heavily wrinkled receptionist whose whitish-blonde hair looked like a helmet of cotton candy, very puffy and feathery. She sat behind an oak desk in the middle of the small carpeted room. Metal filing cabinets lined the wall to the right; a few wooden chairs were set to the left.

Roger swallowed hard to clear his throat, to calm his nerves. "Good afternoon. I have a four-o'clock appointment with Mrs. Hubbert. Is she in?"

Setting her pen down on a notepad, the secretary asked, "Are you Mr. Grahame?"

He nodded. "Yes, Roger Grahame."

The woman's slight smile exposed crooked front teeth. "She's expecting you. I will let her know you're here." She picked up the phone, pressed a button on it, and then said, "Hello, Mrs. Hubbert. I have Mr. Grahame in the office."

Almost as soon as she hung up, the door behind the receptionist's desk opened. In the doorway appeared a slender woman wearing a low-cut blue dress with a hemline halfway up her thighs. Her mousy brown hair was fashioned into a French twist. Taken aback, Roger pressed his lips tightly together and suppressed a frown. This woman seemed ready for the Friday happy hour—not exactly an appropriate look for the head of a substance abuse program—but he decided to wait until they had their private chat before passing any judgments on her character.

"Good afternoon, Mr. Grahame," Mrs. Hubbert said in a silvery voice. "Please come in and have a seat." In the next room, the Director pointed to the coffee pot on a glass table, inquiring, "Coffee?"  Roger shook his head. "No thanks." She closed the office door.

While she poured herself a cup, he sat down on a padded chair in front of her desk, still feeling nervous. He glanced around, taking a brief survey of creamy yellow walls, potted plants on decorative stands, and a narrow bookshelf crammed with books. On top of the bookcase was a gilt-framed document—a certificate or award of some kind? Squinting, he tried to make out what it said. Other than the large fancy letters at the top—CERTIFICATE Of EXCELLENCE (and right below that) Awarded to Michelle

*Hubbert*—he couldn't read the rest of the words on it. Giving up, he focused back on Mrs. Hubbert, who was now sipping coffee at her desk and leafing through a file.

As she looked up, he asked, "How is Ashley?"

Mrs. Hubbert flashed a wide smile. "She's doing quite well. She's the star of our new program."

"Star of a new program?"

Setting down her coffee cup, the Director returned her gaze to the file. With her finger, she traced a line of writing on a sheet of paper, saying, "Just reading the most recent notes by the social worker."   Looking up again, she explained, "Yes, our work-therapy program. During the day, Ashley works on a farm in the area, supervised by her sponsor, and then attends support meetings in the evening. According to the progress logs, she is doing quite well— hasn't mentioned craving a drink in several months."

Roger's bushy eyebrows rose almost to his hairline. "Ashley didn't mention anything about working on a farm in her recent letter."

"I wasn't aware of any letter. We carefully monitor all communication sent from—" Mrs. Hubbert broke off, drumming her pretty red nails anxiously against the edge of the desk.

"You mean she didn't discuss asking me to visit with you or her therapists?"

"She hasn't said anything to me—nor her therapist, to my knowledge." As if falling into sudden contemplation, Mrs. Hubbert pressed her lips tightly together for a moment. "In fact, I didn't even know she *could* get ahold of you. Your number has been disconnected, and our letters to you were never answered."

He hunched his shoulders and stared down at his jeans, feeling ashamed. "I didn't mean to be an absent husband, not visiting and attending her meetings, but I've been going through my own hell. I didn't want my problems to compromise her adjustment or treatment in any way."

The Director folded her hands atop the desk. "I'm not here to judge—"

Looking up, Roger broke in again: "You see, shortly after Ashley's admission, I was laid off. When you're facing the harsh possibility of living on the streets, your focus has to be on finding employment. I knew my wife would be properly cared for at Victory House. Ashley must be content here, or she would've been writing complaint-filled letters all along. Last week's letter was the first I've heard a peep of her in all this time."

In a calm, concerned voice, the Director inquired: "And how are things for you now?"

"After enduring months of crushing disappointments, I'm finally working again—but still struggling." To emphasize his tribulations, he let out a prolonged sigh. "That's why I wanted to meet with you—before I see Ashley. Her letter was real brief, just asking how I was and stating we needed to talk . . . and I'm wondering . . . now that I'm only making entry-level wages and will be relocating to a much smaller place. . ." Realizing his words sounded like rambling, he paused to condense his thoughts. "What I'm trying to find out is when she might be released and how she feels about living with me again. There was a lot of bitterness between us before we separated, and I wonder if we could ever be happy together again, even if she's 'cured' of her alcoholism. Has Ashley spoken about her future plans to you or her therapist? What does she want to do with her life?"

The woman gazed at him with a forced smile, clasping her hands tighter, conveying that his concerns put her on edge. "Ashley is ready to be released from our facility. She has the option of continuing to work on the farm and moving in with the farmer's family. When Ashley and I talked about it last week—since you've been out of the picture—we didn't discuss her feelings about you or the marriage. The focus was more on the immediate issue of where she could go after here." Mrs. Hubbert straightened her back against the padded-leather chair. "As Director, I never terminate my residents from the program without offering them a way to be supported on the outside again. The Dunkirks have helped several of my other former residents and would ensure that Ashley continued to attend weekly AA meetings—the key to remaining sober—after she left Victory House."

"If you believe it's best for Ashley to stay in the area . . . well, then, I'll . . . I'll agree to it." Hearing the hesitation in his own voice, he realized he really missed his wife. Too easily, he had let the bad overshadow all the *good*: times when they had cuddled in front of the TV after an early dinner, or had taken turns massaging each other after an early morning workout. He had especially relished those evenings when Satin & Suede was between gigs and Ashley stayed home in the evening. Singing along to the living-room stereo music, she amazed him with her ability to imitate her favorite female pop stars' vocal styles. Damn him for being so self-absorbed! Why couldn't he have at least sent her a card now and then, to say she was in his thoughts? He had a lot of making up to do.

The Director opened her hands, shrugged her shoulders. "I wish it was all as simple as agreeing to this or that. But I can only give post-treatment recommendations for my clients. Ultimately, what happens after they leave here is up to them. As far as I know, Ashley has not made a final decision. Obviously, you two have a lot to talk about. I didn't inform Ashley that you were coming today—didn't want to disappoint her in case you didn't appear. She should be back from the farm by now. Shall I have my secretary get her? There's a patio in the back where you and your wife can speak privately."

Mrs. Hubbert reached for the phone, but Roger held up his index finger. "Before you do that," he sighed, "we should have our own chat about the unpaid bills. I intend to take responsibility for them. I'd like to arrange a payment plan . . . if possible." Any day now, he was expecting a reissued (and much fatter) check from the guy who had liquidated his clocks and watches. Though the money would put a substantial dent in Ashley's treatment costs, he also had to use it to start satisfying the credit card company whose overdue account notices had been filling up his mailbox. In his mind, it would be best to negotiate with both Victory House and MasterCard instead of neglecting one in favor of the other.

Mrs. Hubbert began tapping her nails again on the desk. "Most of the balance has been taken care of—thanks to donations and the farm work—so no need to worry. It sounds like you've had enough of your own problems to deal with," she added in a rushed voice.

Fidgeting in the chair, he questioned, "Seriously? Most of it taken care of . . . ?" as if he needed what he had heard to be reaffirmed.

"Yes," she replied, looking toward the door.

At the same moment, the secretary came into the room. Mrs. Hubbert said to Roger, "Please excuse me." At the door, the secretary whispered something into the woman's ear. Turning briefly toward Roger, the Director said, "I'll be back in a few moments. Something I have to deal with real quick. I hope you won't mind." Roger nodded that it was fine.

As he stood up to stretch, his gaze shifted from the door left slightly ajar to the manila folder atop the desk. *I'll be back in a few moments,* she had said: just enough time for him to glance over his wife's progress notes. As a journalist, he had always regarded other's secondhand reports with a bit of skepticism. He found it hard to believe Ashley had so perfectly transformed into a rational and model patient. Calling his wife the "star" of the new program seemed like the Director's embellishment.

As if any rash move would sound an alarm, Roger carefully, slowly opened the file. A photo of Ashley was taped to the left side. Handwritten below it: *Admission 12/16/90*. It pained him to see *that* look in her face again, vacant and dazed, her gray eyes appearing as lackluster as worn-out coins, which he blamed on the awful events of last fall. Fed up with working long hours and earning so little money, her band's bassist had quit in late October; the lead guitarist had followed suit. While Ashley had scrambled, with no luck, to audition and hire their replacements, the drummer had gotten busted for peddling drugs. Ashley had had no choice but to cancel the band's future shows. In response, the local venue owners had claimed they wouldn't book Satin & Suede ever again. Shattered, Ashley had turned to the bottle, drinking more heavily than ever. Besides her morning liquor-store runs, she had vegetated in front of the TV, preparing and consuming one Screwdriver after another, refusing to bathe or change her clothes. Roger had had to hospitalize her. If it hadn't been for the compassionate psychiatrist there who had recommended Victory House, Roger would've been clueless about what to do for his wife.

He shivered, recalling the mid-December morning he had driven Ashley the three-hour distance from their suburban town to this remote part of the state, in the hope she'd be far away from the temptations of bars and liquor stores. Perhaps because of her weakened state, Ashley hadn't objected about coming to Victory House, had kept quiet while they had sat in the near-empty dining room and Roger and Mrs. Hubbert had gone over the admission paperwork. When a female attendant had shown up to fetch Ashley's bags and escort her away, Roger had said, "Honey, I have some rewrites on an article due first thing in the morning. I must go. You'll be well taken care of here." Ashley at first had met his words with an impassive stare; but then, watching him get up from the table, she had asked matter-of-factly, "Will I?" Emphatically, he had replied, "Yes. Trust me." As reassuring gestures, he had kissed the crown of her head and gently patted her shoulder before leaving.

Scratching his chin, he presently wondered if reminding her of their last exchange of words would be a good way to break the ice during their visit. A good way to handle the situation if she flared about feeling "dumped" or "neglected." And perhaps rehashing that memory would also be the perfect lead-in to talk about his own misfortunes: "Please forgive, honey, for being missing in action, but your stay here has spared you from a lot of grief . . . On January the second, the manager at the *Daily Courier* handed me a lay-off notice, claiming he was forced to cut corners. Quite a blow—as devastating as your loss of your band! I was one of the paper's best employees—you know that—hardly ever taking time off and always meeting my deadlines. With no job, I spent days in bed— felt like giving up. But for *our* sake, I rallied . . ."

Roger's attention veered from the Polaroid of Ashley to the paperwork clipped to the folder's top right side. The first page was a lined yellow sheet, dated 3/22/91, about a month and a half ago. He read: *Quite a confession from Ashley Grahame tonight! A very sad life. Past sexual relationship with older stepbrother, starting at age 12 and continuing until she left home at 17, fleeing from an abusive father and stepmother. Struggled to support herself for many years. Got involved in escorting, prostitution, drinking, and experimented with various drugs. Loved best the warm "buzz" from alcohol. Expressed disgust with how most clients were much older men who "begged" for it. Stated that husband was too much like previous clients: significantly older, demanding, repulsive. Tears streaming down her face through most of the session.* The signature at the end of the summary read: *Muriel Lessing, MSW.*

Shocked and sickened by what he had read, he drew a deep breath. He gripped the front of his cotton sweater, pressing his fist against the left side of his chest, as if to keep his heart from sinking into his stomach. He had believed her alcoholism mostly stemmed from the lack of success with her band. This social work report showed he missed the mark with that observation. Because she had lied—claiming she was an only child raised by a loving aunt and uncle now both deceased—he had no idea she had had such a troubled childhood. He felt more estranged from her than ever. . . .

Though he wasn't sure if he could handle it, Roger couldn't help wondering what else Muriel Lessing, the social worker, had written about his wife. With shaky hands, he turned to the next page: a pink copy of an incident report. Dated 3/20/91. The incident type identified as *Inappropriate sexual conduct.* The short description said: *A.H. discovered in greenhouse at 5:20 p.m. engaging in sexual intercourse with T.L. Consumed wine bottles found nearby, under steel workbench. A.H. and T.L. were taken to the Director for questioning and disciplinary action.* Actions taken read: *A.H.'s room inspected—no substances found. Unstructured time suspended; individual therapy sessions increased; T.L. to be dismissed from the program.*

Before Roger could fully process the details of his wife's infidelity, he heard the Director talking with the secretary just outside the door. He closed the file and sprang back to his seat.

Within moments, the Director was sitting at her desk again. "Sorry about that. My day has been filled with interruptions. Where were we . . .?" she asked, her forced smile revealing frustrations.

He gripped his knees so she wouldn't notice how badly his hands were shaking. Settling in the pit of his stomach was this cold, uncomfortable, almost painful feeling, as if he had swallowed a glass full of ice cubes. "Uh . . . my wife . . . Ashley." He almost choked uttering her name.

"Oh yes." She fiddled with the folder. "Ashley's treatment and the unpaid bills. As a private institution, Victory House fortunately receives a good amount of funding from grants, endowments, and donations. Without these sources of income, the facility wouldn't be able to treat our residents as long as we do. Many insurance plans cover little . . ."

His concentration had drifted from her words. Too many disquieting thoughts were pecking at his skull, breaking into his mind . . . and one thought in particular threatened to consume him: *To endure sleeping with her husband, had Ashley fantasized being intimate with her stepbrother?* He needed to get out of the office—leave this place—head for home. He was no longer in the mood to discuss financial matters, or see his wife. He doubted whether he would care to set his eyes on Ashley ever again.

He stood up, saying, "Sorry, but I must—"

Thwarting his immediate escape plan, the secretary knocked at the half-opened door, then came into the room. Tension filled the blonde woman's face as she said, "Mrs. Hubbert, I have to speak with you." Her eyes darted toward the door.

Jumping up, the Director said, "So sorry, Mr. Grahame. Please excuse me—*again*."

The women neglected to close the door all the way. Overwrought with anguish, he paid little attention to what the secretary was telling Mrs. Hubbert . . . until he overheard Ashley's name spoken with heated emotion. Tuning in, he listened to the secretary say: "—Dunkirk was beside himself, yelling into the phone. A short while ago, Thomas showed up at the farm—drove right through the field where Ashley was working. She jumped in his truck, and off they went"— Hubbert shushed the woman to lower her voice. Straining his ears, he was able to hear the secretary continue in a quieter voice: "What should I do . . . ?" In an aggravated yet soft voice, Hubbert replied, "That damn Thomas Lindstrom strikes again. Of all days for this to happen—when her husband's in my office. While I contact the police, I need you, Clara, to get Ashley's social worker and other members of the team together. I don't want to be alone when I tell—"

Bursting into the room, Roger fumed, "—tell me what— that you lied about how wonderful my wife was doing—that she's really a whore and has now run with the guy she was caught screwing? Yeah, you don't want to be alone with me. I might go off on you—or go crazy—or maybe do both!"

A grave expression distorted the Director's pretty face. She motioned toward her office, saying, "Mr. Grahame, I know you're upset—and rightly so. But please go back and have a seat. I'll be with you shortly."

He stared past the women, focusing on the plain oak door to the hallway. A few steps and he would be there. From the hallway, he could bolt to the main entrance and then to the parking lot. In his Chevy Corsica, he could speed away and never look back. A new life . . . finally free from a dysfunctional and unfaithful wife. His own form of victory. He had suffered enough.

"Please go have a seat, Mr. Grahame," the Director calmly requested again. "We must approach this situation keeping our cool . . ."

Perhaps because he didn't respond, her voice took on a more assertive tone: "We must act rationally . . . and not doing anything that—that would hinder your wife's recovery and—and—"

Sounding dazed, he interjected: "And bring new negative publicity to your program—that's what you're most worried about . . ."

"Now, Mr. Grahame—"

He walked right through the women, ignoring their gazes, as if they weren't even there. His mind so consumed with leaving, he saw nothing but the shiny lever handle of the front door until he almost collided with the custodian in the front foyer. No "oh, excuse me" came from his lips. For once, it was all about him and to hell with anyone else. In the parking lot, he couldn't wait to jump in his vehicle and kick up the gravel, aimed back at Victory House, as he hit the accelerator.

But as soon as he got in the Corsica, his plans went awry. A queasy sensation gripped him . . . changing quickly from uncomfortable to almost unbearable. Almost at the same time, he felt short of breath—felt a strange tightness settling in his chest and also in his back, accompanied with bursts of sharp pain in his ribs. Signs of a heart attack? Or more like heart ache? He pressed his hands against his chest. He tried forcing himself to breathe normally, but something seemed caught in his throat. Tears welled up in his eyes. Without warning, he began to sob. To his relief, the bawling helped to loosen up his throat muscles and improve his breathing.

About an hour ago, he had parked here with the hope of . . . starting over with a *recovered* Ashley. A fool's dream.

He couldn't remember a time when he had felt more humiliated . . . and more wronged. During his career, he had written numerous articles about victims of all kinds of crimes—robberies, assaults, kidnappings—admiring their ability to recover and move on; yet, as it turned out, he had absorbed little to nothing of their coping mechanisms. He was ready to crumble like a brick wall suddenly stripped of its mortar.

Still weeping, he leaned forward, his head hung low, grasping the front of the velvety upholstered seat, waiting for the nausea to dissipate. Minutes passed. The sickness persisted. As a distraction, he withdrew from the present . . . forcing his mind to jump back to another time, another place . . . to an occasion early in his marriage when he and Ashley had fought but then quickly reconciled through sex . . . How he wanted to relive finding pleasure and comfort caressing his wife's silky skin, luscious mouth, and soft breasts that molded so perfectly against his firm chest. How he especially loved to hear her excited moans as he gently raked her thighs with his fingers . . . the way her moans turned to panting as she gripped his shoulders and, spreading her legs on the soft cotton sheets, pulled his body into hers . . .

Someone tapping on the car window drew him out of the beguiling past—and into the dreaded present. Straightening his back, he saw it was the Director, and behind her stood two young men, both dressed neatly in pleated pants and white shirts. "Mr. Grahame—Mr. Grahame?" she repeated, still tapping on the glass with her knuckle. "*Please* come back with us. We're concerned about you. We want to help . . ."

Who were the *"we"* she was referring to—the two men standing with her? Were they attendants? Or members of the team she wanted to assemble? It didn't really matter who they were. He knew all he cared to know: men with the same, or almost the same, mindset as hers—more concerned about their reputations and awards—their "victories"—than his suffering. There was no victory for him to be had in this situation. Only retreat . . .

Starting the car, he hurriedly backed out of the parking lot, turned onto the main road, and headed out into the almost-blinding sunny afternoon. The dark sunglasses he put on failed to keep the tears from welling up in his eyes—and shield him from the booming headache that was sure to follow.

\* \* \*

Several miles down the road, where dirt and gravel turned to concrete, he encountered an overturned semi, not far from the expressway entrance. Forced to take a detour, he turned down one country road, then another and another, with no idea how to get back to the route leading homeward. Frustrated, cursing under his breath, he pulled into a strip-mall parking lot, nestled between some cornfields and the poured-concrete beginnings of a new subdivision. The mall—a one-story rustic brick structure with canopied windows—housed a convenience store, a pancake place, a fabric and craft shop, a pharmacy, and a bar. The bar caught his attention because the neon words HORSESHOE TAVERN were shaped like a horseshoe and flashed above an arched doorway.

After five-thirty now, several of the businesses had CLOSED signs in the windows. The convenience store was still open, though. Climbing out of the car, he decided he would go in there, ask for directions while buying a coffee. The caffeine, he figured, would ease the persistent throbbing in his forehead. Crossing the uneven asphalt lot, he took off his sunglasses and wiped his watery eyes with the bands of his sleeves. He was just about to step onto the sidewalk when the glasses slipped out of his moist fingers. The glasses smacked the edge of the curb before landing on the asphalt.

Reaching down with one hand, shielding the glaring sun with the other, he discovered the lenses had popped out of the frames. Straightening up, he wailed, "Dammit, dammit, *dammit!*" Angrily, he flung the lenses along with the frames across the lot, where they skidded by a few cars and settled into a cluster of weeds growing through some cracks. Instead of turning to the left, toward the convenience store's sliding-glass entry, he made an abrupt right and headed for the bar's recessed knotty pine door. Crazy to resist the Horseshoe Tavern's magnetic draw, he decided. More than ever, he needed a couple of beers—and a bartender's sympathetic ear. It would be the beginning of his own therapy—telling others his story, and explaining why Victory House should be renamed House of Failure.

# OLD FRIENDS

*Back in 2006 . . .*

From: H_Morgen218@aol.com     Sun, Mar 12  6:31 pm
To: GeoffWillets76@yahoo.com
Subject: Remember me?

Hi there! This is Hannah Morgen reaching out to you. (Attached is a scanned image of my old EMU ID to jog your memory.) I happened to come across a spiral notebook the other day with your number and email addy on the back cover. We talked about keeping in touch when Abnormal Psych ended. Recalling the last time we sat together in class, exchanging disgusted looks over the lengthy final exam, I asked myself, "Where has the time gone? Has it really been five years? I wonder how this guy is doing."

So how've you been, Geoff? What have you been up to?

From: GeoffWillets76@yahoo.com    Mon, Mar 12 7:15 pm
To: H_Morgen218@aol.com
Subject: What a surprise!

Hannah Morgen—I'd recognize that curly blonde hair and ready-for-a-toothpaste-commercial smile anywhere! You're right—it has been a lot of years. How in the heck are you?

That was one exhausting semester I'll never forget—I stretched myself too thin by taking 18 credit hrs. *and* working part-time. You provided some much-needed entertainment, a definite diversion from my struggles. I loved watching you ruffle our professor's feathers with your constant comments and questions, making him trip over his own words. Each time you interrupted or challenged that SOB, I swear his face turned redder and redder—until it resembled a damn tomato. I kept waiting for his head to explode. Too bad it didn't happen.

If it wasn't for our study sessions at the Student Center to review and compare notes—yours were always better than mine—I doubt I would've passed those hard-as-hell tests. I'll also be forever grateful for the times we got together at the library and you helped me with the research paper that old prick (I'll stop now with the putdowns) assigned. Lacking focus, I was all over the place with my writing. Your ideas and good editing made my work something worthy to turn in.

Well, enough of the past. On to the present. I hope the details don't bore you, but you asked. I'm still living in Ypsilanti. Last year, I finished my MSW degree and now I'm a social worker at a nursing home close to my apartment. Unfortunately, the pay is crappy and the hours are long. I'm supposed to get out each day by 5 p.m.; but often I'm held up by paperwork, phone calls, and meetings with clients and their families. The lack of a consistent 9-to-5 schedule is just as bad, I hear, for social workers employed at hospitals and mental health organizations. I'd like to find a gig where I'll be appropriately compensated for the hours I work. Maybe I should try private practice—just not sure how to drum up the clientele.

Tell me about you. . . .

From: GeoWillets76@yahoo.com      Mon, Mar 13  8:19 pm
To: H_Morgen218@aol.com
Subject: Another Question

After replying to your message, I sat down in front of the TV to unwind and caught the last half of *Entertainment Tonight*. According to the fancy-schmancy Hollywood hairdresser on the program, short hair for women will be "the thing for the spring." In your ID, you hair is exactly as I remember it: long, blonde, and parted down the middle, with big curls draping your shoulders. Is it still the same way? Or did Peter finally let you cut and straighten it, like you always wanted?

Curious how you look now.

From: H_Morgen218@aol.com      Tues, Mar 14  1:58 pm
To: GeoffWillets76@yahoo.com
Subject: Lucky Day!

Geoff, it seems that I should play the lottery today. First, no work because of the ice storm (which turned out not to be nearly as bad as predicted, but caused our building to lose power nevertheless). Second, had sense enough to go grocery shopping the night before. Third, made a shot in the dark and struck a bull's-eye with your messages. It's great to hear from you! I'm surprised to you're still in the area—you talked so much about fleeing the MI winters and moving down to FL. What happened with your plans to relocate? It sounds like you're unhappy with your job at the moment, but you are a gentle and compassionate person, so I'm sure you're helping more people at the nursing home than you realize.

Here's my story: Switching from social work to education, I graduated with my bachelor's a couple of years ago and landed an elementary teaching job at Ypsi schools. I teach 2nd grade. Presently, I'm back at Eastern working on a master's in education. Like you, I'm pretty unhappy with my work. I spend most of my free time surfing the web for exciting lessons for my students; grading papers; analyzing data from their test scores; and submitting weekly reports to my principal about how I will improve my teaching and my students' test scores. My principal—a real witch (that's the nicest word I can use to describe her)—is always on my case about one thing or another. I'm about ready to drop out of the education program and go back into social work.

For a slight change of scenery, I recently moved out of Ypsi into an apartment in the outskirts of Ann Arbor, about 15-20 mins. from work. I still have boxes piled up in one part of the living room. Most of the contents are childhood knickknacks, photo albums, old books and other stuff from undergrad. I've been trying to sort through the boxes and determine what I want to keep or throw out or donate. When I was with Peter, we lived in a two-bedroom flat in downtown Ypsi with ample storage closets. "Out of sight, out of mind," was my motto then. "In my sight, on my to-do list," should be my motto now, if only I had the energy.

As for how I look now, I did cut my hair a few months ago. It felt liberating. It's parted now on the right, comes down to earlobes on the side, and has a sweeping fringe for bangs in the front. The hairstyle requires some effort straightening it in the morning with a round brush and a blow dryer . . . I don't want to *bore* you with too many primping details. I recall that you're a no-fuss, no-muss kinda guy. Your sandy-colored hair was always cut short, resembling a brush cut, and you didn't sport that popular goatee. Around campus, guys with goatees were probably as rampant as girls with platinum hair and hoop earrings. As a natural blonde, I was the envy of my female friends who spent hours stripping the brunette out of their hair. Now that my heavy workload is graying me prematurely, I've become the object of their pity.

Any changes with you?

From: GeoffWillets76@yahoo.com    Tues, Mar 14  7:54 pm
To: H_Morgen218@aol.com
Subject: Changes

Yes, Hannah, I've changed. I'm no longer that no-fuss, no-muss kinda guy. I haven't kept my hair short like a brush cut in a while. More aware of current trends, I have let my thick mane grow out on top, which allows me to comb it up and backwards into a pompadour. No longer clean shaven, I boast a full light-brown beard. After turning 30 last summer, I discarded most of my tattered jeans, rock-band t-shirts, and zippered sweatshirts—and instead started going out looking like a grownup, wearing regular pants or chinos with silk or cotton button-up shirts. My waistline changed too around that time—not for the better. When you knew me, my body was trim and fit. Now I  have somewhat of a . . . belly. It bothers me to admit it.

What led to these changes? This pretty woman named Andrea I met last year at a fundraising event for a homeless shelter. Unlike me, she comes from wealth and privilege. But she doesn't let her background go to her  head. Socially conscious, she belongs to several organizations that help people. Due to her upbringing, she *does* love the high life—

buying new clothes all the time, dining out at 5-star restaurants, outfitting her place with the latest electronics— all courtesy of her parents, since she only works part-time at her daddy's marketing consulting firm. To keep up with Andrea, I started taking more of an interest in my hair and wardrobe—and probably I *did* need to improve in those areas. The eating out, though, was a definite downside to our relationship—the reason why I'm wider around the middle. A bigger concern was her parents, who turned up their noses at me because I didn't fit their dream of some hot-shot businessman or lawyer pursuing their only daughter. That really got to me . . . and so did Andrea's constant insistence on picking up the bill whenever we went out. She couldn't understand why I had feelings of inadequacy. A few months ago, I decided to end it. Call me old-fashioned. Call me prideful. Just don't call me a gigolo.

OK, that last one may seem in poor taste, considering Andrea's generosity, but you need to hear more of the story to appreciate why it's a good thing I can poke fun at myself. On the day I told her it was over, she threw in my face that her parents referred to me as the *gigolo* because she was the one wining and dining me and not vice versa. I'm not the type to be easily offended, but I was hurt because she went on and on about it. What did I say in my defense? Nothing really because I felt like she had pierced me with an ego-deflating dart. It took a while for my self-esteem to rebound.

While I'm on the subject of relationship troubles: you stated in your last email, "when I was with Peter, we lived in a two-bedroom flat . . ." So, I deduce you two are no longer an item. Care to share what happened? Sorry for coming across as nosey but . . . misery loves company.

From: H_Morgen218@aol.com     Tues, Mar 14   10:18 pm
To: GeoffWillets76@yahoo.com
Subject: Companion in Misery

Geoff, you are not alone in trying to get over a failed relationship. Pointing this out may not seem comforting right now, but at least you only invested a year in yours before you decided you had to break up with Andrea. Before we split up this winter, Peter and I had been together for almost 6 years (technically, a little over 6 if I include when he and I started hanging out as friends—friends with benefits—hard to believe we were so hot for each other back in those days). Now at age 27, I'm filled with regrets . . . that I had been so wrapped up in him I let my other relationships with friends and family take a backseat. An example: my grandma (whom I was closer with than my own parents) passed away in an assisted-living facility the previous winter; and I can't help regretting how much time I devoted to Peter and my schoolwork—and how infrequently I visited her.

Now to your question: What happened? It was the culmination of a lot of things. His controlling behavior got old. Never wanting me out of his sight for very long, he had the nerve to insinuate I was up to something questionable with friends or co-workers when I had to meet them somewhere and he couldn't tag along—you must remember how I had to take a break every half-hour during our library sessions to call  and assure him I was still studying. Another issue was his lack of help when it came to cleaning and shopping. He couldn't even be bothered to pick up milk and cereal for us on days when I was busy from morning to night and he was off—he wanted me to do it all. Compounding our troubles was his inconsistent performance under the sheets. (I'm suddenly hearing in my head Mick Jagger of the Rolling Stones sing, "I can't get no satisfaction." Sorry if that's too much info, but it's been a while for me.)

Taking a serious a look back now, I wonder if Peter's problems in life stemmed from his lack of ambition, the fact he couldn't decide what he wanted to do career-wise, just content to jump from one minimum-wage job to another without any concern for the future. That's why marriage never entered into the picture. He didn't have any dreams, I guess you could say, and he didn't support mine. Geoff, I'm sure you're ready to point out: "Well, Hannah, you don't sound thrilled with teaching at the moment and haven't mentioned what you're planning to do about it." Yes, you can make that comparison—I wouldn't deny you or anyone else that. I'm the type of person who sets a goal and sees it through. I decided my third year at Eastern that I wanted to be teacher. I accomplished that. Last year, I enrolled in the Master's of Ed program with a concentration in reading strategies. Only three more classes after this semester and I'll be done with my master's. As with school, I made a commitment to Peter. I gave him plenty of time and opportunities to "find" himself, until he proved he was a lost cause. I'm rambling a bit, I realize. What I'm trying to say is that I stick with something even when the going gets tough. Not a quitter here and hopefully never will be.

While I may seem like a glutton for punishment, doomed for the next 28 years to toil away in the teaching profession, I actually do have an alternate plan—my other dream of becoming a professional writer. Remember when I entered into Eastern's annual student creative-writing contest and won Honorable Mention for one of my short stories? Since then, I've had other successes that say my dream could be a reality: one of my short stories published in a literary magazine, several freelance articles featured in the local newspapers, and most recently a research paper appearing in the summer issue of a scholarly journal. Additionally, I'm only a few chapters away from finishing a novel. Perhaps out of insecurity, Peter laughed at me when I told him someday I wanted to be on the *NY Times* Best Seller list, murmuring his usual trite comment, "The competition for unknown writers is steep—most never make it—so don't quit your day job." He didn't believe I had much talent. You, though, would always praise my writing.

Before signing off, I must tell you how much better I feel airing my private woes. I feel as if you've released me from the shackles of shame—the shame of having made a big mistake—wasting all those years with a man before I had the courage to end it. How did I finally gather this courage? To be honest, it developed from circumstances. Last fall, Peter got a job with a crew that cleaned office buildings in the afternoon. Around eleven or so after work, he and his coworkers would usually end up at our flat, playing cards and smoking joints in the living room. Their loud voices and that awful skunky pot smell, penetrating my bedroom door, often kept me up until the early morning hours. I complained like hell to Peter, but he didn't seem to care. What an inconsiderate jerk he'd become! Before our lease ran out in late January, I went ahead and secured this new place. One Saturday afternoon, while Peter was at work, my parents and brother showed up to help me move out. When he came home that evening, I handed him the keys and a check covering my part of the monthly expenses. As he stood speechless in the middle of the empty living room, I uttered a simple goodbye. He didn't try to stop me from leaving—my stony facial expression told him loud and clear we were *through* in every respect—no way would I even want to go back to being a cordial acquaintance of his. Sorry if this sounds like more rambling or too many details. . . . Time to get myself to bed before you lose faith in my writing skills.

Thanks for asking (and caring about) what happened.

From: H_Morgen218@aol.com     Tues, Mar 14   11:28 pm
To: GeoffWillets76@yahoo.com
Subject: Friday

Yes, Geoff, I said I was signing off an hour ago, but I find myself drawn back to my laptop. I have so much I want to finish by the weekend. I'm taking two grad courses this semester; one is Children's Lit, the other is Informational Reading Strategies. As I type this, my eyes keep shifting to my binder and textbooks on my desk. Only two classes but the amount of work the instructors require is enough for four. Every week, I have journal articles to summarize and critique, detailed charts to create showing connections between the research and my teaching techniques, reflection papers to write on topics covered in the textbooks. So much homework to complete by next Tuesday and Wednesday (the evenings my classes are held), but I can't seem to focus on any of it. Instead of emotionally draining me, my confession about Peter has left me full of restless energy.

All I keep thinking about is that Friday is St. Patrick's Day and I don't want to spend that evening sitting around my apartment. I've had my fill of moping and hanging out here by myself. What are you doing after work that day? If you don't have plans, let's get dolled up in our finest green attire and meet somewhere in Ypsi or Ann Arbor to celebrate it. We can reminisce on our college days, commiserate about our failed relationships, or just enjoy some drinks and talk about whatever. The choice is yours. It would be good to see you again. What do you say, old friend?

From:GeoffWillets76@yahoo.com    Wed, Mar 15 6:52 pm
To: H_Morgen218@aol.com
Subject: Friday

OK, Hannah—let's say 8 o'clock this Friday, so I'll have time to unwind and clean up after work. Let's meet at Clooney's Pub in downtown Ypsi. The beers at Clooney's are cheap, and a not-too-loud jukebox will be playing a good mix of old-school and new music tunes. Its casual atmosphere is just what you need after a stressful week.

This afternoon, I dug my best green threads out of the closet. Even though we haven't seen each other in a while, you should have no trouble spotting me at the bar. I'll be wearing a satin lime-green dress shirt with a wide collar that I wore to a '70s-themed party last year. The shirt is almost the same shade as the Converse high-top sneakers I got for next to nothing off a clearance rack—I couldn't resist it. Now I'll have a reason to wear them. As an added touch, I might pick up this lime-green flat cap I saw in a resale store's window. So that I won't appear totally weird, looking like a tall lumpy piece of green candy, I'll have on jeans and a black leather coat for contrast.

Promise me this—no staring or commenting on my belly.

From: H_Morgen218@aol.com      Wed, Mar 15  9:17 pm
To: GeoffWillets76@yahoo.com
Subject: My Threads

OK, Geoff, Clooney's at 8 p.m. on Friday. I can hardly wait!

I have to admit I'm in a bit of a quandary over what to wear. I don't have much greenery in my closet. I do have this tight stretchy green Henley with pearl buttons down the front, the perfect top for a causal place, but *my* figure ain't what it used to be either. The stress of work, my college classes, and relocating to a new apartment has made me turn to comfort food: bagels with cream cheese, cheddar-&-sour cream potato chips, chocolate muffins, fried cheese sticks. Because I've packed on a few pounds; my clothes don't complement my body the way they did last year. So trust me, there will be no judgment from me about any changes in your physique.

My other options are this mint-colored sweatshirt with a sparkling silver shamrock on the front or an emerald hip-length sweater with shoulder buttons and a honeycomb-stitching pattern. There are a couple of problems with these choices: I'm planning on wearing the sweatshirt to work on Friday and the sweater seems matronly for a night out at a bar.

Well, I have over a day to decide. Until Friday. . . .

From: GeoffWillets76@yahoo.com   Thurs, Mar 16  9:09 pm
To: H_Morgen218@aol.com
Subject: Decision Made

Since you're having such trouble deciding what to wear, I'll help you out, old friend. When you described the mint sweatshirt, I immediately pictured something an elementary teacher of mine wore back in the day. As for the emerald sweater, I think you should save it for parent-teacher conferences or another professional event you have coming up. As we get reacquainted, I don't want to feel like I'm hangin' with a schoolteacher who's ready to correct me if I speak a sentence ending with a preposition. (My attempts at humor may be weak, but I'm sure you're at least smiling somewhat by now.)

That leaves the Henley. I say go with it. So what if it divulges a few bulges? From what I can recall, you have other attributes that easily draws one's attention away from any imperfections you believe you have. Yes, I'm speaking of your . . . You know what I mean. Please excuse my crass talk. The hour is late, and I'm engaging in a pre-St. Patty's Day celebration. In other words: two beers down and a third on its way.

See you in 23 hours and 51 minutes. . . .

From: GeoffWillets76@yahoo.com      Fri, Mar 17  6:38 am
To: H_Morgen218@aol.com
Subject: An apology

When I woke up this morning, I immediately thought about what I sent you last night. I was way out of line in the 2nd paragraph. Though I could blame on it on the beers, you probably wouldn't believe that. My last email was too coherent-sounding to be a drunk's rambling. My only excuse, albeit a lame one, is that I'm a lonely guy. Promise me you'll overlook it—and I promise *you* I won't speak with sentences ending in prepositions. In order words: I'll be on my best behavior.

I'm really sorry about what I said yesterday. Tell me I'm forgiven.

From: H_Morgen218@aol.com          Fri, Mar 17  7:24 am
To: GeoffWillets76@yahoo.com
Subject: Forgiven

Oh, Geoff, you little perv you. I understood what you meant by my other "attributes." No offense taken—not now or five years ago. Yes, I noticed how your big brown eyes used to roam back and forth between my notes and my chest during out study sessions. (Hope you're smiling now.) I noticed some other things about you as well . . .

More to be revealed in 10 hours, 36 minutes. . . .

Please get your mind out of the gutter. By "more to be revealed," I'm not referring to unbuttoning some buttons on my top at Clooney's. (Hope you're laughing now.)

From: H_Morgen218@aol.com          Sat, Mar 18  12:11 am
To: GeoffWillets76@yahoo.com
Subject: Thank you

Definitely had one too many beers. . .  but wanted to write this before bed . . . to say what a great guy you are and what a great time I had tonight. You're a good listener and ask questions, we really talked. Not ever like that with Peter. And you're much handsomer, with much more adorable little belly, loved rubbing it. And I Love the beard. Soft and silky as fur . . . as the dog, the Maltese's I had growing up. You condition it? Peter's scruff was like sandpaper. Yours felt so nice against my cheeks as we made out in your CAr..You are really something, an A+ KISSER. And a good ear nibbler. And so very fast with buttons. The Henley gave you easy access to my bra :-) . . . the sensation from your fingers massaging my nipples electrified me—my head almost hit the roof. I'm sounding like a sillyyyy teen. Glad I admitted that to you, though, about this crush on you. My secret all these years—a secret no more.

Drinking always make me hungry. WHY I don't do IT much, am a major lightweight. Speaking of food, Im looking forward to Sunday at the Asian GARdens place. Five or six to meet? Best veggie egg rolls around.

Must eat a snack then go to bed. Homework and schoolwork all day tomorrow. Promise me no matter what that no other eyes except yours ever reads this email. Too hungry and tired to proofread or try fix anything. No one will or would ever believe me—me with any talent in the writing department.

Forgive any mention of Peter the JERK. No way he compares.

Until Sunday, my sxy bearded one. . . .

From: GeoffWillets76@yahoo.com     Sat, Mar 1  12:27  am
To: H_Morgen218@aol.com
Subject: Home Sweet Home

Hannah my girl just about to call you when I saw this email. relieved you made it home OK. This chilly night—morning—Im turning up the heat. I wish you had taken me up on my offer to drive you back to your apartment. But then again—I think Im quite buzzed here too. Probably should've called a cab. But we're both Home Sweet home so that's all that matters.

Had no idea about the crush—no I kinda knew. You look good with some meat on your bones. Your big boobs got me alll HOT and bothered :) Wheres my manners? This should sound more gentlemanly: Your lips tasted sweeter than fresh honey. How's that for some fancy talk? Best I can do. No Shakespeare here. Just one F___ked up dude.

Ill call tomorrow. The evening. I promise. Sleep tight, sweet lips. . . . . . . .

From: H_Morgen218@aol.com      Sun, Mar 19   11:18 pm
To: GeoffWillets76@yahoo.com
Subject: Another wonderful night

Only about half an hour passed since I left your apartment, but I'm missing your company already, Geoff. Thanks again for treating me to dinner. The depth of our conversations shows we connect with one another. I appreciate that you opened up about the *actual* reason you and Andrea stopped seeing each other. It was good you were honest with her about not ever wanting children. If you had waited to reveal it at a much later date, perhaps after getting engaged or married, she would've felt lied to—cheated—no matter how well you rationalized your point of view. When your mind is set on something, like having babies and raising a family, you can't understand an opposing opinion.

Trust me, you won't have to convince me about the problems of raising kids in our current society. Don't mean to sound like a granny—but the world isn't what it used to be. We are definitely living in more challenging times than ever. The problems in our country—unspeakable crimes against people and animals, heart-wrenching poverty and homelessness, continual environmental disasters—seem overwhelming. I rarely watch the news these days because of the horrific stories happening all over. Do I want to bring up a child in a world of escalating turmoil? The answer is *no.*

I'll get off my soapbox—for now.

What I really want to tell you is how much I enjoyed the time we spent together back at your apartment. (I'll have you over to see my place as soon as my stuff is in better order.) I could've kissed you all night—just love all the passion, how your tongue works its way into my mouth, running its tip along the bottom edges of my teeth, then extending past my teeth until our tongues meet . . . I'm feeling aroused again. Along with kissing, you're pretty damn good with your hands. You have such a gentle massaging touch. As you caressed my arms and legs, the most pleasurable sensation flowed like a current through my body, warming me all over. Too bad we didn't go any further than kissing and touching. But we both had quite a few those of delicious Tsingtao beers—a few too many. That can certainly affect things in our bodies, what we're able to do. Next time we hang out, we'll steer clear of any alcoholic drinks. I don't mean to sound demanding—not my intention. I'm in no rush for us to have sex. It'll happen when it's meant to happen.

I look forward to your call on Monday. I have a staff meeting after work, so any time after 6 is good. Until then . . . handsome guy!

From: H_Morgen218@aol.com    Mon, Mar 20    4:40 pm
To: GeoffWillets76@yahoo.com
Subject: What a day!

Hello again, Geoff. I hope your day went well. Mine was something else. I suppose I could wait until your call later to tell you about it—but I need to vent. It's days like today that cause me to doubt whether I have the ability to continue teaching. Throughout the morning, I struggled to maintain my students' attention on anything I presented, resorting to yelling and threatening no recess after lunch. Instead of punishing them, I allowed them to go outside. Big mistake! When recess was over, they returned to class louder than ever. I knew there was no way they'd pay attention to the afternoon social studies or science lesson I had scheduled.

So I went with a backup plan: a cooperative activity allowing the students to socialize and move about at their tables by making healthy-eating paper-plate collages. (As part of our school's mission to promote health and safety, teachers are required to teach life skills along with academics.) Working in pairs, the students had to find healthy food pictures from old *Taste of Home* and *Good Housekeeping* magazines and then cut out and glue the pictures onto the paper plates to illustrate a balanced meal. Another big mistake! The students roamed around the room and fought over which magazines had the best pictures and which containers had the better markers, their yelling and screeching reaching an almost-deafening level. Materials ended up everywhere, including puddles of spilled glue and markers with missing caps on the floor. In desperation, I turned off the lights for a few seconds and shrieked that they were in danger of losing their recess tomorrow. It got their attention. But when I turned the lights back on and demanded they clean up their work areas, more chaos erupted. Several students began matches of tugs o' war with the magazines, while others dueled it out using markers and rulers as pretend swords.

I was at my wit's end until the school counselor (a friend and ally) happened to walk down the hallway and overhear the riot. Intervening, she burst in and established order by warning the kids she was ready to make a list of names of anyone who didn't quiet down and follow my directions. Those on the list would not only have their parents called but would lose media privileges for the rest of the month— meaning no computer time in the library and checking out any materials (the students love to take DVDs, CDs, and books home). Her approach was more effective than mine: the students calmed down and picked up their messes. The counselor also contacted one of the custodians to remove the drying-up glue on the floor tiles. The day—and my job— was saved! I shudder to think what would have happened if the principal had witnessed the anarchy. If she had, I would've been told to either stay after school or come in early tomorrow for a meeting with her and the union rep. Believe me, the principal would have no qualms about documenting the incident and citing it as proof of my ineffectiveness on my end-of-the-year evaluation.

You'd think I'd be too tired after all that—to sit here and describe what happened at school—but surprisingly, writing it down has given me a second wind. Before it dissipates, I'm going to finish an assignment for my lit class tomorrow while I await your call.

One last comment: I don't know how my colleagues who are parents can do work with bratty kids all day and then go home to their own "darlings" afterward. I wouldn't have the energy—another reason you won't ever hear me say I want to have a baby. Just putting it out there.

Talk soon . . .

From:  H_Morgen218@aol.com      Mon, Mar 20  10:07 pm
To: GeoffWillets76@yahoo.com
Subject:  Where are you?

Hey, Geoff, it's after 10 and I thought I would've heard from you by now. I called you about 15 mins. ago—no rings but straight to voicemail. Is everything all right?

From:  H_Morgen218@aol.com      Mon, Mar 2  11:50 pm
To: GeoffWillets76@yahoo.com
Subject:  Worried :-(

It's almost midnight and still no word from you, Geoff. I'm very concerned something happened to you. I'm going to bed—but keeping my phone on.
Call me no matter how late.

From: GeoffWillets76@yahoo.com    Tues, Mar 21  10:05 pm
To: H_Morgen218@aol.com
Subject: Apology

Hannah, I'm very sorry about not calling you last night. I owe you a good explanation why. I'm not that great with words in situations like this, knowing I'm about to disappoint and upset someone, but I will do my best to express myself. So here it goes: Instead of being straightforward and explaining my feelings on the phone, I decided to take the coward's way out and just disappear out of your life. My conscience, though, told me that wasn't right. Because you're a great person—bright, talented, funny, a definite hottie—and you don't deserve that kind of treatment. I appreciate the affection you've shown me over the last few days and wish I could be *the* right one for you. Unfortunately, I can't reciprocate right now.

I could say the reason is that I'm not over Andrea quite yet. I could also say I feel guilty about trying to replace her with another woman seemingly overnight (maybe why I didn't rise to the occasion Sun. evening). While both scenarios sound so logical, I can say with more assurance I don't sense a special chemistry between us that would spark anything other than *lust* on my end. As much as I don't want to hurt you, Hannah, I have to be honest. Who in the hell wants to be led on? I think we need to give each other some space for the time being.

Again, I'm sorry. :-(

From:  H_Morgen218@aol.com     Tues, Mar 21  10:59 pm
To: GeoffWillets76@yahoo.com
Subject:  :-(

Thanks for your honesty, **PLAYER**!!!


From: H_Morgen218@aol.com        Sun, Apr 29   7:32 pm
To: GeoffWillets76@yahoo.com
Subject: My apology


Geoff, it's been over a month since we talked . . . and each day my regret grows stronger. I promised myself I would leave you alone. I promised myself I would never call or email you again. In fact, I planned to hold a grudge against you for the rest of my life. But I can't!

My reply to your last email was so hostile—and immature. But as you could tell, I was hurt that you wouldn't even give me a chance. I felt as if you were forcing me to retreat into some lonely corner of the world and my only recourse was calling you a spiteful name that would send you reeling into another such place.

Now that I've re-read your email, analyzed it, I think I understand your message. You weren't saying, "I'm just looking to mess around—and since you're looking for more, we should avoid temptation. So, good luck and goodbye." What you actually said was that I was moving too fast and not allowing us enough opportunity to get to know each other. Naturally, your reaction was to put some distance between us. No one likes to feel coerced into something he or she isn't certain about. (I know—how awful of me to end the sentence with a preposition—a prime example of my many flaws—at least my subject and verbs agree—so I have some redeeming qualities.)

When I reached out to you with the first email, I suppose a part of me was eager to fill a void. But it wasn't my intention to get reacquainted because I was on the rebound. I don't love or miss Peter anymore. However, I do care about you. If you're only comfortable with keeping in touch for the time being through emails, I can accept that. As proof, I haven't tried calling or texting you, or stopping by your place. I respect your need for some space.

Can you forgive a flawed friend?

From: Mail Delivery System              Sun, Apr 29   7:34 pm
To: H_Morgen218@aol.com
Subject: Undelivered Mail Returned to Sender

I'm sorry to have to inform you that your message could not be delivered to one or more recipients below:

<GeoffWillets76@yahoo.com> This user does not have a yahoo account . . . .

From: GWillets_2176@yahoo.com    Wed, May 17  6:19 pm
To: H_Morgen218@aol.com
Subject: Please read, don't delete

Hello, Hannah. It's me, Geoff, contacting you from a new account. Why am I bothering . . . ? Because not a day goes by when I don't think about you and how callously I blocked you out of my life. Why did I do it? My fear of intimacy, of falling in love with you and then things not working out, like what had happened with Andrea. You're probably saying to yourself: "What the hell? Why did he jump the gun like that? There's no reason for him to assume that." Hopefully, you'll understand once I give you more details about my breakup. Here they are: Meeting Andrea out for dinner that last time, I tried to steer the conversation around to how we were incompatible in several important aspects and that we'd be better off as friends. I couldn't get a word in because she was bubbling over with her brother's acceptance into med school and how it fulfilled her parent's dream of having a doctor in the family. At her apartment, I was finally able to drop the bomb. She went ballistic! She scared the hell out of me—smashing expensive pottery pieces and ceramic lamps, knocking her plasma TV off the stand onto the wooden floor. She stomped on that beautiful state-of-art TV with her heeled boots until the screen scattered like a frozen pond breaking into a hundred icy shards (can't believe I came up with this simile on my own— maybe a little Shakespeare in me after all). For leading her on, she screamed every nasty name you could imagine and then some at me—her obscenities would've made a crude stand-up comedian blush. She claimed she had no idea I was unhappy. Which was crazy—we hadn't been getting along for a while, arguing over everything from my position of no kids to my lack of enthusiasm over her dad's offer to send me back for a business degree so I could work for him. Unable to calm her down, I decided to escape. As I hurried to the door, she chucked a heavy bookend at me, narrowly missing the back of my head with it. . . .

I should've told you all this. Talking about it would've eased my nervousness about starting a new relationship. If I could go back in time and unsend my last email to you, I definitely would. But I can't change the past. All I can change is the future.

You're probably also saying right now, "If he wanted to change the future, he would pick up the damn phone instead of emailing me. That would show he really had some balls." Shamefully, I deleted your number out of my cell phone contacts and can't for the life of me remember the last 4 digits. Maybe that's just as well. In composing this message, I took the time to gather my thoughts and express myself openly without worrying you'd hang up. Not that I wouldn't deserve it.

And if you had hung up on me, there'd be no chance to tell you about my wonderful find. On my way home from work yesterday, I happened to stop at a garage sale and found this book entitled *Getting Your Manuscript to the Top of the Pile*, a sturdy hardcover with a bright, cheery dust jacket. I got it for you! There is an extensive list of publishers and what kinds of manuscripts they accept toward the back. This resource may be just the ticket to help you accomplish your dreams of publishing your first novel. It's what I needed to gather the courage to try talking to you again—and to show I believe in you.

In the next several paragraphs, I could spill my guts out why I've missed you so much, but I'd rather save it for when I see you in person. Let me say, though, that I've been in agony without you—I'm not sleeping or eating much.

Please say you'll see me again. If you agree to meet, you'll get a delicious meal and a nice book out of it :-).

From:MAILER-DAEMON@yahoo.com Wed, Mar 17 6:53pm
To: GWillets_2176@yahoo.com
Subject: Failure Notice

Sorry, we were unable to deliver your message to the following address.

<H_Morgen218@aol.com>
    <H_Morgen218@aol.com>: Recipient address rejected: aol.com . . .

From: JPStanley48187@gmail.com  Thurs, May18 10:22 pm
To: H_Morgen218@gmail.com
Subject: Great reconnecting!

Hannah, a note here before bed to say how much fun it was meeting you for coffee this evening. It was good catching up and seeing how far we've come from the days when we had to slave away at Sam's Corner Coney, both of us struggling to put ourselves through school. On the day I quit Sam's, I handed you that slip of paper with my phone number on a whim, hoping that someday . . . I'm very glad you never forgot about me.

Even though you never spoke of your troubles with Peter, I somehow picked up this vibe that all was not well. As it turns out, my suspicions were right. It sounds like he let you down time and time again. If that wasn't bad enough, your next foray into dating—with that Geoff guy you mentioned—ended up being another disappointment. But, like you, I refuse to allow some lousy experiences to transform me into a relationship pessimist. As they say— plenty of fish in the sea.

By the way, how do you like your new Gmail account? I've had one for a while. I was surprised when you told me you had had an AOL account for almost ten years, not bothering until recently to try out other email services. But I understand where you're coming from—when I'm comfortable with one thing, I don't want to bother learning anything new and supposedly "easier." It could be that we're both a little shy of technology . . . probably the reason why we've shunned chat rooms and online dating sites . . . or maybe we hang onto something for so long because we're the sentimental types . . . or is "traditionalists" a better label for us . . . in the sense that we both play it safe with our traditions, our own ways of doing things? I'm being repetitive now—my heavy eyelids are telling me to talk about this more another time.

Leaving the coffee shop, we talked about hanging out again. I'd invite you over to see my house, but things are in a disarray here because I've been painting. You mentioned your place resembles a storage unit—boxes piled up–so I'm sure you'd prefer we didn't hang out there either.  How about meeting out for dinner on Saturday? Halfway between us is this Chinese place I like—quiet and low-key atmosphere, best-tasting eggrolls, and a good selection of authentic and Americanized cuisine. Maybe take in a movie afterward?

I'll call you tomorrow after work.

Good night—pleasant dreams!

From: H_Morgen218@gmail.com  Thurs, May 19  10:49 pm
To: JPStanley48187@gmail.com
To: Subject: Great reconnecting!

Sure, Jon, I'm free this Saturday. The Chinese place and a movie afterward sounds good. I'll check what's showing around town in the morning.

Just to let you know: my goal this summer is to make my apartment suitable for company. It just takes time to organize. In my defense, there are some advantages to being a packrat: If I wasn't one, I wouldn't have come across your number in an old address book—I wouldn't be getting reacquainted right now with a handsome old friend :-).

I look forward to talking tomorrow. Pleasant dreams . . .

# TWO ON THE TOWN

Craving chocolate, Carol went for a treat at El Gran Café, the new coffee shop in town. She ordered a caffè mocha with chocolate sprinkles and whipped cream and a big chocolate chip cookie—her favorites—and sat down at the center table. Yet after only taking a few bites from her cookie and a few sips from her drink, she lost her appetite, and pushed her glass mug and plate aside. *Another evening sitting around alone*, she thought. Feeling sorry for herself, she sighed as she slumped over in her chair.

In the past, she buffered her problems by bingeing on sweets. But such self-therapy couldn't begin to relieve her present grief. Carol's parents, who were her best friends, had moved a week ago to a seniors' community in Nevada, more than two thousand miles away. For the time being, her established career as a hematology lab manager at Glenwood General Hospital made it impossible for her to relocate closer to them. Within the same week, she ended a three-year relationship with her boyfriend, Bob, when he finally decided he could not commit to marriage. At forty, she had yet to fulfill her dream of being married with children.

Minutes passed before Carol straightened her back and looked around. Though the coffee shop was located in a northern Ohio community, El Gran Café simulated a tropical climate. Artificial palm trees in brown pots were situated between some of the bamboo-legged tables; on the walls were murals depicting scenes from such exotic places as the Florida Keys, South America, and the Caribbean. She was surprised she was the only patron. After all, it was a Friday evening—hadn't the owners advertised their grand opening?

From another table, she picked up a local newspaper but put it down when she heard the door chime. Carol's eyes went wide. A woman clad in clothing appropriate for a costume party entered and approached the counter. But it was early July—so what was the occasion?

There was quite a mismatch between this woman and Carol, who was wearing jeans and a gray V-neck pullover. The woman's attire reminded Carol of the late 1950s or early '60s. She wore a diamond choker, elbow-length gloves, and a black lace dress with an oval neckline and a swirling skirt. Draped across her shoulders was a white fur stole. The woman's long blonde hair was so thick and perfectly curled that it had to be a wig; the youthful hairstyle sharply contrasted with her prominent crow's-feet and deep forehead creases. Narrowing her eyes, Carol could see some short gray hairs poke out from underneath the glossy yellow bangs.

Carrying a steaming cup of tea, the oddly dressed woman smiled at Carol with her heavily painted red lips. She headed straight for Carol's table.

*Oh, great!* Carol thought. *Now I'm going to be stuck entertaining a weirdo for a while.* She had an urge to get up and leave.

"May I join you?" the woman asked before Carol had time to react. "Are you expecting someone?"

Carol nearly replied *yes,* but the woman's speech was calm and friendly. Maybe the woman wasn't weird—just a little eccentric. It wouldn't hurt to be pleasant for a few minutes.

"Sure—sit down," Carol said, though she hoped no one would come in and see them together.

The woman quickly sank down across from Carol, removed her gloves, and extended her hand. "I'm Loretta." Her smile widened, revealing yellowish crooked teeth.

Shaking the woman's boney hand, Carol introduced herself.

"So what brings you out tonight?" Loretta asked. She kept her eyes fixed on Carol's face as she took a few sips from her tea.

"About a month ago," Carol explained, "I read an article in the paper about a couple who were renovating a bakery in downtown Glenwood and turning it into a coffee shop. Today is their grand opening, so I decided to stop by and check it out. What about you?"

"I had some time to kill before my movie starts at the Cinemaplex—the theatre up the street."

"Which movie?"

"At ten o'clock, I'm seeing *The Diary of Anne Frank*. It's the 1959 version, starring Millie Perkins and Shelley Winters. The outfit I have on is similar to the one Shelley Winters wore to the Academy Awards in 1960 when she received the Best Supporting Actress Oscar for her role in the film."

*So she's not a kook after all, just a film enthusiast.* "Wow, you must be a real movie buff!" Carol exclaimed. "Do you often emulate your favorite stars when you go to the movies? I don't recall Shelley Winters ever having a hairstyle like yours, but I could be wrong."

"Yes, you're right," Loretta said, her smile dissipating. Perhaps finding Carol too picky about an unimportant fact, the woman pointed out, "But Shelley Winters was a blonde on the screen, and it's the only decent blonde wig I own."

"How often does the Cinemaplex show old movies?"

"Every two weeks, it presents a classic film on a Friday night. I've been attending these special showings for over two years now and have yet to miss *one*."

"Good for you!" Carol said. "I should be more dedicated to a hobby. I haven't been to a movie in ages."

She looked shocked by Carol's comment. "Would you care to accompany me tonight?" Loretta unexpectedly asked.

Fluttering her long red nails in front of her face, she clearly expected a *yes*.

Uncertain how to respond, Carol turned her head away. Loretta's gaze was overpowering. For a moment, it was as if Carol was looking into a mirror and saw a reflection of her own loneliness and sadness.

"I don't know . . . Didn't you say the movie doesn't start until ten? That's about an hour from now. I usually don't stay out real late."

"I understand," Loretta said, smiling again. "But if you went, I bet you'd have fun. I own a clothing store a few blocks down the street called Glitzy Garb. With your trim figure and graying dark hair pulled back in a twist, I have just the dress you can borrow if you'd like to go. It's made of blue satin with large buttons along the sleeves and sides, and wearing it would give you a sleek, sophisticated look. You'd look as though you were ready for the Oscars."

Carol sensed her body tightening. It was one thing to invite a stranger to a movie, but it was quite another for Loretta to suggest that she change her attire for the occasion. *What kind of person tells you to come into her store and change clothes when she just met you?* She didn't know what to make of Loretta.

"I appreciate the offer, but I'm going home," Carol replied and stood up. "It was nice meeting you, and if you ever see me out again, please say hi."

"And you do the same," Loretta said with a frown, looking down into her tea.

Carol quickly emerged from the coffee shop onto the street. She walked to the next block; there she halted in front of a bar named THE *IN* SCENE, where she was enticed by the pleasing dance music penetrating the double-wooden doors.

She glanced at her watch:   9:10 p.m. Not tired, she wasn't really in the mood to head home. Actually, a cocktail over hot chocolate appealed to her. Maybe she could strike up a conversation with someone inside—but, she hoped, not with anyone as peculiar as Loretta.

Momentarily, Carol closed her eyes and envisioned how later on people would stare at Loretta in the lobby of the movie theatre. What a sight Loretta would be with that awful wig and outdated dress! Laughing silently, Carol pictured men and woman dropping their popcorn and gagging on their sodas while Loretta moved past them.

After applying a coat of lipstick from her purse, Carol entered the building and then traversed the small, nearly empty dance floor to the other end of the bar. She slid onto one of the swivel stools. The bartender took Carol's order, a Kahlúa and cream. After receiving her drink, she sipped slowly from the glass and surveyed the sparse crowd. The men were all wearing dark pants and bright silky shirts; many of the women had on tight glittery pants and bright tank tops. Carol felt a little out of place in her drab clothes.

A tall man with a shaved head sat down beside Carol. Titling her head, she noticed his large dark eyes and perfectly trimmed goatee. He seemed normal. Perhaps talking to him would help to ease her nervousness.

"Hi," Carol said, looking directly at him. "How are you doing? Have you ever been here before? Does it get busier later?"

The man shrugged his shoulders. "I'm not sure. I don't come here too often."

Carol pressed onward. "Where do you like to hang out? Are you meeting some friends here later?"

The man contorted his face to show his annoyance. "When I came out tonight, I had no idea I was going to be interviewed. What's your deal?"

Carol shrank back, embarrassed. "I'm sorry. I was just trying to be friendly."

"Look, lady, I don't know what you're looking for tonight, but *I'm* not it," he flared. "I'm here for a drink— nothing else."

Carol stood up, glass in hand, and backed away. "I'm only looking for a conversation," she shot back. "Since you're in no mood to have one, I'll search elsewhere." The temptation to call him a *jerk* was very strong, but she decided against it. She didn't want to reveal how much he had upset her.

Carol stopped at the metal railing surrounding the dance floor. A few young men and women were now swaying and bouncing to the lively music. Two blonde women wearing low-cut blouses and tight jeans stood beside Carol.

Still yearning to talk to someone, Carol tapped the one woman whose hair was long and layered on the shoulder. She put her hand against the woman's ear and said: "I like your outfit. Where'd you buy that nice blue top?" Though it wasn't exactly the style Carol would get for herself, she admired the embroidery of white flowers around the neckline and bell sleeves.

The woman raised her eyebrows and stepped back, as if Carol had said something horrifying. Pointing out Carol, she quickly moved to the other side of her friend with the jaw-length bob. The women talked briefly back and forth in each other's ears—then erupted into laughter that roared above the music.

Feeling awkward, Carol headed for the lady's room. In the mirror, she noticed that her drink had smeared her lipstick into the corners of her mouth. Since the Kleenex and towel holders were empty, she went into one of the stalls. With the metal partition door propped against her shoulder, she bent down and rolled some toilet paper around her fingers.

Hearing two women walk in, she straightened up and glanced sideways into the mirror.  They were the two blondes who had been in front on the dance floor. She quickly shut the stall door, hoping the barricade would shield her from further rudeness.

One of the blondes said: "We should've gone somewhere else tonight. This place has a pathetic crowd. I still can't get over that woman asking me about my blouse. With what she had on, it's obvious she has no clue about style. Can you imagine her thin, shapeless body in what I'm wearing? Please. I have an hourglass figure. She was Olive Oyl—a Twiggy."

The other said, laughing: "Maybe if she was a lot younger and had a boob job. She definitely needs a reality check."

Shocked by the women's cruelty, Carol froze. She tried to think of something to say in retaliation. Since nothing came to her, she stayed inside the stall, listening to the women fuss with the makeup containers inside their purses. It seemed as though several minutes passed before the women finished fixing their faces.

When Carol emerged from the stall, she returned to the mirror and wiped clean the edges of her lips. Slowly opening the restroom door, she was relieved to see that the two blondes were at the bar and had their backs to her. She hurried out of the establishment, without glancing back.

She headed in the direction of her car parked a few blocks away. But she halted, thinking, *What's the rush to get back to a lonely condo? Not even a pet is there to greet me.*

Carol retraced her steps back to El Gran Café. With eager eyes, she looked through the large front windows, searching for the lady in the blonde wig. However, Loretta was gone.

Recalling the location of the woman's shop and thinking that Loretta had become bored and returned to her store for a while before going to the movie, Carol headed down the street in that direction. When she was just a few blocks from her destination, she glanced at her watch, noticing the movie was starting in twenty-five minutes. Carol's feet thudded against the pavement, breaking into a run.

Near the end of the third block, she paused to catch her breath. The bright-pink neon sign for GLITZY GARB was directly above her. The business was housed in a brown-brick building that stood between two other brown-brick store spaces of similar size. There could be no doubt that Loretta was the owner. Headless mannequins displayed in the window were dressed in garish attire . . . a gold polyester shirt paired with silver bell-bottom pants, a purple velvet gown belted at the waist with strings of decorative beads . . . an aqua floor-length fur coat.

Carol peered through the glass door and knocked a few times. When Loretta failed to appear, she knocked louder. It was dim inside, but she saw some clothes racks on wheels being pushed to the side. And there was Loretta! She gazed at Carol with a wide smile.

Loretta strode to the door and unlocked it. "Wow, you surprised me!" she exclaimed as Carol entered the store. "I wasn't expecting to see you again."

"I wanted to stop by and apologize," Carol explained. "I felt bad about being so abrupt with you."

"It's okay," Loretta replied. "No need to apologize."

"Are you still going to the movie?"

"Yes, I just came back to my shop because I forgot to feed my canary. In the evening, I put her cage in the back room."

Carol looked raring to go. "You still want some company?"

By how rapidly Loretta fluttered her fingers, Carol could tell her questions delighted the older woman.

"Of course," Loretta replied. "Would you like to wear the blue dress I suggested? Or maybe another vintage outfit?" She turned on the lights.

Scanning the store, Carol noticed a knee-length, beige glittery coat with large silver buttons. The coat was hanging all by itself on a small rack; it reminded her of what her favorite aunt used to wear for holidays and other special occasions. When her aunt passed away a year ago, Carol had meant to ask her cousin if she could have it as a memento. But by the time she got around to inquiring about it, her cousin had already sold the garment.

"What a dazzling coat!" Carol cried, reaching out to touch it. "Where did you find it?"

"I bought it at an estate sale I attended last year. Sometimes you can discover great bargains at them. You want to try it on?"

"Sure," Carol said, taking the coat off the white padded hanger. She tried it on before a full-length mirror. Turning from side to side, she discovered it was a perfect fit. *Olive Oyl couldn't wear anything like this.* "Where was the estate sale?" she asked.

"In the next town over—Pleasant Pointe," Loretta answered.

That was where Carol's aunt had lived. Growing excited, she asked, "Do you remember what street?"

"Grove Street."

"My aunt lived on that street. Do you recall the address? What did the house look like?"

"Hmmm . . . let me think." Loretta paused, concentrating. "I believe it was a white ranch with big windows and . . . a big front porch."

"It had to have been my aunt's house. Hers was the only white dwelling on the street, and this coat looks just like the one my aunt owned."

"Do you want it? In the last hour, the temperature has really dropped. The air is cool now. You should wear it tonight."

Carol countered, shaking her head: "But trying on dresses to go with it would take up too much time. And it certainly wouldn't look good with my jeans and shirt."

Loretta winked at Carol and handed her the coat. "Remember—it's the Oscars tonight! Anything goes—so long as you sparkle."

As Carol and Loretta headed up the street, toward the Cinemaplex, they passed by a small group of people outside a restaurant. Even though it was dark, the street lights illuminated their faces. They narrowed their eyes and scrunched their foreheads, showing they weren't sure what to make of the two women. "Look at those two!" a man in the group remarked. "They must think they're belles of the ball."

Carol laughed aloud at his small-minded comment. In fact, she continued to laugh as she approached the club where she had suffered her earlier humiliation.

She stopped with Loretta in front of the doors. She was half-tempted to drag Loretta inside, to prove that anyone's mean stares or words inside the bar meant nothing to her.

Loretta grabbed Carol's arm, saying, "Let's not be late for the movie."

Carol followed the older woman's lead: she couldn't have agreed with Loretta more. What people thought of Carol no longer mattered. Loretta was carefree and lively. She lived life. Qualities not apparent when they met in the coffee shop. Carol realized that her loneliness had nothing to do with her parents moving away or her break-up with her lover. She shut a part of herself off, placing herself on a high pedestal, above others like the two blondes in the bar. But tonight opened Carol's eyes, and from now on, she would be like her aunt and Loretta, living life. All Carol's worries slipped away with her newfound comprehension. She smiled at her new friend because no one else mattered.

Tonight, it would be just two on the town.

# THE UNEXPECTED

In the heart of bustling Midtown Atlanta, I am standing at an intersection, waiting for the light to change, when I happen to turn my head and observe a young woman fast approaching. Watching her weave through the clusters of pedestrians behind me, I fixate on her striking burgundy hair, its luxurious waves framing her shoulders, and fail to see the intent of her maneuvers. It isn't until she gets close to the corner and our gazes meet that I regret letting my guard down. Her excited—or perhaps more accurate to say *manic*—grin clenches my stomach with an uneasy feeling.

In her black high-heel boots, she teeters on the uneven concrete slab near the curb, panting, "Why, hello—hello there—sexy." She almost stumbles into me, but regains her balance in an instant.

Although good sense says to ignore this pasty-complexioned woman, I say, "Hello," in a cautious but cordial tone. Politeness is part of my nature. As the eldest child and only son of emotionally-absent parents, I assumed the role, at an early age, of teaching manners to my two sisters.

With choppy speech, she reveals: "Excuse me for my clumsiness—and forwardness—but you see—you caught my eye—from afar—at the park." Pausing to take a deep breath, she straightens the beige silky scarf around her neck, its fringy tails draped halfway down her back. "I've been following you—for quite a distance. You're a fast walker."

To placate her, I nod in reply. Several long blocks down the street, north of our present location, is Piedmont Park. To check out the meadow, the monuments, and naturally other attractions like pretty women exercising, I took a walk through it on the way back to my hotel. The circular pathways were full of people, many just strolling along. If her pursuit of me was obscured and hindered by others, it made sense that I wouldn't have noticed her.

"A *very* fast walker," she emphasizes. "So glad I never lost sight of you."

When a stranger approaches me on the street, I expect him/her to ask for something, like directions or a handout, or perhaps to address me by a name showing I've been mistaken for someone else. This lady has me puzzled. I wonder who I'm dealing with—an eccentric or nutcase?—a horny stalker—a combination of both?

I decided to ask, with a creased forehead, "Can I help you with something . . . ?"

"Yes, as a matter of fact, you can." She breathes deeply again. Her voice sounds as Midwestern as mine, so she clearly isn't a Georgia native. "Please say you'll have dinner with me!"

Taken aback, I point at myself and restate her offer sounding stunned, "You want to have dinner with *me*?"

She regards me intensely. "Please say yes!"

People start to pass us because the traffic sign has changed from DONT WALK to WALK. Some of them pause before crossing and give us strange looks. With a jerk of my head and twitch of my brow, I motion to them—a signal that her excitement and high volume are attracting unwanted attention.

Unconcerned (or oblivious to the hint), she continues on passionately: "I've been living here now for well over a month and have yet to meet anyone. This city is a lonely place. I don't know if I can stand spending another afternoon . . . another evening alone in my apartment, eating another meal all by myself, trying to pass the time." In a flirtatious manner, she licks her lips. "There's something about you that intrigues me. I'd love to get to know you better. Let me fix you dinner tonight. I'm a good cook with well-stock cupboards." She loosens the scarf, revealing her slender, pale neck.

Touched by her declaration of loneliness, I stare at her for a few moments, contemplating her offer. She isn't exactly what I'd call pretty: her brown eyes are too close-set and her mouth too thin for her broad face. However, she is sporting a knockout figure in her tight jeans and white V-neck sweater: her slender waist, full hips, and well-endowed chest can rival the physical attributes of a Hollywood sex goddess. The old me would have said *yes* to her invitation right away, anticipating that dinner would be a lead-in to an even more pleasurable experience. The new me, for some very good reasons, has become a wary person.

As I ponder my answer, her concentration shifts from me to the flow of cars traveling eastbound on Tenth. Gesturing in that direction, she says, "My place is close by. What do you say?"

Speaking quietly, hoping she'll notice and follow suit, I reply with an extended hand, "Let's start off with introductions—I'm Gunnar." Anticipating a reaction, I add, "I know what you're thinking—kinda sounds like a porn star's name. I blame my parents for it every day." I laugh and smile. "And you are?"

She takes my hand and shakes it eagerly. "Gunnar, Gunnar, Gunnar," she cries, her eyes widening and beaming with enthusiasm. "I love that name! It really suits you: with your silvery-blond hair and ocean-blue eyes, you look like you come from Nordic stock." As her gaze wanders down to my taut-fitting white turtleneck, zeroing in on my broad, muscular chest, she gushes, "I don't mean an average Nordic background. With those massively ripped pecs of yours, I would dare to assume you descend from a Viking warrior.

How do you maintain your  powerful physique—lift heavy stones like your ancestors?"

I roll my eyes . . . if only she would notice the puzzled looks we're getting. Once again, I reply in a volume much lower than hers: "No Viking-warrior lineage that I'm aware of. Just a lot of working out—at a gym—using *equipment*, not large stones."

As if puzzled by my response, she rubs the side of her porcelain-smooth face, then tugs at her ear a couple of times. In a less exuberant tone, she asks, "So, what *is* your ethnicity then?" She steps closer until we're almost nose-to-nose.

I move back, finding her demanding tone and sudden invasion of my personal space unsettling. Nevertheless, I manage to reveal in a polite tone: "Actually, Austrian—on both sides."

"Both sides, you say . . ." Her eyes blink rapidly. Even though the afternoon sky is cloudy, she shields her eyes with her hand.

"Are you all right?"

Her other hand goes to her heart. She pats her chest several times. "To be honest—*no*. I'm feeling overpowered in the presence of a Viking warrior."

Giving her an annoyed look, I can't help but ask: "Are you normally this sarcastic with strangers?"

Her eyes grow narrow, her face turns tense, as if my question was off base. "No—never—I mean I'm not being sarcastic." This time, *she* takes a step back.

Our conversation going nowhere, I decide it's time to make my exit. "Uh . . . sorry but I didn't catch your name."

"Audrey."

"Well, Audrey, thanks for the compliments and the offer to hang out at—unfortunately, I have a few things to take care of now and have other plans for the evening," I lie, unable to think of any courteous yet honest way of declining her advances. "Enjoy the rest of your day." I wave goodbye, then quickly turn around. A lucky break, the sign flashes WALK again. I cross without looking back.

At the next corner is a bookstore. I pause at the window, my eyes drawn to a display of mystery novels, meticulously arranged on a stand whose shelves are covered with red satin. I start glancing at the titles . . . *Dressed for Death . . . Lethal Love . . . Dominic's Downfall . . .* but stop because of what I see reflected in the glass. Audrey is still standing across the street, watching me. Noticing that I'm staring back at her, she waves at me. I nearly jump out of my skin. Despite the pleasant mid-March breeze, my forehead breaks out in a cold sweat.

I swallow hard, wondering what her problem is. Why doesn't she get the message that I do not want to be bothered?

Looking away, I consider how I might evade her. My hotel is a few blocks away, but if I cross the other corner and head in that direction, she will probably follow me and then learn where I'm staying. If I duck into the bookstore, she will probably wait for me until I come out. Several restaurants line the next block. Perhaps I could hang out in one of them for an hour or so, eating an early dinner while perusing a local entertainment rag. By the time I finish my meal, this crazy woman—Audrey—will have moved on to some other guy in the area.

I pivot away from the window, then start walking straight ahead. I don't glance back to see what Audrey is doing, whether she's trailing me. The less attention she receives, the better. My body language, my actions, need to give the impression she isn't worrying me in the least. With a confident posture, I quicken my pace, passing a dilapidated bar, liquor store, hair salon,  and computer-repair shop. In comparison to the previous block, the number of pedestrians approaching or passing by me has dwindled to only a few. None of them, fortunately, are Audrey.

At the next intersection, I stop at the corner restaurant, the first in a string of eating places. Called Mae's Cafe, it has a dark oak exterior offset by several quaint features. The more snobbish members of my circle of friends back in Michigan would turn their noses up at the red-and-white checkered canopies hanging over the two wide downstairs windows. I   can picture them shaking their heads with displeasure at the soft violin music flowing out of the speaker above the light-blue wooden front door. They would judge the place as too "old-fashioned" or "retro" for their tastes. But I like the nostalgic feel . . . delighting especially in the mum-filled flower boxes adorning the smaller second-story windows.

Stepping closer, I am about to inspect the menu posted on the window to the right of the door, but I feel a soft tapping on my shoulder, and my body freezes. *Please, tell me no . . . please, please tell me that isn't Audrey behind me . . . I thought the coast was clear.* The only way to either confirm or deny my dismay is to turn around, but I hesitate. If it is *her*, how to get rid of her—get rid of her once and for all? Politely expressing my lack of interest seems to have no effect on her. Perhaps I just need to be very direct and say, "Look, Audrey, I told you *no*. And if you don't leave me alone, I'm going to take out my cell phone and contact the—"

More light tapping on my shoulder . . . In preparation, I fold my arms and contort my face into a hostile expression. Swinging around, I face her. She is standing there with a slight smile, her arms and hands resting firmly against her side, waiting for my reaction. I can't judge from her body language whether she's playing some kind of game or sincerely wants to get to know me, unaware of how off-putting her stalking behavior really is. In my head, I can hear my friend Lee say: *Just tell her you're happily married with five kids. She'll scurry away like a mouse.* I doubt that will deter her. Not only will she question why I didn't mention that from the start, she'll see through those lies with her penetrating espresso eyes.

I am about to proceed with my plan of threatening to call the police when I see a taxi cab pull up on the other side of the street. My getaway vehicle. After quickly scanning the street to make sure no cars are coming, I dart across to the cab. Jumping in, I give the Hispanic-looking driver an address. And we head off.

*   *   *

Back at my hotel room, I pace back and forth across the plush carpet, covering the path between the long computer desk and the two queen-sized beds, trying to make sense of Audrey's audacity. Judging by the way she had ogled me so amorously, I have little doubt that her offer to become acquainted over dinner was only a prelude to what she really desired: an evening of passionate sex. Sure, she stated she was attracted to me—or, rather, my muscular physique—yet that didn't explain her persistence. Why was she so unrelenting? It seems that she sensed something about me . . . that said her efforts wouldn't be in vain. But how could she have known? What tipped her off that I was once serially promiscuous . . . and might be persuaded  back into that lifestyle?

I have no answers to those questions. I am certain, though, about one thing: alone now, I regret not hanging out with her. I regret not proving to myself, and to a few close friends who know about my struggles, that I have truly conquered my *bad* habit. Though they advised me to seek professional help, insinuating my frequent trysts meant I was a true sex addict, I proved them wrong by going cold turkey almost a year ago . . . and have yet to falter, remaining steadfast in the belief that within me is the power to abstain until that special someone comes along . . . a woman with whom I feel that certain chemistry bonding us into a loving and committed relationship.

Or is my thinking too immature—too naïve? Maybe temptation, proving stronger than my resolve, would've led me astray in Audrey's company despite my long period of celibacy.

Lying on the bed closest to the bathroom, propping up my head on a stack of fluffy down pillows, I stare at the digital clock on the desk—a few minutes past four—and ponder what I will do for the rest of the afternoon and the evening. My two-day urban planning conference ended yesterday, but I reserved my room until Saturday, tomorrow, so that I would have all day Friday for sightseeing. So far, I have been to two art museums, visited Martin Luther King's childhood home, and taken my fateful stroll in the historic yet modern-looking Piedmont Park, where Audrey claimed to have spotted me. The Margaret Mitchell House and Museum, a block away, was next on my list, but I have suddenly lost interest in viewing it, for my mind is still too consumed with Audrey's proposition (most likely an indecent proposal) to listen to a tour guide or concentrate on any exhibits.

To get my mind off that strange-acting Audrey, I pick up the TV remote from the nightstand and start surfing the channels. So many channels . . . but nothing much on I will enjoy. A fan of "The Master of Suspense," I settle on a Hitchcock film called *Rebecca*, which I've never seen before. Though I missed the first twenty minutes of it, I easily grasp the storyline: a young woman who has recently married an older man, moves into an eerie English mansion and feels increasingly concerned (alarmed?) over her husband's hostile attitude whenever she brings up his first (and dead) wife. Despite the actors' dramatic performances, the movie fails to maintain my interest. I prefer the suspenseful action of his later thrillers, like *Topaz* or *Torn Curtain*.

Stretching my legs as I wielded the remote again, I search for another program to watch. Finding not much else of interest, I begin viewing the comedy/action/thriller movie *Adventures in Babysitting*. I saw it once before with my high-school girlfriend when it first came out. Hard to believe that was almost eleven years ago. Though the film has dated teen lingo and a dated "racy" subplot involving the theft of a *Playboy* magazine (as well as the trite theme that "stealing can get you into more trouble than you ever imagined"), it holds my interest for the next forty-five minutes. Its story of teens venturing from the safety of suburbia to the seedy underworld of Chicago, fleeing from gangsters, and finding themselves in one hilarious yet dangerous situation after another, has me watching through my fingers during several scenes.

As soon as it's over, my thoughts drift to the girl I took to this movie. Kendra and I dated during my junior and senior years and then for five more while we attended Eastern Michigan University together. Sweet and pretty Kendra . . . blonde and green-eyed with a near-flawless peaches-and-cream complexion and a slim yet shapely figure, maintained by weekly aerobics classes and Saturday-night dancing with me and friends at local clubs . . . her physical traits enhanced by her eager soft laugh, warm personality, and intelligence . . . the perfect companion . . . or so I thought until she cheated on me . . . with a mutual male friend just after graduation. The afternoon I caught the two of them in bed—Kendra's and my bed—no doubt about it, that image would probably stay with me until the day I died.

This was my first major romantic betrayal. She offered no real reason as to why she did it, yet—not wanting to break up—she begged forgiveness. To even the score, and save our relationship, she told me to have an affair of my own, recommending a friend of her sister's who had admired me from a far for a long time.

Initially, I refused to even entertain such a ridiculous suggestion. However, the more I thought about it, the more I thought it did have the ring of "poetic justice" to it. Still, I held off on the idea because I had gained weight in college from binge eating while studying late. My baggy shirts concealed quite a gut. If that friend of Kendra's sister laughed at me or rejected me once my clothes were off, that would have been too much. Before anything could happen, I needed to get myself in better shape.

My habitual evening workouts turned my body into a leaner, more muscular machine in about six months. By that time, Kendra and I had stopped seeing each other. I never enjoyed that retaliatory tryst with her sister's friend. No need to—I acquired quite a few female admirers at the gym. For a long time, I navigated a choppy sea of meaningless affairs, not coming to shore until two years ago . . . after having enough of turbulent waters filled with gossipers and stalkers. Funneling my energy in more positive directions, I finished my master's degree and focused on obtaining a promotion within the city department where I worked. Those goals accomplished, I had been contemplating dating again, getting to know someone for a while, deciding if she would make a good long-term partner for me *before* becoming intimate . . . yet . . . a part of me  questioned if that is what life has in store for me. Do I really want a commitment, or am I happier remaining single? All these years alone, yet I'm not unfulfilled. I can bask in contentment with my career, my friends, my workout routines. "The Accomplished Modern Man"—is that me?—active, successful, and *independent*?

Pondering all this, I conclude that perhaps I have, unknowingly, reached a new period in my life . . . one of supreme self-confidence . . . one in which I do not need/want a new woman on my arm every month to reaffirm my attractiveness and vitality. Two years ago, still dwelling in the dark harbor of hurt and resentment over Kendra, I would've gone to dinner with Audrey without reservation, aroused by the prospect of a "casual encounter," free from the worry—since we live so far away from each other—that she might feel differently about the experience and involve me in some romantic entanglement. My brush with temptation confirms I am a changed man. . . .Without second thoughts or regrets, I rejected what seemed like an easy hook-up. Sex . . . I can have it or leave it. A good position to be in . . . a healthy position to be in.

Glancing at the clock again, I see it is now almost six-thirty. A gnawing sensation in my stomach is saying *time to eat*. Where to go . . . ? The restaurant in the hotel? Is that safest? Sitting up, I shake my head. Why worry about what is safest? I am staying in a good section of town, so no need to hide out in the hotel. The odds of being accosted again by someone like Audrey aren't even worth mentioning.

In the bathroom, I change into a faded denim shirt and olive-green dress pants. To freshen up, I brush my teeth and wash my face. Using my fingers, I comb some gel through my wavy hair to achieve a more suitable look for a night on the town: smoothed-back sides, shaggy front, bangs reaching down to my eyebrows. A few sprays of minty-smelling cologne on my body tantalize my nose, bringing a satisfied smile to my face. I am *ready*.

In case the weather gets colder or rainy, I grab my black leather jacket with flapped chest pockets from the closet before heading out.

*    *    *

I treat myself to a delicious meal at Mae's Cafe. Overly hungry, I wolf down a smoked salmon quiche, a generous portion of brown rice, and an ample serving of green beans mixed with almond slivers. (Normally, when eating out with friends or dates, no matter how famished I am, I demonstrate much better table manners.) Although the restaurant has a healthy crowd, only an elderly and energetic man waits on all the tables. Perhaps because I sit at a booth toward the back, it's a while before he returns to take my dessert order—coffee and chocolate cake. It feels like it takes even longer for him to bring it out to me.

By the time I leave Mae's, night has fallen. But the dinner rush, I notice, is still in full force. Many people are waiting to enter the Mexican place across the street and the Greek joint next to it. The generous lighting from the windows illuminates their bundled-up and huddled figures. Feeling the chilliness in the air, I pull the front of my jacket snug against my chest as a cold shiver runs down my back. What I need is another warm drink, maybe another cup of coffee or some hot chocolate. Despite some apprehension, which I force myself to dismiss, I head to the intersection where I first encountered Audrey. I will hang out at the coffee shop across from the bookstore for an hour, and then investigate a couple of the bars in the area. I haven't had a good cocktail in quite some time.

At the corner, my heart flutters rapidly. Another cold shiver comes over me. Whether from nerves or excitement, I couldn't say. Instead of crossing to reach the coffeehouse, I take a couple of steps toward the bookstore, my back to the traffic light, and gaze at the fluorescent-lit displays. My eyes roam over several book covers propped up on the stands, yet do not linger for long on any specific title. A love of books isn't the real reason I'm standing in this spot. I'm back here because of the overwhelming need to relive some moments from the recent past, to see if there will be a different outcome. An opportunity not to let slip away. So I close my eyes, my brow puckered, my hands balled into fists inside my jacket pockets . . . I remain in that pose for several moments . . . maybe more like a couple of minutes . . . centering my thoughts . . . throwing all my concentration into what I want to happen next. My reaction to it will tell if I am "cured" or . . . still tied in some way to my old habits.

Despite believing in the power of suggestion, I feel surprised when it *does* happen:  a couple of taps on the shoulder.

Slowly, I turn around. And there she is! No, not Audrey but another young woman . . . with prettier features . . . bewitchingly lit by the streetlamp's soft glow behind her.  I stare at her lovely dark almond-shaped eyes, curly honey-blonde hair cascading down to her shoulders, moist mouth with well-formed lips. She is tall and trim like an Olympic runner.  Her body may lack curves but more than makes up for it with perky breasts . . . now accentuated by arms folded against her hip-length heavy gray sweater.

"Pardon me," she says with a slight smile, "but do ya happen to have the time?" Her voice, with only a hint of a southern drawl, sounds soft yet strained.

My eyes examine her body again; but this time more fully, from the top of her lovely head, to her off-the-shoulder sweater and fashionably tattered jeans, all the way down to her black canvas sneakers. I delight in her slender neck, delicate shoulders, Scarlett-O'Hara-thin waist, and long legs. Unlike Audrey, her complexion is swarthy and healthy-looking.  A welcome and pleasing sight to behold.

"The time . . . ?" I repeat, feeling somewhat dazed.

"Yeah . . . can ya tell me the time?"

I smile. "Must be after 8 or so."

"Oh," she replies with a frown. She looks around anxiously. "You got a phone on ya to check—to make sure?"

I fish around my pants and coat pockets and find them empty. "Sorry. I seem to have left it behind." Damn, the phone must still be on the charger back in my room. I can be so absentminded, especially when Kendra and the past preoccupy my thoughts.

Her frown turns deeper. "I see."

"Are you all right?

She shakes her head. "Not really," she sighs.

"What's wrong?"

The look of discomfort is all over her face. To ward off the cold air, she narrows her shoulders, hugging herself more tightly. Glancing around, she groans, "Let me put it to you like this: I've had me quite a terrible night. I need to—I mean I need some—" She breaks off into a sob.

Instinct taking over, I reach out for her arm to comfort her, but she jumps back.

I retract my hand. To show that my intentions are honorable, I say, "You look cold. There's a coffee shop across the street. You want a cup of coffee or something?— my treat."

She shakes her head again. "I'm in a bind and wonderin' if ya can help a young woman out." As if to hold back tears, she drops her head into her hands for a moment. Looking up but not meeting my gaze, she explains, "Ya see, I was out tonight with my boyfriend—and he—I mean *we*—we got to arguin' and he took off with the car. Just deserted me here with no coat. I need some money to hitch the train back home."

I stand there, my mouth agape, filled with a mixture of surprise and disappointment. *She was out tonight with a boyfriend.* The jewel that started off as so dazzling has suddenly lost its luster. Though she sounds sincere—and her damsel-in-distress situation is plausible—I question whether she's telling the truth. In the back of my mind a certain hunch grows stronger by the second—that her alleged abandonment is probably a tactic she uses to extract money from unsuspecting sympathetic souls.

Staring at her, I notice how she keeps turning her head from side to side, almost trying to glance over her shoulders but then forcing herself to look straight ahead. Is someone else out there watching her . . . watching us . . . making sure she carries out the plan . . . the plan of swindling the gullible?

"Wish I could help you," I decide to say, "but I don't have any cash on me." Instead of turning back to retrieve my phone, I decide to head for immediate safety. By the time I finish with a cup or two of java inside the coffee shop, this woman will have moved on to panhandling (and maybe ambushing with her concealed accomplice) someone else.

As I walk past her, she commands, "Wait!"

I don't comply. Crossing the street, I hold up a hand and call back, "A few more blocks down, you'll find a lot of people hanging out in front of the restaurants. I'm sure someone there will donate to your cause."

Heatedly, she cries, "Don't get ya—offer me coffee but not even a few damn bucks for train fare. Thanks for nothing, you stupid prick—*asshole!*"

My suspicions confirmed, I wave dismissively, to acknowledge to her but also show I'm not going to stoop to her name-calling level. Once across the street, I fall into a fit of laughter. What the hell was I *thinking* . . . standing around on the corner, pining for some pretty woman to come along and notice me, chat with me, and then to do what . . . ? I smack myself hard in the forehead. For pressing my luck, I got exactly what I deserved—being accosted by another nut case.

In the coffee shop, I settle at a round table in the back with my cafe mocha, behind a display of coffee bean packages and brightly painted mugs, out of view from the front windows. To learn more of what the town has to offer, I leaf through a digest-sized magazine called *Spotlight on Atlanta*, sipping from my drink, enjoying its rich chocolate and bold coffee flavors. I want to find ads on bars and nightclubs in the Midtown area, but, after looking at a few, my focus changes to a feature article on a store specializing in outdoor décor. Last year, I ripped out the rotting wooden deck in my backyard; last month, some masonry workers installed a stamped-concrete porch in its place. (What an improvement to the aesthetics of my backyard! I should've done it much earlier, but waited until I had the money to complete the project.) Though warm weather in Michigan is a few months away, I want to get a jump on the season by getting some decorative pots for planting flowers. The store, according to its address, is a short distance away.

Returning my empty cup to the counter, I ask the young guy behind the register, "Have you heard of Grand Gardens?"

He nods.

"How far from here?"

Pushing his black-rimmed glasses up his nose, he replies, "Just right up the street—exactly two blocks." He points to his left. "It's an all-glass one-story building on the corner of Tenth and Argonne—can't miss it."

Holding up the magazine, I show him the page with interior photos for a Victorian-style pub called Hinshaw's. "This place has an Argonne address. How close to Grand

Gardens?" The ad caught my attention because it boasts that the establishment has a major selection of imported beers.

The worker jerks his head to the side so that his wild mane of curly hair is out of his eyes, then glimpses at the page. "You walking or driving?"

"Walking."

"At the corner of Tenth and Argonne, you make a right and head down eight *long* blocks or so. It's almost to Ponce De Leon Avenue"

"What time is it now?"

After a quick glance down at the computerized register, he replies, "Almost twenty-five to nine. If you want to visit the gardening center before it closes, you best hurry."

\*    \*    \*

Reaching the shop after a brisk walk, I try the G-shaped handles to the metal-frame glass doors, but find them both locked. Gazing inside, I observe the ceiling florescent lights turning off in sections from the back to the front, making it difficult to see the wares down the deep, narrow aisles. I heave a sigh of disappointment. There will be no time tomorrow to come back. So much for checking out the merchandise . . .

No sense in sulking, so it's onward to destination number two. Retrieving the *Spotlight on Atlanta* magazine from my coat pocket, I walk ahead a few feet to be under the corner streetlamp. Methodically, I begin to flip through the pages in search of the ad with the address for Hinshaw's. Where's that ad? Toward the middle maybe—?

Without warning, I am shoved from behind into the streetlamp. My forehead collides with the post, the magazine dropping out of my hand. *What the hell . . . ?* I grip the pole to keep myself from staggering and falling. Recovering my balance, I straighten up and gingerly pat my forehead to learn if I'm bleeding. My head throbs, but I don't feel a cut anywhere.

I turn around and face my assailant: a bald man with a stocky build, slightly shorter than my height of six feet. As if to appear intimidating, he wears all black: leather jacket, jeans, and motorcycle boots. The force of his push left no doubt in my mind he is strong.

Curbing my urge to retaliate, I let my hands fall to my side and address him in a calm voice: "What did you do that for? You could've split my head wide open."

Furrowing his pockmarked forehead, he glares at me . . . with his fierce dark eyes. His contorted face is as ugly as an ogre's. Shaking his fist, he flares, "That's what ya deserve— havin' yur head busted open for being such a—"

Extending the palm of my hand out in front of me, I cut him off: "I have no idea what you're talking about." I take a couple steps back, almost to the edge of the curb. "We don't know each other—so—so I don't know what your problem is."

He raises his arms, as if to lunge forward and push me again—but stays put as he shouts, "I'll tell ya what the problem is"—his scowl growing even harsher—"the problem is assholes like ya—who've got the attitude to go around and say whatever to another guy's gurl."

Across the street, onlookers have gathered. They are just standing around and watching us as if we're performing for their pleasure. I think about calling out to them: "Hey, I'm getting attacked here. If one of you has a phone, call the police." But I hesitate to say that . . . fearing he might take off. Aware now of the source of his hostility, I am curious to find out more. Is he really clueless to fact that his "girlfriend" accosts guys on the street for money using a sad-luck story—or part of a team who preys on the unsuspecting?

"Look," I say with irritation I cannot suppress, "you've got me all wrong. I'm not the type to go around and make rude comments to anyone"—I pause to take a deep breath—"unless the other person says something to me first—"

"Don't act awl innocent and shit with me," he fumes, gritting his uneven teeth. "And don't give me no bullshit excuses." He waves a fist back and forth in the air, as if pounding on an imaginary door. "It's a damn shame my gurl can't even leave the shop for a bit without me—without some joker like *ya* wantin' to pick her up. To make shore it ain't happenin' again, I'm givin' ya two choices: number one, ya git yur ass kicked—or number two, ya go back with me and apologize and . . . and tell her you ain't gonna ever look her way again."

Finding the situation unreal, I can only shake my head. I'm not used to dealing with over-the-top possessive guys (females are another matter). I look away. My stare fixes itself on the crowd across the street. How many stood there now . . . eight . . . nine? A cab has pulled up near them, probably in the hope that someone in the group will need a ride. Most likely, that person will be me if this crazed man does not calm down and listen to what I have to say. My patience is about at its limit.

Gazing into his deranged eyes, I insist, "Listen, buddy, you're mistaken—terribly mistaken." Pausing, I breathe deeply. "I can explain how there's been a misunderstanding. But first I need to make sure about something first. This woman you're talking about—your girlfriend—is a young blonde woman wearing a gray sweater—right?"

"You mean there's been *others*?" he erupts. "Ya bastard—how many victims of yurs err there?" Now, he beats both fists in the air, his too-short bomber jacket riding up on his barrel chest. "I'm gonna stop ya once and fer all. My gurl's gonna be yur last victim."

He swings at me—but, possessing quick reflexes, I duck and jerk my head out of the way. His hand strikes the lamppost instead—strikes it hard. I could swear I heard his knuckles crack against the metal. His eyes, registering his pain, roll back into his head for a moment. Holding his hand at the wrist, he groans as tears stream in a wavy pattern down his face. I watch him collapse to his knees.

I bend down and ask, "Uh . . .you want me to get you some help?" A cold shudder rips through my body, and I almost lose my balance. To keep myself from falling to my knees beside him, I abruptly step forward, widening the stance of my legs, and then take a couple of steps back, straightening my posture.

"Some help? Whatcha think, you damn sonofabitch?" he sobs. "It's awl because of ya. Ya killed it—killed my hand. It hurts—really freakin' hurts." His toughness dissipated, he won't look at me, only stares down at the pavement.

By this time, a couple of the onlookers are crossing the street to check out the scene. The leader is a pear-shaped woman with chin-length black hair. Reaching the curb, she cries, "Oh, dear God, how awful!" gesturing with a shaky hand toward the fallen man. Two older gray-haired men follow her onto the sidewalk. The shorter of the two takes a flip phone out of his khaki pants, stammering, "I—I think—I mean I better call . . . call 9-1-1."

Cupping his wounded hand with the other, my assailant finally looks up at me and wails: "Yeah, call 9-1-1. And—and tell 'em about this asshole—this dickhead who was violatin' my girl . . . he actually tried to . . ."

Unable to listen to any more of this insane man's ravings, I flee . . . jumping into the parked taxi. "Take me to the Hyatt," I direct the male driver. And we head down the street. In a slightly stunned state, I don't pay much attention to my surroundings . . . until we come to a section where the street narrows and becomes one-way because of road construction. The driver, in broken English, mumbles something about going the long way to the hotel. He points to a right turn he's supposed to make which is now blocked off. From the rearview mirror, he looks at me. I meet his gaze and nod to show I understand, and we continue down Argonne.

As I think about where we are heading, a strange tingling sensation sweeps over me. At first, it feels distressing, like being pricked with pins, but then quickly changes and turns more pleasurable, spreading warmth throughout my body the way drinking an intoxicating beverage would. I enjoy the calming it brings. Unfortunately, the pleasant feeling is short-lived . . . and replaced by anxiety, restlessness. I want that relaxing effect back. The easiest means of achieving it again: stopping at Hinshaw's and having a drink.

I don't say anything to the driver about a different destination, though we are approaching another intersection that can be Argonne and Ponce De Leon, the location of the pub. Another urge has come over me, an urge to chastise myself. I hold my arm down, to prevent myself from smacking my forehead and appearing like some kind of crazy passenger to the driver. That's what I am, all right—a crazy passenger, a fool. How can I possibly consider going to the bar? Given all the recent drama, it's best to stick to the plan of an early night back in my room. A safe and sound plan. Yet playing it "safe" and "sound" might rob me of experiencing whatever else the night has in store. The desire to test the future is hard to suppress.

What to do . . . ?

I can't remember the last time I have been so conflicted . . . probably not since all those years ago when I couldn't decide whether to end it with Kendra.

Engrossed in my thoughts, I haven't been paying attention to the street signs. How much farther are we .. ? All I see are fancy houses on either side. With no traffic light in sight now, I figure we have started along a new block. Perhaps we've already gone past Hinshaw's. Perhaps that's a good thing. For a moment, I consider changing my plans and giving the driver the hotel's address.

Though we travel at a slow pace, we move steadily. The row of houses on my right ends, replaced by a small field littered with papers, plastic bottles, and other garbage. A recycling advocate, I shake my head in disgust. I simply can't understand how residents of nicer communities will fail to work together to clean up a trashy property in their midst. Fortunately, my gaze has to linger on the rubbish only for a few seconds. Relieving it is a well-maintained apartment complex—fashioned out of red bricks, surrounded by a black wrought-iron fence, its buildings arranged like two opposite L's around a courtyard.

My eyes almost pop out of my head when I notice a burgundy-haired woman, dressed in black pants and a green velvety-looking camisole, head into the complex by entering an opening in the fence. Can she be—is it really—Audrey? Is this where she lives—alone? And why is she dressed so scantily? She must be cold in a top without sleeves, held up only by spaghetti straps, yet her relaxed posture indicates otherwise. This evening is nothing like I could ever imagine, and I try to make sense of it all. In particular, I try to find the meaning in why I was attacked just a little while ago and why I'm probably seeing Audrey again. One conclusion glares brighter than all others: Karma has bitten me in the butt. To right a wrong, to demonstrate remorse for perhaps passing judgment too quickly (after having been a victim of the same), I decide I must offer an apology.

Past the apartments, just beyond a public parking lot, stands a stone-faced building with a shiny wooden door. Above the door is a sign: HINSHAW'S, illuminated by a goose-neck lighting fixture. "That's it!" I yell to the driver, who isn't slowing down. Reaching my arm over the passenger seat's headrest, I point to the right. "That's the place. Let me out!" Hitting the brakes, the man jarringly pulls over alongside a line of parked cars. Without waiting to hear the fare's total, I throw a couple of twenty-dollar bills in the driver's lap, then jump out.

Instead of checking out the bar, I jog by it and head toward the apartment courtyard entrance where I may have spotted Audrey. "Hey, Audrey! Wait!" I call out repeatedly until I reach the opening. Entering, I run to the courtyard and arrive just in time to catch the burgundy-haired woman fumble with keys to one of the wood-paneled doors of the building behind the sunken pool, calling out again: "Hey! Is that you, Audrey?" As she turns to face me in the darkness, I explain in a softer voice, "It's me, Gunnar—the guy from Piedmont Park," intending not to raise any alarm. The cement walkway around the pool takes me to an intersecting path leading to her apartment.

Twirling the ring of keys on her index finger, she says, "Well, well, well . . . My Viking warrior has returned. What do I owe this pleasure?" She steps forward, the moonlight bathing her face and bringing a startling glow to her chalky complexion.

Not good with apologies, I stammer, "I—I was at the—I mean walking by Hinshaw's—and I—I happened to see you—and I . . ."

Arching her shoulders, she folds her arms and sighs, "Really? I was just at the bar. Some kind of event going on for a bowling league. A lot of sleazy-acting, drunk types—

laughing and yammering on about their pathetic lives above the music—not my scene."

After a deep breath, my voice regains its strength. More relaxed now, I say without stammering: "Not my scene either. I guess I'll skip that place." I laugh and shake my head. "Such a pity . . . because I had my heart set on a good cocktail. Any other bars nearby? I'd like to make up for my rudeness earlier and buy you a drink."

"There's an open bar at my place."

Not wanting to make another mistake, I explain, "Thanks, Audrey, but I'd rather we go somewhere." I slowly move a couple of inches backward, as if to emphasize I have no intention of accompanying her inside. "When we first met, I should've been more up front with you. I should've told you that I don't live here and I'm not looking for anything. I'm heading back to Michigan in the morning."

She reacts with a laugh of disbelief. Her eyes narrow, her mouth twitches, as if irritated; yet she replies in a calm voice: "Don't trust me—is that it? Think I'm going to do something to you." She snorts softly as if suppressing more laughter. "You're so like Eric—another Viking—so scarred to be alone with good-natured me. I don't understand you strong fellows."

*Who's Eric?* I want to ask, but decide I'm not in the mood to hear anymore of her ranting about how some other guy resembles a Viking warrior. Instead, I explain, "I suppose I shouldn't assume anything, but we're adults and we both know how one thing can lead to another."

"I see," she says with a shrug and a shiver. Keeping her shoulders drawn up toward her neck, she clutches her forearm and, slightly extending her other hand, points to a wooden bench beneath a large budding tree in the courtyard. "We can have our drinks out there. That's certainly safe enough." Pausing, she bites at her upper lip. "Never been to

Michigan, so I'd like to learn more about it. I don't have any wine or beer, but I can make you a gin and tonic or a rum and Coke. Which do you prefer?"

I hesitate to respond. Turning toward the street, I ask, "Isn't it a bit chilly to hang out in the courtyard? Wouldn't you be more comfortable indoors? What other bars are close by?"

"The courtyard is much quieter for chatting than any bar would be." She presses her lips together to form a thin smile. "But you're right about it being chilly—I do need to put on a coat or sweater before I come back out. I didn't bother with one because it's a short walk to Hindshaw's and the place always has the heat cranked up."

"Okay."

"So what are you drinking?"

"A gin and tonic sounds good."

"Great choice." She flashes a quick, seemingly phony smile. "I can tell you are a classy guy."

Turning away, she unlocks the door, then heads inside. As a ceiling light switches on, I see that the entrance is not to a hallway or staircase, but to a ceramic-tiled foyer serving as a threshold to the empty carpeted living room. I move closer to get a better look at her place, to watch her fix our drinks, but barren beige walls obstruct my view of the kitchen and other rooms. Waiting, I turn away and look up at the sky, noticing the poor attempt of some wispy clouds to cover the full moon—a beautiful strawberry moon. Although I am well aware of superstitious beliefs about full moons causing people to commit horrible acts, I still do not buy into those ideas despite being assaulted out of nowhere only a little while ago. I feel just the opposite: moons have a calming effect on me. Enjoying a delicious beverage with a nearly clear view of earth's spectacular satellite . . . a great way to spend the evening . . .

"Hey, just don't stand out there," Audrey commands from what I assume is the kitchen. "Give me a hand."

"Okay," I say, crossing the foyer into the living room. "What's up?" I run my tongue along my lips in anticipation of the drink I'm about to consume—the wonderful juniper flavor of the gin mixed with the bittersweet taste of the tonic delighting my mouth—and the tingling, relaxing sensation that will follow.

"I need your help," she cries, her distressed voice coming through a doorway in the far wall. "I can't reach this tray."

Halfway across the enormous living room, I hear someone walk in. Then the front door slams closed. I spin around to see who's responsible. An elderly man, quite tall with disheveled snow-white hair, wearing tattered jeans and a mud-splattered black coat, stands blocking the exit. A deep frown envelops his wrinkled face, and he folds his arms in a hostile gesture. He flares, "You heard her! Don't be another one of those impolite assholes. Help the lady out."

My heart now racing, I whirl back around. "Audrey!" I yell, hurrying toward the doorway with clenched hands. "There's this crazy old guy—at the . . . "

In the kitchen, my voice falters, fails to work; my body freezes in shock from the sight before me. A few feet away, under a flickering light fixture, Audrey stands stripped to her underwear, her body covered with a clear plastic cape, her hair pulled back into a tight ponytail. Pressing her back against the counter, she faces me brandishing a pistol. Sweat drips down my forehead: a silencer is attached to the end of it. Her face contorted (in anger? in concentration?), she aims the gun at the space between my eyebrows.

"I love it when the strong becomes the weak," she says with pursed lips, "when the hunter becomes the hunted."

Still too horrified to respond, react—never expected *this*.

# THE MESSAGE

When her cell phone rang, Debra grabbed it from the coffee table, murmuring, "Oh, please . . . let it be *him*." Mark promised he would call sometime over the weekend. At nine-thirty on Sunday night, time was running out.

"How's it going?" It was Kelly.

"Okay," Debra said, trying to disguise her disappointment. "How about you?"

"I was about to head off to bed," Kelly said. "Then I suddenly remembered that our workshop on stuttering disorders at the Convention Center is tomorrow morning. For the life of me, I can't remember what time. I checked my e-mail, but I must've deleted the message."

Debra and Kelly were speech therapists at Fairfield Developmental School. Located in northeastern Ohio, about ten miles from Lake Erie, the school serviced students with autism and cognitive impairments. Debra enjoyed her job— except for the school's policy that the therapists had to attend an all-day workshop twice a month. Rarely were the speakers inspiring; most of them presented in the same boring way: reading aloud informational slides projected from their laptops onto large screens. Since her professional-journal subscriptions kept her up-to-date with the latest therapy techniques, she believed her time was better spent at school with the kids.

"It's at eight," Debra replied. "So, we report there first thing."

"All right. Thanks."

"I'll see you tomorrow."

Sighing, Debra thought about going to bed, but she wouldn't be able to sleep. Her head was throbbing from the tension in her shoulders and neck.

Dwelling on Mark, she buried her face in her hands. She had met him about three months ago while doing volunteer work at the Fairfield Historical Museum. She sorted mail and cleaned on Saturday afternoons. He monitored the collections of photographs and city documents for tours.

Not long after they began working together, Debra had lost her father to colon cancer. Her mother had passed away ten years earlier; and since Debra had no family left in the area—her sisters lived hundreds of miles away—she wore her loneliness on her face.

Tall and handsome, with a fluffy mat of brown hair and deep brown eyes that complemented his high cheekbones and swarthy complexion, Mark reached out by offering his friendship and support. "If you ever want to talk about anything—I mean *anything*—please feel free," he said when she returned after a temporary leave to handle her father's funeral arrangements. "I'm a great listener." Even though she wasn't able to discuss her sadness with others, she was heartened that he showed he cared.

During their lunch breaks, he often treated her to specialty salads and deli sandwiches at Café Bon Appétit, a few blocks from the museum. At the eatery, she learned about his family: his parents who were glassblowers and ran a local glass studio, his brother and sister who were fine arts professors at different colleges on the East Coast. "I'm not like them," he admitted. "The most artistic thing I've done in years is sponge paint my bathroom. It came out all right, but some of credit goes to having a good sponge." They laughed. Debra related that she was no artist, either. She had once sponge painted an unfinished dresser, but the edges turned out gloppy. When she tried to sand smooth the thick crusts of paint, she dropped one of the drawers and cracked the wood. Deciding it was too much trouble to fix, she threw out the dresser.

On their walks back to the museum, Debra talked about her job. Each year, the school's enrollment increased, thus adding more children to her caseload. She felt as if she needed to be a juggler to ensure she had enough time to test kids for their quarterly reports, see them for individual therapy sessions, and teach large-group language lessons in the classroom. At times, the stress overwhelmed her. Yet whenever she saw progress, or helped students learn new skills, she felt such satisfaction; it reaffirmed that she was in the right career.

About two months ago on a Saturday afternoon, as they closed the museum for the day, Mark made the first move to take their relationship to the next level. "How about meeting me later at Anthony's downtown for dinner?" he asked. "Our lunch breaks are too short for getting to know each other. We're both artistically challenged, but it would be nice to find out what else we have in common." Unsure of his intentions, Debra declined with the excuse that she had to catch up on laundry and cleaning. Yet he insisted: "How does seven o'clock sound? It's only two now. You have plenty of time to get your housework done." When she hesitated, he used it to his advantage: "Very well. I'll see you at seven." He waved good-bye to her and hurried toward his car before she could utter another refusal.

When Debra got home, she considered calling Mark to cancel. He was in his late twenties, but she was almost forty. How much could they *really* have in common? Still, Debra went to her closet and picked out a floral-print dress with a buckle sash that accentuated her small waist. After her dad's funeral, she stopped covering her gray and curling her medium-length hair, letting it drape like a towel across her shoulders. But she wasn't about to show up at an upscale restaurant with a plain hairdo. After dying her hair a warm golden brown, an improvement from her natural mousy color, she used gel and a curling iron give to her locks some flattering waves.

At seven, Mark arrived promptly at Anthony's, an Italian place known for its homemade breads and pasta. He was dressed stylishly in black pants and a silky blue shirt with a striking burgundy tie. During dinner, Debra discovered they indeed shared many common interests. They both had a set of old encyclopedias, which they perused from time to time, fascinated by the way nations and political boundaries had changed over the years. On rainy afternoons, they loved to lounge on the sofa and watch classic Hollywood movies. And what intrigued Debra even more about Mark was that he also enjoyed reading books that analyzed how the Bible affected nations, languages, and cultures. Displayed on the top shelf of her living-room bookcase, Debra shared, were several different books that discussed the history of the King James Bible and the influence this particular text had on the world.

Mark said, laughing, "We are fellow dorks."

Debra laughed, too—for a moment. Putting one hand on her hip, batting her long mascaraed lashes, she reminded him in a playful tone: "I may be a dork, but I'm definitely *not* a fellow."

Mark's eyes widened as they gazed into hers. "Very true."

Hearing how corny they sounded, they fell into a fit of more laughter.

Their first dinner together led to other enjoyable dates— to the weekly mystery-movie night at the library, theatrical productions at the Limelight Theatre, and piano performances at the Heart of Enlightenment Church. At the museum, they collaborated on a couple of articles for its seasonal newsletter: one about the history of families who had lived in the oldest house in the city, another that spotlighted a local man who had recorded folk singers at a nearby studio in the '60s. Before these articles, Debra had never thought much of her writing skills. Back in college, she had earned a few C's in her English courses. But under Mark's tutelage, she learned how to shorten her rambling sentences and put power into them with strong verbs and adjectives.

Several years had passed since she had seriously dated, and she cast aside any cautioning thoughts about getting hurt by Mark. At the end of each date, they embraced with long passionate kisses before parting for the night. Though she never questioned him about his feelings, she believed they were mutually falling in love . . . and would soon be ready to take their relationship to the next level . . . the level that included sexual intimacy. . . .

*Never assume.*

During an evening together three weeks ago, he reached for her hand across her kitchen rustic table where they had been playing the *Ultimate Classic Hollywood Trivia* card game. His grip was softer than usual and he temporarily avoided her gaze, yet these gestures did nothing to prepare her for what he was about to say.

He took a deep breath. "I'm leaving in a few days for Savannah, Georgia!" he exclaimed. "A friend of mine owns several art galleries and framing shops in the area, and he's offered me a job as an accountant for his business. It's just a temporary position. The woman who works for him had to go on maternity leave."

"What about your job at the bank?" she asked. She really wanted to ask *What about us?*—but felt awkward about it.

"Oh, I resigned already," he explained. "I never cared too much for my boss."

Unable to restrain her hurt, she pulled away and tightened her back against her chair.

He gently grabbed her hand again. Stroking it, he said: "I know we won't be able to see each other whenever we want, but we'll only be a call away. I've vacationed in the Savannah several times—it's very beautiful there by the ocean. With this new job, I can test whether I'd want to live there permanently. Maybe when you come down to visit, you might consider relocating there yourself."

His words soothed her with the hope that they could still be a couple in the future.

He then promised that when he returned the following week, they would make the most of their time together before he moved. But he phoned the day he was supposed to come back and said he was postponing his plans for another week. During his call this past Monday, he disappointed her once more by saying he was still searching for an apartment or condo to lease and wasn't sure when he would be returning to Ohio. He seemed in a hurry to get off the phone and said he would call again when he had free time over the weekend.

Since their last short conversation, she had done everything she could think of to prevent herself from watching the hours pass—unfortunately, her ideas were running out . . .

Debra's eyes wandered back to the clock. It was after ten now. Even though she told herself she would give Mark space, she picked up the cell phone and called him. *What's going on, Mark? If you've lost interested, then just say so. I need that closure.* His number rang about seven or eight times, then went to voicemail. She hung up without leaving a message. Disheartened, she let the phone drop to the carpet.

She needed to go to bed, but was too upset to sleep. She had to get out of the house for a while. The emptiness was unbearable. Since it was a damp September evening, she dug into her hall closet for a pair of gym shoes and a hooded nylon jacket before heading out.

With nervous energy, Debra followed along her street for several blocks until it ended. Then she turned onto a longer street that had fewer houses and more businesses. She passed a 24-hour fitness center, a few coffee shops, and several bars.

As the air cleared and turned breezier, she approached a one-story dark brick building that had once been a laundromat. Stopping, she searched the postings on the partially boarded windows to read if any said which new business might be coming into this space. None did: the postings were ads for upcoming concerts and comedy acts at various theatre venues in Fairfield.

Both pizza lovers, she and Mark had been ecstatic when they read in the local newspaper a while back that a Papa Marino's restaurant, a chain well-known for its deep-dish pizza, had planned to open here. The closest one to Fairfield was an hour away—too far for home deliveries or carry-outs after a hard day at work. But then they read later that the prospective owner had decided to shelve his plans for the time being. How disappointed they had been!

Debra heard the sound of a bicycle. Ready to get out of the way, she spun around. Despite the darkness, she saw that the cyclist was an elderly man. She stood flat against the side of the building as he rode past.

He slowed and stopped in front of the next building, a gray stucco bungalow that had been converted into a drab dental office. Keeping the bike between his legs, with his right foot on some grass and his left on the peddle, he leaned against a tall wooden sign. Above the stenciled words Thomas Family Dentistry was a gooseneck light fixture spotlighting his features. With his full head of shaggy grayish-white hair and heavily lined face, he looked to Debra to be in his late sixties to early seventies. The man wore heavily stained khaki pants, and his green wool sweater was unraveling around the cuffs and waistband. His gym shoes were in such rough shape that he had used thick pieces of duct tape to keep them together.

The man simply stared at Debra. Breathing heavily, she stared back. What was the matter? Was he homeless? Was he about to ask for a handout?  She felt her palms sweating.

"Hello . . . ," she said nervously, not truly knowing what drove her to talk to him.

Releasing his grip on the handlebars, he smiled at her, showing a mouthful of crooked, browning teeth.

Again, she felt compelled to speak. "Are you okay, sir?" she asked. "Can I help you?"

His smile widening, he dropped his hands to his side.

Debra abruptly backed away and turned around as if repelled by his grin. Alarmed, she reached into her jacket pocket for her phone, but found only her wallet. Then she remembered she had left it on the living room floor.

"Hey!" he called out to her in a surprisingly gentle tone.

Startled, Debra swung around to see what he wanted, noticing that his face had turned serious. Her eyes locked with his.

"Let go!" he cried.

"What . . . ?"

"Let go!" he repeated. "Even though you feel you can't."

*Let go of what?* Debra wasn't sure how to respond.

Her voice seemed to lose its strength as she asked, "Why are you saying that?"

He didn't reply. Instead, he smiled at her again, but it seemed less offensive, more welcoming.

Confused and scared, she turned and continued her retreat. Shaking her head, she assured herself that this man must be a homeless person who was a little nutty. Too many months—maybe even years—on the streets had obviously affected his mental state. It was the only logical explanation. Why else would he be dressed in ragged clothes and say those things to her?

She considered that, if he was indeed living on the streets, most likely he was hungry. Should she have given him some money? As a child, her mother often warned her about handing money to the homeless. "They'll only use it to buy booze or drugs," her mother said. With an overwhelming sense of guilt, she halted.

Pivoting, she discovered the man was gone. The street was empty. Had he been real? Or had she been only hallucinating? She shook her head. No, she didn't just imagine seeing him. She wasn't a sleepwalker, nor was she a fantasist. Looking along the pavement, she saw the muddy tracks from his bike—physical evidence that he had indeed been there.

As absurd as his words sounded, she couldn't dismiss what he said. What did he mean by *let go*? He spoke with the calmness of a therapist, as if reading her emotions. But how? They hadn't had enough interaction for him to observe the heartache on her face. Could it be possible that he was relaying a message? Had God compelled the man to speak to her? By *let go*, was God telling her to stop agonizing and have some faith? Maybe she had been too hard on Mark by wrongly suspecting that he was distancing himself from her. After all, it wasn't an easy task to move from one part of the country to the other. From what she had heard, reasonable places to rent weren't abundant in Savannah. He probably had been very busy with just searching for a place to live. Most likely, when she returned home, there would be a blinking light coming from her phone, showing she had missed his call.

Debra laughed at her own insecurities. Quickening her pace as she retraced her steps, she couldn't wait to tell Mark her story about the man on the bike. She could hear him say: "Are you sure, Debra? Did that man really say that to you?" and she would say, "Yes, Mark. He *did*." And then they would share a warm laugh over the incident, and Mark would reveal he was actually phoning her around the same time she had spoken to bicycle man. She hoped Mark would say, "I'm so sorry about not being focused lately. It's not like me. I've just been so caught up in the sunny beaches and beautiful scenery. But I realized today none of it matters without you here."

Debra made it home in half the time it had taken her to reach that dilapidated building. She unlocked the door and, anxious to find her phone, practically bounced into the living room.

"Yes!" Debra cried aloud. In the darkness, a small red light flashed in front of her sofa. She eagerly grabbed the phone and activated her voicemail. She was certain it was Mark.

As she heard the number of the missed call, a sinking sensation traveled from her throat into her stomach. Her lips quivered and her hand shook. She almost dropped the phone a second time. Still, she listened.

"Hello, Debra," said her friend Anne, the volunteer coordinator at the museum. "I guess you must be in bed by now. I've had a hectic day and this is the first chance I've had to call. Anyway, I want to invite you to a dinner party at my house on Wednesday evening. There's this man I'd like you to meet. His name is David, and he's publishing a new newsletter for local businesses. He's been raving about your articles for the museum, and said something about you writing for his monthly publication. Let me know if you can make it. 'Bye.'"

Debra turned on the light and glanced at the clock: almost eleven-thirty. She now knew Mark wasn't going to call. Sighing heavily, she set the phone down and then went into the kitchen. After pouring herself a glass of wine, she headed outside to her back deck and sank down on a lawn chair. She sipped the drink slowly.

Gazing up, she saw the sky was illuminated with stars. Some shimmered, others sparkled. The sight of them relaxed her. Staring at the heavens, she recalled a story Mark had once related about his childhood summers on his grandparents' farm. He would sit on the porch glider, relishing the clearness of the country nighttime sky, and try to count all the stars. He never got very far, though, because the process made him sleepy. His grandma or grandpa would awaken him and tell him to go to bed.

While turning her head in several directions, Debra began to count the stars in the sky. She counted ten, twenty, then thirty. Before long, her eyes felt heavy and she surrendered to shutting them. When she opened her eyes a few minutes later, she started counting over again. She only counted twenty stars this time before her yawning distracted her. Sleepiness was overtaking her, so her star counting would have to wait for another night. With half-closed eyes, she headed back inside to get ready for bed, no longer consumed by Mark's broken promise. Thoughts of the next work day and Wednesday's dinner party at Anne's filled her mind. Debra took a moment to glance over her shoulder to stare up at the stars once more, amazed at how counting had relaxed her and helped her to let go.

# THE UNNERVING ARMCHAIR

I was browsing through the furniture department of J. P. Finegood's when I saw something that made me pause. I hadn't thought about it in years. Yet there it was—an object from the past that instantly brought back old feelings of discouragement and despair.

I moved closer to stand in front of it. I pictured the old one in my head as I closely inspected the new. It had the same gray pile fabric and the same straight wooden legs; it was also of the same enormous size. There were, however, a couple of differences between them. This armchair wasn't worn in the slightest, and had matching slipcovers over the armrests and headrest. Otherwise, because of its drab color, it looked just as uninviting (even to a man like me possessing no interior-design skills).

I glanced at the attached ticket and saw a clearance sticker. The other chairs on the floor had floral, plaid, and striped patterns in more vibrant colors. Furthermore, none seemed nearly as large and overbearing as this reduced-priced armchair.

The more I studied the chair, the more my mind became flooded with recollections of Lizbeth Stockton . . .

\* \* \*

I met Lizbeth during my senior year in college. She was twenty-two years old when I first saw her, and at least fifty pounds overweight. Her hair was as frizzy and wild as an untamed landscape: no clip or barrette could keep those chin-length unruly strands from projecting out in all directions. Her skin posed problems for her as well. Despite her use of creams and medication, it was plagued by outbreaks of unsightly blemishes. She subscribed to magazines like *Glamour* and *Woman's Day* for beauty remedies and special diets, but never said how strictly she followed them.

Like Lizbeth, I felt unhappy about my physical features. At twenty-three, the age when men were still youthful and usually quite toned, I could pass for much older than my years. My physique was very thin, with no muscular definition. My dark brown hair had receded across the front into a sharp V, like in a movie I had seen about an aging male vampire, and I had a prominent thinning spot in the back. Because my vision was so poor, I had to wear special eyeglasses that made me feel even more unattractive. At times (I must admit), it took effort not to let my dissatisfactions keep me down.

The night we were introduced, at a party, Lizbeth could talk of nothing but the university's theater-arts department's upcoming dramatization of John Steinbeck's *The Grapes of Wrath*. I remembered her saying, "It's such a lengthy novel, with many so characters and settings throughout. I'm curious to see how effectively the director handles these aspects and how convincingly it will come off on stage. One of my friends is playing the matriarchal role of Ma Joad."

When I mentioned that I also knew someone who would be performing in the production, Lizbeth said, "I have a splendid idea, Andy! Since we both know someone in the play, why don't we go together and see it? Are you doing anything Friday?"

A week later we went on our first date.

The first date led to a second, and then many more dates. I was constantly accompanying Lizbeth to art exhibits, theatrical productions at playhouses, and poetry readings at coffee shops. These places were always what Lizbeth had in mind, what she dictated we should do. I didn't protest much. In her presence, I became as compliant as a well-mannered child.

Nearly three months after we began dating, I finished college and took a job as a social studies teacher in an inner-city school district. (Lizbeth had another year of courses before her graduation.) Correcting papers and preparing lessons soon occupied my evenings. Although these tasks could be tedious and exhausting, I was somewhat grateful for them. They were just the honest excuses I needed to distance myself from Lizbeth's pastimes, which had come to bore me. Going somewhere with Lizbeth once a week, one day on the weekend, was about all I could handle.

One Monday evening in mid-October, Lizbeth unexpectedly stopped by my apartment. We went out to dinner; and, when we returned to my apartment, she said, "My grandmother is getting rid of some of her household possessions. She is putting her house up for sale and planning to move into a smaller town house. Grandma could give you some things—in particular, a gray armchair that she has no use for. My brother could bring it to your place in his truck."

Since my furnishings were sparse, I replied, "That would be great!"

But by the next afternoon, I forgot all about the armchair, despite my initial enthusiasm. While eating my lunch in the staff lounge, I watched tall and shapely Nyasha Jackson walk in. After nodding a hello to me, she sat off by herself in the corner of the room. Usually more talkative and possessing incredible patience, Nyasha worked as a paraprofessional with the special needs children included in the regular classes. Watching her out of the corner of my eye, I could tell something was wrong: she just stared off into space, not bothering to unpack the contents of her cloth lunch bag. Her somber face conflicted with her flattering bright-aqua dress and matching pumps. Since she favored modest colors, I surmised she had worn the outfit hoping to cheer herself up. A colleague had mentioned that her divorce had been finalized not too long ago. A marital split could be messy, but that same colleague said hers had been amicable. Driven by a mixture of curiosity and concern, I waited for the other teachers to leave the room and then walked over to her.

As she turned her head toward me, I noticed that her eyes, which typically shimmered like two dark beads, were missing their luster. "Is something the matter?" I asked. "I don't mean to intrude, but you seem upset."

"Oh . . . I'm good," she replied, and then looked away.

Backing up, I watched her rake some of the thick dark coils of her afro over her forehead, as if trying to cover an imperfection there. Her light brown complexion was flawless, so I gathered she was playing with her hair to sooth her nerves.

About midway between her table and mine, I halted my retreat. "Are you *sure*?" I persisted.

The corners of her eyes moistened as she met my gaze and said, "It's so thoughtful of you to show some concern for me. I—I've been going through a lot lately."

I went up to her again. "Tell me, what's the matter?"

"I don't like to talk about my problems with people at work. Besides, I hardly know you, and it would be unprofessional, Mr. Hughes."

"Call me Andy, and you may consider me a friend." I gave her a reassuring smile, or at least I hoped it was. Self-conscious, I feared my smiles sometimes looked like I was suppressing heartburn rather than being sincere. She didn't seem offended, so I continued, "Please tell me why you're unhappy. I realize that we don't really know one another, but that doesn't mean I don't care."

Nyasha smiled at me as she wiped a couple of tears away with her fingers. "My problem is this: I've recently purchased an apartment-style condo, and on my salary it nearly broke me to do so. I even had to sell the valuable set of jewelry I inherited from my grandmother to cover the closing costs. With real estate prices so low, my dad kept pushing me to buy this little place; now that I'm on my own, I don't have any money left to furnish it—not even with *semi*-decent thrift store stuff. My dad is visiting me this weekend. With his bad back and sciatic nerve trouble, it won't be acceptable for him to sit on one of my folding chairs." Pausing, she quietly sniffled and cleared her throat. "I can already see his face when he looks around—the disappointment in his eyes saying, 'My poor baby girl— almost thirty and not getting too far in life.'"

The warning bell sounded. I could hear students walking quickly in the hallway, talking loudly with one another, outside the door to the staff lounge. The noises made me anxious.

"Don't lose heart," I said, an idea forming in my mind. Nyasha's attempt to smile failed to mask her sadness, so I added, "I think I know how I can help you out. Let me get back to you."

I rushed off to greet my fourth-hour class, but for the remainder of the school day, I found it difficult to concentrate. I was impatient for work to end so that I could race home and call Lizbeth. When I made it home, I practically ran to the phone and dialed Lizbeth's number. She was supposed to be coming to my apartment in an hour with the chair. I was relieved when she answered.

"I was just on my way out the door," Lizbeth said breathily. "What's going on?"

"Oh, Lizbeth, I heard a sad story today," I explained. "Ms. Jackson, one of our parapros, recently moved into a condo and is having financial troubles because of it. Her father is coming to visit, and she doesn't even have a decent chair or sofa for him to sit on. Ms. Jackson is always so kind and helpful to the teachers and students she works with. I feel really sorry for her. Even though my apartment is mostly empty and uncomfortable, I can still manage fine without your grandmother's chair. Would it be all right if we held off bringing the chair here for the time being? I want to find out if Ms. Jackson would like it instead. I plan to give your grandmother some money, of course."

An awkward moment of silence passed before Lizbeth finally replied. "This is my grandmother's chair!" Lizbeth yelled into the phone. "If you gave it away to a stranger, you'd hurt and insult us."

Before I could advocate any further for Nyasha, Lizbeth emphasized that the chair was now *mine*. She was about to drive to her brother's house, and from there they were heading to her grandmother's to fetch the chair *for me*. She abruptly hung up.

I was expecting that Lizbeth and her brother wouldn't arrive for another hour or more, but instead they were ringing the bell to my apartment in less than half an hour. Her brother, a stocky man with large, muscular arms, carried the chair into my apartment. "Thank you," I said, though this piece of furniture wasn't really my taste. The armchair was massive: it occupied about half of the back wall in my little living room. I generally preferred furniture that was smaller in scale and not so overwhelming. To show my gratitude, I offered to take them out to dinner. But Lizbeth had to study for an art history exam, so they declined.

Later on that evening, I sat in the chair and watched TV for an hour. It was roomy and comfortable, yet I wished to remove it from my apartment. When I went off to bed, my sleep was not restful. The image of Nyasha sitting on it, after a more colorful slipcover had been placed over the dull fabric, consumed my thoughts. I decided that even though

Lizbeth said I had to keep it, I could not honor her request. Ms. Jackson was in far greater need. But how would I go about giving it to her? Would Nyasha find my suggestion inappropriate? Or would she appreciate it?

The following school day passed slowly and tediously. I taught my lessons on the events leading up to the American Revolution, but my presentations lacked the usual enthusiasm I tried to display. I was anxious again for three o'clock to come. I wasn't good at being assertive with adults, and I had this fear that I might lose my courage after school to tell Nyasha about the armchair.

Three o'clock finally arrived. With my haphazardly packed briefcase in hand, I approached her in the parking lot, calling her name, just as she was about to get into her rusting-around-the-edges Dodge Neon. Letting go of the door handle, she turned to face me, saying, "Oh, hello, Andy. How are you doing today?" She glanced up at the sunny sky, dangling her vinyl handbag at her side. "Nice afternoon, isn't it?"

"Yes, pretty nice." I swallowed hard, summoning my courage

"Did you need to talk to me about something? Is Ralph still disrupting your third hour?" As if certain that was my motive for detaining her, she continued without waiting for me to respond: "Though they're a little better this year, his parents still aren't too accepting of his autism. If you have a meeting with them, always have the principal there and talk about their son's problems in a roundabout way. The Johnsons are tough customers. Would you like some suggestions?"

"No, it's not a matter of you helping me with anything. Rather, I'm here so that I can be of some help to you."

Nyasha wrinkled her forehead, obviously puzzled by my words. "What's this all about?" she asked.

"Well, when we were in the staff lounge together yesterday, you explained your situation about your condo and having no furniture. Your predicament touched me, and I want to help. I have an overstuffed chair at my apartment which I hardly ever use, and I'd like to offer it to you. I can have it at your new place by Friday, before your father visits. I hope I'm not sounding too forward. You seem like a *very* nice person, and I hate to hear of someone in need when it's within my power to do something."

The sparkle in Nyasha's eyes returned. She said softly, as if fearful someone might overhear us: "I'd be a fool to turn you down. You sure you don't need it for yourself? It's so nice of you to offer it."

"The chair is yours," I assured her.

Nyasha clasped her hands quietly together and shook them in the air. "Your kindness is greatly appreciated. You've relieved my worries now, Andy. There will be nothing preventing me and my dad from having our Saturday afternoon together in the living room. He can sit in that chair and gaze out window, enjoying the nice grounds surrounding the complex. I'll have to repay you somehow in the future. Maybe you can come over for dinner one night. I'm a very good cook."

I smiled inwardly. The thought of having dinner with her would be like a dream come true. I wanted to say, *That would be great*, but fear set in and I uttered something far different than I felt. "*Please* don't trouble yourself about that," I said. "Just keep being a friendly coworker. You're one of the few people here I enjoy talking to."

"You're too kind . . ."

"Let me have the directions to your house." Unzipping my briefcase, I pulled out a notebook and pen to jot down the information. I reiterated that after work on Friday, I would rent a truck and transport the chair.

Considering my slim build, this wasn't an easy task, but I carried out my mission nonetheless. Once I arrived at her house, I was concerned that, as I did, she would find it to be a drab piece of furniture. However, Nyasha expressed a great deal of excitement about having it. She said she would take excellent care of it. Before I left her apartment that evening, she hugged me warmly at the door, giving me a sunny feeling in my soul.

The following morning, I agonized about how I would inform Lizbeth of my actions. She was due at my apartment around six o'clock that afternoon. She would certainly notice right away that the chair was gone. For a little while, I pondered whether to say I had taken it to a special furniture shop to have it cleaned; but the more I entertained the idea in my head, the more ridiculous it sounded. Her grandmother was a clean person, and the chair was spotless. There was no getting around what I had done. Truthfulness would have to be my guide in handling the situation.

Lizbeth promptly appeared at my door at six. She wore strange attire. Her clothes reminded me of what I had observed in books that dealt with the fashions and cultural of Eastern European women from long ago. Her embroidered dress was flowing yet shapeless, and almost reached her ankles. And she had tied a decorative scarf around her head, causing her wild hair to jut upwards like some kind of tall flowering hat. *Eccentric* was the word that started dancing around in my head; it was an adjective that best suited her. As soon as she entered, she kissed me pretentiously on both cheeks. We stood in the short, narrow hallway that led to the other rooms.

"Andrew, you're only wearing jeans and a T-shirt. Didn't you remember that we planned to go to the re-release of *Christiane F.* at the Art Institute this evening, that movie about a Berlin teenager addicted to rock music and drugs?

We will be meeting some of my friends there. Don't you have something more appropriate to wear for a night out? One of these days I'll have to do some shopping for you. I can't let your propensity for mundane clothing go on for much longer."

Lizbeth walked past me into the living room. I hesitated before I followed her. I wasn't looking forward to the discovery she was about to make.

Just as I stepped into the living room, Lizbeth let out a piercing scream. She had her back to me, staring at the blank wall, at the former location of the armchair. "Andrew, get in here!" she commanded roughly. I slowly approached her. Lizbeth put her hands on her hips as she swung around. "Where's the armchair?" she demanded with a knife-like glare. "Tell me you didn't give it away." I attempted to relax her by embracing her, but she remained stiff and unmoving. She backed away from me.

I directed my eyes toward the floor as I said, "Oh, I couldn't keep it, Lizbeth. I felt so sorry for Ms. Jackson. I felt compelled to . . . to give it to her. Please forgive me. I only did it to help out someone. It's a natural inclination of mine."

"How dare you!" she yelled at me. "I doubt I ever want to look upon you again. How could you have thrown away my grandmother's generosity onto some lowly parapro? This Ms. Nobody probably won't even take good care of it." With that, Lizbeth rushed to the door. She flung it open and stomped away into the October darkness.

I retreated like a wounded soldier to my bedroom, where I remained for the rest of weekend. Lizbeth's abrupt departure from my life was more unnerving than I imagined it would be. She had been my first, and might be my only, girlfriend. My realization that I was returning to being alone again was overwhelming. Yet at the same time I felt no desire to telephone Lizbeth and reconcile with her. By Sunday evening, I just stared at the ceiling in the bedroom.

Analyzing my behavior like a psychologist, I recognized that giving the chair away was passive-aggression, which enabled me to assert my independence and thus end our relationship. But had I acted too hastily? Was *her* company better than no company? Over the course of the following week, I was constantly debating whether or not I should pick up the phone and call her. After that week, I made my decision about what I would do . . .

\* \* \*

"Oh, honey!"—a pleasing voice called out to me, drawing me out of my intense reflections on Lizbeth Stockton. "Have you been in the furniture department all this time?"

I turned around and observed my wife striding toward me with another woman who was also tall and well-proportioned.

"Oh, yes, I guess I've been here for quite a while," I said, straightening my face to conceal any unpleasant emotions. "I've been browsing at some armchairs. The one we have in the living room, the one your sister gave us, is beginning to show its wear."

"Andy, do you remember my cousin, Lucinda?" Nyasha asked, gesturing towards the other woman. "She was at the Christmas party we had at our house two years ago, and that was probably the last either you or I have seen of her. She's been keeping such a low profile. Just by chance today I caught sight of her at the perfume and cosmetics counter." I gave Lucinda a warm hug.

I was about to ask what had been going on in her life when my wife said, "Don't tell me, Andrew, you're thinking about replacing our current chair with that one. It's identical to the one we got rid of years ago." Nyasha patted me on the shoulder as she fixed her eyes on that gray monstrosity. "I know you're the sentimental type, but some things are best left in the past," she added, barely suppressing a laugh.

Nyasha had made a valid point. To be sure, my former appearance was one thing I always wanted to stay in the past. About six years ago, I had seized my destiny with my own hands. I ate better and exercised at a local fitness center. My body increased in mass. I also underwent an eye operation that allowed me to be free of those hideous eyeglasses I was once forced to wear. Lastly, using inheritance money, I was able to restore my hair to its former full glory. Because of my improved confidence (though I might've done it even if I hadn't changed), I had the courage to ask out another woman, a far more worthy and balanced woman than Lizbeth ever was.

"You're right, Nyasha," I said. "I don't really care for the selection of chairs here. Why don't we try another store? Would your cousin like to accompany us? Maybe a family member's opinion is just what we need."

As we moved toward the exit, more memories suddenly emerged. I recalled the week before my wedding when I took the chair to an upholsterer, to have it redone to reflect the changes in my life. But, soon after I got there, I had a change of heart, realizing the chair would never be a reflection of me. I brought it back to my place; the next morning, I posted an ad for it on the bulletin board inside a local coffee shop. I sold it a few days later—the evening before Nyasha and I both said, "I do." My face brightened with a smile as I relived helping that elderly man, the buyer, load the armchair into his truck and then watching him drive away. How relieved and grateful I was on that day to finally be rid of that unnerving armchair and the awkward memories attached to it!

# NIGHT OF THE PARTY

*W*hat should I do? Lorelei wondered. *I'm not sure if I'm up for a party tonight. Could I call him with some excuse so I wouldn't have to go . . .?*

Anxiously, she drummed her fingers against the arm of the plum-colored velour sofa, bored with the gardening show on TV. As a diversion, she glanced at her friend Myra sitting quietly next to her, thinking about how nice it would be to turn off the program and listen to some pleasant pop music instead. The soothing beautiful voices of Adele or Amy Winehouse would really help calm her nerves. But she said nothing about it because Myra seemed so engrossed in watching what was on the screen—a young couple in filthy jeans and t-shirts hauling and planting shrubbery around the perimeter of their Georgian colonial's corner lot. Such dirty and exhausting work! When Lorelei got around to beautifying her own yard, she would definitely hire someone to do it.

Though she and Myra were both in their mid-thirties, Lorelei looked much younger—with her long silky blonde hair, creamy smooth skin, vivid blue eyes, and brightly painted nails. In contrast, her friend had rugged features. The wrinkles around her dark eyes were almost as prominent as her deep forehead ridges. Years of alcohol abuse and too much sunbathing had aged her once-smooth olive complexion. Lorelei spent hours at an expensive beauty salon twice a month. Myra went to a friend in the neighborhood who cut her jet-black hair chin-length short in a simple style, with modest bangs and a part down the middle. She never bothered to buff or polish her nails, just clipped them short. Lorelei wished she could be more like her friend—less preoccupied with her appearance.

*Maybe if I was less superficial, that would solve my dilemma about Lyle—and about what to wear if I do go to the party?*

Nudging Lorelei with her elbow, Myra said, "Okay . . . I get the hint."

"The hint. What hint?"

Myra mimicked Lorelei's finger-drumming, then pointed to the silver clock with three-dimensional numbers displayed beside the wall-mounted TV. "It's almost six— time for me to head out so you can get ready for the party. Thanks for having me over for dinner. That almond chicken you got from the Chinese place was good," she added with a smile, making the A-ok sign with her right-hand thumb and forefinger.

Lorelei sighed deeply. Picking up the remote from the silver-mirrored end table, she switched the TV off.

Narrowing her eyebrows, Myra scrutinized her friend's face. "Anything wrong?" she asked.

Frowning, Lorelei shrugged her shoulders. "I'm having second thoughts."

"Hmmm. When you called yesterday, you sounded excited about the party. Now you act as if you'd rather not go." Pausing, she motioned to Lorelei's prize-winning golden retriever, Sammy Joe, curled up on the patchwork accent rug in front of the door wall. "Honestly, Lorelei, I know how much you love him, but I've taken care of Sammy Joe before. If you get back real late and want to just pick him up in the morning, that's fine. You have nothing to worry about." Matching her look of concern, Myra's voice turned motherly. "Since your divorce, you spend too much time at home with the dog. You need to get out more—mix and mingle, as they say."

Lorelei nodded. "I know. But it's not that I don't trust you—it's Lyle I'm worried about."

Myra turned, facing her friend, and laid her hands in her lap. "Explain."

Lorelei took a deep breath. "A few hours ago, shortly before you came over, he called me to say he and his friends were doing some preparations for the party." She paused for emphasis. With a look of uneasiness, she continued, "Then he said something that upset me—he said he could hardly wait for the night ahead of us."

Smirking, Myra shook her head. "What's so awful about that? It sounds like he has some *fun* in store for you. Maybe he and his friends know some cool party games."

Lorelei sighed louder than before. "How can you be so naïve, Myra? I was looking forward to the party because it was chance to go out on a Saturday night, to meet new people and get to know Lyle a little better—not to spend the night with him."

"Is he moving too fast for you?"

"Kind of . . ." Lorelei's voice trailed off as she gathered her thoughts. "But it's more than that. When I went out to that wine pub last Friday, my motive wasn't to meet a guy. After a long day at work, I was in the mood for a glass of good Chardonnay. Then Lyle sat down at the counter beside me and struck up a conversation. He was very personable, and I discovered we had a few things in common—art, love of good wine, indie films, clothes shopping . . ."

Myra patted her friend's knee. "So what's the problem then?"

Frowning again, Lorelei rubbed her forehead. "The problem is, I'm not sure if there if there is any chemistry between us. With my ex, Zach, it was instantaneous but also mostly physical. With Lyle, it didn't seem to be there in the beginning. But I know attraction can develop over time." She fell silent, jiggling her leg, then continued, "He isn't a gym rat like my ex, and he doesn't have Zach's exquisitely thick wavy hair. But he has other things going for him—a great smile and beautiful brown eyes and a neatly trimmed goatee complementing his intelligent face . . . And I admire that he's a college literature instructor. English was one of my favorite subjects. "

Myra threw her hands up. "Not following you. You're contradicting yourself."

Lorelei relaxed her frown, nodding. "You see, since that night at the pub, he's been calling or texting me almost every night. It's been a while since a man has been so attentive to me. Should I feel flattered or uncomfortable?" Bewildered, she shook her head.

"He's probably just trying to get to know *you* a little better," Myra pointed out. "Nothing wrong with that."

"I know. But then he made that comment about hardly waiting for the night ahead of us. Now I'm thinking that going to this party isn't such a good idea. If I only were telepathic, then I'd know what his true intentions are."

Myra stood up and turned around, facing Lorelei. "Don't make this into something bigger than it really is. If he tries to put the moves on you, you know what to say: 'I came out tonight to get to know you and meet your friends. I'm sorry if you thought something more was going to happen. I like to take it slow.'"

"But I—"

Myra stepped back and looked at the clock, which now read six-thirty. "Stop being such a worrier. Go to the party. Maybe you'll like one of his friends. You're constantly saying you'd like to leave Michigan and relocate down South with a guy. Here's your chance."

"He doesn't live that much farther south." Lorelei laughed at how absurd her friend could be: traveling the city roads and stretch of I-75 S highway from Pleasant Ridge to Toledo, just across the Ohio border, only took about an hour.

"But it's a start," Myra said as Lorelei stood up.

"I wish you could come with me."

"My AA sponsor says I can't be in a situation where people are consuming alcohol. I've been sober for too many months now to risk the temptation of drinking again and suffering a setback." Glancing at Lorelei's bright-red cell phone on the glass coffee table, she added, "Did you call Laurie or Susan to see if they could come with you?"

Firmly patting her thigh to rouse Sammy Joe, Lorelei said, "Laurie had other plans. Susan said she'd be there around nine-thirty or so. We're meeting there separately because she went to visit her dad in Perrysburg, south of Toledo, and will be coming from the opposite direction."

Sounding motherly again, Myra said with hand on hip, "I'm glad you took my advice and invited another friend. You'll be all right, then."

Fully awake, Sammy Joe rushed over to Lorelei, who put on his leash. She bent down to gently hug the dog's neck. Responding to her affection, he licked her face.

Myra took the leash and softly patted the dog's head. "Time's a-wastin'. Once I get home, I'll take him for a nice long walk. He'll be all tired out when we get back. I'll give him a treat and he'll probably go right to sleep."

"Thank you."

Lorelei saw Myra to the door, then waved good-bye, watching her friend back down the driveway. As she drove away, Sammy Joe stuck his head out the passenger window of Myra's green Jeep Wrangler.

The quietness in the house heightened Lorelei's anxiety. Still uncertain about what to do, she sat back down on the sofa and picked up her phone. She sent Lyle a text: "Hey."

A minute later, he responded: "Hey there."

"How's it going? What r u up 2?"

Several minutes passed before he replied: "Snacks n uncorkin wine."

"Question 4 u."

"Sure. Shoot."

"What did u mean by this: can't wait for nite ahead?"

"Good friends n wine. Why?"

His explanation put her at ease. "Just askin. How many will b there?"

Lyle didn't respond right away. Waiting, she went into her recently remodeled Euro-modern kitchen to empty the stainless steel dishwasher. When she was about halfway done, he finally texted back: "10 or so. Work folks n friends."

"OK."

"C u @ 9?"

"Yes ☺"

After finishing with the dishes, she opened her wall-to-wall bedroom closet. Like an archeologist hoping to uncover an amazing discovery, Lorelei was on a mission to find just the right outfit for the party. As a buyer for Nordstrom, she appreciated fashion and had a wide-range of styles. During her three-year marriage to Zach, she acquired quite a selection of bright tight-fitting dresses and stiletto heels, trying to keep his wandering eye in check. She had a lean figure and perky pear-shaped breasts, and it often turned him on when she flaunted her cleavage privately or publicly. But to be on the safe side with Lyle, she would steer clear of an outfit too revealing. Instead, she examined the pant suits and professional-looking dresses, hung toward one side, that she wore to work. Quickly, she concluded her work attire wasn't appropriate either: too bland for an informal get-together. After all, it wasn't her intention to come across as too conservative and thus seem boring to Lyle or any other man at the party.

Sighing, she pushed hanger after hanger aside—then stopped when she came to the *right* dress. Taking it off the padded hanger, she held it against herself. *This is the one!* A knit gray dress with kimono sleeves and a beaded black belt. It was casual and dressy at the same time, and had the right sleeve and skirt length for a late September evening. She wouldn't have to bother with a coat.

In the bathroom, after changing into the dress, she brushed her hair until it shined and then put into in a simple ponytail. Digging through the vinyl bag on the counter, she pulled out her makeup brush and lip gloss. Methodically, she put on a light layer of foundation, blush, and lip gloss. As a finishing touch, she applied a single coat of mascara to her long lashes. Turning from side to side in front of the gold-leaf vanity mirror, she was satisfied with the results. She looked sophisticated—and not overly sexy.

Shortly before eight, she headed out in her pristine Lexus. Within approximately four miles, she was cruising down I-75. To pass the time, she turned on her favorite radio station, 93.9 FM, which played a pleasing mix of retro and current pop music. Before long, her thoughts drifted to her mom, who had been married to her father for almost forty years. Her parents had their share of disagreements over the years, yet their love remained strong. What was their secret for longevity? With his tall muscular frame and handsome face, Zach had enough sex appeal to keep her in for the long haul. Unfortunately, her feelings weren't reciprocated. On two separate occasions, she forgave Zach's unfaithfulness, but after his third indiscretion with yet another woman from his gym, she couldn't accept his promise of *it'll never happen again.* Earlier in the week, Lyle confided on the phone that he, too, had ended his last relationship because of deceitfulness. The more she thought about the differences between Zach and Lyle, the more a conversation between her and her mother from long ago whirled around in her head:

\* \* \*

*"I didn't think much of your father when I first met him,"* her mother revealed to her one morning during breakfast, when Lorelei was fifteen. *"I was only twenty years old at the time and hadn't really dated much. Frankly, I wasn't attracted to your father at first and believed I could do better, so I turned him down when he asked me out."*

After a brief pause, her mom continued: *"Between the ages of twenty and twenty-two, I dated my share of men. I don't know . . . maybe as many as ten. Of course, not all of them were jerks. The relationships just didn't work out. Some acted as if they liked me—some even professed their love. They would shower me with flowers and gifts, taking me out to nice places. Then when I talked about marriage, they stepped backwards. A couple of them wanted me to give up my virginity without being married. When I said 'absolutely no,' the games started. They told me they would call but they would stand me up for dates. By the time I was twenty-three, I was watchful of men and much wiser. And I realized your father was the kindest man I had met out of all of them."*

*"Why are you telling me this?"* Lorelei asked, feeling awkward that her mom was sharing her own past. Since her mom was so domestic and old-fashioned—usually in the kitchen donned in flowery aprons, baking and preparing meals—Lorelei had a hard time envisioning her dating all kinds of men and having to ward off their sexual advances.

*"Last night I heard you talking to one of your friends on the phone. You were talking about some of the boys at school. It was awful to hear you refer to them as ugly and hideous and utterly horrifying. You're a smart girl, Lorelei, and mature for your age. I expect better from you than this."*

*"Okay, okay. But all people judge by what they see . . . whether they'll admit to it or not,"* Lorelei asserted firmly.

Her mother eyed her with disappointment, saying: *"Your father may not be handsome in the worldly sense, but he's kind and caring and loving. If I had continued to care about a guy's physical attractiveness, and not seen anything deeper, I would've never agreed to go out with him when he re-entered my life a few years later."* She paused, reaching across the table to lovingly stroke her daughter's hand. *"And you wouldn't be sitting here with me today!"* her mother emphasized with a smile.

Lorelei finally could not resist the delight of her mother's story, and mother and daughter burst into laughter at her mother's last statement.

* * *

As she exited the expressway, rolling down the window to enjoy the crisp night air, she decided to heed her mother's advice and considered Lyle's finer points: his impeccable appearance at the pub—violet polo and crisp khaki linen pants— and his ability to draw her into a meaningful conversation. During their initial meeting, she was fascinated with how much he knew about indie film directors—specifically, the way they used subtle symbolism to portray the human condition. For fun, Lyle was taking a film editing class at the university where he worked. His ambition was to one day make a movie out of one of the three scripts he had written. Creativity, she was beginning to see, was an attractive trait. Time would tell if she and Lyle were compatible as friends or something more . . .

Her thoughts were interrupted as a call came in through the vehicle's Bluetooth device. The name on the dashboard display screen was *Susan*.

"Hi, Susan," Lorelei answered. "Are you on your way?"

"Actually, no. There's been a problem."

"What's going on?" She slowed her speed slightly, but her heartbeat accelerated. Susan couldn't be cancelling.

"My dad's not feeling too good. I'm going to stay here overnight to keep an eye on him. Hope you understand."

Hiding her disappointment, Lorelei said mumbled, "Yes, I understand."

"Thanks. Gotta run. Enjoy the party."

Susan ended the call before Lorelei could say anything more. Facing her now was the decision: either attending the party without a safety net—or calling Lyle with some excuse and saying she couldn't make it.

*But if I call, will my voice betray my nervousness? Will he read any excuse I come up with as flimsy?*

Consulting the map on the car's GPS device, she discovered his house was a short distance away and she had no trouble finding it. His place stood in the middle of a winding tree-lined street. The dwelling was a spacious two-story colonial. The landscape lanterns hanging on decorative stakes, along with the porch light, illuminated his lovely perennial beds of ornamental grass, sedums, and silver mounds. By the looks of things, Lyle seemed to be doing well for himself. Because vehicles filled his cobblestone driveway, she parked in front on the street. Still feeling a little anxious, she put on another coat of lip gloss before getting out of the car. On the porch doorstep, she paused to practice a pleasant and confident greeting, then rang the bell.

Moments passed but no one answered the door. Lorelei could hear '90s grunge music—Nirvana? Soundgarden? Stone Temple Pilots?—and loud voices inside. Were those noises muffling the sound of the doorbell? What should her next move be? Her internal voice gave her conflicting advice:

*If you have any reservations, now is your chance. You can slip away. If Lyle calls you and asks why you never showed up, you can honestly say you rang the bell but no one answered.*

*But you've traveled all this way. You can't turn back now. You won't be happy until you reach a conclusion. That's why you're never satisfied with mystery novels until you come to the end. Besides, Lyle will surely ask why you didn't call him so he would know you had arrived. He wouldn't believe you drove from Pleasant Ridge to Toledo without your phone.*

She reached into her quilted black handbag and pulled out her phone. When Lyle picked up, she enthusiastically said, "I'm here. I didn't feel comfortable with just walking in."

"Just a sec," he said, then ended the call.

Several minutes went by. On edge again, she shifted her weight from one foot to another in her black low-heel boots. What was going on? What was taking so long? She was about to ready to pound at the door.

Finally, the door opened—but an unfamiliar face greeted her.   She felt her throat muscles tighten and her eyes twitched. She could only say, "Uh, um . . . I'm Lyle's friend." The sight of him shocked her: he looked as disheveled as a homeless person or drunkard she might encounter in an alley. Tiny pieces of crackers were enmeshed in his unkempt blondish goatee; his blue silk shirt was completely unbuttoned, exposing a dingy grayish-white T-shirt that failed to cover his hairy navel. Glancing down, she noticed he had been just as careless with his black dress pants: the zipper was down and the leather belt was twisted haphazardly in the loops. As he stared at her, he rubbed his reddened nose. What was wrong with him? Was he drinking or binging on cocaine? Drug or alcohol use must be the explanation for this. What exactly was going on at this party?

"Why—why—what'cha doin' out here? Come on—on—on in," he said with slurred, broken speech. He seized her by the hand and pulled her inside.

Still stunned, she followed him into the first room off the hallway—the handsomely furnished living room. Loud chatter and music were coming from the back of the house. He pushed her so that she fell into the brown-leather love seat. Fuming with irritation, she barely noticed the Impressionistic paintings on the walls and other tasteful décor displayed around her.

"You need—need—drink—baby," he said, staggering away. "Lyle be back."

*You might've had a chance tonight, Lyle. But not now.*

Almost in tears, she stood up angrily clutching her purse. She had to get out. She felt humiliated beyond belief.

Lyle appeared in the doorway, with a half-empty glass of red wine in his hand. Like the other guy, cracker crumbs were matted in his goatee. Down the chest and protruding stomach of his heather gray turtleneck were flecks of crumbs and cheese spread smears. Holding up the glass, he said with a silly grin, "Hey, Lori, you want—want some wine?" His speech sounded like he had had one drink too many.

She shook her head. Though they were a few feet from one another, she turned up her nose at his smell: a sickening pine scent reminding her of marijuana. Closing her eyes for a moment, she envisioned the expressway and roads leading back to Pleasant Ridge. Never did concrete and asphalt appear so welcoming to her.

"So, Lori, what—what it'll be?" he asked, running his fingers through his thinning blondish-brown crew cut.

"You asshole, my name's Lorelei, not Lori." she said, stepping forward. "Get out of my way. I'm out of here." She held up her fist, ready to strike him if he tried to block her exit.

"Now—that's no—no way," he said, still grinning at her, as if he thought her words were a joke.

As he staggered toward her, her heart drummed furiously. She was about to punch him in the face, maybe kick him in the shin; but to her surprise and satisfaction, he tripped over the edge of the large beige wool rug covering most of the wood floor. As he fell forward onto his stomach, he dropped his glass and the wine splashed onto the rug. The other day, Lyle had sent her a picture of this rug on his phone. He claimed he had spent a couple thousand on it—had it shipped all the way from New Zealand! And now the rug had several dark red stains.

Dropping her hand to her side, Lorelei said, "Serves the idiot right." She gazed down at his still body. His arms were sprawled forward; the unbroken wine glass lay near his left hand. With the side of his face pressing awkwardly against the rug, and the one visible eye shut, he definitely looked passed out.

She stepped over him and tiptoed away, wanting to make an inconspicuous getaway; but the music turned considerably lower, indicating the other guests must've heard the commotion. She halted in the living-room doorway as two women—a tall brunette and a shorter red head—rushed down the hall, splashing the wine from their glasses onto the wood floor. Typically a keen observer of others' fashion sense, Lorelei would've taken a few seconds to scrutinize their attire; at that moment, she couldn't have cared less about what they were wearing. Instead, her focus was on their faces, zooming in like a camera lens on their bloodshot, watery eyes and reddened noses. The brunette's lipstick was smeared like a clown's around her mouth. Lorelei didn't care to ponder how that had happened.

"Your friend isn't doing so well," she told the women, her voice oozing with disgust. Stepping into the hallway, she moved out of their way so they could have a look at him.

"What's up with him?" snickered the red head, pointing to Lyle lying on the rug, as if she hadn't heard Lorelei.

Reaching back, the brunette roughly grabbed Lorelei's arm, saying, "Oh, forget him. Let's go to the back den where the real fun is."

"I don't know what's going on at this party—what kind of substances you're on," fumed Lorelei, "but I'm not sticking around to find out." She jerked her arm out of the brunette's grip, then bolted out the door to her car.

As she drove off into the starry night, she wasn't sure how to react—pull over somewhere and then laugh, cry, or scream at the absurdity of what had just happened. But she told herself to stay calm. Her attention had to be on her driving, on arriving to Myra's place in Ferndale safely. She would save her emotions until she saw her friend. When they sat in her living room, with Sammy Joe at their feet, she would know then what to do.

# THE SOUL-MATE SEARCH

I'll never forget the sunny January afternoon I met Amy.

It was my first day back at the university after a two-week holiday break. Around four-thirty, I walked into Rebecca Chandler's office and was awed by a striking young woman sitting in front of my colleague's desk. The pretty woman had flawless skin the color of alabaster, and her pale blonde hair was meticulously curled, hanging about her shoulders like a stylish accessory.

What intrigued me the most was her shyness. She never made eye contact with me, barely glancing in my direction from the moment I entered the room. Tilting my head in different directions, I attempted to get her to look at me. But she just stared at the floor and fidgeted with her burgundy blouse and skirt, both made of a silky material. I found myself fighting the urge to comfort her, assuring her that she was among friends.

"David, I'd like you to meet our new secretary. Her name is Amy Dupree," Rebecca said with her usual bright eyes and wide smile. She loved to show her bleached white teeth. "Isn't *Dupree* such a pleasant-sounding name?"

I nodded, saying, "A delightful name."

Rebecca snapped her fingers, signaling for Amy to lift her head up. "Amy, this is, Dr. Dempsey."

Ignoring Amy's embarrassment, Rebecca continued, "Before coming to Kingswood, she worked at Marchmont, a private college in Massachusetts. I'm sure she'll enjoy the warmer weather here in Georgia."

I reached over and shook Amy's soft hand, holding her fingers gently, while gazing into her lovely blue eyes. "Nice to meet you," I said, wondering if she would respond. "Are you here temporarily—or for longer?" I felt somewhat ashamed by my eagerness to hear if Amy was here permanently. Judith had been our departmental secretary for over ten years, rarely missing a day of work, and was very efficient. I hoped Amy's secretarial skills matched her exceptional looks.

Rebecca answered for Amy. "She's here for the winter, spring, and summer terms." In a somber voice, Rebecca explained: "Right before break, Judith got a call from her sister Karen in Washington. Karen's emphysema has seriously worsened. She has no one nearby to care for her, so Judith flew out to Seattle to be with her. When I spoke to Judith a few days ago, she said she doubts she'll be back until next fall."

Again, Rebecca's face brightened with a wide smile. "Fortunately, the temp agency was able to find a suitable replacement for her right away. At Marchmont, Amy was the English department's receptionist."

Glancing at the wall clock, she finished: "Well, I better get going. I don't want to start the new semester off on the wrong foot and be late for the first session of my afternoon seminar." She laughed pretentiously and stood, shoving a stack of file folders into an already crammed briefcase.

In the hall, Rebecca said, "David, I'd appreciate it if you'd take Amy around to meet the other faculty."

"Sure thing," I replied, happy for the opportunity to spend more time with Amy.

Once Rebecca was out of earshot, I turned to Amy and said, "We don't have to do this now. I can tell you're a little nervous today. A new job can be overwhelming." I smiled at her, hoping she would reciprocate.

"It's fine," she said, nodding. Her expression remained unreadable.

The history department tour was brief. Dr. Trennor was the only other faculty member around at the time, but because she was on the phone and had a student in her office, I didn't want to interrupt.

In the main reception area, as we stood at her desk, I said, "I'm sorry, Amy, I couldn't introduce you to anyone today."

"No problem," she said flatly.

"Well, it looks as though your work day is about to end," I said, pointing to the wall clock. It was almost five. "I was thinking about grabbing a drink at Starbucks around the corner. Care to accompany me? It'll be my treat. I've never been to Marchmont College—nor Massachusetts. You can tell me all about them."

"Thank you, but I'm not thirsty," she replied, then added in a businesslike tone, "I still have to finish typing a few letters for Dr. Chandler. Have a good afternoon, Dr. Dempsey."

"Please call me *David*," I requested.

She nodded shyly, looking away, then sat down at her computer without glancing up.

Leaving the office, I thought about how Rebecca had said Amy's last name was *pleasant*. Well, maybe her last name was, but her personality didn't seem to be. Amy was polite enough, but a more befitting word would be *standoffish*. She was the exact opposite of the overly pleasant Judith.

I spent a quiet evening at home updating my syllabi for my three introductory European history courses. Instead of assigning research papers, like I always did in the past, I gave my students the options of either completing several book reviews that expanded on one of my lectures, or researching a historical person and writing some journal entries as if they were that individual. I hoped the changes would make their work more interesting to read.

That night, I had trouble drifting off. Tossing and turning, I was unable to get comfortable enough to sleep. My thoughts were of Amy, with her blonde hair and delicate lips. Her face, untouched by makeup, radiated a bewitching glow. Yet Amy interested me for more than her looks or my strong attraction to her. In my experience, shy people often had something to hide, and I enjoyed inventing scenarios that explained their secretiveness. Even if she wasn't attracted to me, she might serve as a character study for one of my short stories.

The next morning, despite restless sleep, I wasn't tired. Anxious to get to work, I quickly ate my cereal and toast, and skipped my perusal of the morning newspaper. I couldn't wait to see Amy, to be close to her again. It had been a while since a woman had intrigued me the way she had.

My last obsession was with a woman who wasn't real. Three years ago, I frequented a gallery not too far from home, in another Atlanta suburb, where a painting of a beautiful 19th-century lady, entitled *Amelia,* captivated me. I put aside money out of every paycheck until I saved enough to buy it. Amy was having the same effect on me. I knew nothing about her, yet I wanted to possess her.

How those feelings excited me!

After showering and shaving, I gazed at my reflection in the mirror. Like my good friend and former colleague Mark, I was almost fifty. Last spring, he accepted a professorship at the University of San Diego. Recently, he emailed me a picture of himself outside his new townhouse. With his whitish hair and heavy wrinkles, Mark looked much older that he was. Yet I could pass for a man in his early forties, or even late thirties. The majority of my hair was brown, not gray. Although I had a few fine lines across my forehead, the rest of my face was smooth. Using gel, I styled my hair in spiky bangs and sleek sides. With my updated appearance, I dressed in black pants and a woven sport shirt with purple and gray stripes, both Christmas gifts from my brother.

I arrived on campus just after eight. The history department offices were housed on the fourth (top) floor of Rodney Hall. Like many university buildings, it was a multi-storied, white brick structure, with an overhanging roof supported by Corinthian pillars. In an energetic mood, I took the stairs to my office instead of the elevator. I looked for Amy, hoping I would have a chance to talk to her before she became too engrossed in her work. But she wasn't at her desk.

On my way down the hall, I paused in the lounge doorway. Amy was inside, standing in front of the tall bookcase, browsing the books. She methodically leafed through the pages of what I thought was an English history text about the Tudor period. More than before, I was drawn to her, to her quietness, to the way she seemed so content with her endeavor. I cleared my throat. Amy abruptly closed the book and turned around.

I didn't know what to say at first, except to apologize for startling her. I took the book from her. "*England and the Tudor Dynasty*," I remarked, reading the book's complete title. "My favorite period in history."

"Mine as well," she said. "In my opinion, the story of Henry VIII and his relationships with his six wives is far more suspenseful and romantic than any novel I've ever read."

"I agree," I said, enthused. "I did my dissertation on how the political climate in fifteenth-century England set the stage for the establishment of the Tudor dynasty. You see, before the Tudor dynasty rose to power, two other prominent dynastic houses—Lancaster and York—were involved in a military dispute as to which should rule the country. Henry Tudor descended from the Lancastrians and—"

"Yes," she interjected, averting my gaze, "I know quite a bit about the Tudors' background."

"Why don't you accompany me to lunch?" I said. "I'm sure I can enlighten you on something from history. What do you know about Geoffrey Chaucer and how he came to write *The Canterbury Tales?*"

"Not much, actually," she said, giving me eye contact. "When are you thinking?"

"I have an hour and a half break between my morning and afternoon classes at noon," I said. "How about then?"

She nodded, smiling, and said, "Okay."

At noon, we went to Corner Crêpes because it was close, just a block from Rodney Hall. As we ate our crêpes at a metal pub table, Amy's coyness dissipated and she opened up to me. Forgetting about Geoffrey Chaucer, we talked about our backgrounds. Interestingly, we were both born and raised in Ohio. I grew up outside of Cleveland, but she spent her childhood in Toledo. After high school, Amy attended college for a few years but dropped out after meeting the "man of her dreams"; she married him, and they relocated to Roanoke, Virginia. Just before their second anniversary, he was driving home late after an evening of beer drinking with his sports buddies, and fell asleep at the wheel. His car, moving into the opposite lane, was struck by an on-coming truck. He died instantly. At age twenty-three, Amy became a widow. Unable to bear the painful memories Roanoke evoked for her, she decided to move again and found a job with an Atlanta-based temp agency. She had been in the Atlanta area for almost a year now.

"How do you like living here?" I asked.

"Let's say I'm content at the moment," she replied. "I do like Kingswood's quaintness and its interesting stores, especially the antique places. I live downtown, and I enjoy browsing in them on the weekends."

Amy glanced at her watch. "It's almost one. We better head back."

I nodded, venturing, "I had a really nice time chatting with you. Can we do this again?"

"I'd like that," Amy said encouragingly.

\* \* \*

A week passed before I had an opportunity to ask her out again. I was called away to help my father, who lived alone outside Savannah, recuperate from an accident: while cleaning out his gutters, he slipped off the ladder and sprained both his ankles.

At my father's, not a day went by when I didn't think about Amy. My growing obsession with her was rather alarming. After all, I barely knew her. But on the few occasions I had been with her, I felt as though I were in the presence of the elegant 19th-century *Amelia*, which hung in my living room. Amy had the qualities of maturity, refinement, and modest beauty that seemed missing in the women I had come across. The women I dated in the past claimed they wanted marriage and monogamy, but I would discover later they were seeing other men on the sly. In my heart, I believed Amy would not disappoint me in that way.

Naturally, I had reservations about pursuing her. My colleagues, I was sure, would frown upon me dating her, viewing it as inappropriate. "Why couldn't David find someone his own age?" I imagined them whispering behind my back. My other concerns were about Amy. Once I made my intentions known, would she reciprocate? But if she did show interest, would I eventually be hurt anyway? Only twenty-four, would her feelings wane if she met a younger man? To find out, I would have to get closer to her.

On Tuesday morning, my younger brother, Charles, drove up from northern Florida to take over my father's care. I had been at Dad's beck and call all week, even cleaning his townhouse from top to bottom, yet my father practically leaped across the living room with his crutches when Charles walked through the front door. Long ago, I had resigned myself to the fact that I would never be his *most* beloved son, but I'd be lying if I said my secondary status didn't still irk me.

After returning to work the following day, I stopped by Amy's desk in the afternoon. She was tidying some papers and preparing to leave for the day. "Heading out?" I asked.

She nodded with a concerned look. "How's your father? Dr. Chandler mentioned he had some kind of accident—that Dr. Trennor was teaching your classes for the week."

"He's much better. The doctor has him on the right medicine to relieve his pain. My brother is watching him now and taking him to his physical therapy appointments."

As she grabbed the purse from the desk, I said, "I was hoping we could go out for a bite. But I can tell you have to get going."

"I just have some errands to run. They won't take me longer than an hour. When are you thinking?"

"Seven?"

"Sure," she replied. "I have a craving for Italian food. Let's meet at Rosa's."

I returned to my office and passed the time by re? and editing my notes for upcoming lectures on the Revolution. Many of my colleagues extolled the using PowerPoint or some other software p program in class. But I believed in the old-fash? of teaching: engaging students by posing thought-provoking questions before, immediately following my lectures.

At six-thirty, I cleared my desk and headed out. Theoretically, Rosa's was ten minutes away—but since the restaurant was located on Pine Street, a busy thoroughfare in downtown Kingswood, I wanted to give myself enough time to find parking.

I arrived downtown at ten to seven, and was fortunate to get a spot right in front of Rosa's. Though it had a stone façade like the other properties on the block, the restaurant stood out because of its purple canopy over the wooden double doors. Instead of passing the time window shopping, I decided to enter Rosa's and see if Amy was already there. Scanning the tables, I discovered she was not. I told the hostess I was expecting a friend. Looking around again, I was puzzled why Amy had picked this particular place. It was drab and dismal inside. The walls were painted a deep burgundy; the tablecloths and chair coverings were almost as dark. Adding to the dreariness was the absence of artwork on the walls. The hostess seated me at a quiet table for two away from the kitchen and restrooms.

Amy walked in promptly at seven. How she was dressed— it astonished me. It was as if she had stepped out of a picture from the turn of the last century. She wore a frilly white blouse buttoned to the top and a black skirt that fell almost to the floor. Her footwear was wingtip low-heeled boots. In my khaki cargo pants and blue cotton sweater, I suddenly felt underdressed.

"Have you been waiting long?" she asked.

"Uh . . . no, not long at all," I replied, pulling out the chair for her.

She sat down, saying, "You look a little startled."

Returning to my seat with raised eyebrows, I said: "I ust admit you've surprised me. Unless I'm in a vintage ıthing store, I typically don't see clothing likes yours."

"Your book *The Lives of European Women in the Early 1900s* was my inspiration. I came across it in the lounge and read a few chapters last week during my lunch breaks. You wrote about the style of the period so eloquently that I searched several antique shops to find an outfit that matched one of your fashion descriptions. You see, studying history has been an interest of mine—it was always my best subject. When I go back to school, I want to major in history. I'm not sure what I'll do with it after graduation, but at least I'll have a degree."

I smiled. "I'm pleased you enjoyed my book. It did not sell well, but that didn't matter to me. All that mattered was the book got good reviews and cemented my tenure status. It's been six years since the book was published. I need to get back to writing again."

The waitress came and took our orders. Amy requested the Fettuccine Alfredo—I did the same. Eating our salads, we fell into a discussion about our inspiring high school history teachers. Hers was a Mr. Stephens, who taught U.S. history at the Toledo high school she attended. "Whenever he talked about battles, he acted out the scenes dressed as a general," Amy said. "It really made history come alive for me." I told her about mine—Ms. Breen—who had been my ninth-grade world-history teacher. "She had traveled all over and had a massive collection of slides," I said. "During her lessons—whether she was lecturing on ancient Persia or the Vikings—she always showed pictures she had taken of historical artifacts from different cultures." As we veered into talking about our worst teachers, the waitress arrived with our pasta dishes.

Given the few customers, the dark atmosphere, and inexpensive prices at Rosa's, I had believed I was in store for a sub-par meal. How wrong I was! The fettuccine was delicious! It had just the right combination of butter, pepper, and garlic flavors. I would have to try some other menu items to decide if I had indeed judged the establishment too hastily.

We ate our meals in silence. I could not say why Amy was suddenly quiet. My excuse was my fixation on Amy. I could barely take my eyes off her as I thought about my living-room painting. Although the *Amelia* in the portrait looked a little older and had darker hair, I kept seeing Amy in that picture. I envisioned coming home tonight, turning on the gas fireplace, and having that woman (Amy) step out of the frame. I would pull her into a gentle embrace, kissing and caressing her softly, then snuggling with her throughout the night.

Feeling awkward by my intense gaze, Amy stared back at me quizzically. A cold shiver went up my spine. If she could read my thoughts, what would she think of me? An "eccentric," a little "off-balanced," or worse—a middle-aged "pervert"? But maybe I was berating myself too severely for my imagination. There was no sexual act in my fantasy. I had held my hormones in check. At least for now.

Leaving the restaurant, we decided to walk off our meals. It was after eight; the businesses were closed. Passing several clothing and home-goods stores, we window-shopped for several blocks. At the end of the third block, we lingered in front of Thom's Tantalizing Treasures, which specialized in art deco furniture and collectibles.

"I could use one of those right now," Amy remarked, pointing to the vintage space heater in the store's window. She crossed her arms against her hooded black trench coat, then hugged her body, shivering. "Dr. Chandler repeatedly tells me the winters are so much better in the south. That may be true. But forty-some degrees feels like forty-some degrees, no matter where you are."

I nodded in agreement, clutching the collar of my woolen coat. "It definitely has gotten chilly." I took off my long scarf and wrapped it around her neck and shoulders.

She pulled the cell phone out of her purse and said, "It's going toward nine. I should be on my way home."

"Let me walk you to your car," I offered.

"No need," she said. "I walked from my apartment to Rosa's."

"Let me drive you back. I insist."

Amy's apartment building was five blocks east of the restaurant, on a residential side street, in a section of town I deemed as "questionable," judging from how the properties were maintained. Most of the buildings, including Amy's, had fallen into disrepair. The sight of hers, with its depressing ambiance, tugged painfully at my heart. The siding on her three-storied building was loose and pulling away in several sections. Additionally, the window frames were rotten and the roofing shingles were buckling.

I parked behind the building to let Amy out, but she surprised me by asking, "Care to come in for a bit?"

Because she was eyeing me cautiously, I asked, "Are you sure—are you sure it isn't too late for you?"

"I'm sure," she said, slowly smiling. "I made some chocolate cake yesterday. Would you care for a piece?"

"I've never been one to turn down chocolate," I said, my heartbeat quickening.

Her apartment was on the top floor, at the end of a dimly lit narrow hallway. Once inside, she switched on the lights and said, "Have a seat in the living room. Do you want coffee or milk with your cake?" Shaking my head, I said, "No, thank you."

On the faded loveseat, I looked around the apartment, observing the sparseness of her living arrangements: a worn-out armchair across from me; two floor lamps strategically placed at opposite ends of the room; and a wooden desk beside me, cluttered with books, papers, and dirty dishes. Except for a large calendar hung by a nail, the walls were bare.

Amy came out of the kitchen without any cake, her nose twisted, clearly annoyed. "I have to apologize," she said. "I can't offer you any cake. My roommate, Justine, must've polished it off. But I have a box of peanut butter cookies."

I waved my hand in front of my face, saying, "I'm good. If your roommate has a sweet tooth, I don't want to deprive her of anything." My eyes wandered to the short hallway off the living room. I could see two doors and assumed one opened to a bedroom, the other to a bathroom. "Is Justine home?"

Amy sank down on the armchair. "No, I don't expect her tonight. When I was home earlier, she was heading out the door with this new guy she's seeing. For the past week, she's been spending every night at his place."

"Sounds like the start of a whirlwind romance."

Amy laughed. "Maybe. She's dated four guys since I moved in with her two months ago. The longest she's been single was three days. During that brief time, she was on her computer constantly, posting and responding to personal ads. She thought nothing of leaving the apartment at midnight to meet some man at the bar. Risky behavior, in my opinion. I just hope she stays with this new guy."

I shook my head. "Justine must be something else. You shouldn't have to live with someone who has men coming and going at all hours. It's just not her safety at risk."

"I agree, but she doesn't hang out with them here. She doesn't have a car, so they just come here to pick her up. In fact, I like that she's gone a lot. I like having the place to *myself*."

"So you prefer being alone?" I asked with arched eyebrows.

"Oh, I wouldn't say that. I just love the quietness. It gives me the chance to read undisturbed."

"That's wonderful to hear! I admire a woman who devotes her free time to improving her mind." Standing up, I was overtaken by an urge to stroke her hair, to caress her face.

But before I could get close enough to touch her, she jumped up and yawned loudly. "Suddenly, I'm sleepy," she claimed, rubbing her eyes. "I don't mean to kick you out. But we have work tomorrow, and I'm no good in the morning unless I get a full night's sleep."

"I'll see you tomorrow, then," I said, suppressing a sigh, trying to conceal my disappointment.

We only shook hands before I left.

\* \* \*

In the weeks following our first date, Amy and I spent more and more time together. We often dined out, took long walks, and browsed in and outside of bookstores. On weekends, we relaxed in my living room while I read aloud poetry books and Amy knitted scarves. "When you have six brothers and sisters, and many nieces and nephews," she said, "it's economical to make birthday gifts." Her eyes grew wide and brightened whenever I read poetry by Emily Brontë. In her opinion, the themes in Brontë's verse expertly entwined the unpredictability of weather with the wayward nature of love.

I had been worried the other professors would snub me if they discovered I was dating her, but my fears proved unnecessary. As the weeks passed, Dr. Chandler and the others did not look upon Amy and me any differently than before. Whenever they saw me hanging around Amy's desk, they did not frown at me. And whenever Amy and I entered the lounge to eat our lunch, the sight of us together did not bring my colleagues' conversations to a sudden halt. If the staff *were* aware of my more-than-friendly interest in Amy, they kept their opinions to themselves.

In bed, I tried imagining what their reactions would be, were I to announce one afternoon in the lounge that Amy and I had become engaged. I saw two main possibilities: they would either quickly express congratulations with warm smiles, or their initial speechlessness would give way to phony happy wishes. Naturally, I preferred the first scenario. Before drifting off, I would chide myself for even caring how they would receive the news. I didn't need their support. So what if there were large age and educational differences between Amy and me? Age and college degrees shouldn't dictate our feelings.

However, by late March, I feared that an engagement announcement would never come to fruition. Whenever I asked her, "Are you sure you enjoy being with me?" she would assure me, saying, "Of course," with a gentle squeeze of my hand. But even after almost three months of dating, our relationship had yet to move beyond virtuous. On the sofa, we snuggled in the evenings, but, when I kissed her, although she reciprocated, it was with considerably less passion than I put into it. As I massaged her shoulders and arms, she stiffened if my caresses lasted too long or if they veered toward her breasts. As a result, we hadn't reached the point of intimacy where I felt comfortable asking her to spend the night. I pondered what I could do to break down this barrier between us. After all, I was falling in love—but was she?

One morning in early April, an idea struck me how I could take our relationship to the next level. The suggestion titillated my mind like an exotic perfume. In a week it would be spring break at the university. During that time, I was going to visit my father and Charles, who was still staying at my father's place in Mandeville, Florida. Thirty minutes away from Mandeville was my brother's house, a ranch, in St. Ciro, a community abundant with Spanish moss and cypress trees, close to the Georgia border. For the last few days of my vacation, I considered relaxing at his place and taking in the nearby sights. But my arrangements could be reversed—and could include Amy. Inviting her along, I would drive to Charles' unoccupied ranch and spend the first couple days of our break there. In St. Ciro's lush setting, removed from the possibility of retreating to her home, Amy might loosen up and discard the modest front she presented. In other words, I hoped she might finally allow me to explore more than just her arms and shoulders.

The following evening, as we cuddled in front of my fireplace, I asked: "What are you doing over the break? Do you have any plans?"

"No plans at the present," Amy replied. "I thought about driving up to Ohio to see my parents, but they have a lot to do that week and probably wouldn't have much time for me."

"I have a great idea!" I exclaimed, as if it suddenly popped up in my head. "How about driving to Florida with me? We both could use a change of scenery from these gray skies."

"Doesn't your family live in Florida?" she asked.

"Yes, most of them do now—including my father's favorite—*Charles*," I said, my voice betraying my irritation with this fact.

"I can tell your brother isn't *your* favorite," she said, her forehead creased. "Whenever you mention him, you grit your teeth."

"I shouldn't blame Charles," I explained, "but my father has always shown him preferential treatment. As kids,

Charles got better grades than I did.  He won many awards, especially for his athletic achievements.  My father was constantly showering him with gifts.  When I finished high school, I only got a used Ford Escort.  But at Charles' graduation party, my father presented him with the keys to a brand-new Mustang.  How fair is that?"

"Not very," she agreed.

"What irks me most is that my father continues to favor Charles, even though my brother spends most of his free time on a golf course and hasn't put his medical degree to use in years.  I'm a tenured professor, a published writer, yet my father gives me little recognition."

"How does your brother make his living?"

"About ten years ago, he put his money into some sound investments and now lives off those earnings.  It's not a lot.  His ranch is modest, only two bedrooms, and he doesn't own any animals.  But he lives comfortably."

I then sprung my complete trip proposal on Amy.  First, we were to stay a few days in St. Ciro, where we could experience the local parks, natural warm springs, and wildlife.  Once we had enough of that, we could explore downtown St. Ciro, which had antique boutiques offering one-of-a-kind wares.  Later in the week, we would stop by my father's so that she could meet my family.

"We wouldn't have to spend more than a day or two with him and Charles," I said.  "We could be back by Saturday evening.  You'd have a day to rest before returning to work.  What do you think?"

"I'd love to get away!" was her enthusiastic reply.

* * *

By the following week, once we arrived at my brother's place, her attitude changed.  She appeared riddled with anxiety—and she wouldn't tell me why.  During the day, she complained of headaches and sudden fatigue, and refused to leave the ranch with me. In the evening, instead of reading or knitting as she did in Kingswood, she restlessly paced the house, glancing out the double-hung windows, as if she didn't know what to do with herself.

Another difference was her style of dress. Although she usually wore blouses and skirts on our dates, I expected her to don more casual attire for the trip. Nevertheless, she surprised me with her new wardrobe—an array of tight-fitting jeans and revealing V-neck pullovers.

But she wasn't dressing sexy to please me. When I commented how well her clothes accentuated her trim shape, she said, "Thank you"—without smiling. Sitting on the sofa one night, I tried to distract her pacing by patting the empty cushion beside me. "Instead of admiring you from afar," I teased, "it would be nice to have a closer look." She didn't appreciate my attempt at humor:  as she passed by, her glower told me there was no changing the sleeping arrangement of separate rooms.

On Thursday morning, our last full day in St. Ciro, I tried once more to get Amy to accompany me downtown, to view some art galleries and museums, but she wasn't interested. "If you don't mind," she said, "I'd rather be alone for a while." Again, I questioned her, asking if something was wrong, but she insisted she was fine.

On my return that afternoon, she was less agitated than before. Taking out her yarn and knitting needles, she sat down beside me on the sofa. While we watched a documentary about the U.S. Founding Fathers, she added more rows to an afghan.

During a commercial break, showing my gratitude for having her in my life, I gently stroked the side of her face. I could sense her shoulders and back tighten, yet I continued since she didn't pull away. When I tried to brush my lips against her cheek, she jumped up and said she heard someone lightly knocking at the door. "Shouldn't you answer it?" she demanded. Complying with her request, I went into the vestibule and squinted through the peephole in the door. I didn't see anyone.

Returning, I shrugged my shoulders and said: "No one was there. Are you sure you heard knocking?"

"I know what I heard," she replied peevishly. Picking up her knitting, she moved to an armchair at the other end of the room.

By this point, I had had enough of her crankiness. "I think I'll take a drive to the mall," I said, not bothering to ask if you wanted to go along. "Do you need anything while I'm out?"

"No, thank you," she said, without glancing up from her knitting.

*  *  *

The St. Ciro Outlet Mall, a one-level yellow stucco building, was just a mile from the house. The only store I went in was The Look, which specialized in men's clothing. After browsing, I took five brightly striped shirts into the fitting room. While modeling the first two shirts in the dressing room mirror, I discovered both were tight through the chest and shoulders. The size medium didn't fit me as well it had last year. I definitely needed to stop ordering heavy meals and desserts when I went out to dinner. Disgusted, I piled the shirts on the chair in the dressing room, and left. Not ready to head back, I walked around the mall parking lot for an hour, enjoying the pleasant breeze.

Back at the house, I parked my car under the carport and entered through the side door. "Amy!—I'm back!" I called out, heading for the living room.

The armchair where she had sat was empty. But lying on the sofa was someone I hadn't expected to find—my father! Lifting his head from the pillow, he rubbed his watery eyes, then smoothed down his tussled gray hair. He had obviously fallen asleep.

"Uh—Dad—what—what are you doing here?" I stammered. "Did Charles bring you here? Where's Amy?"

He yawned loudly. "Yes, Charles did. He had to come back to the house to pick up something. He told me this morning what it was—but I can't recall now. We were to meet your new lady friend and then go out to dinner later—"

"What are you talking about? Don't you remember our phone conversation a few days ago? I said I was bringing her by tomorrow so you could meet her. Didn't you tell Charles that? Why didn't he call me earlier to say he was coming by?"

"I have no idea why he didn't call," he sighed, shaking his head. "I wish you and your bother would get your plans straight." He sat up and rubbed his ankles. "You both know I haven't been feeling the greatest lately. I don't need any stress in my life."

Looking out the window, I asked, "So where are Charles and Amy?"

"As soon as we got here, that lady friend of yours said she had to go to the store for something. Charles offered to drive her." My father paused, massaging his neck. "I'm sure they'll back any minute. Save your questions for him."

The queasiness at the pit of my stomach, though, told me Amy wasn't coming back. I wandered into the guest bedroom to see if she had taken her things. My survey of the room confirmed my fears. Her two suitcases, which had rested atop the oak dresser, were gone. On the bed was an envelope addressed to me. With trembling hands, I opened and read the note inside:

*Dear David,*

*I apologize for leaving you so abruptly. I wanted to get home, and Charles has offered to drive me to the bus station. As you could tell, it was not working out between us. I wish I could fully explain why, but I am not the writer you are. This morning, I realized I could never respond to your affections in the way you wanted, and that there was no sense in continuing our relationship.*

*You're a wonderful man and deserve a woman better than me.*

*Amy*

Pulling out the cell phone from my pocket, I tried to reach her. But the call went directly to her voicemail. Then I tried Charles' number. He didn't pick up either. Without leaving messages, I tossed my phone onto the carpet. My head throbbing, I collapsed on the bed. All I could think of was how wrong I had been about Amy. She wasn't mature—she was nothing more than a drama-seeking child. She could've just said she wanted to go back to Atlanta, and I would've taken her at any point. There was no reason to play games—no reason to involve my brother. Humiliated, I lay there for a while, my extremities turning numb, as if my body was being encased in ice.

But my anger—my outrage at the betrayal—had a thawing effect. Sitting up with clenched fists, I pounded the bed. I scowled at my reflection in the mirror above the dresser. How could I have been such a fool? Knowing little about Amy, how could I have trusted her without reservations? How could she have charmed me into believing she was my ideal, my *Amelia*?

I vowed then and there I would be more cautious in the future: I never wanted to be *had* by someone like her again.

* * *

The following Thursday afternoon, around five, I knocked at Rebecca's office door. That morning, she had sent an email out to everyone in the department that her latest article, "How the Georgia Institute of Technology Put Atlanta Back on the Map in 1888," had been accepted by the *Journal of U.S. Urban Development*. Congratulations were in order on her accomplishment.

"Hello, David," she said as I walked in. "Please sit down."

Taking a seat, I said, "I got your email. That's great about the article! When is it supposed to appear?"

"In the fall," she said, walking around me to the door. She closed it and sat back down at her desk. "You're the first person to acknowledge my email. Thank you for that." She paused, leaning forward, her face growing serious. "I wish my news was creating the stir that you have the last couple of days. The department is still abuzz about Amy's sudden resignation on Monday. Do you know why she left? I'm asking because you seemed like *good* friends."

I thought about my answer. But by the way Rebecca emphasized the word *good*, telling me that she (and most likely my other colleagues) suspected Amy and I were more than "chummy," I decided I would come off as deceitful if I said I had no idea. Consequently, I settled on a half-truth, a story devoid of details that would tarnish my reputation.

I swallowed hard and cleared my throat, hoping to avoid sounding nervous or distressed in my reply. "Well . . . she's . . . with my brother. They are living together now."

"Really? How did that come about?"

"Over break, I introduced them. Needless to say, they hit it off pretty well." I laughed to conceal my bitterness toward

Charles—the ultimate lowlife. My father urged me to contact him, saying I should hear his side of what had happened, but I wouldn't be able to listen impartially without uttering obscenities. I wasn't sure how I could find it within myself to forgive him for taking advantage of my troubles and seducing Amy.

"I feel bad now," Rebecca sighed, leaning back. "I misjudged her—and you."

"Why? What do you mean?"

Rebecca laughed, shaking her head. "The day after she started here, Amy was in my office, and I had out some photos from my fourth-of-July party last year. In the stack was a picture of you with your father and brother in my dining room. What Amy said about Charles took me by surprise. But when I pondered her words later, I felt she said those things to throw me off track, to fool me into believing you two weren't an item. Some people like to keep their office romances private."

"What did she say, exactly?"

"At first, she didn't say anything. She just stroked the picture with her finger." Rebecca closed her eyes for a moment, as if visualizing the scene. "I asked her, 'See anything you like?' She replied, 'Oh yes, who is this handsome man?' I peered over her shoulder and saw she was touching Charles' face. I told her that he was your brother. 'He's the sexiest!' she said. 'I love his dark features—his wavy hair and goatee.' Then she went on and on about his amazing smile and physique, comparing him to some model she had seen on a magazine cover. 'I'm going to marry that man,' she said. 'That's the man I want, and I'm going to marry him,' she emphasized. Like I mentioned, I thought she was saying all that to take the spotlight off you both." Rebecca shook her head again. "I couldn't have been more wrong."

She stood up and went to the window, looking out. "When did Amy reveal her feelings to you about Charles? Did you play matchmaker?"

Stunned by her disclosure, I left Rebecca's office without uttering a word. Realizing I would be too distraught to teach, I sat down at the computer and made two signs saying my afternoon class was cancelled. I posted one on my office door, the other on the classroom door.

In a daze, I wandered down the stairs, out the building, and crossed the street, heading for the parking structure a few blocks away. I stared straight ahead, not paying attention to anyone I passed. My focus was on getting in my car and taking off somewhere, driving to a state where there were no memories of Amy.

* * *

Two hours north of Kingswood, I stopped at the Ruby Café and Tavern in Chattanooga, Tennessee. I read about the restaurant in an online article a while back. Built over a hundred years ago and sided with cedar shingles, the two-storied bright-red establishment was something of a historic landmark in the city and boasted of its "remarkable" service.

Upstairs at the bar, sipping a rum and Coke, I struck up a conversation with the blonde woman sitting next me. Marnie was a native of the area, worked as an interior decorator, and spoke with a charming southern drawl. She seemed to possess the three traits I was seeking—fair skin and blonde hair, friendliness, and financial security.

Why was it so hard to find a woman like that around Kingswood?

Opposite the bar was a small dance floor. At nine o'clock, the DJ arrived and started spinning a mix of '70s and '80s songs, which drew some patrons onto the floor. When he played "Copacabana" by Barry Manilow, the song immediately lifted my spirits. I grabbed Marnie's hand and

we joined the others dancing. In her tight-fitting, blue V-
neck sweater and jeans, she showed she had rhythm, moving
her arms and hips in time with the song's varying beats.
Though inexperienced, I did my best to keep up with her. An
arm's length away was a young bearded man wearing a
cowboy hat and leather boots. Dancing alone, he winked at
Marnie, wildly swaying his arms and hips, as if putting on a
show for her benefit.

Next was "Rapture" by Blondie. I had always been a fan
of Deborah Harry's seductive voice, but not of this particular
song. Cupping Marnie's ear, I told her I'd be back in a
minute with fresh drinks.

At the bar, after ordering two rum and Cokes, I turned
around to look at Marnie—and couldn't believe what I saw.
She was grinding with the young man who had been dancing
by himself! Her arms were wrapped around his biceps
bulging underneath his white western-style shirt. She was
clearly enjoying herself. To quote a line from a country song
I heard earlier on my car radio: "Her smile was as wide as
the Chattahoochee River in spring."

Yet I wasn't going to let this discourage me. I wasn't
going to retreat quietly, like I had when Amy left me for
Charles. Holding the drinks above my head, I wriggled my
way onto the dance floor. Then I elbowed my way between
Marine and the cowboy. Still smiling, she grabbed one of the
drinks from my hand. The cowboy stepped back, but his
hostile glare told me I had to think fast to get him to leave us.

After taking a quick sip from the other glass, I cupped
Marnie's ear: "All these people dancing and I bet no one
understands the meaning. You see, as a history professor,
I've studied these things. . ." Drinking, Marnie motioned for
me to continue. "The purpose of dance through the ages has
been to tell stories, to entertain . . . and . . ."—summoning
courage, I took a fast gulp and swallowed hard—"to make

love." I playfully arched my eyebrows, then kissed her full on the lips.

Out of the corner of my eye, I peered at my rival. At the same moment, a tall woman with a strawberry blonde beehive pulled up his beefy arms to rest atop the wide straps of her lime-green halter dress. As if copying me, she kissed him. And to my delight, he passionately kissed her back while they danced to the next, very fitting disco song, "Bizarre Love Triangle," by New Order.

"I love this song," Marnie said, snapping her fingers to the electronic beat.

My shoulders swaying, I took her hand. "So do I," I said, my feet moving in time with the music, managing somehow not to spill a drop from my drink.

# HERR HAUPTMANN

When you get to be my age, with more years behind you than ahead, you'll probably find yourself reflecting often on the past. During my quiet moments alone, my thoughts turn to my childhood—particularly to one event from my teenage years I feel compelled to talk about. It had the greatest impact on my adult life, and I hope the telling of it will enrich yours. Let me paint the scenery so that you can visualize that time along with me.

Traveling back to 1965, I am seventeen years old again in Havensville, a quaint Upstate New York town with more working-class neighborhoods than affluent. It is just past four-thirty, or maybe closer to five, on a warm afternoon in late August. The place is a bedroom on the second floor of a large house clad with weathered cedar shingles.

I am sitting on the bed with Timothy, my best friend ever since the day we started sixth grade. Everything around me is neat and tidy, no papers or other items on his desk, no clothes on the floor. I particularly enjoy gazing at the unique bedspread on the full-size bed; on it is a colorful map of Europe, the continent I hope to visit one day. Although we are very trustworthy, almost adults, Timothy still has to keep his door wide open. Checking on us, his mother or father will walk by every fifteen minutes or so. Timothy and I laugh at that. There's nothing romantic in our relationship, although I admit Timothy has been the boy of my dreams for several years. I'm attracted to his gentleness, warmth—and, yes, handsome face with its squarely cut jaw and perfectly formed nose. I would like to "go out" with him, but my parents frown on the idea of me dating. "If your mind is too much on having a boyfriend, then you won't get things done around here," is their diluted rationale.

Out of nowhere, Timothy says, leaning forward, "Nance"—my friends and family always call me "Nance," never Nancy—"we're getting a new German teacher. Frau Kramer has moved away—left the state." He pushes wavy auburn bangs away from his emerald eyes. "Apparently, Frau accepted a new position at some private school in Massachusetts. The school board has hired a man to take her place. His name is Mr. . . . or, rather, Herr Hauptmann. My father just told me about it this morning. Unlike Frau Kramer, he's a native German—but he's been in this country now for a while. I wonder if our pronunciations will get better this year because of him."

Timothy's father is the high school principal. He has an imposing presence, and he lets you know it with his deep, intimidating voice. Students at Havensville High may try the patience of their teachers, but they rarely, rarely challenge Timothy's father.

"Wow, that's great!" I exclaim in reply, swinging my legs and arms in the air as if dancing. "You know that Frau Kramer wasn't a favorite of mine. I won't miss her."

Timothy nods, agreeing with me. "I gathered as much. For some reason she liked to pick on some of her students—*you* in particular."

Frau certainly did. Knowing I was shy, she called on me most often to stand in front of the class and read story selections *auf Deutsch*. Whenever I made blunders with pronunciations, she shook her head and smacked her ruler against her desk. She rarely did that with other struggling classmates. And when she went over homework or tests, she always displayed my paper, full of red marks, on the board as an example of what not to do, even though others had as many mistakes.

Shuddering to shake off the unpleasant memories, I look directly into his eyes. "Timothy, *please*. I don't need to be reminded of what a nightmare last year was for me. I almost considered dropping out of German, and not going on to the next level."

"What? I had no idea. After studying a language for three years, it would be a shame to give it up now and not take the final course."

"Yes . . . glad I decided to keep going. I can only wish for the best with this new teacher." I pause, pondering an analogy to express my feeling. "This news is like finding a gift left on your doorstep—as you begin to unwrap it, you're hoping to find something decent inside the box."

I hear the grandfather clock in the hallway strike five times, reminding me I need to get home. Before I left, my mother told me to be back around five to help out with dinner. But I really want to stay here with Timothy. His room is very peaceful, painted in a pale blue that shows off the custom-made maple Amish furniture. Needless to say, his stuff is far superior to the well-worn odds and ends in my room. At home, I never seem to get any rest, my head often throbbing from the endless noise created by my brothers and sisters.

How lucky Timothy is, I realize for the umpteenth time, to be an only child. His parents lavish all of their love onto him, and they provide whatever he wants. As the oldest of eight kids, I'm lucky if my parents even notice me—unless something needs to be done around the house. My father is rarely home because he has to work two jobs to support such a large family; after dinner, my mother always complains she's too exhausted from working around the house all day and just wants to watch television. Whenever I ask my mother for extra money to buy a new outfit or go out with a girl friend to the movies, there's about a seventy-five percent chance she'll say *no*. Timothy's mother and father are always friendly and considerate towards me. My own parents leave a lot to be desired.

Timothy now gazes into my eyes, sensing that I will probably make my exit soon. "Do you need to leave?" he asks, frowning. "I can always tell when you have to go. You get this anxious look, and you always start cracking your knuckles."

He knows me so well, I think, as I get up and move away from the bed. I brush away the wrinkles from my jeans; with my slender fingers I pull at the tight collar of my t-shirt as we head downstairs.

"When will we hang out again?" Timothy says, holding the front door. "We still have tomorrow and the weekend before school starts."

"Not sure," I ponder. "This weekend my mom is planning to clean out the basement. She wants to have a yard or garage sale. We'll have to play it by ear."

"Okay." Timothy's face is full of disappointment.

"Maybe I can find a way to sneak away tomorrow or Saturday afternoon," I suggest. "I'll volunteer for an errand so I can get out of the house for a while."

His eyes light up. "Looking forward to it," he says. One of the politest guys I know, he gives me a firm but abrupt handshake. I'm working on changing that a little. Turning my head in different directions, listening for any sounds, I discover the coast is clear—no Mom or Dad around. My heart is pounding; my face heats up. Testing to see if he really likes me, I kiss him quickly on the lips. Then I step back to see his reaction. Smiling, he takes a step toward me, pursing his lips, about to return my kiss. Startled by the sound of his mother or father coming down the stairs, we jump back from each other. After calling up to his parents to have a good afternoon, I depart and hurry home.

The evening goes by at record speed. There is so much for me to do: dishes to wash and put away, clothes to fold, floors to sweep and mop. No chance to take a break and listen to the latest Beatles record my cousin Caroline gave me for my birthday last month, knowing how much I love Paul McCartney's light tenor voice. By the time it's ten o'clock, I am anxious to go to sleep, to escape the commotion downstairs. I brush my teeth, change into a nightgown, and literally jump into bed.

Before I drift off, the memory of Frau Kramer floods my mind: her constant scowl, her huge black-framed glasses, her dark hair pulled into an unattractive bun at the base of her neck. She was my German teacher for the past three years and also was, in my opinion, the most detestable person I had ever known. Like a vicious animal, she was ready to strike and pounce at my every mistake.

I complained to my school counselor about the situation, but he told me to either withdraw from the class or tolerate the woman—neither of which I really wanted to do. Despite Frau Kramer's terrible treatment, I persevered and managed to pass her classes with a C or D. With a German class on my schedule, it was guaranteed Timothy and I would be enrolled together and consequently could spend more time together. Each year, I found more enjoyment in reading stories and poems written by different German authors, whose themes and use of symbolism intrigued me and filled me with insights into human emotions. Nevertheless, Frau Kramer almost won: I came very, very close to giving up on learning this foreign language.

As the coolness from the night air enters my bedroom through the screen, I suddenly cry out to myself, "How wonderful that she's gone!"—elated by the prospect of Herr Hauptmann.

But the next moment I am riddled with fears. What will Hauptmann think if I fail to accurately translate a certain passage into German? And what will he think of me if I unexpectedly freeze in the middle of reciting a German poem? Will he be a gentle and compassionate teacher, and coach me through it? Or will he belittle me like Kramer?

There is no sense in dwelling on this, I reason. In six more days school will begin, and then I'll be able to see for myself what kind of teacher Herr Hauptmann will be.

It may be silly to believe in this superstition, but I decide to keep my fingers crossed for the next several days whenever I have the chance.

\* \* \*

On the first day of my senior year, I wake up with a jolt, with a mixture of anxiety and eagerness about school, anticipating what Herr Hauptmann will be like. I say a silent prayer that he'll at least be some improvement over the past. As if to impress him, I exert a lot of energy into creating a fashionable shoulder-length flip hairstyle. Unfortunately, all the teasing and extra hair spray makes my brown hair look like an overly used mop. Luckily, I have already dressed. Otherwise, a struggle might've ensued when I put my head through the narrow collar on my short-sleeve ribbed green dress.

During the bus ride to school, I look out the window, observing the cloudy, dismal sky; however, as we near the school some rays from the sun are attempting to break through. Glimmers of hope, I think. When I pick up my schedule from my homeroom teacher, I gaze at Herr Hauptmann's name written in black ink on the stiff paper. I won't have to wait much longer to see what he's about; I have him first period.

When homeroom is dismissed, I head down the hall and then enter what is no longer Frau Kramer's room but now

Herr Hauptmann's. In comparison with Frau Kramer's decorating efforts—all she ever displayed was the bell schedule and the calendar by the door—Herr has enlivened things with some nice touches. Posters of various German cities adorn the yellowed walls (how I long to escape the monotony of my present life and travel to these distant places). Potted plants, some of which are flowering, now sit atop the bookcases lining both sides of the room, just the kind of sprucing up these worn dark oak furniture needs. Behind the dark oak teacher's desk are several four-drawer metal filing cabinets, heavily dented and scratched—but my eyes only focus for a moment on these imperfections because I'm more interested in inspecting the tall and colorful wooden figures, resembling historical Germans, standing atop the cabinets. Hanging on the wall above the models of an old-fashioned Bavarian couple is a traditional cuckoo clock framed by carvings of birds, leaves, and berries. Of all the improvements, I like this timepiece addition the best—so neat!

I am becoming comfortable and relaxed as I take my seat. Within seconds, looking as preppy as ever in his khaki pants and blue lightweight-cotton sweater tied over the shoulders of his white oxford-cloth shirt, Timothy occupies the desk behind me. We gaze into each other's eyes and exchange warm smiles. From my secondhand beat-up leather purse, I pull out a note written on a half-sheet of lined paper and hand it to him. In it, I have expressed my unhappiness about not seeing him over the weekend. As if she could read my mind about wanting to slip away, my mother kept me occupied until Sunday evening with a long list of chores.

After reading the note, Timothy turns the paper over and writes a reply, then hands the paper back to me. Much to my delight, he responds: *Let's "miss" the bus after school and stop at the park on our walk home. I want to show you how much I liked that kiss!*

I'm about to reply with *Sounds good!* but the warning bell rings, distracting me. Herr Hauptmann has yet to make his appearance. My gaze returns to his narrow desk. Unlike Frau Kramer who kept her papers and folders stacked on it in rigid piles, Herr has a somewhat messy, cluttered surface on his. I take this as another good sign: that he'll be laid back and approachable. As I glance toward the door, the last bell sounds and the cuckoo strikes that it's eight-thirty—but still no Herr.

Finally, after another minute or so, he rushes into the room, saying pleasantly, "*Guten Morgen, Klasse. Wie geht es heute. Es tut mir lied, dass ich so spät bin.*" Greeting us, he apologizes for being late. Then he proceeds to pass out a stack of packets, which are copies of a short story entitled "Ash Girl," a German folktale—in an English translation thank heavens—written by Jacob and Wilhelm Grimm. Offering little help, Frau would've expected us to read long German passages on the first day.

I look up from the story and stare at my new German teacher. His average height, slender build, wavy brown hair, and neatly trimmed beard make him appear non-threatening. His periodic smiles indicate that he has a pleasant demeanor.

"Class, I am aware that your German is probably rusty after your summer vacation," Herr begins. "Consequently, I would like for you to translate the first two pages of this story in German for tomorrow—a good review for you. Attached are three questions I want you to answer about the story's symbolism . . . *Auf Deutsch, bitte* . . ." He wants our responses to be written in German. And then after he takes attendance he reads the entire story with us. From there, he talks about the lives of Jacob and Wilhelm Grimm, about how they took several oral sources of a particular tale and fashioned them into one. It's a rather lengthy lecture. The bell rings again, and he dismisses us.

The rest of the school day passes quickly. Except for having Mr. Tyler for physics—he has as much personality as a rock—I am pleased with my other teachers.

Thwarting my plans with Timothy, my mother arrives in her silver '58 Chevy to pick me up, just as I exit out the door onto the sidewalk facing the parking lot. With all its frontend chrome and the prominent tailfins, the car resembles an enormous fish smiling with dental braces. I see my little brother Johnny sitting next to my mother. As I walk toward the car, she rolls down the passenger side window. "Johnny isn't feeling that great today," she says, brushing her wispy chestnut bangs out of her eyes. "I need you to watch him while I run into the grocery store." The fact that she hasn't put on any makeup tells me she's in a sour mood and that I should do as she says.

For a moment, I stand immobile and glance to the flagpole about ten yards away, in front of the school, where I'm supposed to meet Timothy. Leaning against the pole with books under his arm, he is too far away to notice me.

"Nance," my mother says, "I don't have *all* day. Let's go." With a stern look, she motions for me to get into the car. I have no choice but to obey, to hop into the back. As we drive past the flagpole, I wave to Timothy. He sees me. Frowning, he shakes his head. I helplessly throw up my hands to show him the situation is beyond my control.

\* \* \*

At my desk that evening, I start with the German assignment. Once I have finished rereading the story and picked up my German dictionary, I translate those first two pages. The story enthralls me. I can empathize with Ash Girl's plight. As the oldest, I know firsthand what it is like to have so many responsibilities, while not nearly as many expectations are placed on the other siblings. In fact, the story interests me so much that I continue and translate all four pages; then I answer the accompanying questions.

I try to complete my other homework as well; but my mother calls up the stairs: "Nancy, I need you. Please get down here." What is it *now*? I wonder. What do I have to do this time? Why can't Lizzie, Susan, Marcie, George, or Billy help her? I close my geometry and physics texts, knowing I won't be back here for at least another two hours.

* * *

The next morning in class, Herr Hauptmann asks us for the analysis of the fairytale. I discover that I know the answers to the questions, and after class he calls me over to his desk.

"You amaze me with your interpretations," he says, and I am ecstatic to hear his praise. "I liked how you explained that the broken twig in the story was symbolic of the severed relationship between the girl and her father. How did you become so good at understanding symbolism? *Ich bin sehr stölz auf dich*," he adds, meaning that he is proud of me.

I brag without pausing to catch my breath, as though all my thoughts are contained in one sentence: "Oh, symbolism is easy for me. I simply read the story as a whole and then go back to the descriptive passages. I compare these passages with the overall plot of the story and make my conclusions from there. It's just a process of figuring out parts of the story that seem to not make sense, or that seem overly descriptive and unnecessary but really aren't."

I've only dreamt about being able to honestly say such things at once.

"That's one way of doing it," he agrees. "I'm glad that you have a fine mind for this sort of work. As a part of this advanced course, we will be doing a lot of translations and interpretations of stories."

"That sounds great! I love stories."

"Well, I don't wish to detain you any further. You're already late for your next class. Let me write you a pass." Herr pauses and looks up from pad of hall passes. I remain patiently standing at the side of his desk. Tapping his chin with a pencil, he says, "I'm pleased to see that even though it's only my second day at this school, I've already unearthed a talented student like you studying German. I look forward to having you in class this year and seeing your continued growth with the language."

His words are like personalized lyrics from a song. They mean so much to me, especially with a turbulent home life like mine.

At the end of the day, though I have about three hours of homework in addition to a couple of hours of chores ahead of me, I walk alongside Timothy in the bus-filled parking lot with a steady grin on my face. "What's up with you?" Timothy asks. "What are you so happy about? Herr has assigned us several pages to translate from English into German tonight. And then we have those new words to learn and verbs to conjugate for tomorrow's quiz. It'll take forever . . ." Nodding, I listen to him, but his frustrations have no effect on me. I continue to smile.

"Yes, but I'm enjoying Herr's assignments," I reply. "I don't mind them at all."

"That's probably because you've become the rising star in class." He says this matter-of-factly, staring straight ahead without a smile or frown, so I can't read whether he's being sarcastic or sincere.

I slow down as we near our buses. When he does not say anything, I come to a full stop. It takes a moment for him to notice, to stop. Turning around, he steps back toward me. He scrunches his forehead, gazes at me with a puzzled expression. Clearly, he has no idea what I'm waiting for.

"What?" he asks rather impatiently.

Trying to soften his edginess, I smile and say, "Am I going to 'miss' the bus today?"

"*Miss* the bus?" he asks, his jaw dropping as if surprised by my question. "Why would you do that? With all this homework, we better get home and start on it as soon as we can."

"Okay," I sigh disappointedly. "I suppose I'll take a rain check then." Although I added the *I'll have a rain check then* to brush off his rejection, to make light of it, I feel hurt that he doesn't at least say he regrets not heading for the park.

He glances ahead to where his bus is parked next to mine. Kids pass us by, hurrying to their buses. The strong breeze bristles the fine hairs on my forearms. One by one, the drivers turn on the ignitions. The obnoxious humming of the engines helps to fuel my irritation with Timothy. If only he'd pacify me somehow. Maybe with smile or wink or quick hug and then say he'll try to make good on that kiss tomorrow.

But none of that happens.

Acting responsible, too darn responsible, he says, "Let's get moving. We have buses to catch."

Without saying good-bye, I walk away and climb onto the bus almost in tears, with my shoulders slumped, my head hanging low. I am wondering whether his eagerness to get home means his interest in me has cooled. *What a jerk!* I mouth to myself as I flop into a seat next to some freshman girl, my forehead and cheeks turning hot. Not wanting anyone to see my anger and watering eyes, I drop my head in the crook of my arm and press my forehead and elbow against the vinyl backrest of the seat in front of me. I pretend to rest—"sleep." My immaturity, my inexperience in the world, means I haven't a clue that Timothy's cold shoulder that afternoon will warm me for the years of hard work to come.

\* \* \*

I now lift my eyes away from the computer screen and look up at the framed copies of my master's and Ph.D. in German hanging on the wall. Both degrees received from the University of Vienna. I also gaze at the framed photograph of Herr Hauptmann and me standing outside of my brownstone apartment building here in New York City. It was taken last year when he came for dinner one evening. (Last week Herr celebrated his ninety-sixth birthday, still in good health!) Yes, I reaffirm, my drive and ambition has taken my life in many wonderful directions since the age of seventeen.

"Nance, you've been sitting at that machine today for hours." Timothy, my husband of thirty years, approaches me from behind. He motions to the pages of text coming out of the printer. "What are you working on?"

"Just reflecting on some childhood memories," I explain.

"Oh, yeah . . . ? What have you been writing?"

"About an uplifting event that you and I shared in high school. . . . Our daughter and granddaughters seem to have adjusted to their new lives, although I can still sense this sadness about them. Ilsa and Tanja have had a lot to deal with since their parents' divorce and their move to a new city. Neither of them likes their new high school—or their teachers. When they came to visit a few weeks ago, they were so quiet. I decided that the next time Veronika brings them over, I'd have an inspiring story for them."

My husband smiles. "Well, all of us need a little hope in our lives to encourage us, to carry us through." He gives my shoulder a gentle, reassuring squeeze.

"*Du bist rictig,*" I tell him, and how right he is!

# LIGHT IN THE DARKNESS

Confined to a stiff hospital bed that barely accommodated his bulky frame and five-foot-eleven height, Mathew lost awareness of the passing of time, the minutes and the hours, the staff coming and going through the doorway, the nurses and attendants who occasionally stopped at the footboard and chatted with each other about his condition. With nothing to do, not even able to look out the window because of the dark heavy-duty screen over it, he resigned himself to staring at the tiled ceiling, trying to grasp how complicated and tangled everything had become. . . .

Mathew didn't snap out of his daze until he heard his doctor in the hallway quietly ask one of the nurses, "How's he doing?" Dr. Pederson's voice sounded deep yet gentle—paternal.

"Okay for now," the nurse said. "I mean, he's stable, but earlier Morrison said he wouldn't advise letting him out of his restraints just yet."

"Definitely not," Dr. Pedersen agreed.

It had been six hours since Mathew had been admitted to the Rosewood Psychiatric Hospital and only maybe an hour since he had stopped thrashing. The pain in his left wrist throbbed with a burning sensation. The bandage had come off the wound when he pulled at the tough leather cuffs. It no longer bled. In the movies, his cut would be nothing. Hell, in the movies you could get cut, stabbed, and shot and walk away with just a limp. He loved those kinds of movies as a kid. But this was not the early '50s; this was now, real life, and there was no walking away from it, even with a limp.

The nurse with the pretty brunette hair and pleasant oval face came into the room and went to the clipboard at the foot of his bed. She scribbled a notation, then looked up and smiled. "How are you feeling? Would you like some water? A snack?" she asked.

Mathew didn't answer. Instead, reading her nametag, he said sarcastically, "Glad to know I'm stable now, Tracy. What drug did that for me?"

Probably sensing the anger bubbling in his words, Tracy only repeated her offer. "Are you sure you don't want something? You haven't had anything to eat or drink in several hours."

A tall man in a white hospital coat, with glossy brown hair and a bushy beard, knocked at the open door. "Can I come in?" he asked in a deep but friendly voice.

"I can't slam the door on you."

Not expecting Mathew's sarcastic remark, the tall man shot the nurse a sideways glance as he walked in, as if a little leery about Mathew's state of mind. To assuage any worries, the nurse nodded and smiled.

"Hi, Mathew . . . I'm Doctor . . ."

"Pedersen," Mathew said. "I already know. I heard someone mention you'd be in to see me."

"You know why you're here, don't you?"

"Dr. Morrison thinks I'm a schizo—a crazy man."

"But do *you*?"

"By definition I am, maybe. Probably." Disgusted with himself, with the medical profession's lack of understanding, Mathew balled his fists and violently shook his restraints.

"So you personally don't feel you are?" the doctor asked, his brow furrowed, stepping closer to the bed. The nurse took a nervous step backward toward the door.

Mathew shook his head, moving his wavy, sweaty bangs away from his eyes. Then he stretched his long legs beneath the white covers. "What's your reality?" he asked the doctor. "I bet it's not mine. But there's no way tell—is there?" He continued without waiting for the doctor to respond. "Your reality is filtered through your professional jargon, your training, and thus is supposed to become my reality—or the reality you're hoping I'll eventually believe in. The trouble lies in my perceptions—which can't be controlled at times—and you can't exactly get inside my head and make me believe what you or others tell me. Only drugs can do that—but only for a short time." Frustrated, finding no comfort in expressing his thoughts, he paused to shake his head again. "Since your mind doesn't work anything like mine, there's no way to prove what I've seen and heard and felt. And whether it is or isn't true. The only way you could probably ever cure me is for you to see and hear and feel what I have. So either we both have to see it or I'm screwed."

"Well put," the doctor said with a slow smile. "But you're not the first patient to logically work out something like that."

Mathew nodded. "Maybe so, Pedersen . . . but I'm sure I'm not like the others. The drugs and therapy and such probably helped them, but they haven't helped me. Why am I so different?"

"Everyone in this world is different," the doctor sighed, folding his arms. "Your situation may take longer to help, that's all. Besides, you haven't participated in any long-term therapy program during your other visits, and according to your blood work, it doesn't appear that you've been taking your medications."

Mathew turned his head away and stared at the wall.

"It's getting late," the doctor said. "I'll be off duty soon. Is there anything you need? Are you in any pain?"

Although the pain in his wrist vacillated between a burning sensation and needle-like stabs, Mathew said nothing and lowered his eyes to half-mast. There was one thing that would dull the pain, but they wouldn't let him have it.

"Mathew, an attendant and I will be back to check on you later," the nurse said in a soothing voice.

They left, their lab coats quickly blending into the fuzzy white light of the hallway.

Again, he heard them in the hall. It was the usual lines. With a tinge of sadness, the doctor said, "He's only twenty-eight and extremely intelligent. It's such a shame."

He could picture the nurse shaking her head as she said, "And no family in the area."

Then he heard new words. "I'm going to talk to Dr. Morrison first thing in the morning about committing him here for a much longer period," the doctor said. "This time, he only lasted about a month on the outside before he had another occurrence. According to the report, two police officers picked him up downtown. He was wandering down the alley at two in the morning in his underwear, clutching an old teddy bear, claiming some voice in the alley kept calling his name. But the alley was deserted. When the officers approached, he used a knife to slit his wrists. Fortunately, the cuts weren't deep."

"That's awful," the nurse said.

Mathew cringed as their voices faded along with their footsteps. They were gone. He was alone now. He didn't like being alone, not anymore. Why hadn't he asked the doctor for something more so he could fall asleep? He buried his head deep into the pillow. He wasn't thinking clearly because of the tranquilizers. The lights, though low, bothered his eyes. He was very tired, yet now the pain in his wrist kept him awake. Was the pain in his wrist real? *The cuts weren't deep*, the doctor said. So was he just imagining the pain? Was he imagining the confusion?

He had no memory of how he happened to be wandering around downtown this morning. Why the pocketknife in his briefs? And why wasn't he wearing any clothes? However, he did recall the two burly policemen rushing toward him on First Street, yelling at him. The voices, those hostile tones.

He heard them as the sound of his mother's shrill complaining. The voices enraged him and caused him to grab the knife from his underwear. He slashed at his wrist, crudely. The next thing he knew, he was pushing these men away. They put him into those restraints and dragged him to a white van.

This was Mathew's third stay at "Hotel Crazy." The first two were for what Dr. Morrison had described as "psychotic episodes." In Mathew's mind, they were just overblown temper tantrums. The first episode, about five months ago, took place when he was in his office at Suffolk University, reading through some articles on existentialism to prepare for an upcoming lecture. He taught several sections of Intro to Philosophy at the university. As if being taken over by an unknown force, he could feel anger and frustration pouring out from his arms and hands, eager to be vented. Even in childhood, he had worked hard to control his wayward emotions—no matter how upset his mother became for stupid things like neglecting his chores and not following her rules. He resented her telling him when to go to bed, how to keep his room neat and tidy. Her rules couldn't control him, not really. Even at the age of nine, while he lay in bed and read Shakespeare, he recognized he was above her. He understood things, eloquent words and symbolism. She never could.

The more he thought about his mother, the more he needed to release his pent-up rage. He pushed the binders and papers off the desk, watching them scatter across the beige carpet. Stepping over the materials, he went to the tall metal bookcase next to the door. With tears welling up in his eyes, he emptied the two top shelves as he hurled books across the room. The noise he made that afternoon alerted Janice, his colleague whose office was next door. Hurrying into the room, she saw books and papers everywhere.

Mathew was sobbing at his desk, his face buried in the crook of his arm. "Mathew? Mathew?" she repeated, standing over him, finally yelling, "Mathew!" to get him to look up. But he was too distressed to respond to her. After several minutes, she gave up and left him. Ashamed of what he had done, he stopped crying. Without bothering to pick up the mess on the floor, he packed up his briefcase and then headed for home.

The following day, he cancelled the three classes he taught, and stayed home. Despite feeling incredibly depressed, he managed to haul himself out of bed around noon and, sitting at the round oak kitchen table, forced himself to catch up on grading essays. His department head, Donald Phillips, called later in the afternoon and said he had heard about the incident. Expressing deep concern, he told Mathew to seek professional help before he could return to work. Donald recommended Dr. Morrison. After a session, Mathew was admitted to the hospital for a few days for observation. After his release, he never took the two prescribed antipsychotic meds. Why did he need pills? There was nothing wrong with his mood, or his grasp on reality. The incident in the office was freakish. At the time, he believed nothing like that would ever happen again.

The second episode occurred two months ago, when he was home alone one evening in his apartment, about two blocks from the university. One minute he was sitting in a chair at the kitchen table, the next he was face-down on the floor, basking in the chemical odor of the waxy yellow linoleum. There was a slight interval between the two moments when he saw nothing. He lay there for several minutes, too stunned to move or notice the small pool of blood forming around his head. It wasn't until he tasted it— the mixture of the metallic and salty flavors—that he "woke up." He turned over and touched his face. His nose and lips were dripping blood.  Getting to his feet, feeling lightheaded, he staggered into the bathroom, where a blood-streaked face stared back at him in the mirror. What the hell had happened? With trembling hands, he washed his face in the sink. He rinsed the towel in cold water and hung it back on the bar; then he splashed water around the sink until it was clean. From the cabinet beneath the sink, he pulled out an older dark towel and pinched his nose with it.

In his starkly furnished bedroom, still pinching his nose with the towel, he sat down on his bed as he picked up the teddy bear resting on the stack of down pillows. He gazed at the matted brown fur and dull black buttons for its eyes and nose. He had disposed of his old music records, books, movie posters, academic-achievement awards from middle and high school—but not the teddy bear. It was the only childhood remembrance he cared to keep around. He was five when the young girl living next door, who was probably about eight or nine, gave it to him. He was playing in the backyard with his toy trucks when she called him to the fence. "Here," she said, handing it to him. "I'm moving away next month with my dad. He says I'm too old for it now. But I can't just throw it away. Please take good care of it." He nodded he would. His mother told him the girl left the area because her parents divorced and her father wanted to start a new life in another state. The girl's mother, an alcoholic, continued living in the house until the place sold.

Twenty-three years had passed since he had last seen the girl. He could only vaguely recall what she looked like: skinny with long blond hair and wide-set eyes. If he passed her on the street today, he would have no idea who she was. Which was a shame. More than anything else in the world—besides getting out of Hotel Crazy again—he wished he could find the girl, a woman now, and tell her *thank you*. The teddy bear, the welcomed gift, had seen him through some very difficult times. The bear had been therapeutic when his father had disappeared not long after Mathew's sixth birthday. He had hugged the bear at night, which gave him some relief from the anger and frustration he felt toward the man who had taken off without saying good-bye, who was no longer there to play catch in the field behind the house or play checkers at the dining-room table.

Whenever he asked about his father, his mother's face tightened, letting him know it was a topic she would not willingly discuss. She gave him brief answers to his probing questions. Initially, she told him that his father had been called away unexpectedly on business and never came back. He was a missing person. When Mathew got a little older, his mother finally divulged more of the truth: his father had suffered some sort of mental breakdown at work. His doctor thought it was the result of stress and the long hours he worked as an automotive engineer. That same doctor prescribed a short rest in a hospital like Rosewood. His father was supposed to be gone a few weeks. But, when he was discharged, he disappeared without any word regarding his whereabouts. His mother claimed she had contacted the police and filed a missing person's report. They had no leads in the case. "Your dad doesn't want to be found," his mother had said once, heatedly, "so forget about him, Matt. Obviously, he doesn't care about me or *you*."

Even though his parents were technically still married, his mother lived her life like a single person, going to parties and dance clubs on weekends. She even had guys show up at the house to take her out to dinner. Actually dating. How that enraged him at first! Before long, he discovered he liked it much better when she was gone. Then only his aunt, who had moved in to help raise him, was around to nag. And she wasn't as much of a pain in the ass as his mother. His aunt's soft voice had no authority. Who cared about the dishes piled in the kitchen sink, or about the overstuffed bag of trash in the sink cabinet? With just his aunt in the house, he could sing along to pop music on his stereo without being told to "knock it off"; eat cookies and read as long as he wanted while lying on his bed with the teddy bear; talk as long as he wanted on the phone to his friend Jesse, whose obsession with horror comic books, like *Tales from the Crypt*, equaled his.

Although the remaining details of his *second* fit were still sketchy in his mind, Mathew remembered his flood of childhood memories being interrupted by the phone ringing on his cluttered nightstand. Tossing the towel onto the floor, he answered it. Much to his annoyance, he heard his mother say hello. As soon as he responded peevishly with "Oh, hi," she started harassing him: "Okay, Mathew, I can already tell something's wrong. Are you keeping in contact with Dr. Morrison? Are you taking your meds? If you screw up and lose your job, don't think I'll be taking you in. My child-rearing days are over . . ."

Mathew responded to her questions by slamming down the receiver. Firmly clutching the teddy bear, he rocked himself on the bed, his gaze fixed on the Trimline phone. His head thudded like a washing machine that was off-balance. He sensed his face and hands turning hot. Unable to contain his rage, he let out a prolonged scream—then shorter screams with tears streaming down his face and saturating the front of his blue oxford shirt. After that, he seemed to remember rushing around the alleys behind his apartment building, still holding the bear. He retraced his path over and over around those alleys. Whether he did so silently or continued to scream, he didn't know.

He also didn't know how long he ran. When several police officers stopped him, he faintly heard them ask, "What's your name, guy?" "You all right—anything wrong?" "Is there someone we can call?" Trying to catch his breath, Mathew thought he said, "No, no one. Just leave me alone." But they couldn't leave him alone—it was their job, their duty, to take him away . . . Probably recognizing how important the stuffed animal was to Mathew, the two officers who drove him to the station allowed him to hold onto it until he was released into Morrison's care at the hospital.

After a few days of emotional stability, Mathew was sent home. For several weeks, he felt fine— carried on as he normally did, teaching during the day, reviewing lecture notes and grading papers at night. Not once did he open the brown-tinted plastic bottles in the medicine cabinets and swallow any of those pills. *Not once.*

However, this third time at Rosewood was different. He could tell from the moment a nurse took the bear away as he lay on the stretcher. That was hours ago in the emergency room. That had set him off. Screaming at the top of his lungs, he thrashed about, kicking in the air, while two attendants attempted to hold him down. His outburst failed to persuade the ER doctor that he needed the stuffed animal. Instead of trying to reason with Mathew, the doctor administered an injection that drained him of all his energy, putting him into a catatonic state. And he hadn't come out of the stupor until an hour ago, when a male attendant showed up to change his diaper and clean his private parts. (If the diaper had been soiled with urine or feces, he hadn't noticed.)

Now the bear sat in plain view on the wooden visitor's chair, opposite the foot of his bed. Mathew's arms still ached to touch the bear, to hold it close against his chest, the way a father's arms would for a kidnapped child.

Emotionally exhausted, giving up on pretty Tracy coming back to check on him, Mathew drifted off to sleep. He slept dreamlessly. He awoke to someone saying his name and patting him on the shoulder. The glaring fluorescent lights assaulted his eyes. Because his surroundings were a blur, he couldn't make out who had said his name. He blinked fiercely until his hazy vision cleared. Then he saw a new doctor with a male attendant standing beside his bed. The doctor was an attractive woman with wide-set large eyes whose blond hair was fashioned neatly into a bun at the base of her neck. He also noticed the doctor's complexion was quite tan. Clutching a clipboard, she smiled warmly, putting him at ease.

"Good morning, Mathew," the doctor said. "I'm Dr. Lila Canfield. This is Jeremy." She glanced at the stocky gray-haired man next to her. "We've come to check on you this morning."

The man, leaning over Mathew, pushed down the safety rails and untied his wrists. Then the attendant scooped his arm under Mathew's neck, slowly helping him to sit up. The man took a step back, as did the doctor, giving Mathew room to swing his legs around and stand.

"How are you feeling?" the doctor asked with a look of genuine concern. "You need Jeremy's help getting into the bathroom?"

Groggily, Mathew replied, "I'll let you know in a second." Pivoting on his buttocks, he scooted across the bed until his legs were dangling off the side. Slowly, he pushed himself up with his hands pressing against the stiff mattress until he was standing. The uncomfortable pressure of his full bladder made him hunch over a bit as he tottered toward the bathroom.

As he passed her, she took another step back and asked, "So how are you feeling?"

"I'll let you know in a minute—or two," Mathew said.

From the pocket in his smock, the attendant took out a pair of latex gloves. He followed Mathew across the cold tile, past the wooden chair and plain oak dresser, until they reached the bathroom, where there was no door for privacy. Mathew waved the man away. Entering, he pulled up his white gown and pulled off the diaper, letting it drop to the floor, as he headed straight for the toilet. As soon as he flopped down on the seat, the urine flowed out of him in a heavy stream, quickly relieving the tension. He stood and straightened his gown.

At the sink, he washed his hands and gazed in the mirror. *What a mess!* Dark stubble protruded from his sallow cheeks and chin, and formed the beginnings of a crude mustache above his upper lip. The dark circles underneath his green, blood-shot eyes were so prominent that they looked like someone had stamped them on his face. And with his natural cowlick standing up from the crown of his head, he resembled a cartoon character brought to life. *A mess!* He wanted to shower. At Rosewood, however, none of the bathrooms in the patients' rooms had showers or tubs. The hospital policy was that patients' showers had to be monitored by attendants in the showering rooms (separated according to gender) at the end of the halls. Mathew hoped Jeremy or another attendant would allow him to shower soon.

From behind, Mathew heard a knock on the doorway molding, followed by Jeremy asking, "May I come in?"

Turning around, he replied, "Okay."

The attendant entered the bathroom holding a pair of gleaming-white underwear. "Fresh from the laundry this morning," the man said as he handed Mathew his briefs.

Mathew gave a nod of thanks. Returning his nod, Jeremy bent down and picked up the diaper with his gloved hand. After tossing it in the metal waste can, the attendant left him and rejoined the doctor.

As he put on his briefs, Mathew let out a sigh of relief that he had them back. Wearing a diaper was humiliating. He went back to the bed. Sitting down on it, he told Canfield, "Much better now." His words brought another smile to her face. With his thumb, he pointed toward Jeremy standing beside her. "So, is he going to put me back in the restraints?"

"What do you think?" the doctor asked calmly. "Do you think it's necessary?"

"Hell no," he replied, staring down at his forearm, his wrist, resting across his lap. The partially blood-soaked bandage had moved down to just below where the cut was. It didn't seem to hurt. The rough line of the cut had turned a deep brownish-red. Already healing. And itching. Not wanting the cut to bleed again, he didn't dare scratch it.

Canfield said, "Mathew, you must be hungry. Are you ready for your breakfast tray?"

He shook his head no.

The doctor dismissed Jeremy with a wave of her hand. "I've looked through your file," she told Mathew, "and it says you're a teacher."

"Professor," he corrected her. "That's quite different from being a grade-school teacher," he added sharply.

"Please excuse me," the doctor said, casually folding her arms, pressing the clipboard against her lab coat. "What do you teach?"

"Philosophy. Recently, one of my articles was published in the *Journal of Western Philosophy.* Not many *schoolteachers* can boast of that."

"Very interesting," the doctor replied with a nod. "Mathew, do you know why you're here? When you were admitted yesterday, you were in quite a disoriented state. I'm just making sure you understand."

"Yes, Doc. I understand. Dr. Morrison thinks I'm schizophrenic . . . nuts."

"Dr. Morrison was called out of the country because of a family emergency—and isn't sure when he'll be back,"

Canfield said with a serious expression. "I'll be your new doctor now." She took a step forward. "I've reviewed your file. Dr. Morrison hasn't made any official diagnosis yet. Given the problems you've been having—and no clear cause, I think it's best I observe you for a while."

Mathew's lips tightened with frustration as he spoke. "And try to dope me up with more meds—to see how I react to them. And then release me in a couple of days."

With the clipboard under her arm, the doctor took another step closer. "Mathew, Dr. Pedersen contacted your mother last night. She arrived early this morning in the company of a police officer, who submitted incident reports and witnesses' statements about your recent behavior. Your mother–who has power of attorney–signed the necessary paperwork to extend your stay. She's very worried about you."

Dr. Canfield's information didn't surprise Mathew. His mother had always wanted him confined. Jealous of his intellect and success in school—"Too intelligent for your own good and should be locked up," his mother often said smirking—it was only natural that she would get back at him. This must be her revenge: she barely made it out of high school and worked for years in a doll factory.

"What do you mean by *extend your stay*?" Mathew asked. "Are you talking about a week? More than a week?" He gazed into the doctor's face. There was something familiar, uneasily familiar, about her wide-set eyes. He had never met Dr. Canfield before—yet it seemed as though he had once stared into those blue eyes before—eyes possessing a certain softness yet commanding power.

"I can't give an exact answer right now," the doctor said slowly, gently, as if worried about upsetting him.

"The truth is, I'm going to be here for a very long time," Mathew snapped, clenching his fists as he rocked on the bed.

His temper was starting to flare. "You and the rest of the doctors assume that what I see and hear is within the realm of being treatable by your medicinal gods. But what if it isn't? I realize my perceptions are *off* at times, that I might not always be credible, but that doesn't mean I'm out of control. Just because I don't act and sense things the same way others—the way so-called *normal* people do—what right do doctors have to stop my feelings with pills? What if my senses, my 'tempers,' are necessary for my survival? You doctors are fighting something you can't even explain."

"Mathew," she said, glancing down briefly at her shiny white leather shoes, "those are not easy questions to answer." She looked up with a slow, cautious smile, which drew his attention to the fine lines across her forehead and around her eyes. "But in therapy tomorrow, we can explore some answers—and perhaps talk about how your behavior affects you and others."

"No one can answer my questions," Mathew said. Turning his lower lip up in disgust, he swung himself around on the bed until he was lying down again.

Canfield continued to smile at him warily. "One of the attendants should be by real soon with your breakfast tray. Please try to eat—or at least drink something this morning."

Perturbed that his questions were being brushed aside, Mathew was silent. He stared at his teddy bear on the chair.

The doctor clapped her hands together softly to get his attention. "Mathew," she said, motioning toward the chair, "I see you looking at your bear. I'm not sure why it was put here." She fell silent for a moment, as if contemplating different thoughts. "Dr. Pedersen made a note on your chart that it would be best if we put it in storage for a while. He believes it has become a substitute for human relationships—and he's not alone in thinking that. In fact, your mother mentioned this morning that—"

"What do you doctors know?" Mathew asserted, the inflection in his words sounding more like a statement than a question.

He was about to add w*hat does my mother know?*—but a red right started to spread across the wall above the bear. The light glared at him. Within that light, he saw an image of his mother's face. It jutted out at him like a hologram. He sat up, his heart pounding, his eyes twitching. His hands shook uncontrollably. He loathed the image—those stern eyes and that creased forehead, that sharp chin and nose, the thin lips arched downward into a frown, especially that mess of gray hair piled high atop her head. Not wanting to see it, he closed his eyes and hugged himself, rocking back and forth.

"Mathew! *Mathew!"* he could hear Canfield cry.

He opened his eyes. The doctor was standing in front of him, holding the bear. Her face brightened into a mesmerizing white light. Staring into the light, he watched her face transform. Her skin became as smooth as porcelain, almost doll-like, while her rosy cheeks widened and her lips narrowed. Her eyes, though watery and swollen as if sad, were recognizable. He had gazed into their piercing blueness at least once before. "How—how can this be?" he stammered. But at the same time, it all seemed to make sense. It was time. It was finally time to say what he had always wanted but couldn't. Once he said it, maybe, just maybe, he could be well—or at least "well" as others understood it. Lying back, he took the bear into his arms.

He was about to speak to the light, to pour out his loneliness to the face of the young girl, when a prick and burning sensation in his upper arm took him by surprise, rendering him speechless. He held the bear firmly against his chest. He felt his heartbeat and breathing slow. The bright glowing light in the room dimmed, followed by a calming darkness. Overpowered, he couldn't help but close his eyes.

* * *

The room was dark, except for a wedge of light forcing its way through the door left slightly ajar. The beam illuminated the teddy bear resting atop the thin cotton blanket covering him. He tried to sit up, but an intense pressure throbbed in his forehead. Flopping back against the pillow, he shuddered trying to shake off the strange tingling in his arms and legs. His bear slid down his chest safely into the crook of his arm. With heavy eyelids, he was ready to drift off to sleep again. *The effect of my drugs . . . ?*

Just outside his door, he could hear voices—a man and a woman talking. He shook his head almost violently on the pillow to stay awake. Though the throbbing in his forehead resumed, he forced himself to listen to what they were saying.

". . . I can't believe you gave him back that bear," said the man, whose voice Mathew recognized as Pedersen's. "Didn't you read Morrison's recommendations?"

"I did read them," calmly replied the woman, whose gentle tone belonged to Canfield. "I chose not to follow them."

"But why? According to what Morrison wrote about Mathew's history, it's obvious the poor guy is socially inept—no friends really, never been in a romantic relationship, often abrupt and standoffish with his colleagues and his students. He's pushing thirty. It's time for him to stop clinging to a bear."

"As Mathew's assigned psychiatrist, I can't see how taking away an object of comfort will solve his problems. Right now, my goal is to ensure he's stable, out of the restraints, and more secure so he'll open up during therapy . . ."

Canfield's voice faded as she walked away with Pedersen. Mathew collapsed back into the pillow. Sleepiness was overpowering him again: each eyelid felt that it weighed as much as a lead brick. He gave up the fight to keep his eyes open. Hugging the bear against his side, he murmured, "Thank you," and then dropped off into a deep sleep.

# CLOSE ENCOUNTERS OF THE MALE KIND
## Part One

*O*n a starry night, I come upon him sitting all alone on a bench. Venus, in full view, is assuring me the time is right. Licking my lips, making them even glossier, I cross the street to him.

*"Why, hello there," he says with an eager smile, standing up.*

*"Hello," I reply in a breathy voice. Seductively, I run my fingers through my long tresses, brushing hair away from my eyes.*

*He reaches out and takes my anxious hand. He holds it between his thick fingers. A strong touch. A manly touch. I shudder from the thrill of it! He steps closer. I can sense his desire—a desire that matches my own.*

*Neither of us speaks. He brings my hand to his chest and holds it there. I can feel his thudding heartbeat through his nylon bomber jacket. I bat my long eyelashes as I place his other hand on my chest, letting him feel the thumping of my own heart through my woolen cardigan.*

*He grasps my elbow and pulls my body into his. I tilt my head anticipating that we are about to. . .*

\* \* \*

". . .What adjective do you think best describes our gal? Spirited—indecent—naïve? Or, given her actions, is just plain old *stupid* the most fitting? Who's ready with a comment?"

The instructor was walking down the aisle, coming close to her desk. Worried he had noticed she hadn't been paying attention to the lecture, Annette straightened her back and reopened the paperback. She traced her finger along the sentences of a random paragraph, appearing to be searching for a passage that would answer the man's questions. The words on the page looked like a blur.

Much to her relief, the woman two desks ahead, at the front, raised her hand and offered a reply. Mr. Leland, quickly passing by Annette, responded to what her gray-haired classmate had to say. Annette heard very little of the discussion. The urge to turn around and stare at Kenneth was as overpowering as ever. Resisting, she closed her eyes for a moment as she mouthed to herself, *Don't fantasize—don't glance behind.* She took a deep breath, then exhaled slowly, quietly. Looking straight ahead, she poised her pen over her spiral notebook.

Back at the podium, the tall, middle-aged instructor provided an analysis of *Daisy Miller.* The assigned reading was about a late-nineteenth-century American girl traveling abroad. Because of her striking attractiveness and flirtatious personality, Daisy Miller initially captivated the European men she encountered. But once they got to know the *real* Daisy, they were put off by her lack of modesty.

With his gaze wandering about the room, Mr. Leland said: "Many reviewers simplify the character of Daisy Miller by stressing that she failed to follow the Victorian code of decency, thus bringing about her own downfall." He paused indicating what he said next would be on the upcoming exam. "But there's much more to her story than that. She was young and inexperienced. In other words, she didn't see how flirtations—especially such seemingly innocent flirtations—can be taken too seriously and lead to situations with uncertain outcomes. Daisy played a risky game for attention, and without a role model to teach her the rules, she was destined to lose in the end . . ."

Annette set down her pen. Giving into temptation, she turned her head and glanced at where Kenneth was sitting three desks behind. With his fingers combing through his dark wavy hair, he stared off into the corner of the classroom. Sighing, Annette thought, *I guess I'm not the only one having trouble. Too bad I'm not the reason he's distracted.* Her eyes darted to the wall clock. It was almost eight. *Not much longer. You can do this.* She pulled at her chin until she was facing Mr. Leland again, and listened.

Scratching his nearly-bald head, the instructor said, ". . . now that you've heard my opinion and some scholars', *whom* do you blame for Daisy Miller's untimely death? Perhaps Mr. Winterbourne, her cold-hearted suitor, who turns his back on her? Or maybe her dim-witted mother, who seems to care little about what her daughter does? Or is the culprit her other suitor, the Italian stud Mr. Giovanelli, who escorts her to the Coliseum where she contracts Roman fever? Or does Daisy, so unhappy with the way others have treated her, will her own death . . .?"

The woman sitting next to Annette raised her hand, but Mr. Leland gestured for her to put it down. "I don't want your answers now," he explained. "Instead, I want two pages next week stating your opinion with support from the text." He glanced at the clock, looking almost as relieved as Annette felt that his time was up. That didn't hinder him from adding more instructions: "When you get home, jot down your ideas while this lecture is still fresh in your mind. Class dismissed."

Annette slid her copy of *Daisy Miller* and her notebook into her leather tote bag, then put on her black wide-neck cardigan. While the classroom emptied, she waited at her desk for Kenneth. When he walked past her, she stood up, holding the bag at her side, and allowed a few others to get between them as she followed him out the door. She was dressed in form-fitting jeans, black two-inch high heels, and a silky merlot-colored blouse. She hoped the blouse complemented her brunette hair, whose loose curls flowed over the ruffled V-shaped collar onto her shoulders. Normally, her nicer clothes were saved for better occasions than class, but she was on a mission to impress. *Take the first step tonight and try talking to him—no more excuses,* she told herself, though she sensed knots forming in her stomach.

Along with the other students, Kenneth descended the flight of stairs at the end of the narrow hall, but he turned away from the crowd and exited out a door onto a side street, *alone.* Annette trailed close behind. He didn't seem to notice her, didn't even look back as he adjusted the straps on the backpack across his shoulders. She shadowed him as he rounded the parking lot and continued walking. *Hmm— maybe he lives close to campus like me.* The thought sent a shiver of excitement through her.

The October night air was cool yet balmy, and the sidewalk glistened from patches of wet concrete beneath the street lights. While they were in class, it must've rained. Slinging the braided tote straps over her shoulder, she noticed thick patches of grayish-black clouds in the sky. No visible moon or stars tonight. Earlier in the afternoon, the sun had been out, and it had felt almost like summer. The temperature could vary dramatically during the fall, yet Annette didn't mind this time of year. What she dreaded was the Michigan winter with its endless weeks of gray skies and frigid air. Whenever heavy snowfalls or ice-covered sidewalks prevented her evening walks, she developed intense cabin fever from being cooped up in her tiny apartment.

Pausing in the heart of Washington Street's shopping district, she watched Kenneth gaze at the window display of Preston's Fine Clothier. From a few store fronts away, she studied him more intensely as the display lights illuminated his masculine yet boyish features. She estimated he was twenty-three, her age. With his tall physique, angular face, and hair cut short with wavy bangs, he looked as though he'd stepped out of a fashion magazine. He was *that* handsome! Kenneth, she noticed, was a careful dresser. He always wore designer jeans or dark dress pants, never wore tennis shoes, and sported shirts that were always crisp and neat. She also noticed he never wore jewelry, not even a watch. The absence of a ring was no definite indication he was unmarried. Throughout her life, she had known several married men, including her own father, who never wore a wedding band. Wanting to learn more about Kenneth, especially his relationship status, she had googled one night "Kenneth Dorsey" (his last name she had heard during roll call on the first day of class), but nothing had come up pertaining to him. She had also tried to hunt him down on social media sites. Once again, her search had uncovered no accounts, profiles, or images featuring him. Talking to Kenneth would be the only way to find out if he was *available. . . .*

Moving on from the clothing store, he crossed the street, and she followed him as he headed down Fourth and turned onto Main. She was enthralled with the way his trim-fitting gray jacket with contrasting black ribbing outlined his broad, muscular shoulders. She wondered if his jacket had been tailored to accentuate his physique. *Money well spent if it indeed had been. . . .* Once, on the next block, he almost turned around. Fearing he might discover her stalking him, she let more walkers get between them, pursuing him from a safer distance. When she approached him, it had to appear unplanned, spontaneous . . . as in her fantasy.

Her cheeks and forehead burned. Not only did she feel feverish, but her stomach was acting up again, its contents dancing around in agitated motions and seeming about to travel up her throat. She definitely wished she hadn't eaten so much spaghetti earlier for dinner. The longer she walked, the more nauseous she became. She pressed her hand against her stomach. She needed to sit down somewhere until the sickness passed.

*My body is saying I'm not ready. I don't have the confidence yet to talk to him.*

Collapsing onto the nearest wrought-iron bench, she dropped her tote into her lap. She took a tissue from the bag and wiped her face with it. The queasiness subsided. Looking up the street, she found she had lost sight of Kenneth. She shook her head and pounded her knee with her fist.

*Why so afraid? What's the worst he could say?*

*Is my real worry that he wouldn't understand how emotionally fragile I am—that he could do me a lot of harm?*

\* \* \*

The following morning, Annette took a bus to the edge of Hazel Park bordering Detroit, to visit her mother and sister, Lorna. After the twenty-minute bus ride, she walked several blocks, passing through a neighborhood of run-down bungalows and dilapidated apartment buildings. She was so grateful not to live in this neighborhood anymore. The street dead-ended near a small field and railroad tracks. At the last house, cream-colored with dingy white shutters and moldy brown roof shingles, she went around to the back porch and then climbed the rickety wooden steps leading up to her mother's flat. On the balcony, as she knocked at the rusty door, a gloomy feeling quickly settled over her, despite the bright sun rising in the sky. How she dreaded spending time with her family.

Answering in a tattered robe, her mother stepped aside to let Annette in, not making eye contact. Her mother's shoulders were hunched over, and she looked exhausted.

"You want anything to drink?" her mother asked.

Annette shook her head no. The apartment's appearance took away her appetite. Empty plastic shopping bags, opened cracker boxes, and crumpled candy-bar wrappers littered the living-room carpet. The furniture needed dusting, and cobwebs crisscrossed every corner. In the open kitchen were dirty, smelly dishes stacked high in the sink and along the counters. Annette knew her mother had never been an immaculate housekeeper, but all of this was worse than ever before. Had her mother stopped taking her meds?

While her mother fixed herself a cup of coffee, Annette sat down at the round glass table in the dinette, between the living room and the kitchen. Her gaze fell on the door to the other room, opened just a crack. She pictured her sister lazily lying on the bed. From her small cloth handbag, Annette pulled out a wet disinfecting wipe and cleaned the streaks off the glass. She saw her mother's reflection in the glass giving her a dirty look. After a bit of hesitation, her mother sat down across from her. Watching her stir the coffee with slow, methodical strokes, Annette couldn't help but feel sorry for her. Merely forty-three, her mother was letting her apartment and appearance deteriorate. With her wiry eyebrows and mostly gray hair pinned into a bun at the nape of her neck, she resembled Annette's late grandmother.

Her mother's expression seemed pensive, preoccupied. Since she didn't seem eager to talk, Annette started the conversation with, "Poor Lorna. She never seems to learn by her mistakes. How long was she gone this time?" Two days ago, her mother had called to say Lorna had shown up at her doorstep the previous morning after a long disappearance. (Annette had had no idea her sister was missing because she hadn't talked to her mother in months.) Lorna frequently ran off with one guy or another for long periods of time. This pattern of behavior had begun when she was sixteen. And their mother always took Lorna back without question.

After taking a couple of sips of coffee, she said, "I know, Annette, you don't go out much—but, at your age, you can't expect me to take you by the hand and lead you through every fact of life. Don't you realize that some guys seem kind and caring when you first meet them—but after a while turn into complete jerks?" Her lips twisted into an exasperated expression.

In response, Annette shrugged her shoulders. Not wanting to indulge her mother's incessant need to argue, she diverted her stare to the only bedroom in the flat. Lorna still hadn't stirred, and now she started to wonder whether her younger sister was even there.

After taking a few more sips, her mother looked past the cup. For the first time, she met her daughter's gaze and said, "Keep being a good girl, Annette, and stay away from men. They'll only bring you trouble in the end."

A shiver traveled up Annette's spine. It was true she didn't have much experience with men—was still a virgin. As a "good girl," she set limits to where passionate kissing with a guy in the car or on the sofa could lead, pushing away hands that tried fondling the crotch of her pants or reaching under her shirt to touch her breasts. But her chastity also led to lonely evenings when dates stopped asking her out. Her last date was over a year ago. Hungry for affection, she was more than ready to shed her "innocence," yet feared the outcome. What if she ended up like her sister—sexually uninhibited, always choosing the wrong guy?

"Well," her mother said expectantly, "how about we go in the bedroom and see if Lorna needs anything other than your judgmental attitude?"

Though she was fairly sure of the answer, Annette asked, "So what happened to her?"

Making light of it, her mother said, "Nothing that some good rest won't cure. She's been through a lot, like I have, and just needs time to get better."

Annette's eyes narrowed. "You mean . . . she's sick?"

Her intense gaze apparently annoyed her mother. Replying in a hostile voice, her mother said, "Didn't you hear me?" She paused. "Lorna needs to relax, sleep—must have her family right now. That's why I called you. I—we need your help. It's time you stopped turning your back on your family."

"What—?"

"Oh, don't deny it." Her mother leaned back, eyebrows raised in a challenge. "As soon as you could, you packed up and moved out—started your own life with as little to do with me as possible. I'm tired of being all alone, with no one to rely on."

Her mother's words reverberated in Annette's head: *It's time you stopped turning your back on your family.* She pushed her body hard against the vinyl-padded backing of her metal chair, nearly knocking it over, hardly able to contain her rage and guilt. How could her mother say such a thing? Annette had never deserted her family. If she really had, she wouldn't have taken her mother's call the other day. But Annette had stopped extending herself unnecessarily, preferring instead to keep her distance from her sister and mother at times, since neither seemed to want to get ahead. Her mother had a hard time holding down a job for longer than a year and preferred to live on unemployment. Even though her mother never divulged the reason to Annette, she was finally granted Social Security Disability last year. Annette suspected her mother's disability was mental illness because of her history of depression and wild mood swings. Lorna seemed to have inherited their mother's poor work ethic. Her sister worked occasional waitress jobs that never lasted more than a few months. Instead, she hunted for a man to take care of her. So far all she had found were abusive jerks.

"Annette!" her mother shouted, snapping her fingers to rein back Annette's focus. "Go in the bathroom and look at yourself. Your face is flushed. Are *you* feeling sick? You need water or pop or something? With her hand pressed against her cheek, she added, "The last thing I need right now is for you to get sick on me."

Annette shook her head. "I'm okay."

Accompanying her mother into the bedroom, she winced at the musty smell. Grimy half-filled drinking glasses cluttered the nightstand. Dirty clothes and bed sheets lay in heaps on the floor. The drapes over the window had been pulled tightly together. Annette crossed over a path of mismatched shoes and clothes to reach the shabby curtains, hoping some outside light and fresh air would change the dreary atmosphere of the apartment—but a disapproving look from her mother stopped her.

Lorna sat up. The top of the beige bedspread dropped to her lap, revealing she was wearing one of her mother's billowy white nightgowns with a wide neckline and snap closures down the front. To support Lorna's head and back, her mother fluffed and stacked the pillows behind her. Lorna had a blank expression on her face, her eyes staring off into nowhere.

Annette sighed as she stepped away from the window. Sitting on the edge of the bed, she put her hand on Lorna's forearm. Her sister's skin felt cool and clammy. As she stroked Lorna's long brown hair, she stared at her sister's trembling hands. She tried to meet Lorna's gaze, but her sister wouldn't look at her.

"Talk to her, Annette," her mother said. "Tell her about your job."

Annette couldn't get over how much Lorna resembled their mother . . . resembled her from that time when she'd been in a hospital psychiatric unit. Overwhelmed, Annette couldn't utter a word. After clearing her throat a few times, she said, "My job is going pretty well, Lorna. A couple of months ago, I got promoted to the position of Head Library Tech at the Royal Oak Library. The administration promoted me even though I haven't finished my associate's degree yet. I'm eligible for some scholarships the city offers, so I can go back for my bachelor's degree and then maybe a master's in Library and Information Science—" She broke off suddenly, regretting she had mentioned her promotion. Most likely, her mother would hit her up for money later.

"That's wonderful!" her mother cried, but then shot Annette a disappointed glance to show her unhappiness about just now learning this news.

"How are you feeling, Lorna?" Annette asked. Their eyes met briefly—too briefly for her to read whether her sister was pretending or indeed sick. "Do you want anything?"

"No," Lorna mumbled, turning away.

"What do you mean *no*?" her mother asked with clasped hands. "I went to the market earlier and bought some coffee cake, your favorite. I'm going to wash some dishes, then cut you and Annette a slice." She quickly left the room.

Uncomfortable silence permeated the air. It bothered Annette to be alone with Lorna. Like never before, she sensed the distance between them, as if they were two objects on opposite sides of a widening river. At the same time, there was an alarming closeness between them that threatened to shatter this image. How could this be? She was nothing like Lorna, who'd do anything to get attention, especially from guys. When they attended middle school together, it was Annette at lunchtime who sat either alone or with a couple of friends, other girls like herself, who were quiet and reserved. But a large group of kids, mostly boys, sat at her sister's table, their voices loud and affable. In high school, it was the same story: Annette was usually quiet, passed from class to class with her head down and her arms filled with books, while Lorna loitered in the hallways to fool around with her friends.

Waiting for her mother to return, Annette straightened a couple of piles of clothes. Whirling around in her head were questions she wanted to ask her sister: *Why did you run away with those men? Did they say you were special—that they loved you? Or did you hope one day they would say that to you? Is that why you tolerated their mistreatment?* The answers might help Annette understand abusive relationships. Lorna, though, seemed in no condition to talk.

Annette's mother suddenly appeared in the doorway, holding a tray of cake slices. The sternness in her face jolted Annette, and she dropped the clothes in her hand.

"Annette," her mother snapped, "don't bother with the laundry. I'll deal with that later. It's time for cake."

Sitting on the bed with the tray in her lap, her mother tried to hand Lorna a dish with cake. "Here, take it. It's delicious." But her sister pushed the plate away. "Honey, please stop this. You need to eat something for breakfast." Again, she tried to put the dish into Lorna's hand, but her daughter resisted, folding her arms. "Okay," her mother sighed. "You win. I'll wrap it up for later."

Her mother held up the plate for Annette.

"No, thanks, Mom. I'm still full from cereal and toast this morning."

Standing up, her mother shrugged and said, "I guess you girls are all about your figures." With the tray balanced on one hand, she patted her slightly bulging stomach, adding, "More for me then."

Annette glanced at Lorna one more time, not knowing what to say but realizing she needed to say something. Finally she said, "Hang in there, Lorna. You're tough. Get better soon." She turned around and left the bedroom secretly hoping never to enter it again.

In the living room, she took her purse from the table. "I should head out now," she said. "It's my day off, and I'm devoting it to homework."

Setting the tray down on the table, her mother followed her to the door.

"If I had a day off," her mother said, "homework would be the last thing I'd want to do."

Annette turned the subject back to her sister. "Do you think Lorna's going to be okay?" she asked. "I noticed how her hands trembled. Maybe you should take her to a doctor?"

Her mother's face turned red. "How in the hell am I supposed to afford some fancy doctor?" she flared. "I'm on Social Security, and you know how much that pays? Not very much. And Lorna is out of work and without insurance." After a few deep breaths, she regained her composure. "Oh, Lorna will be just fine. She's just brokenhearted that it didn't work out with this last guy she was seeing. Give her time—she'll realize he was no good. Then she'll move on to a new boyfriend. She always does."

"Okay," Annette said, trying to be agreeable, eager to leave.

In an abrupt change of tone, her voice now full of sweetness, her mother asked, "Dearest, can I ask a favor?"

"What is it?" Annette already knew what was coming next.

Her mother gently stroked Annette's arms. "My bills are really piling up. Social Security doesn't pay enough to cover the expenses. I've even had to cut back on my own meds. Is there any way you could spare some extra dough?"

"Hmm. I don't know," Annette said, clutching her purse handles more firmly. "Money is tight for me, too."

"I wouldn't ask if things weren't bad for me," insisted her mother.

Annette rolled her eyes, then opened her purse and pulled out two twenty-dollar bills. "It's all I have on me."

"Thanks. I can use it for some groceries." her mother said, snatching the money out of Annette's hand. "You mind sticking around while I run to the store? I hate to leave Lorna alone for too long."

"I can't—I've got to work this afternoon." Saying nothing more, she hurried off to catch the bus.

During the ride home, she made a mental note to bring an empty wallet next time she visited her family.

*   *   *

*Descending the library steps, I find him standing a few yards away, in front of the tall decorative fountain. He waves at me. He's been waiting for me to get off work. I stand motionless for a moment: I'm not used to this kind of male attentiveness.*

*I rush to throw my arms around him. The paperback in my hand drops to the brick pavers. After several kisses, he reaches down and picks up the book. He studies the cover: a picture of an old English manor.*

*"A classic?" he asks.*

*"Yes," I reply. "An old story with a not-so-old plot."*

*He sets the book back in my hand. "Reading for school?"*

*"No, just for me." I shake my head. "When family problems arise, I reread it. Not so much as a boost, but as a reminder that, when times get tough, I can persevere."*

*He grips me softly about the shoulders. "Why haven't you told me about this?"*

*Demurely, I glance down at my leather slip-on shoes. "To spare you."*

*With his index finger, he pulls up my chin until our eyes meet again.* "Let's go back to my place. I have Chinese carry-out for us sitting on my kitchen counter. After dinner, you can tell me all about it."

"Without judgment?"

*He nods.*

*In front of the fire in his living room, he holds my back against his chest and nuzzles my neck. There's something about the warmth of his hug coupled with the beguiling flames that relaxes me enough to open up. Motioning toward my copy of* The Tenant of Wildfell Hall *on his end table, I talk about the connection between the book and my childhood:*

"I first read the book when I was eleven, in the sixth grade. My English teacher had a poster of the Brontë sisters on the wall behind her desk. She was a fan of these women and that intrigued me. At the public library—the school didn't own any Brontë novels—I checked out the novel."

*He brushes his lips along my earlobe.* "Why that particular book?"

"Because it was written by Anne Brontë—Anne coming before Charlotte and Emily, alphabetically." *I laugh softly.* "It was the first Brontë book I came to on the shelf. When I read its description, I couldn't believe the story shared many of the same themes as my childhood."

"Such as?" *Tightening his hold, he squeezes the words right out of me.*

"Ohhh . . . .like adultery and alcoholism and . . . .uh, marital separation—to name a few."

"Sounds like quite a childhood . . . Can you tell me more? I'd to like to know more about you."

*I hesitate, fearing I've shared too much. Will he really want to get involved long-term with a woman who's had such a turbulent life?*

But he's insistent: "If we are to grow as a couple, we shouldn't have any secrets." Softly, he rubs my arms, relaxing me. "No worries about being judged"

I smile. I like that he's referred to us as a couple. After a deep breath, I begin by describing my dad who, despite his problems with alcohol, was kind to me and my sister. When it came to either Lorna's or my birthdays, he showered us with thoughtful gifts and dinners at expensive restaurants, undaunted by the low pay he made as a custodian. Off the booze, or drinking moderately, he could be a lot of fun to be around . . . entertaining me with his hearty laughter, his piggyback rides, the endearing way he strummed his guitar as he sang the Irish folk songs his grandparents taught him.

Lost in those memories, I fall silent for a bit.

"What was your dad like when he was drinking heavily?" he presses me. "Was he mean to your mom? Is that why they separated?"

My voice loses its warmth as I talk about my mom. To give him a sense of what she's like, I emphasize her history of instability. How her wild mood swings, inability to hold down a job, and flirtatious behavior with guys in the neighborhood drove my dad to hit the bottle more and more. From observing my parents' heated arguments, I swear my mom received a certain satisfaction from inflaming my dad— the way she smirked as he yelled at her spoke volumes.

I reveal: "Most kids at age twelve would've been devastated if their fathers moved out, but I was actually happy that mine did. In my heart, I knew it was for the best."

He kisses me several times on the forehead. "I bet it was hard to talk about, but I'm glad you shared." Now, he kisses me lovingly on the lips, as if to assure me his feelings have not changed.

## Part Two

Taking a break from her studies, Annette braced a cushion behind her head as she reclined on the futon. She propped her feet up on the coffee table and read another chapter from *The Tenant of Wildfell Hall*. Despite having read it many times, she never tired of the book's dramatic dialogue, well-drawn characters, and wonderful descriptions of the English countryside. Annette spoke so highly of the story that many of her library co-workers had even started reading it.

One thing Annette didn't discuss with her co-workers was the personal connection she felt with the novel's heroine. Helen in *The Tenant* fled from an abusive husband, Annette in her past from a demanding and castigating mother. Like Helen, she struggled to be independent. And the struggle was well worth it. She loved living away from her mom. She also loved attending the local community college, in walking distance of both home and work. Her life was the best it had ever been. She had a great group of friends at the library who shared some common interests: reading classic novels, watching foreign films, hanging out in coffee shops. Yet something was missing, and she believed *that* something was a meaningful relationship. A while back, one friend had suggested a trial membership to an Internet dating site; but as much as Annette had enjoyed browsing the profiles of local men, it hadn't taken long for her sour on the idea of finding someone online, especially after spending a few weeks emailing, texting, and phone-chatting with a guy who had backed out at the last minute on their plans to meet face to face. *Wasted effort!* She much preferred to find desire and romance in a natural setting. How wonderful it would be to hit it off with a nice, handsome guy like Kenneth she either approached or was approached by at a park, bar, or some kind of social event. The only way to make that happen was to stop fantasizing and try putting herself out there. . . .

Setting down her book, she stretched and rubbed her eyes. Reading was making her sleepy. She wandered over to the window, where she could view downtown Royal Oak. Unlike Hazel Park's downtown, whose main attractions were dollar stores and mostly boarded-up shopping centers, the center of Royal Oak was filled with trendy bars, restaurants, and coffee shops. The artificial glow of the city at night mesmerized her. No matter how late, she enjoyed sitting on the benches downtown, watching the people, focusing her attention on couples stylishly dressed. Like models on a sidewalk runway, the women walked by Annette in an array of tight glittery tops, jeans decorated with fancy stitching, and high heels. The men paraded by in dark pants and silky shirts in a variety of styles and patterns. Laughing and talking loudly, the couples wandered in and out of the nightspots, usually in groups. The man often held his date's hands. Or he had one of his hands across the woman's back or shoulder. The expressions on the couples' faces were typically wide-eyed and excited as they entered an establishment, as if each place promised to be fun.

Annette yearned to be part of that scene. But her friends were all female, and none of them liked bars. She couldn't bring herself to go into one of those places alone.

A restless fire stirred inside her again. In her bedroom, she changed from her bathrobe, dressing in straight-legged jeans and a multicolored blouse with three-quarter length sleeves and a scoop neckline. Standing in front of the bathroom mirror, she straightened her dark wavy hair with a flat iron until it flowed gently onto her blouse. She applied her makeup, starting with luscious wine-colored lipstick and rose blush, complementing that with creamy beige eye shadow followed by black eyeliner and mascara.

Studying her reflection, she was transfixed by what she saw. She used to believe she was unattractive because of her high forehead and elongated face. However, with cosmetics bringing out the richness of her hair and olive complexion, she saw an image staring back that wasn't plain. *There's hope.*

Outside, the sky was clear; the air was cool with just a touch of a breeze. Wearing a burgundy cotton pea coat with big gold buttons, Annette headed up Eleven Mile Road. Once she reached Main Street, she browsed at the window displays of coffee shops, bakeries, and clothing stores. From there, she wandered to Washington Street, where she sat down on the bench facing a public parking lot. For more than fifteen minutes, she watched small crowds of noticeably tired and drunk people leave the night spots and head for their cars.

Although it was almost midnight, she continued sitting on the bench even though she had to get up early tomorrow for an 8:30 a.m. class. The calming yellowish glow from the street lights felt almost mesmerizing. Closing her eyes, she imagined Kenneth approaching her out of nowhere and saying, *Hey, aren't you the woman from my lit class? It's good to run into you. Have you started on your paper yet? Wanna have a drink somewhere and talk about it?* At the bar, they would chat until closing, discovering they had many things in common, and afterwards go back to his place and maybe . . . She opened her eyes, but there was no Kenneth standing before her. Nothing but a nearly empty parking lot. Sighing, she stood up and headed back.

Halfway down Main heading toward Eleven Mile, she lingered in front of a women's shoe store. In the window were tiered shelves displaying four-inch heels. Annette had no idea how women could comfortably walk around in them. The best she could muster were those two-inch heels she'd worn to class the other day in the hope of impressing Kenneth. *Just as well I didn't run into him. One look at these shabby shoes and he would've just passed me by.* She laughed to herself.

Hearing a car slowing behind her, she turned around to see a sporty white sedan pulling up alongside her. As the passenger-side window lowered, she saw a male driver.

"Hey there," he said. "How's it going?"

Caught by surprise, she just stared and didn't respond.

"Are you okay?" he asked. "Sorry if I startled you."

She peered more closely into the car. In the dim light, she had a difficult time seeing exactly what he looked like. From what she could tell, he had a thin nose but a wide mouth and bulging chin.

"I—um—I'm fine," she stammered.

"You sure you're okay?" he persisted. "You need a ride somewhere?"

His impatient tone both pleased and unnerved her. "Uh, thanks—but I'm fine," she replied.

"Honey, it's late," he said. "You don't want to be standing around at this hour. It's not safe for a young lady to be wandering around this late all alone. The cops may think you're working the streets—if you know what I mean?" When she didn't answer, he continued, "You live nearby? I'd be glad to drive you home. I'm not crazy, just concerned. Don't want anything to happen to you." His voice was deep and intimidating, but also a bit titillating.

Annette walked up to the Hyundai's passenger door, to have a better look at him, and daringly placed her hands atop the lowered window. Leaning her head down, she noticed the man had puffy cheeks and large forehead over which he combed a short fringe of hair. His tight-fitting blue T-shirt revealed his massive shoulders and muscular arms.

He reached over and stroked her hand with his meaty fingers. "So, what are you up to?" he asked.

"Just hanging out." His touch sent shivers up her back. She pulled her hands away, unsure where his attention was heading.

"Nothing going on—?"

"No."

"You want to hang out somewhere?"

She glanced up and down the street. "Like where?"

"How about my place? My house isn't too far from here."

"I don't know," she said, taking a step back.

"Come on in," he persisted. "I'll park somewhere and we can talk in the car."

"I'm more in the mood to hang out downtown." She pointed to the pub across the street. "We could walk to that bar over there and talk for a while. I've never been there but would like to check it out."

"I'm not much of a drinker." He opened the passenger door and motioned for her to sit down inside the car.

She took another step back. "You could get a soft drink."

He bit his lower lip and looked away, as if concealing his annoyance. "Well, I'm going to take off." He shut the door abruptly. "Another time, sweetheart." With that, he drove away.

During the walk home, Annette's heart pounded wildly, her ears roared, and her breathing turned into partial panting. She looked behind her now and then to see if the man was coming back. But no white cars drove by. She didn't relax until she reached the doorway of her apartment.

Half an hour later in bed, she tossed and turned, still full of nervous excitement, contemplating whom she would tell about her encounter with the man. The incident was the most bizarre yet equally exciting thing to happen to her in a while. She considered telling one of her friends at work about it, but she worried that talking about the guy might give them the wrong idea about her. *What were you doing walking around Royal Oak alone at that hour? What's the matter with you? It sounds like you were trying to get picked up.* Still, she felt she had to tell someone. So, that left her mother, who seemed to like drama. Annette was tired of being seen as the "good" daughter in the family and dealing with her mother's sarcasm because of that. Maybe telling her mother would show she wasn't destined to be a perpetual virgin. And maybe that would earn Annette a little respect.

\* \* \*

Two days later, on her day off, Annette stopped by her mother's with two bags of groceries, a surprise to put her mother in a good mood. To Annette's relief, her mother opened the door wearing a clean light-blue sweatshirt and jeans. Her mother's hair, loosely pulled into a ponytail, looked fuller than usual, as if it had just been washed and blown dry. Eyeing the bags with a smile, her mother said excitedly, "How nice! You want some help with that?"

Annette shook her head, saying, "I'm fine." She stepped past her mother, then through the dinette area, to enter the kitchen. After setting the bags on the counter, she turned around and said, "I'm going to put the groceries away. Go ahead and sit down, Mom. I'll be done in no time."

"Okay," her mom said, still smiling.

As Annette put the food away in the mostly empty cupboards, she pondered how she would bring up the man in the Fusion when she joined her mother in the living room. *Mom, you say I don't go out much, and there's good reason for that. You're not going to believe what happened to me the other night . . .* That might sound critical of her mother, so Annette considered introducing the subject with humor: *Mom, my status as "dateless" might be changing pretty soon. A couple days ago, I discovered a new way of a getting date—all I have to do is take a stroll around downtown Royal Oak. Listen to this . . .*

"If you want anything," her mother called from the living room, "help yourself. There's some lunch meat and bread in the fridge."

Annette glanced at the dirty dishes—plates streaked with ketchup and grease, rims of cups stained with coffee and soda—piled still on the counter and in the sink. The sight of them turned her stomach. She stuck out her tongue in disgust.

"Thanks, but I'm not hungry," she replied. Quickly finishing with the groceries, she folded the bags and tossed them in the cabinet under the sink.

In the living room, Annette found her mother sitting on the faded brown-and-white plaid sofa, going through envelopes spread across the coffee table. It appeared she was trying to sort them into two piles, probably one for bills and the other for miscellaneous mail.

Looking up, her mother pushed her half-moon reading glasses down to the edge of her nose. "Do me a favor, Annette?" she asked. "Check in on Lorna and say hi. I'll be done here shortly."

"Okay."

The bedroom door was ajar, and peering in, Annette saw that her sister was sitting in an overstuffed chair in the corner, with a blue cotton blanket haphazardly covering her jeans and white T-shirt. Lorna was sipping from a glass of soda, watching TV. Annette wondered if her drink was mixed with vodka or rum, her sister's two favorite liquors.

Entering the room, Annette said, "What'cha doing, Lorna?"

"Watching a talk show," she replied, looking up.

Like her mother, her sister had a cleaner appearance than two days ago. Her hair had been washed and combed, fluffed into layers about her shoulders. She wasn't wearing makeup, but her face looked smooth and clear.

"How are you feeling?" Annette asked, approaching Lorna.

"Better," she replied with a half-smile.

Annette slipped onto the edge of the bed and, trying to be casual, watched TV. The show's female host was talking with a male psychologist about how to tell if you've found the perfect mate. The psychologist mentioned obvious examples like common interests and goals, as well as friends who like your new partner. According to the man, it was healthy for couples to maintain their independence, but also to think of the future in terms of *we*, meaning the potential for a long-term relationship. The show's topic turned Annette's mind to Kenneth. She wondered if he might be her ideal mate. Since they hadn't gone on a date, or even talked, she felt frustrated. Before long, the semester would be over, and she might never see him again. What was the best way to get to know him?

"Hey, Lorna," Annette said. She waited for her sister to look at her, then continued, "I've got a question for you."

"Yeah? What is it?"

"There's this guy—in my night class. He seems like an interesting guy—and I wanted to get your opinion about—"

Lorna snickered. "Annette, after all my relationship fiascos, I'm probably the last person you want to ask for advice about guys." Instead of sipping, she took a big gulp from her glass. "If I were you, I'd stick to your studies at school. But if you really want to go out with a guy, I'd find one who's quiet and bookish like you. Are there any guys at work?"

Annette shook her head. The only male employee she worked with at the library was the director, and he was fifty years old with a wife and two kids. Anyhow, she didn't care to date a man who was quiet and bookish. She needed someone just a little bit daring, who would stimulate and excite her. Kenneth wasn't reserved. During class breaks, he hung around the hallway vending machines, chatting and laughing with a group of classmates. Often, she stood nearby them and overheard his jokes. Some of them were pretty bad: *Hey, I've got a new one for ya. What would happen if you cut off your left side? You'd be all right.* But his comedic attempts made her laugh nonetheless.

Getting to her feet, Annette smoothed the wrinkles on her black pants. Changing the subject, she said, "I'm going to see what Mom is up to. You want anything?"

Lorna's eyes were back on the TV screen. "I'm good."

Closing the door, Annette returned to the living room. Now finished with arranging the mail, her mother was reading a letter. Not wanting to interrupt, Annette quietly step over two small piles of snack wrappers and plastic soda bottles, and headed for the brown corduroy armchair across from the sofa. Partially covering the chair was a frayed blue-knit blanket. After brushing off some cracker crumbs from the blanket, she sat down on the chair and waited for her mother to look up.

Before long, her mother did. Setting her glasses on the coffee table, she asked, "What's Lorna doing?"

"Just watching TV," Annette said. "She said she didn't need anything." Suddenly feeling anxious, she rubbed her hands on the armrests and softly tapped her feet on the carpet.

"How about you?" her mother said. "You ready for something to eat? Maybe something to drink? I can offer you orange juice or Coke."

Annette shook her head.

"So what's up? You off today?" her mother asked, folding her arms, eyeing Annette a little suspiciously. "I wasn't expecting you today."

Annette nodded, drumming her fingers against the armrests. "It's my day off, but I'm never really *off* work. My classes are more demanding than last semester—endless reading and papers to write. I'm just taking a break from my studies for a few hours."

"Oh, you and your studies," she sighed with a frown.

"What does that mean?"

"I mean—it must be nice to take college classes, to pursue your dreams. I never could." Her mother paused, her frown deepening. "I got married at eighteen, barely out of high school, and then you and you sister came along. When you two were a little older, I tried to go to community college, but your father wouldn't hear of it. He claimed I'd neglect my duties at home—yet it was okay for him to go out almost every evening and drink the night away."

Annoyed by her mother's rehashing of the past, Annette scowled with a furrowed brow. "What does that have to do with me?"

"I'm saying this: I wish writing a paper or reading a book was my only problem."

"Well," Annette flared, leaning forward, "my life isn't exactly stress free. I almost got—"

With a hand wave, her mother cut her off. "I'm sorry— but your life can't compare with mine. At least you're *not* living in a run-down flat in a run-down neighborhood. You're living the good life over there in Royal Oak. When I went to see your place last year, I saw all those well-dressed people walking around the downtown area. Their only worries are whether their shoes match their clothes." Clearly agitated, her mother picked at her fingernails.

Annette moved to the edge of the chair. "Listen, Mom," she said more calmly. "Bad things can happen to people anywhere. The other night, I was walking around by myself downtown, minding my own business, when this guy pulled up alongside me." For effect, her eyes widened. "And then he asked me to get into the car . . . He scared me somewhat because he was persistent about it. What do you think I should do? Report him to the police?"

Her mother shook her head. "Seriously, Annette. I don't have time right now for a crazy story. I'm too busy working out the details of my plan."

"What plan?"

"To help your sister," her mother explained in a low voice. "Tomorrow, I'm taking her to the doctor to see about putting her on some meds."

"Really?" Annette replied excitedly. "I thought you didn't have any money for that."

Her mother drew her index finger to her lips. "Shh, Annette, I don't want Lorna to hear all this." She paused until Annette nodded for her to continue. Quietly, she explained, "Your aunt Vera loaned me some money so that I could take her to this shrink. The sooner she's on the right pills, the sooner she'll be ready to date again—hopefully in a month or so. Once she's seeing someone new, she'll forget all about Charles."

Annette arched her eyebrows, saying, "You sound like you have a guy already lined up for her."

"In fact, I do. His name is Todd. My friend Helene knows his family, and she tells me he's a respectable guy. He's got a nice house in Madison Heights and makes good money fixing cars. At night, he goes to Wayne State to finish his engineering degree. Helene and I are being matchmakers this time—to keep her away from more losers.”

Annette was taken aback by what she was hearing. Though her heart pounded wildly and her face flushed, Annette kept her voice down as she said, “I can’t believe you, Mom! You’re trying to pimp out your daughter to make life easier for you.”

Her mother’s face turned red as well. “Annette, I’m only trying to—”

Annette jumped to her feet, looking her mother in the eyes. “I know what you’re trying to do, but you’re living in a fantasy world. Even if he and Lorna got married, do you think he’d want his mother-in-law living with him?”

Her mother turned her gaze toward the corner of the room. “Jeez, Annette—let me finish, will you? I’m doing this for all of us—Lorna, you, and me. Once Lorna and I are situated somewhere nice, you wouldn’t have us as a burden. No more calls from me in need of anything. I know how much you hate coming here.”

Annette waved her hands angrily in front of her mother’s face. “Please stop—don’t pretend your matchmaking has anything to do with me. Let’s just say how it is: you only care about me when I can help you out in some way.”

“Annette, that’s not true.”

“Oh, it is true. If you really cared, you could’ve at least listened to my story. The man who—”

Her mother interjected, “You’re calling me a liar when you’re the one trying to act like some story you probably heard off the news actually happened to you. C’mon, Annette. Do you really expect me to believe you’re that dumb to walk around alone at night? Do you need attention that badly?”

Rather than utter words she'd later regret, Annette stormed out.

* * *

*I arrive home near tears. I'm about to call him, but he phones first. Right away, he senses my distress: "I'm on my way over."*

*Before I know it, he's at my doorstep. In the living room, we head for the futon, where he sits with his arm around my shoulder. Holding my hand, he gazes with deep concern into my watery eyes. He tries smiling, but his knitted eyebrows and wrinkled forehead overrule it.*

*"I'm sorry that seeing your mom is so upsetting," he says, unable to conceal his melancholy tone. "Visiting her beats you down into such a state of dejection. . . I hope someday you two will have a better relationship."*

*I stare down at my lap, shaking my head. "She doesn't love me and I definitely don't love her."*

*"Sweetheart, don't say that."*

*To back up my claim, I go back in time for my boyfriend, to the months following my parents' separation. With my dad temporarily out of the picture, my mom worked hard to tarnish his character. "Look at those worn-out gym shoes," my mom snapped one morning, pointing to my feet, before I was about to run an errand. "If your dad really cared, he'd send me what I need to provide for you." On another morning, in an even fouler mood, she flared, "Once again, Annette, your father is behind with his child support. So forget about seeing a play with your class today. I'll call the school and say you're sick—to save you any embarrassment."*

*My thoughts swell with many other examples of my mom's lies, intended to hurt an innocent teen. Such despicable lies! I saw my dad's checks come regularly in the mail.*

*As time went on, my mom won Lorna over to her side, but not me. It irked her to no end that I spent more and more weekends with my dad. Almost every Friday afternoon, it was the same scene: standing in the bedroom doorway and watching me pack my duffle bag, my mom taunted, "Anxious to check out already, I see. Sorry I don't have the means to turn the apartment into a five-star hotel. Hope your stay wasn't too unpleasant." When I didn't respond, she would glare and try to goad me into an argument: "It must be nice to have two places to live. When you don't feel like helping out at one, you can run off to the other. I wonder how many kids in your class have it this easy."*

*Why did she always expect me to stick around and do the cleaning and laundry? No fun in that. Rarely did she tell Lorna to do her share.*

*My dad knew how miserable I was and managed to wrestle custody of me away from her. I moved in with him full-time the summer before I started high school. Things were going well in his life: he seemed to have curtailed his drinking and found a better job as a manager at a tire shop. In early August, he and I went away for a few days to Mackinac Island, a resort area between Michigan's Lower and Upper Peninsulas. I had the most fun in my life: eating fudge, riding horses, taking boat and carriage tours. The experience, though, taught me how fleeting happiness can be. One week later, my dad suffered a massive heart attack at work. He died in the ambulance on the way to the hospital.*

*Recounting all this chokes me up with tears—makes my head pound like a drum machine. I rub my eyes, then press my palm against my forehead. I suffered terribly from headaches and fits of crying like this after my dad's funeral. I felt so guilty wishing it had been my mom, not my dad, who had dropped over.*

*That wish is one detail I don't tell my boyfriend, worrying he will find me cold-hearted and withdraw his love.*

*Allaying my fears, he hugs me more securely and gently kisses my earlobe, my cheek. I grip his knees. Then I turn my head until our lips meet. We kiss passionately, our tongues inside each other's mouth. Bathing in his big handsome eyes, I rub his muscular thighs, back and forth, over and over. Responding to my arousal, he caresses my breasts, making my nipples hard. I close my eyes and listen to the voice in my head. Saying now is the time, don't wait any longer. More than ever, I want him . . . I want my body under his, with our hands intertwined, our legs wrapped around each other. . . reveling in our closeness, an intense closeness that will drive away these painful memories.*

*He stands suddenly, pulling me to my feet. His gaze shifts from me to the futon. "Shall we . . . ?"*

*Yes, I nod. Kissing again, we tear at the buttons, snaps, and zippers of each other's clothes, which end up in a heap on the floor. Our lips part only long enough for him to unroll the futon and then lower me onto it . . . .*

\* \* \*

Later that evening, Annette sat on her futon cross-legged with her laptop on her lap. The computer screen remained blank as she mulled over what the introduction to her paper on *Daisy Miller* would be. Several minutes passed before she typed the words that expressed her thoughts: *Taking place during the 19th century, the novella* Daisy Miller *by Henry James is a study of this hypocritical time. European women during the Victorian era were very restricted; they were expected to follow a rigid code of respectability. Since Daisy Miller's mother fails to grasp the code and teach her daughter acceptable behavior, Daisy experiences a fatal blow to her reputation by the story's conclusion.*

Annette paused, her fingers dancing over the keyboard, uncertain what to write next. If she went with the view of blaming Daisy's death on her mother, she worried if her disgust with her own mother would show through as she wrote additional paragraphs. She sympathized with the character of Daisy Miller, who was more concerned with matters of the heart than society's conventions. Although Mr. Leland had marked Annette's essays down when her writing wasn't objective—evident by the C-plus she had received on the last paper—she found it difficult not to let emotions dictate what she wrote.

Frustrated, she set her laptop on the coffee table. At the window, she opened the blinds and, looking up, saw the sky was brilliantly clear, dotted with stars. She rocked from heel to toe, her heart fluttering. She took several deep breaths, but her restlessness grew stronger and stronger. It was almost midnight. She didn't want to take any breaks until her paper was finished, so she wouldn't have to worry about it over the weekend. But there was no way she could do that now.

Dressed in a maroon boat-neck cotton top, denim mini skirt, and plain black stockings that matched her belt and high-heeled boots, she put on her makeup in the bathroom. Then she brushed her hair, letting her waves fall loosely about her shoulders. For pizzazz, she pulled out a pair of long gold-fringe earrings from the wooden box on her bedroom dresser, and looped them into her earlobes. After grabbing her coat and purse from the closet, she headed out toward downtown, determined to participate in Royal Oak's nightlife.

On the corner of Eleven Mile and Main, the Mexican restaurant was bustling with people. Pausing at the door, she considered going inside, figuring she could order a margarita and check out the people. She reached for the wooden door handle, hesitated, then dropped her hand. *No, the purpose of being out tonight was to go to an actual bar, not a restaurant where you probably won't meet anyone. Don't be a coward!*

After walking a few more blocks, she stood in front of Tom's Oyster Bar, staring through the window. The place was dimly lit inside and had a low-key atmosphere; couples were sitting at tables with black-and-white checkered tablecloths. Entering, she headed straight for the rustic dark-stained bar, drawn to where a blond man with a trim physique was sitting alone. He was wearing a silky blue diamond-print shirt, almost identical to one Kenneth had worn on the first day of class. She slipped onto the stool next to him and ordered a Kahlúa and cream. Almost immediately, as if knowing her intentions and displaying his lack of interest, the man gulped his beer, got up and left.

*Damn*, she thought. *So much for trying to talk to him.*

Setting down her drink, the bartender said, "That'll be eight dollars." She handed him two fives, telling him to keep the change. She sipped her drink, savoring the sweet and dense coffee flavor. A tingling sensation, starting in her head, quickly spread throughout her body. She enjoyed the sensation and took bigger sips. A pleasant warm feeling replaced the tingling. When she finished the drink, the bartender asked if she wanted another. Standing up, she said, "No thanks." Her head seemed a little fuzzy, her balance a bit unsteady, so she walked with careful steps toward the door, to avoid bumping into one of the tables.

Once she was outside, her natural stride returned. She took a deep breath and smiled. *I did it—I really did it! I can now say I've experienced some of the nightlife.*

Turning the corner onto Fourth Street, she stopped smiling. Her body froze. Approaching the intersection was a sleek-looking white sedan. It looked just like the Hyundai from the other night! To avoid being recognized, she pivoted so that her back was facing the street. In front of her was

Deco Doug, a store specializing in art-deco wares. Pretending to window-shop, she studied the car's reflection in the glass. At the light, the vehicle stopped. The driver's image was blurry; she couldn't tell if it was the same man who had accosted her. Patiently, she waited. The light changed and the car drove away. She sighed with relief.

Around the next corner on Center Street, she heard rock music coming from Gusoline Alley, a neighborhood bar that attracted a varying crowd. *Maybe this place.* The closer she came to the warped-looking wooden door, the louder the music became. As she looped her fingers around the metal door handle, her hand felt the vibrations from the hard rock beat. She opened the door just a couple inches to test whether her ears could tolerate the music. The volume was deafening. Doubting she could have a decent conversation with anyone inside, she let go of the door and walked away. Back on Fourth Street, she shook her head, thinking, *Tonight doesn't seem to be my night for meeting anyone.*

Her disappointment quickly dissipated as she eyed the man sitting on the wrought-iron bench across the street. Even though he was turned toward the small, near-empty parking lot with his back to her, she recognized the distinctive style of his dark wavy hair. To be sure, she crossed the street, then stepped sideways to get a good glimpse of his profile. She kept a reasonable distance and stared at him for a few seconds. It was Kenneth all right. His features—the handsome nose, high cheek bones, and square-like jaw—were etched in her mind.

It was as if it were meant to be: he was all alone, sitting under the stars. Now was her chance to talk to him. Her heartbeat quickened, pounding rapidly. She breathed deeply to keep her anxiety under control. *Kenneth, you're the one to help me break free. I can't go on like this . . . in this empty bubble. If something doesn't happen soon to pop the bubble, I fear I might lose my mind.*

Her thoughts seemed crazy. Was it the effect of the Kahlúa? Annette shook her head to clear it. How could she think such things? Yet they empowered her to take the next step.

Approaching the bench, she swallowed hard, then said, "Hey, how's it going?"

Kenneth nodded with a puzzled expression, as if he had some dim recollection of who she was.

Standing in front of him, she said, "I'm Annette—from night class—with Mr. Leland."

He nodded again, without the bemused look.

"How's it going?" she repeated with a smile. "I saw you out tonight and wanted to say hi. What are you up to?"

"Just hanging out."

To keep the conversation going, she asked, "What do you think of Mr. Leland? I like him—just not sure I'd take another class with him. His tests aren't too bad, but he grades pretty hard on the writing assignments. Have you started your paper yet for next week?"

He nodded with a smile (or was it more of a smirk?). "Not yet."

She didn't know how to read him. He was pleasant enough, but his short responses to her questions weren't encouraging. Still, she rationalized that their chat here on the street, no matter how brief, could serve as an ice breaker for talking more in class next week. Not wanting to come across as too intrusive, she decided to ask him about Leland's assignment to wrap up their conversation before saying good night.

"Any ideas on what you're going to write?" she asked. "I haven't decided yet who I'll blame for Daisy Miller's death. Probably one of her suitors. I suppose I could put the blame on Daisy herself. After all, she didn't use the best judgment going to the Coliseum at night when she'd been warned about catching Roman Fever there." Annette laughed nervously.

"Yeah," he said, "I suppose—"

"Kenneth! Kenneth! There you are!"

Annette and Kenneth simultaneously turned their heads to see the blonde woman across the street who was calling to him.

Transfixed by the woman's beauty, Annette stared at her as she headed toward them. The woman's long hair was styled with charming waves and curls, which bounced against her shoulders as she approached them. Hugging her hourglass shape, her knee-length black dress was cut low in the front and showed off her ample cleavage.

Kenneth stood up to greet her. "Hi, Olivia."

"Where've you been?" Olivia said, playfully arching her eyebrows and waving her phone. "I've been texting and calling you for the last hours—to see if you wanted to meet up for a drink."

"Sorry about that," he said. "My phone has been doing weird things lately—not ringing or receiving texts. I'm going to take it in and get it fixed."

"Anyway," Olivia said, "I'm meeting Jackie for a drink at the Black Finn. You want to join us?"

"Sure," he said. "I don't have to be into work until the afternoon."

The woman eyed Annette up and down. "Who's this?" Olivia asked him, casually pointing to Annette, who had taken a few steps back. "A friend of yours?"

"Just someone from my night class," he replied.

After nodding a good-bye to Annette, he put his arm on Olivia's shoulder and steered her up the street. Annette watched them with the intensity of an owl. They didn't hold hands or display any other mannerisms that indicated they were a couple, so it might be safe to say. . . . Annette shook her head at herself. *Best to stop speculating and move on*, she decided. Yet, she couldn't tear her eyes from them until, at Fourth and Main, they turned the corner, out of sight.

A wave of numbness swept over her body, leaving her weak in the knees. She flopped down on the bench, her legs stretched out in front of her. Moments passed before the sensation went away . . . replaced by feelings of hurt and sadness. Kenneth's indifference toward her was evident; he hadn't even bothered to introduce her to Olivia. Essentially, she was (and would remain) a stranger to him. Wiping stinging tears away with the back of her hand, she reflected on how she acted around Kenneth. How could she have allowed herself to become infatuated with him? He had done nothing to encourage her: only once had she, maybe, observed him looking her way in class. Still, her expectations had been high—the result of silly fantasies.

She rubbed her eyes. *Well, it's done and over with.*

She drifted in the opposite direction, toward Washington Street. Turning the corner, she walked several blocks along the street without a destination in mind. Although she had to be up early for work, she wasn't ready to go home.

At the resale clothing shop, at the intersection of Washington and Lincoln, a car pulled up beside her. Glancing to her side, she saw it was a white sedan. *Is that man inside?* She squinted. It was a male driver with dark hair, but the burned-out street light prevented her from being certain whether it was that strange guy from the other night.

The passenger window rolled down. "What are you doing, sweetheart?" he asked. His voice, deep and baritone, sounded the same as *that* man's! But she wasn't going to stick around to be sure. She crossed the intersection and headed back toward Fourth.

The driver did a U-turn and followed her. Though her internal alarm went off, his persistence aroused her. After a few blocks, she slowed her pace. Her hands shook from nervousness, so she folded her arms to steady them. She walked a little farther to a lighted area, then stopped to see who the driver was.

The car pulled into an empty parking spot in front of her. The man leaned his head partly out the window, saying, "Hey, baby. What are you doing out here all alone? You want a ride?"

Annette recognized the man's profile: the round cheeks and jaw, the broad forehead, the slender nose. His thinning hair was combed straight back. It was indeed that guy. Against her better judgment, she drew closer to the car. She bent her knees slightly to peer inside, to get a good look at him. He wore a gray short-sleeved shirt that was buttoned halfway up, exposing hard chest muscles beneath a light sprinkling of brown chest hairs. As he adjusted his posture, his large biceps flexed. He was no Kenneth but he wasn't unattractive. She could do a lot worse. He reached over and opened the passenger door, and she got in.

"Where'd you want to go?" he asked.

In a mechanical voice, she replied, "Your place." Her earlier humiliation had left her feeling dazed.

He made another U-turn and drove. "You doing okay?" he asked, rubbing his hand against her knee. "You looked a little upset walking around by yourself. Anything happen? Feel like talking about it?"

"I'm okay."

"I remember you from the other night," he said, withdrawing his hand from her knee. "You're very pretty. What's your name?"

"Annette," she answered. She didn't ask his name.

They fell silent as they left downtown and entered a residential area of bungalow-lined streets. His driving followed a maze-like pattern. She had no idea where they were. Near a small park, he pulled into a brick driveway leading to a white cottage-style dwelling with a steep roof and shuttered windows. They got out and she accompanied him up the driveway. Outwardly calm, she waited for him to unlock the door and then hold it open for her. She stepped inside and stood in the dark foyer, her heart quivering from mounting anxiety even as she strove to suppress her reservations.

*This is it. I can't turn back now. . . I'm finally going to know what it's like,* she assured herself. A shiver of anticipation traveled up her spine.

But as soon as he locked the door behind them, and brushed Annette's hand away as she reached for the light switch, she realized what a mistake she was making. Perspiration broke out around her forehead and under her arms, and her heart pounded wildly.

"I—uh—I don't know—don't know about this," she stammered, feeling short of breath.

"What?" he cried, creasing his forehead. "You have to be kidding . . ."

"I'm sorry. I don't feel comfortable." She fumbled with the door lock. "I don't know you."

Playfully, he slapped her hand away from the door, then reached his hands underneath her shirt and cuddled her breasts. "Relax," he said.

She backed away and his arms fell away. Undeterred, he encircled her with his arms, drawing her against his firm chest. About her height, around five feet nine, he tugged her hair and positioned her face to kiss him. He tried to smother her mouth with his, but she reeled back as much in fear as disgust. His breath had a pungent rotten meat odor. She flailed and tried to push herself away from him, dropping her purse, but he held her against him, even though she dug her nails into his arms.

"You're a wild one," he said into her ears. "A real feisty bitch. It turns me on."

"Let me go!" she pleaded. "This was a mistake. Please let me out of here."

He released her but then slapped her face hard, knocking her to the floor. Her left cheek burned like fire, as if branded with a hot iron. Rebounding, she quickly stood up and groped for the door lock. He smacked her hard again on the back of the head, knocking her down. Landing on her face, she tasted the dirt on the ceramic floor, her lips puckering as the flavor of blood mixed with the dirt. Her head throbbed with pain. Gasping, she attempted to crawl. He laughed while she made her way to the corner, near another door, and a tall decorative vase. Using the door handle, she hauled herself up, her breath now in short bursts, blood oozing down from her lips. Behind her, he laughed.

Adrenaline raced through her body. A survival instinct took over. Though the vase was heavy, she picked it up. Raising it over her head, she rushed toward him, while he laughed, "You can't hurt me, you bitch."

With all her strength, she slammed the vessel down, catching him on the crown of his head. The vase shattered. Large pieces crashed across the tile. The man's blood splattered across her face and on her clothes. He collapsed, hitting the floor with a hard thud. She stood frozen, eyes agape, looking down at his motionless body. Despite the near darkness, she could see blood pool around his head.

Moments passed. Her shock dissipated. Wiping her face with her coat sleeves, she turned on the lights. Her eyes darted. Where was her purse? She spotted it behind her, resting in the middle of the foyer. She tiptoed through the broken pottery pieces and grabbed her purse. Without checking to see if her attacker was alive or dead, she fumbled with the lock, then flung herself out the door.

Halting at the edge of the driveway, she thought, *You can't just run off. You've gotta call the police.* After taking her phone out of her handbag, she dialed 9-1-1 while continuing to wipe her mouth.

When someone answered, Annette's voice came alive, gushing forth like unstoppable water. "Oh, God!" she sobbed. "There's been a terrible accident . . . I mean, not an accident.. . .I didn't mean for it to happen. It wasn't my fault. *Please* believe me—I didn't want this to happen. It was because of him—the guy from night class. If only he talked to me, if only that woman hadn't shown up. . .I would've never gotten into the car. I'm not that kind of person. I don't do these things—I've never done anything like this before—"

Annette stopped. She tried to listen to what the person on the other end was saying. It was a man's voice. A warm voice. A comforting voice. He was telling her to slow down, to calm down. It seemed as though she hadn't heard a voice like this in many years, not since her father's passing. She pressed the phone more firmly against her ear. She listened. Then she took a deep breath and began to answer his questions, while assuring him that she was all right.

# ANIMAL LOVER

Growing up in a Dutch colonial with two affectionate and protective Bouvier des Flanders, in Michigan's thumb area, Mason thought his destiny was to always be a dog lover. That notion changed one September morning during his sophomore year. On the ride home from the Saturday Farmer's Market, Mason saw a man holding a cat over a winding creek. What was the guy going to do with it? Throw the poor thing in? Try to drown it? The scene tore at Mason's heart.

Estimating the creek to be about a hundred yards away, Mason believed he could save the animal before it was too late. "Dad, stop!" he yelled, pointing to the gravel shoulder of the country road.

Hitting the brakes, his dad pulled the Chrysler minivan over. "What the hell, Mason? What's the matter? You sick or something?"

Without responding, he jumped out of the van, not bothering to shut the door. Waving his arms, he screamed, "Hey, Mister! Please—please don't do that! Don't hurt that cat!" In excellent physical shape, he ran effortlessly as muddy water shot up from the rain-saturated field, soaking his tennis shoes and jeans.

Seeing six-foot-three Mason heading toward him, the much shorter man dropped the cat on the grass. As the man leaped over the creek, his sports cap fell off his head and landed in the water. Without pausing to retrieve the hat, the bald stranger headed up a small hill, then disappeared into a cluster of trees.

Carefully, Mason picked up the orange-and-white-striped cat, inspecting it to see if it was hurt anywhere. Appearing unharmed, the cat purred in his arms. As he cuddled it like a baby, it nuzzled the shoulder of his fleece jacket. "You're so beautiful—handsome," Mason told it, unsure if it was a boy or a girl.

Red-faced and gasping for breath, his father caught up with him, saying, "Son, you almost made lose me control of the car." His father looked down and pointed to his muddy boots. "And you made a mess of these."

Mason set the cat on his shoulder, petting its soft back. "Can I keep it?"

His father shook his head.

"At least until we find out if it belongs to anyone other than that crazy guy . . ."

Rubbing his forehead, his father was silent for a moment, then said, "Okay—but if no one claims the cat in a month, I'll have to hand it over to the Humane Society. Your mom won't put up with two dogs and a cat under the same roof for very long."

To their surprise, his mom said she didn't mind the new addition. She even helped make the missing-cat flyers that Mason and his dad posted around town and the neighboring communities.

Concerned about the animal's health, he convinced his dad to take the cat to the vet, who told them it was a neutered male. Calling the cat "Burr-boy"—because that might've been the animal's fate in that cold creek—Mason kept the feline in his bedroom, away from the cat-skeptical dogs. With balls of yarn and stuffed toys, he spent many evenings playing with the animal. Often, his red-haired and freckle-faced girlfriend, Laurie, joined him.

"Cats are so cool," he told her, watching Burr-boy bat his paw at the pretend stuffed mouse on the floor and knock it across the imitation-wood laminate. "I like how Burr-boy can be with me without being all over me. When one of those beefy Bouviers tries to get on my lap, I feel suffocated."

Reclining with Mason against a headboard of pillows, she combed her piano fingers through his fine sandy hair. "And I like how his fur is as soft as your hair."

*And what I like even better,* he thought, *is that the cat seems to bring us closer together.* Their month-long relationship still had its awkward moments. Without a lot in common—he enjoyed long hikes in the woods; she preferred being indoors—they struggled at times to have a conversation. At their disposal for discussion was gossip about mutual friends, or the brewing scandal concerning the school principal's affair with one of their teachers and  . . . yet they exhausted those topics within minutes. Now, when they were alone, Burr-boy relieved the pressure of what to do, what to say.

As his attachment to the feline grew, so did his gratitude that no one ever contacted his parents about a lost cat. After school, he often went with Laurie to the public library to read and check out cat care books while she studied. (He found he did his best studying on his bed with his back against a stack of pillows and Burr-boy curled up on his lap.) In a book entitled *How to Keep Your Kitty Meowing* were several fun exercise games for cats. One game called Catching the Light became Burr-boy's favorite. In his darkened bedroom, laughing so hard that his stomach hurt, he shined a flashlight around and watched the cat jump on the bed, the desk chair, the desk, the clothes hamper in his attempt to paw at the light. In order not to frustrate Burr-boy too much, Mason allowed him to actually "catch" the light once in a while.

Feeling guilty about neglecting Duke and Duchess, the dogs, he changed his weekend plans to devote more attention to them. Instead of going with their friends to the Port Huron Factory Shops, a discount outlet, he went on walks with Laurie and the dogs to the nearby park. In the area designated as a dog run, they unleashed the Bouviers and threw soft balls for the animals to fetch. The game lasted about thirty minutes, until Duke and Duchess flopped down in front of the bench on which he and Laurie sat. To quench their thirst, the dogs drank the water in a rectangular plastic container set at their feet.

It was on a late-October afternoon at the park that Laurie told him the upsetting news:

"Mason," she said, looking into his eyes, "I've been wondering about *us*." She brushed her long straight hair back behind her ears. "I mean we're sorta 'going out,' but it doesn't really feel like it. It kinda feels like we're connecting more as friends."

Though he somewhat agreed with what she said—going out for three months and no make-out sessions, only awkward kisses—her revelation stunned him. Then angered him, heating his face up like a hot poker. This skinny backstabber was actually rejecting him. Did she really think she could find something better, with her pug-like nose and pointed chin like a witch, with her outdated and baggy-fitting clothes looking like hand-me-downs? She was nothing so special that she could reject him first. And he hadn't even wanted to date her in the first place, got pushed into it by their mutual friends, Jay and Tina. Trying to fit in, to be "cool," he wanted to be in a relationship like the rest of his friends.

His immaturity getting the best of him, he shook his head, flaring, "Look, if you weren't interested, you should've said it two months ago. Why play games and waste time?"

As he stood up and hopped over the dogs, she reached for his hand, but he backed far enough away that she couldn't touch him. "Sorry," she said, "I like you—I really do. At first, I thought maybe a little more than just *like*. Don't be upset. What's wrong with being friends?"

"Nothin'—I guess," he said with bitterness, pulling the dogs up with their leashes. "I gotta go." He tugged gently at each dog's leash until Duke and Duchess were standing. With the dogs leading the way, he hurried out of the park.

"Hey!" she called after him. "What about the container you brought? What do you want me to do with it?"

"Stick your head in it!" he yelled. He crossed the gravel parking lot, then the road to the dirt path on the other side, grateful for the breeze cooling his face. Jogging along that path, he reached his house in about fifteen minutes. On the front porch, the dogs bent their heads, as trained, so that he could easily unleash them.

Once inside, the dogs headed straight for their rugs in the den. Mason was about to head upstairs, but his mom's frantic voice drew him into the kitchen. Entering the room, he discovered her cries were coming through the fully-opened French doors in the dining area. He followed it outside, onto the deck, where he saw his mother standing on the edge of the steps, shaking a cat-treats bag and calling across the yard, "Here, Burr-boy. Here, baby. Come home, Burr-boy. Got a treat for you."

"Mom," he said excitedly, "what's happened? Where's Burr-boy?"

Turning to face him, she let out a loud sigh. Clutching the treats bag against the skirt of her purple dress (his father's favorite because it complemented her blue-black hair so well), she explained, "Oh, honey, since you were gone with the dogs, I made the mistake of bringing Burr-boy downstairs. He's been cooped up in your room so much."

She took a deep breath. "He was having a great time exploring the kitchen, finding the treats I left around. For just a moment, I had the doors open, to check out the weather, when Burr-boy bolted past me and scurried away, into the woods." She patted him on the shoulder. "Don't get upset, Mason. I'm sure he'll be back before nightfall. He knows he has a good home here."

Overcome with worry, he ran past his mom, down the sloping lawn, into the woods. For what seemed like hours, he jogged, then walked along the overgrown paths crisscrossing the half square mile of forest. Thorny plants and sharp twigs tore at his pant legs. Frequently, he paused to crouch and stick his head through the low tree branches, looking and calling for Burr-boy. Sweat drenched his hooded sweatshirt and plastered his hair across his forehead. His leg muscles ached; his head reeled from exhaustion. Not seeing Burr-boy anywhere, he gave up and went home.

He collapsed into a supine position on the deck, staring at the sky, with his hands folded underneath his head. He observed quick-moving gray clouds, threatening to pour rain, settle overhead. *Poor Burr-boy!* he thought, his eyes turning tearful. *Two months ago, I rescued you from that crazy guy, and now you're gone. All alone in the woods. I hope you're taking cover wherever you are, in case a storm erupts. And most of all, I hope you come back to me.*

The sound of his mother's high heels smacking across the wood planks interrupted Mason's thoughts. Rolling onto his side, he saw that she was approaching with the cordless phone in her hands, her fingers covering the handset's transmitter, as if she didn't want whoever was on the other end to hear them. He sat up, crossing his legs Indian-style.

"Any luck finding Burr-boy?" his mom asked, her brow creased with concern.

Mason shook his head.

"Honey, Laurie's on the phone. She says she really needs to talk to you—that it's important. I know you're pretty upset right now. Do you feel up to talking to her?"

He pulled at his chin, thinking, *What to do? What to say?*

Just then, Burr-boy hopped through the railing onto the deck. As if to answer Mason's questions, another cat, tiger-striped with a mixture of sandy and gray tones, followed Burr-boy. The felines made their way toward him, but stopped at his feet. They stared at him, as if they, too, wondered what he would do and say.

"Oh, honey, I told you Burr-boy would come home," his mother said. "And look, he's got a friend with him."

Mason stretched his arm until his mom set the phone in his hand. Then, putting the receiver to his ear, he said, "Hello, Laurie. . . Yes, we need to talk. Long story—but the day got a lot worse after I ran off at the park. Can I call you back in a while? I'll explain more then. Probably in about an hour. Okay?" However, she kept him on the phone, clearly not ready to hang up until he uttered, "No worries, Laurie. I'm the one who should be sorry." Which he did say because he was.

# MORELAND PARK

"Are we almost there, Alex?" my grandmother asked, letting out a loud sigh.

"We're close," I assured her.

We were traveling along a winding road. The occasional sighting of boarded-up farm buildings and empty corrals broke up the view of grassy fields on either side. Momentarily, I allowed my gaze to wander from the approaching curve so that I could glance at my grandmother. As I turned my attention back to the road, the steering wheel jerked in my hand.

"Be careful," she scolded, her brow puckered.

"Sorry. Just checking on you."

"This place better be as breathtaking as you claim. It seems as though we've been trapped in this car for hours. I don't know if my back will be the same again."

"You won't be disappointed—I promise."

My upbeat voice masked the anxiety I felt. Before the doctor diagnosed her with Parkinson's two years ago, my grandmother could pass for ten to fifteen years younger than her actual age. *Not anymore.* Her hair had turned almost as white as Arctic snow; her face had sagged, with heavy bags under the eyes, perhaps from the combination of fatigue and all the medication she now took. Embarrassed by her hand tremors, she stopped participating in church activities and sold her interest in the decorative pillow-making business she owned with a friend. Most days, she lay on the sofa, just watching TV, and aging.

To halt her rapid decline, I was taking her to Moreland Park. A visit had done wonders for my friend Kevin's elderly mother. "At the fountain, something magical happened," he claimed. "When she splashed her hand around in the water, her face started to glow, and the sparkle came back in her eyes." (My friend's story may've sounded too good to be true, but I believe in keeping an open mind.)

The road straightened and turned into a residential street. Sighting the wrought-iron park entrance, I slowed and pulled into a parking spot in front of it. As I helped her out of the car, I noticed the roughness of her hand. Grimacing, she complained, "Oh, Alex, I can barely stand up. I must've been out of my mind to let you talk me into this." Frustrated, taking deep breaths, I waited for what seemed like nearly a minute as she stood on the sidewalk and rubbed her lower back. She nodded when she was ready. With slouched shoulders, she walked beside me, taking measured steps with her cane, toward the gates. Before the mid-morning sun's brightness could bother her eyes, I handed her my wire-framed sunglasses. To shield my eyes, I held my right hand above my brow.

As we passed through the front entrance, the whistles and squeaks of starlings flying overhead filled our ears. The breeze was light and refreshing. We ambled along a brick path boarded on both sides with daylilies. The birds' chatter faded away. I tried to point out an impressive rock garden coming up on our right, but my grandmother showed no interest in it because she kept fiddling with the sunglasses, pushing them up and down on her nose. Once again, I breathed deeply to calm my anxiety. *Have some patience*, I told myself.

The brick path stopped where a manicured lawn and a row of wooden benches faced a vast garden of flowering perennials—such as coneflowers, bee balm, and Asters. The healthy plants glistened, as if they had just been watered. Ready to take a break, my grandmother motioned to one of the benches. We sat down.

She removed the sunglasses and rubbed the bridge of her nose. Squinting, she said, "I can't take these anymore. They bother me." I wasn't about to let the expensive aviator-style sunglasses go to waste, so I put them on.

About twenty yards ahead, the meandering dirt pathways through the garden converged and became another brick walk. After a few more yards, it forked to encircle a magnificent fountain. The structure reminded me of something from Ancient Rome. Surrounded by statues of toga-clad maidens, the fountain was housed in a wide marble basin. Great bursts of water shot up in arching formations and traveled from one edge of the pool to the other. As I pointed to it, I turned my head to see her reaction. Instead of gazing at the fountain, her sunken eyes stared at the cluster of colorful magnolia trees and vibrant conifers to the left of it. I had no intention of redirecting her, for I was just grateful she was looking outward—rather than inward.

Several minutes of silence passed. Since the sun was directly overhead, I was getting warm. Little beads of sweat formed along my forehead; I regretted not bring a hat to keep the sun off my balding head. Staring down at my khaki shorts and the pale skin exposed on my legs, I also wished I had put on sunscreen earlier to ensure I wouldn't burn.

"Beyond the fountain and the trees is an old-fashioned pavilion," I said. "We could head over there and enjoy the shade." My T-shirt clung to my chest. I hooked two fingers underneath the ribbed collar, then loosened and flapped it for ventilation.

"We can—in a few minutes, Alex. For now, I want to stay right here."

To find out whether the park's atmosphere was having the desired effect, I asked, "Do you still think I was wasting your time—bringing you here?"

"Oh, I don't know . . ." Her voice trailed off as she fell silent. "Why are you bothering with an old lady like me? You should be here with your new girlfriend." Resting her cane between the knees of her light-blue cotton pants suit, she gazed at me critically, as if she were trying to understand my intentions. "Is there something you're not telling me? Are things all right between the two of you? Have you been paying her way when you go out? Sometimes, you can be a bit too frugal."

Rolling my eyes behind my glasses, I sighed with exasperation. "Oh, Grandma, everything is okay. But I don't always pay her way. I have to be frugal to save up for the new house." Worried my tone sounded a little too harsh, I added, "Besides, I believe in supporting Jennifer's independence."

Not responding to my attempt at humor, she shook her head with a furrowed brow. "At thirty-two, you should know by now a woman will lose interest in a guy who's too cheap. With that attitude, how do you expect to get married someday?"

Very gently, I jabbed her bony upper arm with my elbow. "Grandma, I'm just teasing. And enough worrying about me. You've done too much of that in my life."

She patted my knee. "Not too much, really."

"Oh, c'mon." I took a deep breath, then began my list: "Watching me after school and during summer vacation as a youngster. Pushing me to get good grades. And after Dad walked out on Mom, persuading me to join after-school clubs so I wouldn't isolate myself. Later, helping me with college expenses. Need I say more?"

She picked up her hand, holding up her shaking index finger. "Actually, I could use a little more explaining about something. Even though I don't go out much these days, I know that many recreational spots in our area are being neglected or sold off to developers. So I realize we had to drive a certain distance for a decent park. But an hour's drive? There isn't one closer?"

"You're right—but many of the parks by us have either closed or aren't well-maintained, like the grounds at the church." I paused, giving her a few moments to mull over what I had said, before continuing with, "Besides, you haven't traveled anywhere in a long time. It never hurts to have a different view on your horizon."

She nodded. "After living in a neighborhood of row houses for so long, with no yards to speak of, I've almost forgotten the fact that gardeners and landscapers are artists in their own right. They have the power to turn the most unkempt field into a site we can enjoy." She cupped her chin with her hand, as if falling into deep thought.

I took off my sunglasses, clipping them onto the collar of my T-shirt, and gazed at my grandmother's face. Observing the return of color to her cheeks, the gleam in her hazel eyes, I felt confident to press with, "Doesn't being here inspire you in some way?"

"Yes, it does," my grandmother said. To my surprise, she stood up, purposefully setting her cane against the side of the bench, and turned to face me. "Now that summer is almost here, I'm thinking about that small empty field across from Heart of Enlightenment's parking lot. It's been two years or more since Lena Wimsley and her sisters resigned from their spots on the Beautification Committee, just before leaving the church. I realize the Committee has become inactive since then, but that's still no excuse for letting weeds and debris overrun the property. I can't believe the Council—that none of the members seem to care about tidying it up." She shook her head in disgust.

My eyes widening with enthusiasm, heartened she was taking interest in something again, I asked, "Any idea how to motivate them?"

Her smile told me that several were now dancing around in her head. "It's time for someone to talk to Pastor Mike about restarting the Beautification Committee. With help from volunteers, the committee could clear up the lot and plant some flowers and perennial beds." To emphasize her excitement, she clapped her steady hands together. "And I could paint those wooden benches stored in my garage—and have your cousin Bill bring them to the new park in his truck. People could use them after Sunday service to relax, socialize, and admire the volunteers' handiwork."

Standing up, I reached out and took her hand. It felt different from when we arrived. *No longer cold and trembling.* In fact, her palm was warm—filled with life.

"I see I have a mission now," she said.

# THE TROUBLES OF KAITLYN BROOKS

*Troubles come in threes.* Though Kaitlyn Brooks had been aware of that saying for years—who used to say it in the family?—Great Aunt Betsy?—she had regarded the superstition as silly or meaningless, despite enduring a childhood filled with hardships, until the summer of 2001. That summer, shortly after her twenty-third birthday, her life seemed to crumble before her.

In early July, her father succumbed to complications from diabetes and heart disease, passing away at age sixty-one.

A month later, her mother had a sudden stroke. She fought valiantly to recover for several weeks, until a second one claimed victory, causing her death at age fifty-nine.

After her mother's funeral, she started worrying obsessively about what terrible thing would happen next. What other tragedy would she have to endure? And it took effort—outlining the chapters in her dry textbooks, working out each morning and most evenings at the community recreation center—to keep herself from constantly thinking that *a third trouble could strike any day now.*

As more weeks passed, she prepared for future, and her new plans helped to lessen her anxiety. Before long, she was almost ready to put her fears to rest. *Just stop dwelling on the past . . . look ahead and happiness will come. . . . It will . . .* She was forcing herself to be optimistic—and thus not initially concerned when elderly Mr. Jamison came by one late afternoon, near dusk, at the end of September.

Kaitlyn and her parents had lived in the same brick ranch in Wayne, Michigan, since she was ten, but they had always been renters with a month-to-month lease. As she greeted the hunchbacked landlord on the crumbling cement porch, he apologized for not returning her call from a few days earlier and about just dropping by. He happened to be driving through the area and, wanting to express his condolences in person, decided to take a chance on Kaitlyn being home. For several minutes, he reminisced about what good tenants her parents had been, quiet people who never needed reminders about snow removal and maintaining the yard. Missing several teeth, Jamison spoke with a lisp, forcing Kaitlyn to crane her neck and ears uncomfortably close to his wrinkled face, to hear him better.

As if his mind suddenly switched gears, he stopped talking and motioned across the street using with the tip of an aluminum cane. Without asking, she knew he was drawing her attention to the other dilapidated properties in the neighborhood: a mix of ranches and bungalows (bricked and wood-framed) with decaying chimneys and porches, moldy roofs, collapsing wooden fences. Then he pointed to the weathered wooden door behind her and said, "As ya know, I haven't been doing much to this here rental for a long time—only what's necessary. If the others around here ain't bothering with paintin' and fixin', why should I? Besides, your parents didn't mind because no home improvements meant no rent raises."

Jamison paused to gesture again at the dwellings across the street. Anxious for him to get to the point, Kaitlyn nodded to indicate she was listening. He resumed with, "The neighborhood's definitely gone downhill, so next month, Kaitlyn, I'll be putting the house up for sale. You'll have about five weeks to move out." He waited a moment for her reaction, but she gave none. "I wish I coulda let you stay on longer, but, with the market pickin' up again, it's best to put the house up for sale. I'm too old to be worryin' about this property and the other ones I got. The missus and me want to hightail it outta here to the Georgia, where we're originally from." He shook his head. "Last winter here was a real doozy. My bones just can't take that kind of cold anymore."

Kaitlyn nodded to show she understood his reasoning. His notice didn't come as much of a surprise. As a believer in the motto *those who fail to plan, plan to fail*, she had already made arrangements to vacate by early September. Still dazed from burying two parents in such a short time, she hoped he would stop rambling and say *goodbye*. She wasn't in the mood for a conversation.

Unfortunately, he made no sign of leaving. Probably feeling guilty about the eviction, he quizzed her about her future plans. Where did she think she might go? Could she afford her own apartment? Or was she going to stay with her older brother, Justin—or maybe another family member or friend?

"With Justin," Kaitlyn said, taking a couple of steps back to show she was ready to go back inside. "I was planning to call tomorrow and tell you. I should be out of the house within a few weeks."

Once again, the old man didn't take the hint. Leaning forward on his aluminum cane with the padded grip, he lisped on with more questions. How was managing without her parents? Was she going to take their personal property with her? Or donate them? He had connections with the manager of a local thrift store. If needed, he could arrange for the man and some of his employees to swing by with their trucks and remove any of her parents' things that she no longer wanted. In turn, she would receive a receipt she could claim as a deduction on her taxes.

Jamison's talk only intensified her sadness. Despite the growing lump in her throat, indicating she might burst into tears at any moment, she swallowed hard and took a deep breath before responding again. "Thanks for your concern, but I'll be all right. Justin and a friend of his will be helping out. There isn't a lot of stuff, and most of it is going to the curb. "

She took another step back, about to say goodbye and that she'd be in touch, but his gaze kept shifting between her face and the well-defined cleavage of her V-neck Henley top. This weak-looking man who'd been so kind to her parents, not raising the rent in years and never penalizing them when they fell behind . . . could he be . . . was he some kind of pervert? The idea forced the lump in her throat to travel down into her stomach, transforming it into a tight knot of uneasiness.

What he said next confirmed her suspicions: "Glad to hear someone's looking out for ya. I hate to think of a pretty thing like you dealing with everything by her—herself. You let old—old Jamison know what ya need." He winked at her. "I'd love to help you out with wha—what—whatever I can—" As if choking on his words, he lapsed into a brief coughing fit. From the pocket of his suspender pants, he pulled out a handkerchief to cover his mouth

Repulsed by the sound of phlegm in his throat, she closed her eyes for a moment, wishing she hadn't answered the door when he rang. She began, "Well, I should start my—" Her second attempt at getting away was drowned out by the loud and obnoxious way he blew his nose.

Not quite ready to let her go, he went on with, "Sorry for taking up your time. I just can't get over how much you've grown up, lookin' just like your ma. She was such a purdy thing, too, passing down her copper hair and big violet-colored eyes down to ya." He winked again and smiled—his gap-toothed and unsightly grin reminding her of a jack-o-lantern's. "Ya also got her same high cheekbone, them cheekbones that kept her from aging despite all the smoking she did."

Her anxiety turning to anger, Kaitlyn wanted to tell him off. How dare he bring up her mother's smoking habit, as if he knew the extent of it! Last year, she had been working hard to quit, smoking only *one* cigarette every couple of days. Rolling her eyes, Kaitlyn began, "Really, Mr. Jamison, I'd rather not—"

The ringing of the phone inside the house saved her from the uncomfortable situation. "Please excuse me," she said. "Justin will let you know when my exact move-out date will be. Please contact him if you have any questions." With that, she hurried inside, quickly shutting the door and locking the deadbolt. Racing into the kitchen, she retrieved her cell phone from the gray Formica counter. The number appearing on the screen was her brother's.

"Justin, I'm so glad it's you," she gasped with relief, leaning against the heavily scratched porcelain sink. "You really saved me and you're not going to believe from who."

"Tell me who," he said in an impatient tone. As a kid, he never liked guessing games, and, as an adult, he still didn't.

"The landlord—Mr. Jamison!" she replied excitedly. He dropped by to say he was selling the house and that he wants me out in a few weeks, just like we anticipated. But he was acting weird—asking all kinds of questions and leering at me with those squinty, baggy eyes. It was like he was trying to feel me out, trying to gauge my reaction to his flattery. If I hadn't cut him off—telling him you'd be in touch fairly soon with my move-out date—he probably would've propositioned me."

Like a social worker (though he was actually a traveling Premium Coffees sales rep), Justin analyzed her concerns. "Come on, Kaitlyn, let's put Jamison and whatever he said into perspective. The guy's older than dirt. If he had tried anything, one push or shove from you would've sent him falling straight to the ground."

Her brother had made a valid point, so she replied more calmly, "Okay, Justin—you're right. Just can't help being upset. Mom and Dad considered Jamison a friend." Her voice quavered. "And I considered him to be like a great uncle, or grandfather. It goes to show that you never can really trust anyone, no matter how long you've known that person."

"Seriously, Kaitlyn, you're being a bit *extreme*. Like I said, the guy is old as hell and probably doesn't think too clearly, says things without considering how offensive his words might be."

"His remarks were offensive—that's for sure," she interjected, her fingers and palm tightening like a vice on the receiver. "Jamison must realize I'm still grieving, yet he had the nerve to say something unflattering about Mom— insinuated she was a chain-smoker. He wasn't around her all the time. He had no right to draw that conclusion!"

"Stop getting carried away, Kaitlyn." He paused; she could envision a wide frown spreading across his swarthy face. "Just think about how fortunate you are. In about two weeks from now, you'll be outta that neighborhood and living in a much better one, in Livonia. So settle down and stay positive."

"I'm sorry," she sighed. "You know how anxious I can get." She paused, wondering if she should tell him all.

"Yes, I know. You've always been uptight . . . been that way ever since you were real young . . . anxious about what you'd get for your birthday and Christmas, constantly worrying about how you did on this test or that one, pacing the floor when you couldn't get ahold of one of your friends. You have a habit of working yourself up into a 'real dither,' as Mom would say."

Her brother's comments provided a lead-in to get her deepest fear off her chest. "Do you think I take after Great

Aunt Betsy? It's been years since her death, but I can still remember her agonizing over every little thing. And—and wasn't she always the one who said troubles come in *threes?*" She paused again to emphasize her point. "First Dad, then Mom, and now Jamison with his sleazy offer of help. I'm thinking now Jamison might be that third trouble about to rear its ugly head. He may be elderly and sickly, but that wouldn't stop him from coming back tonight—using a master key to enter the house while I'm sleeping and try to—try to—" She stammered with disgust envisioning Jamison sneaking into her bedroom and stripping to reveal his doughy body.

"Enough of that," Justin flared. "Promise me you won't mention Jamison—and whatever you imaging he did or will do—to Suzanne when you meet her."

She straightened her back, as if worried her brother could somehow tell she was slouching and chastise her for that, too. "Who's Suzanne? Your new girlfriend?"

"Kind of," he replied. "More like a friend/girlfriend. Nothing too serious. With all my traveling, I can't keep up a steady relationship. It's too demanding. Suzanne realizes this and doesn't put a lot of pressure on me. But we have been spending more and more time together. Perhaps down the road, it could become more serious."

"What's she like?"

"I was calling to invite you out to dinner this week so you can meet her. She's very sophisticated and used to level-headed people. I'd like you two to hit it off, since she'll be coming around the house a lot. But, if you start talking about all your troubles and worries, she might get the impression you're a drama queen or suffering from paranoia."

After promising she wouldn't say another word about Great Aunt Bessie's favorite saying or anything else that sounded absurd, Kaitlyn offered some available times when she would be free for dinner. Like her brother, she also had a hectic schedule. Along with being a full-time retail assistant manager, she attended the local community college, pursuing, part-time, an associate's degree in business administration. And, like her brother, the furthest thing from her mind was getting involved in a committed relationship with someone. Her focus had to be on work and her college classes. *The only way not to repeat past mistakes . . . and the only way not to dwell on superstitions.*

*   *   *

As it turned out, Jamison posed no further problems. He only phoned the following week to say she didn't need to bother with the last two months of unpaid rent and that she could mail him the keys after she vacated the house, rather than deliver them in person, if it were more convenient. Kaitlyn took him up on both offers.

Her sigh of relief was short-lived. A new threat to her ambitions came shortly after she moved into her brother's vinyl-sided colonial with three bedrooms. One Thursday evening, while Justin was away on business, Suzanne called to invite herself over for decaf coffee and some conversation, pleading boredom: "With my boyfriend *and* my housemate out of town, I just don't know what do with myself. Would you mind if we hung out for a little while?" Kaitlyn *reluctantly* agreed, knowing it would please Justin if she were hospitable to his "girlfriend" during his absence.

Suzanne arrived within twenty minutes, her green eyes and red-lipsticked smile aglow with what seemed like a mix of curiosity and mischief. In the living room, she abruptly pushed aside Kaitlyn's economics textbook and spiral notebook, making room for herself on the brown-leather sofa. Sitting down on the middle cushion, she said, "I've changed my mind about the coffee. Let's go out and have a real drink."

Despite feeling agitated, Kaitlyn calmly declared, "But I have class in the morning."

Suzanne shook her head. "No excuses. Your brother told me you have Fridays off from work, so you can take a nap after class." She flashed a cheesy grin as if to also say: *So there!* "Where would you like to go? Downtown Royal Oak or Ann Arbor? Or one of the bars at the Novi Fountain Walk? It's time to loosen you up a bit with a cocktail or two—I'm treating—and find out why an attractive girl like you doesn't have a boyfriend."

Taken aback, Kaitlyn stood speechless in front of her. Although Suzanne had been polite and respectful when they initially met at dinner, apologizing for not being able to make it for either of her parents' funerals and not asking or offering anything too personal, she was acting just the opposite now: being too intrusive. But, because Suzanne was dressed up in black high heels and a black low-cut cocktail dress, her short blonde hair meticulously styled to look alluring with big soft curls, Kaitlyn hated to disappoint her by saying *no* to the bar-hopping proposal.

Suzanne, eager for a response, was making the situation more difficult. "Well? Which shall it be?" she asked, her voice shrill with impatience. "The longer we stay here, the less fun we'll be having."

A quick thinker under pressure, Kaitlyn came up with a plan that would end the evening as quickly as possible. Because it was a school night, she said she'd only have time for *one* drink. The perfect place would be a nearby Mexican restaurant, where they could grab a margarita. It closed in an hour, so there was no time for her to change out of her jeans and t-shirt. Having worked a twelve-hour shift at the Shoe Depot, she wasn't in the mood to dress up. In response, Suzanne let out a rankled sigh, then shook her head to show she wasn't too thrilled with what Kaitlyn wanted.

Nevertheless, they headed out to Rosa's Grill and Cantina in Suzanne's metallic gray Ford Contour. During the ten-minute drive, they said little to one another: Suzanne was too busy singing along harmoniously to a Christina Aguilera CD, showing off her ability to hit some of the famous singer's high notes. But once they pulled into the dimly lit restaurant parking lot, Suzanne turned off the stereo and began to bombard her with questions: "Tell me, Kaitlyn, what kind of men do you like? Tall, dark, and handsome? Or maybe blonde, buff, and tanned like a California beach guy? Or would you rather be with another red-head like yourself?"

To get through this evening, Kaitlyn needed a drink more quickly than she thought. "No sense in hanging out in the car," she said in a forced polite tone. "Let's talk more about it inside."

Agreeing, Suzanne nodded with a smile. "You must be as thirsty for a margarita as I am."

But once they got settled into the red-leather swiveling stools at the mirrored bar, Suzanne started in with more questions before even taking a sip from her drink. "I have to know one thing: which one—you or Justin—had the mailman as a father? Or is one of you adopted? Because you and him don't look anything alike." She reached out and straightened Kaitlyn's mid-shoulder-blade-length ponytail. "I mean you two are like night and day—Justin with the dark hair and eyes, you with the freckles and pale complexion."

Appalled by Suzanne's insinuation, Kaitlyn choked on her margarita and fell into fit of coughing. Suzanne patted her roughly on the back until her coughing stopped. After wiping her mouth with a napkin and taking a deep breath, Kaitlyn calmly said, "I see you're the type that has no problem saying what's on your mind." She had to keep her anger in check. Living under her brother's roof rent-free meant she couldn't afford to get into a confrontation with him or his girlfriend. "To answer your question, our mom was Scots-Irish and our dad mostly Italian." She pointed to her hair. "The mixing of their ethnicities is how they ended up with a red-headed daughter and a dark-haired son—not from cheating on one another."

Much to Kaitlyn's relief, Suzanne explained, "I was only making a joke—to break the ice. You'll come to appreciate my humor: everyone does." She paused to sip from her drink. "But speaking of *types,* you seem like the real serious kind. You and Justin are alike in that respect. He doesn't like to joke around."

Kaitlyn set her drink down on the glass counter. "You're right. We *are* very serious. It's the result of our upbringing."

"Whenever I ask Justin anything about his childhood, he changes the topic. So what's the family story? Why's he so secretive?" As if anxious for Kaitlyn's reply, Suzanne drummed her long red fingernails against her glass.

"How to explain . . . " Her voice trailing off, Kaitlyn glanced around at the mostly empty rows of mahogany tables with turquoise-padded chairs, slowly sipping her drink, savoring the tangy lime flavor, as she considered a good starting point. Several moments of awkward silence passed until her gaze returned to Suzanne. The alcohol loosened Kaitlyn's lips to reveal: "Justin's secretiveness about our parents, I'm pretty sure, boils down to their poor socio-economic status. Unfortunately, our parents were not well-educated—both barely finishing high school. Justin and I watched them struggle year after year trying to appease the bill collectors. Needless to say, Justin and I grew up without a lot of luxuries."

"Like indoor plumbing," Suzanne interjected, laughing under her breath, patting Kaitlyn's knee. "What do you mean by *luxuries?*"

Kaitlyn laughed softly as well, crossing her legs. "Nothing that severe. I'm talking about air-conditioning, cable TV, computer systems, Florida vacations—things other kids at school had. To be frank: Justin was pretty embarrassed by our parents—by their beat-up used cars and the meagerly furnished bungalow we lived in. As a teen, he never brought his friends around, always went out to meet them somewhere. And once he got to college, he rarely came home again, usually too busy with schoolwork, internships, and his entrepreneurship club. But instead of being hurt by how Justin avoided them, Mom and Dad only talked about how proud they were of his accomplishments."

Suzanne nodded to show she had been listening. "I appreciate your frankness. And I'm sorry to hear that Justin and your parents were estranged. They sound like great people." She fell silent for a moment as she gave the establishment a look-over, as if suddenly distracted or pondering an idea. With her elbow resting on the counter, she continued, "But surely Justin wasn't the only one affected. You, too,  must've been influenced by your parent's financial troubles. How did you feel about . . . about growing up in a . . . a less affluent area? "

Her question was a perfect lead-in to what Kaitlyn had been dying to say to her even before they left the house. "Of course I was affected." She took a big sip from her drink. "I saw what can happen when two people marry too young—no matter how much in love—without lucrative careers or the education to achieve them. So that's why I don't have a boyfriend, or really any close friends now. I don't need anyone to make my life more complicated than it already is. My focus has to be on getting my associate's degree and seeing where that takes me—hopefully on a path to a good-paying job."

"That's very commendable," Suzanne said with a skeptical look. "But you must have urges to be with a guy—romantic dinners, cuddling in front of the TV, holding hands on a walk." With a wry smile, she added, "And other fun activities, if you know what I mean."

"Sure, now and then. To satisfy them, I'll watch a movie like *Gone with the Wind* or something more recent, like *Sleepless in Seattle*, and experience romance vicariously via the characters and their love stories. I must say I enjoy the older movies better. They leave more to the imagination. Whenever I watch that scene in *Gone with the Wind* with Clark Gable swooping Vivian Leigh up in his arms and carrying her up that spectacular staircase to the bedroom, my imagination runs wild." Uncrossing her legs, Kaitlyn added, "Far more fulfilling than watching porn," hoping her explanation sounded reasonable, not pathetic.

Clearly not impressed, Suzanne waved her hand and rolled her eyes. "That's a poor substitute for the real McCoy. You must know what I'm saying."

Kaitlyn couldn't help but smile at Suzanne's choice of words (idiomatic yet clear-cut) for the male anatomy. "Oh, I get what you mean. But with juggling school and work, I simply don't have time to put myself out there and get the *real McCoy*," Kaitlyn replied, being only partially truthful. She didn't care to offer Suzanne any more reasons about why she was single. Hearing the story about Kaitlyn's high school sweetheart who dumped her after graduation because he was gay, Suzanne would certainly have something sarcastic to say, like: "All makes sense now. I suppose I wouldn't be dating either if I couldn't tell whether a guy is straight. Fortunately, you now have me to guide you." Although her breakup with Ben had happened several years ago, it would be painful to discuss, especially with someone like Suzanne who easily could twist those details into some kind of mockery: "He surely graduated all right—from one lifestyle to one another. But how did you not know? Were you two not *sexual?*" No sense in reliving the shaming she had once received from former friends. And besides, that information was none of Suzanne's business.

The short, stocky bartender pointed a remote control toward a stereo system perched high on one of the glass shelves behind the bar. Immediately, the level of the instrumental Mexican guitar music playing in the background went from enjoyable to blaring. The middle-aged man dropped the remote into his satin dress shirt's chest pocket and began to dance with a great deal of affectation, one beefy arm raised and moving about in precise circular motions, his full hips swaying in rhythm to the music. His performance, Kaitlyn figured, was an expression of happiness that his shift was almost over. Not wanting to be impolite, she bit her lower lip to keep herself from laughing at him.

Suzanne didn't seem to notice the entertainment, too preoccupied with searching for something in her black quilted-leather purse. "This isn't gonna be easy," she mumbled, pulling out her flip phone. Because of the music, Kaitlyn couldn't be one-hundred percent sure that she had heard Suzanne correctly. Maybe she had said, "I need something cheesy," meaning she wanted to order an appetizer to go with her margarita?

"Can you say that again?" Kaitlyn asked, trying to meet Suzanne's gaze. Instead of responding to the question, Suzanne started texting. After a few seconds, she said quite clearly, "Oh, damn—terrible reception," closing her phone. With device in hand, she stood up, saying, "I'll be back in a bit," and then headed outside, leaving her purse on the counter.

Watching her exit through the mahogany-trimmed glass doors, Kaitlyn resumed sipping her margarita. Although the drink relaxed her, warming her cheeks and making her feel light and tingly all over, she wished she was back home. She hated to have her routine interrupted, and especially hated to be out when she had to be in class early the next morning. Glancing at the wall clock above a shelf of booze bottles, she saw it was already fifteen minutes to ten. Yes, she definitely wished she was back in Justin's living room, either reading a good book or catching an episode of *Murphy Brown* or *Designing Women*, her favorite sitcoms, both rerun each night on cable. Because of the late hour, she would have no time for that—really only time to get ready for bed once Suzanne dropped her off.

Kaitlyn's eyes darted to the double doors. Speaking of Suzanne . . . where in the hell was she . . . ? All appeared dark and quiet outside. Had Suzanne taken off—abandoned her? Kaitlyn's eyes quickly shifted back from the door to the counter. No, Suzanne couldn't have because her purse was still there. So she must be outside texting in the dark and ignoring Kaitlyn? Enough was enough. The restaurant would be closing soon, so Kaitlyn was going to find Suzanne and tell her that she wanted to go home.

From the brown-cloth handbag in her lap, Kaitlyn pulled out a twenty-dollar bill and then held it up for the bartender, who took the money without asking if he was to keep the change. Standing up, she murmured, "Thanks for the treat, Suzanne." After slinging both her purse and Suzanne's over her shoulder, she headed toward the doors.

Outside, there were only about four cars in the parking lot. Suzanne's Contour, to Kaitlyn's relief, was still parked under one of the two dim light poles in the lot. Squinting, Kaitlyn saw that the vehicle was dark inside. Suzanne wasn't sitting in her car, nor visible anywhere else in the lot. Had

Kaitlyn missed seeing her reenter Rosa's to use the restroom?

She was about to retrace her steps, but, from around the corner of the brick building, she now could hear what sounded like Suzanne's voice. Talking with someone . . . on the phone? Straining her ears, Kaitlyn couldn't tell for sure. Although it would seem rude, she decided to walk around to the other side and interrupt whatever was going on.

As she neared the corner, she overheard Suzanne clearly talking on her cell, "Look, Justin, this is a lost cause. I can already tell Kaitlyn and I aren't going to hit it off as friends, and the guys I know aren't going to like her. She's too reserved and bookish—not our idea of a *fun* person to hang around."

Caught up in the excitement of eavesdropping, but furious about the things being said, Kaitlyn could sense her heartbeat racing, her face flushing with heat. Breathing slowly and evenly to maintain composure, she took a couple of steps closer to the edge of the building. Then, with her elbow pressed against the wall, she cupped her hand over her ear and listened closely, craning her neck a little, but careful to keep her face from being exposed. What she heard next infuriated her even more:

"Justin, this plan of finding her some guy to date and then move in with—to get her off your hands—is too unrealistic to work. Just be honest. Tell her that you like your privacy so you can screw your girlfriend as loud as you want." Pausing, she laughed heartily. "Okay, I'll be serious. Why don't you offer to help her out—maybe with some money to secure an apartment? Your relationship may be strained for a while, but she'll come around . . ."

That last sentence propelled Kaitlyn into action. Turning the corner, she strode up to Suzanna and grabbed the phone. With her back to her brother's girlfriend, she put the device up to her face and lashed out into the receiver: "Yeah, I understand something all right—that my brother's a major jerk and a phony. After Mom died, I actually started believing you cared about me. How wrong I was! You're still as self-centered as ever." Justin tried to interrupt by saying something, but she was far too angry to listen. Cutting him off, she continued: "And now that I know what a fake you really are, I'll do my best to be out of your place as soon as possible. Have fun in France or wherever the hell you are," she added in a shrill tone, then abruptly ended the call.

Handing Suzanne back the phone and the black-leather purse, Kaitlyn said with a scowl, "Let's go."

On the way home, they didn't say a word to one another. As soon as Suzanne pulled up in the driveway, Kaitlyn jumped out without waiting for the vehicle to come to a complete stop. After slamming the passenger door, she hurried into the house, then upstairs. Not bothering to undress, she flung herself on the queen-size bed in the guest bedroom, which was supposed to be hers until she finished with her associate's degree, about a year from now. Not only did that arrangement have to end, but also her relationship with her brother. Justin had hurt and betrayed her to the point where she doubted she could tolerate the sight of him (or that meddling Suzanne) ever again.

*Oh, Aunt Betsy, you were wrong about troubles coming in threes,* she felt like crying out. *They can come in fours, fives, or more. Simply unrelenting.*

Foreseeing herself saddled with a lot of bills in the very near future, she worried that she wouldn't be able to afford her tuition in the winter. Her graduation would be delayed and so would her opportunity to move into a more lucrative job. She might be stuck in the meagerly paid retail profession for many years to come, thanks to Justin. Lying on her stomach, she drew the two pillows from the head of the bed until they were firmly underneath her chin and chest, holding on tightly as if they were life preservers preventing her from drowning in her own tears.

*   *   *

Despite not sleeping well, Kaitlyn rose the next morning at the usual time of seven. Hurriedly, she finished her coffee and cereal, determined to begin her apartment searching as soon as possible. Wearing a plain white T-shirt and powder-blue sweatpants, she drove to a local 7-Eleven and picked up a copy of the *Observer*. Once back in her brother's kitchen, sitting on a swiveling leather chair, she spread out the newspaper's classified ads on the rectangular glass table and perused the listings under the section of houses/apartments for rent. Though put off a little at first by the prices of Livonia apartments, she was relieved to find that those in nearby cities and townships were cheaper. At the bottom of the page, one particular ad leapt out at her:

> **Garden City**—One-bedroom apartment in charming historic farmhouse, hardwood floors, updated kitchen and bath. $495 per month + security. Don't wait! Call today!

Enthused by the description, she leaned back and clapped her hands: both the price and location (in a town just south of Livonia) sounded ideal. From the back window, bright sunshine was slicing though partially opened the mini blinds, illuminating the newspaper with a patchy yellowish glow. Turning her head, she gazed out at the beautiful weather. Though the day had greeted her with dark-gray clouds and the possibility of rain, the sky was now clear, blanketed with a cheerful blue. The corners of her mouth curved upward into a smile of satisfaction. She made a mental note: if she ever again felt pessimistic, as she had last night, she only needed to remind herself that, with a little effort, optimism could appear on the horizon by morning.

As if he were suddenly standing before her, she said in a calm voice, "I don't need you, Justin, after all. I'm quite capable of managing by myself." And, should he ever apologize or try to convince her to stay, she would convey those words to him in exactly the same manner. In honoring her parents' legacy of valuing hard work and tenacity, she would show Justin—and the world, for that matter—that she could make it on her own, without his help or any other man's.

But, as she glanced down at the newspaper again, a blast of anxiety struck her. It immediately eroded her confidence. Since none of the other listings were as appealing, what would she do if the Garden City apartment was already rented? Could she handle more disappointment . . . ? A mixture of nervousness and anticipation was making her feel shaky all over. Though it wasn't quite eight o'clock and nine would be a more appropriate time to call, she was afraid she might become a basket case if she waited that long. Taking the newspaper upstairs to the guest bedroom, she grabbed her cell phone from the whitewashed oak dresser. With a trembling hand, she dialed the Garden City contact number, saying a silent prayer, *Please, please, let this apartment be available . . .*

After a couple of rings, a man with a warm, friendly voice answered. "Good morning. This is George Reinholt."

"Hello. I'm Kaitlyn Brooks. I apologize if I'm calling you too early, but I wanted to find out whether the apartment is still for lease."

"The Garden City residence?"

She took a deep breath. Assuming her most confident manner, she said, "Yes, that one."

"You're in luck," he said in a hearty tone, "because *it* is."

"Great! I'd love to have a look at it. When is your earliest convenience?"

"You're in luck *again*. I'm free this morning. Could you meet me there in an hour? I'll give you the grand tour. It's lovely old house that's been divided into private apartments—a good location in a quiet neighborhood, close to a lot of shopping and restaurants."

Kaitlyn had class in an hour, but she decided to skip it. The instructor was supposed to be reviewing for the upcoming test, and she could get answers to the study guide from a classmate either that evening or tomorrow. So, she said, "Sure. I can be there. What's the address?"

Once she had a thorough understanding of the directions, she politely ended the call. Whistling pleasantly, she waltzed up the stairs to shower and change into presentable attire, feeling hopeful again about the future, considering her streak of problems were about to be over.

\* \* \*

Driving along Burton Road in her Ford Escort, approaching her future home, she was struck by how the white farmhouse (probably built in the mid-1800s) stood out like a shiny Cartier pearl necklace displayed among strings of ordinary plastic beads. A real beauty with a manicured lawn. Set spaciously between two vinyl-sided ranches, the Gothic Revival dwelling had a steeply pitched roof with gabled windows and a wrap-around veranda whose decorative gingerbread trim reminded her of the way porches might be described in an old storybook like *Little House on the Prairie*. The property's ambience gave off an impression of serenity, so she knew she'd love living here! After pulling into the pebbled driveway, she followed the path as it curved around to the back where there was a cement parking lot with five spaces. Since none had numbered markings indicating they were reserved for certain apartments, she assumed it was all right to occupy one of the two vacant spots at the far end.

Once parked, she headed down the driveway and then around to the front, where she headed up the brick walkway to the veranda. Sitting midway on the porch steps, she straighten the lopsided elastic waistband of her V-neck white chiffon blouse, then gazed across at the row of wood-framed ranches whose yards sported sculpted bushes and pruned trees. She didn't see any homeowners or their kids around. The strong breeze periodically rusting tree leaves was the only sound disrupting the tranquility. What a difference from where she grew up. Her former neighborhood was full of wild kids running up and down the sidewalk in front of her bedroom windows, their bickering and shrieking penetrating the thin glass, often making it difficult for her to concentrate on her schoolwork during the day or fall asleep at night. Sadly, the kids modeled their behavior on the adults they lived with—usually single moms who thought nothing of having heated arguments with their lovers right in their driveways or on their porches, in plain view of everyone. Consequently, Kaitlyn's favorite part of the year was the dead of winter when the frigid weather kept everyone indoors and the streets quiet. But in this community, once settled in the new apartment, she could become a normal person, preferring the warmer months when she could open windows for fresh air.

Hearing a knocking engine, she turned her head to the right and observed a pickup truck approaching. It was traveling at a speed that seemed rather fast for a residential area. Squinting as the truck got closer, she saw an elderly man in the driver's seat. She took her cell phone out of her jeans pocket and checked the time: a little after nine. *This should be Mr. Reinholt.* Within moments, as if confirming her thought, the man sharply pulled into the driveway, waving at her. He slowed down as he drove around to the back.

Standing up, she silently practiced how to introduce herself. *Hello, I'm Kaitlyn. Thanks for meeting me here this morning. I'm very anxious to see the place.* No, the last sentence wouldn't do. If she seemed too desperate, he might ask a lot of questions. She didn't care to go into much detail about herself or her present living arrangement. *Best to just stick with a simple greeting,* she decided as she combed her fingers through her wavy tresses, ensuring any wind-blown strands were neatly back in place.

From around the side of house, he appeared with a gray suede briefcase in hand. The accessory complemented his black jeans, black sneakers, and heather-gray polo shirt. Crossing the luscious lawn, he smiled and asked, "Ms. Brooks?"

Kaitlyn nodded and said, "Good morning, Mr. Reinholt. How are you today?"

From the chest pocket of his polo, he plucked out a white handkerchief. Wiping the sweat off his wrinkled forehead, he replied, "I'm doing okay, just a bit warm. Thank goodness there's a nice breeze. Please call me George." As he looked down briefly to tuck his handkerchief back in his pocket, Kaitlyn noticed a lot of pinkish-red skin exposed through his thinning gray hair, quite a contrast from his pale complexion. He probably had the same skin-care habits, she thought, as her father, who would forget to wear a hat when doing yard work and end up with an inflamed scalp.

On the stairs, he shook her hand. Motioning with his finger in various directions, he said, "Getting down to business, I wanted to tell you I manage this property and oversee what needs to be improved. In the spring, the outside was repainted, and the parking lot in the back has been repaved. And if you ever see something that's not up to par, let me know about it. I strive to make my tenants happy."

"Oh, yes, I can see that the property is meticulously maintained," she gushed, intending to be complimentary, not syrupy. "And it's so peaceful here, just like you described on the phone."

He nodded. "I'm sure you'll also be pleased with the available apartment upstairs. It has some nice features—too many to list in that ad. Some examples: good amount of counter space in the kitchen with built-in microwave over the stove, a new shower with dual jets, a walk-in bedroom closet."

"Sounds wonderful!" Kaitlyn exclaimed, following him up the steps.

At the door, Reinholt set down his briefcase and reached into his pants pockets, fumbling for what were probably the keys. He said, "All residents have two keys—one for this front door, which locks automatically when closed, and the other for their own apartment." After searching through his pockets several times, he added, "Oh, no . . . can't believe I did this!"

"What's the matter?" she asked, though she had a good idea what the problem was.

He sighed with heavy exasperation, shaking his head. "Your good luck has run out for the moment: I think I left the master keys on the kitchen counter at home. I can't believe I was so forgetful. This isn't like me."

"Oh, dear . . ." That shaky feeling returning, she folded her arms firmly under her chest in case her hands started to tremble again.

"Fortunately," he said with a reassuring smile, "I live close by. Can you stick around for ten minutes or so? I'll be right back with the keys."

"I can do that."

"Okay, then. I'll be back shortly." Reinholt hurried off to the parking lot. In no time, he was shooting down the driveway, kicking up pebbles with his tires. Seemingly unconcerned that there could be any traffic police in the area who might give him a ticket, he flew down the street. She watched him for a couple of blocks, until he turned and was out of sight.

Once again, she said a silent prayer, *Please, please let him find those keys quickly.* She doubted she could handle waiting another day to check out the apartment. All she wanted to do was make sure it looked all right and then sign the lease, her problems solved. Despite the continuing bright sunshine overhead, her mood was clouding with discouragement. *Why can't things work out the way they're supposed to . . .*

Back on the sidewalk, she gazed as far as she could down the street. A few blocks away was a park with playground equipment. She suddenly had a childish urge to get on a swing. How many years had it been since she had last swung on one?

What stopped her from acting on that impulse was the concern that someone might look out a window and catch her on the swing. How embarrassing if she became a topic for conversation around the community, with neighbors saying to one another: "Did you hear the latest about that young woman who lives in the farmhouse? Apparently, she loves playing on the park equipment. Does she think she's a kid? Must be something wrong with her." Worse yet would be if the farmhouse tenants got wind of it. She didn't want them to think they would be living with a mentally ill person.

Because her eyes were watering from the sun, she decided to wait for Reinholt under the porch's protective overhang. She ascended the steps, and, just as she reached the stoop, the oak- paneled door opened to reveal an elderly man with a full head of silver hair, pushing it from the inside. While his face was rather homely, as wrinkled as a Pug's, his smile appeared warm and kind, its fullness and glow very similar to her father's. As he said, "Hello. Good morning," she went up to him to shake his gnarled hand, then returned the greeting.

He introduced himself: "I'm Michael Bentley, one of the tenants. You must be here to look at the apartment for rent upstairs. Are you waiting on George?" She nodded, and he continued, "No need to stand around and wait for him out here. Please join me for a cup of coffee while you have a look at my flat. It's got almost the same layout and updated like the other three." With his free hand, he made a sweeping gesture inviting her to come inside.

Enticed by the invitation, Kaitlyn followed him into a narrow hallway, where a staircase with an ornate banister and wide steps took up a lot of space. The stairs led up to parallel landings that, she assumed, offered access to the upstairs apartments. Running her hand back and forth along the wall, she found the beige linen fabric covering the walls to be simple yet charming. Since the two narrow windows on either side of the front door offered limited brightness, a ceiling fixture with an enormous flower-patterned globe had been installed at the end of a long chain to keep the stairs and upstairs landing well-lit, in consideration of the upstairs occupant's safety. Right across from one another were two oak-paneled doors, the same style as the front. Bentley unlocked the door to the right.

The door opened onto his living room. Though it was box-like, it reasonably accommodated a cherry-stained armoire, a plaid sofa and matching armchair, and a full-sized cherry coffee table. Above the sofa was a lattice window that looked out onto the street. *Nice view*, she thought. The walls were painted off-white; the only adornments on the walls were gilt-framed family photos hanging on either side of the armoire, opposite the sofa.

Bentley motioned for her to keep looking around while he passed through an arched doorway into the kitchen. To the right of the armchair was another arched entryway, and she walked through it to step into the short hallway. On either side were oak paneled doors, one leading to the bathroom, the other to the bedroom. She decided to inspect the bathroom first. Sticking her head through the doorway, she saw it was tastefully decorated with wainscoting halfway up the walls, a pedestal sink, and jetted tub exposed through the opened waffle-fabric shower curtain. Shifting her attention to the bedroom, she found the space was also small but adequate—just big enough to fit a double bed, a nightstand, and narrow chest of drawers without seeming claustrophobic.

Returning to the living room, she observed that Bentley set down on the coffee table a wooden tray holding two mugs. Facing her as he sat on the sofa, he asked, "So, what did you think? Enough space for you?"

"More than enough for my limited furnishings. But before I can firmly commit, I need to survey the kitchen," she replied.

"Be my guest."

Inspecting the L-shaped kitchen, she fell in love with the rustic white-washed cabinets and lantern-style light fixtures hanging from the ceiling. Although Bentley lived alone, nothing was out of place, not a dish of any kind on the granite counters or on the ceramic tile top of his dinette table. As she had witnessed in the other rooms, everything here was very clean, no crumbs or dirt or grease marks anywhere; the appliances sparkled, especially the toaster oven and coffee maker resting side by side next to the sink. *A far cry from Justin's.* Her brother's kitchen, though not cluttered, had had such a dirty and greasy linoleum floor when she moved in that she needed to wash it several times with ammonia to get it clean.

In the living room, Kaitlyn told Bentley, "Very nice! If my apartment is just like yours, as you say, I'll be quite happy here." She looked, past Bentley, out the window. The street was still silent, with no sign of Reinholt. "What is your opinion of the landlord? He seems like a nice guy—but is he as diligent as he claims about fixing things as needed?"

Bentley nodded and said, "Pretty good."

"And responsible?" she pressed, picking up a mug and taking a sip of coffee. "When we met earlier, he discovered he left his keys at home. He said he'd be right back with them, in about ten minutes, yet almost half an hour has passed. I hope he hasn't forgotten me."

Bentley shook his head. "Reinholt'll be here." He pulled out a photo album from a wicker basket beside the sofa. "But I can tell you're anxious." He set the album on the table and patted the velour cover. "This'll help pass the time."

"I think I should call him." She hoped she didn't come across as rude, but there was nothing more boring, in her opinion, than flipping through someone's collection of old photos and/or other memorabilia. Since she didn't know his family, what was the point? Besides, she wanted to learn where Reinholt was.

After sipping more of the coffee, she set down the mug and dialed Reinholt. Much to her relief, he answered after the second ring. After their exchange of hellos, he groaned, "I was just about to call you. There's been a snag in the plans: after I got home, my car wouldn't start. A tow truck is on the way."

Kaitlyn swallowed hard. "Oh, no . . . sorry to hear that. Should I call you later to reschedule the showing?"

"Remember," he said in a more upbeat voice, "I deemed you the *lucky* lady. I've contacted my son. He lives in the building. He will be over to show you the place in about twenty minutes. He will—"

Reinholt's voice cut out, and then the call dropped. Eager to hear the rest of what he intended, she immediately tried calling him but only got his voicemail. "Hi, this Kaitlyn," she said in her message. "We must've had a bad connection, and I  didn't catch the rest of what you were saying about your son. Please call me back and let me know. Thanks." Feeling edgy, she reached for her coffee and took a big swig.

"What's going on with Reinholt?" Bentley asked, holding his mug on the knee of his khakis.

"He's having some car problems," she sighed, "but he says his son will be here in about twenty minutes. So all is not lost." She managed a smile. "As soon as I'm done with your delicious coffee, I'll wait on the porch for him."

Once again, he lightly drummed the photo album cover. "Twenty minutes gives us enough time to humor an old man who is very proud of his grandchildren. Come sit beside me."

*Damn*, she thought, *why did I have to mention twenty minutes? I should've said Reinholt's son would be here any minute—any second. It would've been the perfect excuse to avoid this situation.*

Demonstrating good manners, she sat down beside Bentley, setting down her cell phone and mug on the coffee table. Halfheartedly listening as the man talked about his granddaughter, she began to go through the first half of the album, a haphazard portfolio of a pretty raven-haired and olive-complexioned young woman, who liked posing in anything from evening gowns to traditional Polish peasant garb. At twenty-seven, she was presently living in Warsaw, Poland, and conducting genetic research at a university there.

"Jordana received her doctorate from the University of Michigan at only twenty-three," Bentley said, his eyes wide from amazement. "After her graduation, I expected her to settle into some cushy university job here in the U.S., but she doesn't believe in the mundane. Before Poland, she was a missionary in Russia and helped out in a Moscow orphanage. And before that, she was in Africa doing hospital volunteer work, caring for patients with all kinds of ailments and diseases."

Since the album lacked photos or documents supporting his granddaughter's achievements, Kaitlyn regarded his claims with skeptical ears: Jordana's accomplishments seemed too good to be true. Nevertheless, she said, "You're very fortunate to have such a successful granddaughter. She's clearly blessed with both beauty and brains."

"If you think she's distinguished," Bentley raved, "wait until you have a look at my grandson—he's a real model. At nineteen, Caleb's already been in the business for almost ten years. He's now living in New York City and will soon appear in a shampoo commercial. He has beautiful wavy hair the girls go crazy about." Waving his right hand in a circular pattern over the album, he urged her to skip through Jordana's remaining pages to get to where Caleb's section began. From viewing the first photo, Kaitlyn found Bentley's grandson, with his boyish yet intelligent smile and mane of wavy reddish-brown hair, to be definite eye candy. Tall and slender like his sister, he could look good in anything: double-breasted and other retro-style suits, skin-tight exercise gear, stripped preppy polos with plaid Bermuda shorts, or trendy denim shirts with ripped-up jeans. In one particular magazine clipping, an ad for a Hollywood tours service, Caleb reminded her of a 1930s movie star, as he was standing beside an old-fashioned limousine and dressed in a tuxedo and white gloves, his hair neatly trimmed and slicked back. The caption read: "TINSELTOWN TOURS: CUSTOMIZED HOLLYWOOD VACATIONS. THE SERVICE AND SELECTIONS YOU DESERVE." If she could afford a personal tour of Hollywood with a sexy man like Caleb, she would book it in an instant. *Just because I'm intelligent and a hard worker, Suzanne, doesn't mean I don't know how to have fun.*

Staring at the ad, Kaitlyn recalled pleasant childhood memories of staying up late with her grandparents during summer break and watching old movies from the '30s on their vintage wood-grain Zenith Console TV. The sophisticated ways men courted women in the films impressed her. So, as a young teen, while her female friends lusted after TV's *Beverly Hills 90210* studs Luke Perry and Jason Priestley, she fantasized about herself ballroom dancing with dashing classic Hollywood stars Cary Grant and Clark Gable.

Her former boyfriend, Ben, though not well-built and handsome like those men, had appealed to her idea of romance, initially asking her out on Valentine's Day, and then winning her over with love poems he would compose on flower-bordered stationary and secretly drop into her backpack. Not by her choice, their intimacy had never progressed beyond make-out and cuddling sessions. In other words, he had made excuses about why they needed to postpone having sex. Because she was in love, she had respected his boundaries. When he had gone away to college, he had distanced himself more and more until he finally had revealed his homosexuality to her one winter evening by phone and said their relationship was over . . . The terrible loneliness she had felt following the breakup had been difficult to bear. Trying to ease the sadness, she had had several one-night stands with guys to whom she typically wouldn't give the time of day: scruffy and ill-mannered, risky bar pickups that luckily hadn't turned out to be serial killers. Remembering Ben—his soft gray eyes, goofy but adorable smile, and clipper-cut brown hair with a perfect part on the side—made her eyes watery. Wiping the tears with the back of her hand, she fibbed to Bentley: "My allergies are acting up. Must be a lot of pollen in the air."

As she neared the end of the album, she came upon several pictures of Caleb in swim trucks on the beach, his arms around a curvaceous blonde girl showing off ample cleavage in her tight Bikini top. Kaitlyn pointed to one of the photos and sighed, "They seem like a happy couple," feeling a little jealous.

"Caleb and Maylinda have been dating ever since ninth grade," Bentley informed her, between sips of coffee. "But I'm not sure for how much longer. She's still back here with her parents, and he plans to stay in New York on a permanent basis. A handsome guy like Caleb, with his pick of cosmopolitan women, has been playing the field in the Big Apple, so to speak. In time, she'll be a faded memory. A fact of life."

Bentley's nonchalant attitude toward the situation, as if Caleb's sex appeal meant he could behave as he pleased, irritated Kaitlyn. It struck a raw nerve. Having an over-inflated ego was not an excuse for one to treat others callously, disrespectfully. As she pondered that, the faces of Justin and Suzanne replaced those of Caleb and Maylinda in the pictures. To get their sickening images out of her head, she shut the album and pushed it across the table, toward Bentley.

Glancing at her cell phone, she realized more than half an hour had passed since she had last spoken with Reinholt. It was now after 10:30. Turning her head, she gazed out the window. The only activity outside was a car driving past the house: no sign of anyone hanging around the porch or lawn. Where in the hell was Reinholt's son? Was he really coming by? "Excuse me," she said to Bentley, picking up her cell. "I'm going to try Reinholt again." Pacing, she redialed the landlord; once again, it went straight to voicemail. Frustrated that he must be having phone trouble, she sensed her voice quaver leaving the message: "This is Kaitlyn. I'm presently hanging out with your tenant Mr. Bentley. So far, I haven't seen your son. Please call me—or have your son call—"

There was knocking at the door. From the sofa, Bentley said, "Go ahead and answer it, you poor anxious thing. Must be Dalton—Reinholt's son—at last."

*At last.* The two words brought a smile to her face as she strode to the door. At last, she could view the apartment and sign the lease. At last, she could be secure about the future.

When she opened the door, her joy vanished like fire doused by water. Standing across the threshold was not a man—but a woman . A short, plump woman whose layered bob was honey-colored and frosted with pink streaks, as if she were aiming for a rock singer's look. Because she wore garish makeup—heavy gold eye shadow, ample amounts of peach rouge, a clown-like application of champagne lipstick—it was hard for Kaitlyn to guess her age. Maybe late twenties? Early to mid-thirties? Forty-something was not of the question either.

"Why, hello," the woman said, one hand on the hip of her black floral sundress, the other formed into a fist resting under her chin. She eyed Kaitlyn with a playful stare. "I'm Marina from across the hall. And who might you be? How did you and Michael get to be *friends?*" she emphasized with a grin.

"It's—it's not what you—you think," Kaitlyn stammered, finding the woman's brazenness off-putting. "To make a long story short, I'm Kaitlyn and I'm here to lease the apartment upstairs. I've been passing time with Mr. Bentley until Mr. Reinholt's son arrives to give me the official tour."

"How wonderful," Marina exclaimed, with a pretentious wave of her hand. Grabbing Kaitlyn's elbow, the woman steered her toward the coffee table. "Meet my new friend," she said to Bentley. "It's going to be great having another woman living here. Someone to gossip and share secrets with—listen to all my man troubles."

Marina spoke as if Kaitlyn was supposed to step into the role of therapist, to be available for listening as needed . Unnerved, Kaitlyn eased her elbow out of Marina's grip, wondering, *Is this woman a little crazy or what?* She took a step back, toward the door.

With a furrowed brow, straightening his back, Bentley advised, "Go easy on her, Marina. Katilyn seems like a sweet young woman. Don't scare her away like that other one— Sheila." He pointed to ceiling, indicating to Katilyn that Sheila had been the former tenant living above him. "All of your online chatting and dating stories were too much for her, I fear. She didn't quite last here six months."

"Nonsense, dear Michael," Marina said, shaking her head. "What scared her off was all your bragging about your grandchildren. When is that commercial Caleb's in supposed to finally air? You've been boasting about it for months, it seems."

Taking no apparent offense, Bentley responded with a shrug and an expressionless face. Marina walked around the coffee table and sat down beside him on the sofa. To

Kaitlyn's dismay, she picked up Bentley's mug and gulped the coffee down. After wiping her mouth with the back of her hand, she contorted her lips into a grimace and said, "Speaking of online dating, you wouldn't believe the joker I met this morning. I took off work to spend the day with this fellow. What a mistake! Wasted a personal day for nothing. Even though we had been chatting online and on the phone for almost a month, he failed to mention a few of things." As if for effect, she slammed down her coffee cup on the tray. "In particular, that he's also dating a couple of other women—one of whom is a stripper and drug addict. And then he had the nerve to suggest we head back to his place after breakfast for some other 'delight,' if you know what I mean." She gazed at Kaitlyn with narrowed eyes, perhaps trying to read her reaction. Kaitlyn, though, stood there speechless and motionless, appalled that Marina would be revealing her personal life in front of a stranger.

"He wanted to have sex?" Bentley asked with raised eyebrows.

Marina, sighing, threw up her hands. "That's what he wanted all right—started asking me about my bedroom interests halfway through the meal, to compare them with the other women's. But I wasn't about to mess around with a dude also sleeping with a heroin-addicted stripper and who knows who else. No diseases for me, thank you very much." She sighed again. "Goes to show you that guys can seem so nice online or the phone—but act totally different in person."

Bentley patted Marina on the shoulder. "Poor baby." He gestured toward Kaitlyn. "Maybe our new neighbor can be of some assistance. A pretty woman like her must have a lot of dating experience. She probably can give you some tips." With backward nod of the head, he winked at Kaitlyn, as if signaling for her to chime in with her own dating stories.

"From the way she leered at Caleb's photos, it's obvious she's got good taste."

Marina, crossing her chunky legs, shook her finger at Kaitlyn. "Warning future friend: When Caleb comes to visit next month, I get first dibs. I've been lusting after him for a lot longer." She snickered like a witch.

Kaitlyn could endure no more of this conversation. "Please ex—excuse me," she said in a shaky voice.

*     *     *

In the hallway, she leaned against the banister. Sensing a headache coming on, she massaged her forehead. *Bentley and Marina are a couple of loony tunes*, she thought, pressing her palm hard against her brow. Marina, whose theatrics could test the limits of even a saint's patience, was the worse of the two. And Kaitlyn doubted she would have any peace of mind living in the same building as that woman.

Before deciding whether to leave or continue waiting for Mr. Reinholt's tardy son, she mentally composed an essential list of pluses and minuses about the farmhouse apartment. The pluses: good location and good price. The minuses: unreliable landlord and annoying tenants. One set balanced out the other. Despite the dull pounding in her head, she concentrated hard, trying to determine if there was an feature she had seen that would tip the scale in one direction or the other.

The ringing of her cell interrupted her effort. She hoped it was Reinholt. Pulling out phone, she discovered it was her brother. Should she talk to him? If he was calling to argue or tell her to do something absurd, like apologize to Suzanne, she wasn't sure if she could handle the aggravation. Nevertheless, with curiosity consuming her, she felt compelled to answer the call.

"Hello, Justin," she murmured.

"Hey there, Kaitlyn," he exclaimed. "Hope I didn't catch you at a bad time. Are you out of class now?"

"Yes. What's up?" she asked impatiently.

"I just wanted to call and see how you were doing. I also wanted to apologize for what happened, and level with you—"

"Look, Justin—"

"Let me finish: I know you're a quiet person, but I flipped out about having someone move in with me and losing my privacy. So I concocted this plan, partly for selfish reasons—and—and partly for your benefit. Please believe that. I'm not a total self-centered pig. I thought Suzanne might help you come out of you shell and start dating again. You seem lonely."

His apologetic words soothed some of her hostility. "Okay, Justin. I've listened. I appreciate what you said. To ease *your* anxiety, I think I've found an apartment. I should be able to move out quite soon. Perhaps you can help me again by lending your muscles and your truck?"

"Of course." He sighed with what sounded like relief, indicating he was pleased with the idea of having his house all to himself again. "Just promise me that you won't isolate yourself in the new place and become a stranger. And please promise me that you'll give some consideration to what I— and Suzanne—have said. You never know what'll happen unless you try dating again—take a chance on someone. How long has it been since Ben?"

"Like I told Suzanne, my life is jam-packed these days. Hell, I barely have time to keep up with my friends at school. The only way I could manage a relationship is if the guy either lived with me or right next door . . . "

Katilyn's voice trailed off as her attention switched to the front door. Someone was pulling it open. Reinholt's

son . . . ?   "Hey, Justin, I have to go. I'll call you later."
Abruptly, she ended the call

Entering the foyer was a handsome young man. With his
swarthy complexion, rounded and confident chin, and bushy
yet well-arched eyebrows, he had the same alluring looks as
Tyrone Power. In addition to Gable and Grant, Power was
another of Kaitlyn's favorite 1930s male film stars. Though
she could only imagine what the athletic Power looked like
shirtless—in the movies she had seen, he wore suits or
period costumes exposing little skin—the clinging tank top
of this man flaunted his finely chiseled chest; exposed his
ropey, muscular arms.

"Are you Kaitlyn?" he asked in a deep, seductive voice.

Falling in love with his hearty smile, she nodded as she
tightened her grip on the pineapple newel cap of the banister,
feeling now airy and light-headed.

"Hi, I'm George's son, Dalton," the young man told her.
"I apologize for keeping you waiting. I'm a fitness instructor
and was finishing up a spinning class when Dad called
asking me to show the apartment."

Mesmerized by his deep brown eyes and glossy dark-
brown hair, she merely nodded again.

"Are you all right?" he asked, his gaze meeting hers, as
he pulled a ring of keys out of his pocket. "Hope you aren't
upset with me."

She shook her head.

"Are you sure?"

Relaxing her grip on the post, to put them both at ease,
she came up with a logical excuse for her quiet responses:
"Yes, sorry. Only had one cup of coffee this morning.
Should've had two. My body is not awake yet."

"I understand. I'm a two-cupper-in-the-morning person
myself." With a outstretched hand, he motioned to the stairs.

"Let me know when you're ready. I'm in no rush: don't have to teach again until later this afternoon."

*Admit it: You do want someone special.*

*Yes, I do want that—and more. Just not right now.*

*Timing is never perfect. Take a chance.*

After a hard swallow, she said, "I'm ready."

As they ascended, he said, "I'm sure you'll like it here. I can personally vouch for your neighbor across the hall. A great guy—smart, sexy, and *single*." His smile radiated like the bright bulb in the ceiling fixture.

She gazed at him with lust-filled eyes. Breathily, she said, "And you'll have a great neighbor—who's also smart, sexy, and single."

*See: you don't have to wait until your college graduation for your life to turn around.*

*I'm starting to believe this. An affordable apartment across from a hot guy—and no effort at all for a mutual attraction to spring up between us.*

*For sure. Seems like you and Dalton are about to prove that "love at first sight" is more than a poetic concept.*

Making the first move, she leaned into him. He reciprocated by reaching for her elbow. With a gentle grip, he guided her up the rest of stairs, smiling all the way, until they reached the landing.

He let go of her to step ahead and unlock the door. As she watched him fumble with the keys, her heartbeat raced. Shivers of excitement ran up and down her spine. A tingling sensation pulsated along her arms, quickly settling into her hands and fingers; so eager was she to be touched again, to hold his hand while they crossed the threshold together, to fulfill a long-contemplated fantasy. *At last . . .* In anticipation, she closed her eyes and held out her hand, her fingers almost dancing in the air. To relax, she took a deep breath and counted silently *one . . . two . . . three . . .*

Jolting her eyes and mouth wide open was a shrill voice exploding from the foot of the staircase: "I've been watching you, Dalton Reinholt, and your little love fest with the farmhouse newbie. I'm shocked! I guess I'm not good enough for you, is that it? Why not be honest and tell me you weren't interested? Why keep feeding me the same bullshit for months—about being too busy to date?"

Her body stiffening, Kaitlyn closed her eyes again and clenched her fists. She wasn't ready to turn around and face the territorial and hostile Marina. She didn't want to accept that today's wave of effortless fortune had been some kind of illusion, a mere tease. She especially didn't want to deal with the harsh reality: *Major new troubles lay ahead. . . .*

# DRESSING A DREAM

"Mom, what's the matter?" Allison cried, clutching the front of her robe, seeing the reflected image of her mother bursting into her room.

It wasn't like Lydia not to knock on Allison's door, but she was carried away by the moment. If the evening went as she hoped, her dreams for her daughter would finally come true. In the vanity mirror, Allison watched her as Lydia felt her unrestrained smile widened, showing all her pearly teeth.

"On the way home from work, I walked past Reyna's Boutique and saw the most perfect dress," Lydia said, dramatically laying the silky light-blue dress with its short hemline and flutter sleeves across her daughter's bed. "It was half off—so I had to get it for *you*."

Allison started to turn, but Lydia directed her daughter back toward the mirror. Allison's long chestnut hair was still wet from her shower, so Lydia pushed up the towel from around her daughter's shoulders and dried her wavy tresses. Picking up the pink brush from the vanity table, Lydia slowly groomed her daughter's hair, careful not to damage the ends as she untangled them.

"What's going on?" Allison asked, creasing her brow. "What's all the attention for?"

"Oh, Allison, please don't do that," Lydia said as she massaged the girl's forehead. "If you keep doing that, you'll end up like Aunt Susan—deep forehead ridges before she was even forty." She continued brushing, remarking, "You're such a pretty girl, Allison. You're just as pretty as this actress in the movie I saw last night . . . you could pass for a young Ann—"

"You mean pretty Anne Hathaway—in her first movie *The Princess Diaries*?" Allison asked, arching her eyebrows in anticipation, bringing back lines across her forehead.

With her left-hand fingertips, Lydia smoothed down the skin above her the girl's eyes. "No, dear, not Anne Hathaway. I am talking about Ann Blyth," she explained. "You've probably never heard of her because she was an actress from the 'forties. In *Mildred Pierce*—the old movie I was watching—she played the self-centered daughter of Joan Crawford. Mildred, Joan's character, worked so hard to give Veda, Ann's role, everything in life, and the girl repaid her mother with ingratitude. I'm glad you're not —"

Cutting Lydia off, Allison asked excitedly, "When can I see the new dress?" She tried to turn around again; but Lydia was clasping the top of her head, immobilizing it.

"In a minute," her mother replied, brushing underneath the girl's hair. "I want to make sure your hair is groomed properly. Otherwise, it'll end up frizzy."

"Mom, why are you acting this way? What are you up to?"

"Allison, *really*. What a suspicious mind! I'm not up to anything." Lydia took a deep breath, then exhaled loudly. "It's just that at the office I've been boasting to Mr. Wainwright's handsome son Carlton about my delicious cheese soufflé. A few weeks ago, he fired his personal cook. He said he was tired of eating out at restaurants, so naturally he was more than happy to accept my dinner invitation." After a brief pause, she added with a wink, "You know, Allison, I make the best soufflé around."

"I had no idea you're interested in Carlton Wainwright. Isn't he a little young for you? He's gotta be in his late twenties, and you're forty—"

Lydia softly covered her daughter's mouth. "You know it's not polite to reveal a lady's age—I raised you better than that."

Gently, Allison pushed her mother's arm away. "Do you need me to run to the store for anything?"

Setting down the brush, Lydia shook her head. "Make sure you put on some rouge and lipstick. You need to look as pretty as you can for Carlton."

"What? You have to be kidding! . . . Mom?"

"Allison, you're very pretty and smart—a great catch for any man." Lydia threw her arms around her daughter's shoulders and hugged her briskly. "You'll be eighteen in only a few months, an adult. And many men, older men, will be interested in dating you. When I was your age, I was already married," she reminded Allison, then left the room before her daughter could say anything in reply.

In the kitchen, she took out six eggs and a block of cheese from the refrigerator, a large mixing bowl and grater from the lower cupboards. Within no time, the soufflé was baking in the oven.

While slicing zucchini for a side dish, she daydreamed about her own future if Allison were to marry Carlton Wainwright. Since her husband's death nine years ago, she had been working as an underpaid secretary to Clifford Wainwright, Carlton's father, as well as a weekend chambermaid at the Wainwright Hotel. For almost a year, because she was sick of having to walk everywhere or calling a taxi, her thoughts had been consumed with how she could set aside enough money for a down payment on a halfway-decent used car. (To help pay for her husband's funeral, she had to sell the pickup truck, their only vehicle.) Now, her mind was focused on beautiful clothing, plush furs, fine jewelry, and the shiny black Bentley that Carlton drove around town. Old Mr. Wainwright planned to retire soon, and transfer his ownership of the hotel and other downtown properties to his son. Surely, once Carlton and Allison married, he would be generous to his mother-in-law. After all, Lydia often overheard him brag he had "money to burn." Perhaps he would even invite her to move into his enormous house on Norcrest Street, the most affluent neighborhood in their town of Havensville, New York.

She felt as if her mind were dictating the script of an old Hollywood movie whose female lead went from *rags to riches*—from being a widow who struggled for years to provide for her daughter and pay the mortgage on her dilapidated bungalow, to a prominent citizen in her community enjoying the finer things life offered.

The doorbell rang, abruptly cutting short her fantasy. She put down her knife and answered it.

To her surprise, Allison's classmate and neighbor Hailey stood on the doorstep. Brunette and bug-eyed, her daughter's friend acted at times like a blonde scatterbrain, the type perfected on screen by Marilyn Monroe and Jayne Mansfield. "Good afternoon, Mrs. Dresden. Is Allison around?"

"Yes, but she's very busy right now," Lydia said, barely able to contain her annoyance. "Can she call you later?"

"Oh, please. I tried texting her just a little while ago, but she didn't text back. Can she talk for just a bit?" Hailey pleaded. "I forgot some details for our language arts assignment. Allison is always so good at writing things down. I'm on my way to baby-sit for the Murray kids down the street. It'll just be a minute."

"All right—but promise—don't keep her."

The girl nodded.

Lydia motioned for Hailey to wait in the vestibule. Walking down the hall, she took deep breaths. She knocked at her daughter's bedroom door, more composed. "Allison? Did you put on that new dress yet?"

No response.

"Allison?" she repeated, opening the door, but her daughter wasn't there. The new dress still lay untouched across the bed. She hurried into the adjoining bathroom, where the large frosted-glass window beside the toilet was wide open to the backyard. "So that's where that girl went," she murmured.

Returning to the bedroom, she shook her head, thinking aloud, "Dammit, why did I have to raise a child with such a stubborn streak?" Her rapid heartbeat settled in her forehead, causing her temples to throb. What was she going to do about Wainwright?

The doorbell rang again. She glanced at the clock on her nightstand. It was six o'clock. She couldn't remember if she told Wainwright six or six-thirty.

"Mrs. Dresden—I see this tall, handsome guy on your doorstep," Hailey called down the hall. "He's holding a bouquet of roses. You want me to let him in?"

Lydia had to think quickly. Her favorite stars on the Classic Movies Channel—Joan Crawford, Barbara Stanwyck, Bette Davis—were always resourceful no matter how tricky the situation could be. The same size as Allison, Lydia practically tore off her uniform and changed into the dress.

"Yes, Hailey!" Lydia yelled back, running her daughter's brush through her shoulder-length hair. "But tell him I'll be just a minute!"

Like the determined stars of her favorite old Hollywood stories, she wasn't about to give up on her dreams.

# IN A VIOLENT WORLD

Through Miles's open bedroom window, he heard his sister shouting but couldn't make out what she said. He got up from the bed and groped his way downstairs, calling her name: *Claire? Claire? You all right?* He stumbled into the foyer. Moonlight shone through the open front door, illuminating his sister's silhouetted shape standing on the front porch.

Something was wrong, terribly wrong. Facing Miles, Claire wildly swayed from side to side, as if she were having a seizure and couldn't control her balance. *Stop! You're hurting me!* his sister cried out. Miles rushed to push the screen door open. He yelled, *Claire? What's going on—what's the matter?* A tall muscular man, his face blurred, was now pulling his sister by her waist down the porch steps. With outstretched arms, hands pawing frantically at the air, Claire screamed, *Please! Help me!* Though Miles reached out, she was beyond his grasp.

A rusty sedan that wasn't there before appeared in front of the house, gripping Miles with fear. The shadowy figure flung open the passenger's door and shoved his sister inside. As the car sped off, Miles tried running after it, but his legs froze. The bright rear taillights disappeared as the car rounded the corner. Unable to move, he collapsed on the porch steps . . . .

Waking, Miles jolted upright in bed, his heart thudding wildly. Warm sunlight ambushed his opening eyes. His body was drenched in sweat, and he pulled at his clinging T-shirt, loosening the collar. To calm himself, he patted his chest, breathing deeply, thankful for the refreshing breeze ruffling the sheer curtains. As he brushed the damp brown hair off his forehead, he glanced at the nightstand alarm clock. It was almost 7:00 a.m.

More than anything, he wanted to stop dreaming about his sister, to finally let Claire go.   He remembered her wonderful eyes—bright green and mesmerizing—and her long reddish-brown hair. Claire enjoyed people and had a knack for attracting attention when she was with others. She carried herself with her shoulders straight and head held high, aware of her prettiness, while Miles often slouched and only wanted to blend into the crowd.

When they were young, he and Claire had been inseparable, even though she was almost four years older. Both lovers of sci-fi movies, they created imaginary worlds in their backyard by acting out adventures of people on remote planets. They also played card games, like gin rummy and double solitaire, for hours. They took the bus to faraway Glengarry Plaza because its storefronts were painted in wild colors—magenta, bright orange, lime green. There, they brought pretzels and candy from Drexel's, their favorite drugstore. On a bench outside, shaded by the store's red-and-pink canopy, they shared their treats.

But that all changed when Claire started eighth grade. She pushed her brother away, saying it was no longer "cool" to hang out with him. Too busy and tired after working overtime as a warehouse receiving clerk, their widowed mother did nothing to stop Claire from going out with a troubled kid named Pete. He was a few years older but still an eighth grader. She often skipped classes with him and his friends, drinking beer and smoking weed in the alley behind a cluster of abandoned buildings, not far from the school. During her high school senior year, she dropped out and moved in with Pete, cutting her family out of her life. Their mother grew to accept her daughter's coldness, but each time

Claire refused to talk on the phone or answer her apartment door, Miles was hurt all over again.

*Enough of the past*, he thought, shaking his head. As it was Saturday, he could lie back down, but he feared falling asleep might bring back the same dream. *Oh, Claire, when will your death stop haunting me?*

Though it was mid-April, it was already warm out, so he decided on a pair of denim shorts and a gray polo shirt. Grabbing his wire-framed glasses from the nightstand, he wandered downstairs into the kitchen. He poured a glass of orange juice and slid into a chair at the kitchen table. Looking out the side window, he noticed the sky was covered in blue with occasional patches of clouds.

The peacefulness of this time lasted only minutes, broken by his aunt Glenda coming in to make coffee. She was tall and bony, with cropped gray-streaked brown hair and an endless supply of shapeless, floor-length dresses. If she wanted others to see her as matronly, he pondered, then she had accomplished her mission.

"It's a nice day out, a beautiful morning," his aunt said, following the direction of his gaze. "What do you have planned today? Would you like me to take you somewhere?"

"No, that's all right," Miles said. His plan was to sit in his aunt's backyard, much of which was surrounded by tall shrubbery, and catch up on his English-class readings. "I have a lot of homework to do."

"Okay—if that's what makes you happy."

Miles moved around his aunt and poured his half-empty glass in the sink.

"Aren't you going to have some breakfast? You want some scrambled eggs?" his aunt asked. "You haven't been eating much at all lately. I swear you've probably lost ten pounds in the last month or so. You need to eat to keep your brain and body working."

"I'm not hungry right now," he said, putting the glass in the dishwasher.

* * *

On the back patio, Miles tried reading some of the essays assigned for Monday, but his heart wasn't in it. If he were back in Druryton, he would be out today with his best friend, Brandon, either shooting hoops or kicking around a soccer ball in the vacant lot down the street. But he had no friends in Fairfield, Ohio, where he had lived since October. The students he met at West Fairfield High mostly enjoyed hanging at the mall or working out at the Community Rec Center—activities he avoided. He didn't see the sense in browsing through the stores when he had no money to spend, and he steered clear of the Rec Center because being around his muscular, better-looking male peers only intensified his poor self-image.

Since leaving Druryton, Miles had been back only once, during Christmas, to see his mom and Brandon. The city was over an hour away, and whenever he talked to his mother on the phone and mentioned coming for another visit, she put him off. "It's not a good time right now," she always said. "I've been working extra hours on weekends. Besides, you're better off staying in Fairfield." And Brandon wasn't encouraging Miles to return, either. His friend wasn't much of a talker on the phone, but he did like to text. Which made it all the more puzzling (and hurtful) that he rarely or only randomly responded to Miles's messages. What else could Miles assume other than that Brandon was giving him the brush-off?

He couldn't really figure out Brandon. His mother, though, he understood. In her mind, she was keeping him away in order to protect him. Druryton had some quaint historical dwellings and cool downtown businesses (like the bakery called Dee's Sweet Treats that also sold vintage candy and ice cream); yet the barred windows and security doors on many of the homes and businesses could be an unnerving sight, especially to outsiders. A lot of the Druryton residents and store proprietors took theses extra safety precautions because they were well aware of the dangers lurking in the city. After nine in the evening, the street corners transformed into hangouts for gangs of rough-looking people—young men and women dressed in oversized, tattered clothes with intimidating glares. They acted as if they owned those corners. The park in the center of town (right behind the graffiti-defaced strip mall housing Food Circus, Family Drugs, and Dollar Deluxe) was another place to avoid after dusk because of drug activity. To stay out of trouble, you had to either be *street smart* or stay in at night. Lying in bed at his mother's house, Miles had sometimes heard gunshots coming from the park since he lived five blocks away. He would toss and turn for a long time as he envisioned different faces for the person who might've been injured and possibly killed in a drug-related altercation.

Despite the constant presence of police cars patrolling its streets, Fairfield didn't seem much "safer." Only the other day, the headline of *The Fairfield Daily* at a local drugstore read SERIAL KILLER STRIKES AGAIN. And about a week ago, while taking an evening walk through the downtown area, he watched two men in a confrontation, one man shoving the other against a storefront window, cracking the glass in several places. He didn't stay around to see the outcome of the fight.

Last night on the phone, Miles asked his mother, "Is it possible to get away from violence in this world?"

Much to his surprise, she said, "But you have. You're a lucky young man to be living in Fairfield, in a nice house with an aunt who cares about you." Miles was about to say something more, but his mom cut him off. "You don't see prostitutes and dope dealers standing around outside rundown hotels like you did in Druryton, do you?" she reminded him sharply.

Rather than argue, he said, "Okay . . . got your point."

"As soon as I land a better-paying job, I'm selling this house and finding a new one for us in a nicer area," she asserted, as if to pacify him. "I'm not going to lose another child," she added before saying goodnight.

For years, his mother had been saying she wanted to leave Druryton, yet the house was never put up for sale, nor did she follow through with getting a new job. In his mind, he questioned how serious she was *this time* about relocating. She seemed fairly content with them living apart.

As Miles reopened his book, he saw a young woman watering a newly planted bed of geraniums alongside his aunt's unfenced property. The woman had pale, lightly freckled skin and thick brown hair. Her floral-pattern cotton dress pleasantly hugged her slender figure. When she noticed Miles staring, she set down the hose and smiled.

"Hi there!" she said, her smile widening.

Miles nodded hello.

"What are you reading?" she asked, walking toward him.

Miles showed her the title: *Writing Through the Ages*. "I wish I *was* reading," he confessed. "This book is boring."

With her striking blue eyes, she gazed at him curiously, almost suspiciously. "Your aunt told me that her nephew was moving in, and my husband and I have been meaning to come over and say hello."

Miles laughed nervously as he extended his hand. "I'm Miles. Nice to meet you."

"I'm Lorna."

Their handshake, lasting for just a second or two, felt pleasurable for him.

When a car door slammed shut, she lost her smile, and her gaze flew in the direction of her driveway. "Well, I have to go," she said. "Nice chatting with you. Enjoy your day."

"Thanks."

Lorna disappeared into the abundant foliage of her backyard.

Returning to his book, Miles still couldn't concentrate. Instead of seeing words, the image of Lorna's lovely heart-shaped face leaped up from the pages: her dazzling blue eyes, her full moist lips, and delicate chin. He closed the book, then his eyes, imagining what it would be like to run his hands up along her smooth arms, her slender shoulders, then down to her firm breasts. It had been months since he had experienced any attraction like that to a girl—rather, a woman. The book dropped out of his hand. He wasn't sure how to handle his lustful feelings.

Then the obvious solution came to him. *Of course—a cold shower.*

\* \* \*

Later that night, Miles moved from one side to the other of his bed. It was almost midnight, and he still couldn't sleep. Though he had tried to focus his thoughts on more pleasant things—sitcoms he watched earlier on TV, humorous blogs he read on the Internet—he couldn't shake the memory of the night of his sister's accident.

On that late Friday evening in November, Miles answered the door and let in the officer. "I need to speak to your mom or dad," the man said. His size was intimidating: he was very tall and had a frame as wide as the door. Miles stammered, "I—I'll—I'll get my mom." He raced up the stairs without even thinking to find out why the officer was there.

The man informed them that Claire had been in a terrible car wreck and was being treated at St. Bart's

Hospital. When they pressed the officer about how badly she was hurt, he replied flatly, "You'll have to ask the hospital staff."

Miles and his mother rushed to St. Bart's.

Early the next morning, Claire underwent surgery to repair her skull fracture. While Miles and his mother sat in the waiting room, two men with mustaches approached them. One introduced himself as a police officer, the other a social worker. Miles's mom took some money out of her purse and told Miles to get a snack from the cafeteria down the hall. Miles pretended to leave but lingered within hearing distance in the hallway.

The officer related what had happened. According to witnesses, Claire and her boyfriend, Pete, were drinking and arguing outside a mutual friend's house. This was nothing out of the ordinary for them—they often drank and fought. Claire screamed nasty words at Pete: "You asshole—you asshole jerk—you disgusting pig." Inflamed, he was said to have grabbed her, pulling her in the direction of his car parked on the street. Although Claire tried to free herself, Pete forced her into the vehicle, then drove off at a high speed. He lost control about three blocks away and crashed into a tree. Both went through the windshield. The impact crushed Pete's neck—he died instantly. It was a miracle Claire was still alive.

The social worker spoke about how they might transfer Claire to another facility once she stabilized. This other place had highly trained staff—physical therapists, occupational therapists, speech pathologists—to deal with patients with head injuries. His voice beamed with optimism, though the X-rays revealed Claire's brain was severely damaged.

Hooked up to all kinds of machines, his sister was kept in ICU and never regained consciousness. She lingered for two weeks before slipping away.

The image of his catatonic sister, with her head wrapped in bandages, quickly faded with voices rising up through Miles's opened window. He recognized Lorna's voice. He scrambled to the window, seeing nothing but darkness.

"Get back in the house!" shouted a man. *Lorna's husband?*

"*Please*," Lorna bellowed. "I want to be left alone."

"You'd better get back in here, or you'll regret it!"

Next came what sounded like a wail, followed by a muffled scream. Someone's patio door slid open. Then it abruptly shut. Miles broke out in a cold sweat. *Please . . . this can't be happening again.* His heart frantically pounding, he paced the room for a while with his fists balled in front of him, level with his chin, as if ready to fight. What should he do? What could he do? If he woke up his aunt, would she be angry—would she believe him and want to get involved? And, if he called the police, would he have to identify himself and answer a lot of questions before they would bother to investigate?

Though he felt like a coward, he decided not to act.

Returning to bed, he continued to toss and turn, unable to relax his fists.

\* \* \*

The following Saturday, Miles stood in line at the counter of the IN & OUT convenience store holding a bottle of soda, waiting for his turn to pay, counting and recounting the coins in his hand.

Lorna walked in. Her appearance was impeccable, as before; her white polo shirt and blue drawstring Capri pants had been ironed and looked very crisp, and her hair was pinned along the sides of her head and fashioned into elaborate curls flowing down her back. After taking a bottle of water from one of the back refrigerated cases, she got in line.

Miles turned around and said, "Hi. How's it going? What'cha up to?"

"Oh, hello," Lorna replied warmly. "I was out for a walk."

They paid for their drinks, then together casually headed back home.

Lorna said, "So, tell me about yourself—your family. Even though I've known your aunt for several years, she's never talked about her relatives."

Miles shrugged his shoulders, not sure what to say. Would Lorna really want to hear about his mother's first husband, Claire's father, who ran off one evening with some whore he met at a bar? Or about the second husband, Miles's father, who overdosed on narcotics? And even more depressing, about his sister, whose boyfriend robbed her of life? With all that, it was no wonder his aunt was secretive about them.

Lorna arched her eyebrows.

"What do you want to know?" Miles asked with narrowed eyes.

"Hmmm," she said. "I've hit a touchy subject. So tell me this: what's Fairfield High like? It seems like a really nice school, far better than the dumpy one I went to in Michigan. You made any friends there? You have a girlfriend?"

"It's an okay school. There's a few kids I talk to . . . but no girlfriend yet," Miles said, frowning.

"Why no girlfriend?"

Miles shrugged again. "Maybe because I look dorky. I'm too skinny and shy and don't have cool clothes."

"You look fine to me. Great head of dark hair—very wavy, very shiny. And good skin, nice and smooth."

"I guess . . ."

After falling silent again for a few moments, Lorna said, "So you're from Druryton? What a strange name for a city!

It sounds like *Dreary* Town. I hear a lot of news stories about the crime there—assaults, terrible shootings and murder, robberies." Shaking her head, she looks away for a moment. "The same kinds of crimes happen quite frequently in the area near where my mom lives. She never goes out when it's dark or close to getting dark."

Miles hesitated. "Yeah, there's crime in Druryton—like everywhere else. But as long as you're careful, like staying away from certain areas, you're usually okay."

"What else can you tell me about it?"

"Let me think," Miles said, rubbing his chin with the top of his knuckles. "It's really different from here . . . in some ways. Like how the streets are laid out. The houses in Druryton are smaller and closer to the sidewalks. Most of them have small front yards but big front porches. No matter what the weather is like, people hang out on their porch, talking and smoking cigarettes. It's like a built-in neighborhood watch program. My mom and I have never been broken into."

"Here, people don't sit on their porch."

"Another cool thing about my old neighborhood," Miles continued, "is an old lady named Helen. She's my friend Brandon's grandmother. They live down the street from me and my mom. Helen keeps a close eye on our street. Even when something happens blocks away, Helen knows about it. I'm not sure *how*. Last year, she even knew what this eleven-year-old girl was doing all the way down the street. The girl was calling up boys and sneaking them in through her back door while her mother was at work. Helen was afraid something bad might happen, so she went over to the girl's house and talked to her mother about it. I could go on about Helen . . . she's nosy but helpful."

"She sure sounds like it," Lorna said flatly, not showing the interest Miles hoped he would inspire.

At Lorna's driveway, he noticed some bruises on her face and some scratches on her neck. On the walk, she had perspired, and some of her makeup had washed away, revealing those marks. Driven by instinct, he reached up and stroked the side of her face a few times. She closed her eyes and titled her head into his palm. He could feel her facial muscles relaxing. This aroused him. Embarrassed, he pulled his hand away.

"How'd you get those marks?" Miles asked softly.

Lorna's body and face stiffened, and she quickly stepped away. "What—what are you talking about?" she stammered, her forehead wrinkled.

"I see some bruises on your cheeks, and you've got scratches on your neck."

"Oh, I accidentally whacked myself in the face the other day when I was moving some boxes around in my basement." With her hand, she gently stroked her neck. "And these scratches are from these cats I have. They fight like wildcats, and I'm constantly pulling them apart."

"Oh, okay," Mile said, but he was still skeptical.

"Well, I have to start cooking dinner. Catch you later," she said, hurrying into her house.

With a heavy heart, Miles headed back to his aunt's. He had promised to finish his laundry and pick up his bedroom, but he would've rather stayed with Lorna. The more time he spent with her, the more he wished he wasn't a kid. If only there was a quick way to turn himself into a man—a stronger person she could trust . . . not like her husband.

* * *

Day after day, week after week—Miles became more agitated about the strange happenings next door. In the early hours of the morning, Lorna's husband could be overheard shouting at her. Over and over, he accused her of the same things—of being lazy, of making him look bad in front of his friends, of acting surly. Whenever Lorna raised her voice, her cry of pain was almost certain to follow. No matter how intensely Miles squinted in the darkness, he could never see any of it from his bedroom.

Then in early June as he walked out the front door, Miles caught sight of Lorna standing on her porch. Before he could call to her, a man's arm, which he believed was her husband's reached out from behind her. With his thick, muscular forearm, the man hooked her around the neck and pulled her inside. Lorna shrieked as the door to her house slammed closed.

The next morning, before going off to school, Miles decided to talk to his aunt about what he saw. "Have you ever noticed anything weird about Lorna and her husband?" he asked her.

Aunt Glenda practically slammed her coffee cup down on the kitchen table. "Why do you ask *that*?" She was clearly perturbed.

"Have you . . .? I mean . . . you've never been awakened by noises coming from next door?"

"What noises?" His aunt shook her head. "I've never heard anything."

"But I hear—"

"The Bardells are the perfect couple. Lorna is so sweet, attractive, and domestic. And Todd—well, he may've started out as a mechanic, but now he's a successful engineer designing car parts. They're highly reputable people. You must be imagining things. All those scary movies you watch on TV, those violent video games you play on the computer—they're doing something to your mind."

"But I don't play violent video games. And I don't watch scary movies."

Aunt Glenda changed the subject. "You should eat more," she remarked. "Your cheeks look so sullen under your big brown eyes. You look unhealthy. When your mom sees you next, she'll accuse me of starving you."

* * *

Later, during lunch at school, Miles took a few reluctant bites from his peanut butter-and-jelly sandwich, nibbled at his cheese crackers, but soon put the food aside. He couldn't eat any more, though he tried. When the bell rang, he threw his lunch away and moved on to his next period—U.S. History.

After shuffling through some papers on his desk, Mr. Handleman stood up, and the students instinctively opened their notebooks. The teacher began to lecture about the 1950s—about the arrival of rock-and-roll and how this music affected teenager's leisure activities. Dances called sock hops were often held in high-school gyms, where teenagers shed their shoes before they "jumped" around to the latest rock-and-roll tunes. When his teacher switched to talking about how movie-theatre attendance went down because of television, Miles's mind drifted, and he stopped taking notes.

Oddly, he thought about Druryton High, where the students were often unruly and disrespectful. Teachers typically had students complete worksheets or answer questions out of textbooks. Miles never caused any problems, so he was allowed to escape to the library and do alternate assignments. He read other books on the topics covered in the textbooks and wrote reports. How he thrived in that environment, earning A after A! It was so much better than listening to a teacher drone on and on.

After forty minutes or so, Mr. Handleman sat back down at his desk, indicating that his lecture for the day had ended. Looking down at his paper, Miles discovered that he had written only a few sentences. The other students talked quietly among themselves for the next ten minutes until the bell rang.

After school, he headed to the basement and put in a load of laundry, then sat outside in the backyard. The afternoon, though humid, wasn't as warm as earlier. A pleasant breeze was blowing, hitting him directly but gently, revitalizing him after a long day at school.

He saw Lorna step outside with a book in her hand. Seemingly unaware of him, she flopped down on a wooden chair at the edge of her yard, next to her flower beds. He stared at her, waiting to be noticed. Eventually, her eyes lifted from the book and her gaze traveled in his direction.

"Hello, Lorna," Miles said. "Great weather, isn't it?"

"Yes, I suppose," she said. She abruptly shut her book, as if annoyed that her reading had been interrupted.

He got up and asked, "How's your book? What are you reading?"

Lorna quickly pulled several thick curls of her hair over one eye, as if hiding something. As Miles approached her, she awkwardly covered the title of the book with her thumb. But he could still see the font cover: a picture of a very pretty woman attempting to free herself from a handsome man's grasp as they stood in front of a beautiful mansion.

Lorna reluctantly looked up and said, "It's just a romance."

Standing over her, he asked, "How's your day been?"

"Okay. How was school?"

"School's okay except that finals are coming up next week. I need to start organizing my notes for them. I hate memorizing stuff."

They fell silent for several awkward moments.

"Why do you stay . . . ?" Miles blurted out, unable to stand the stillness any longer. A choking sensation gripped his throat, and he had to swallow hard several times.

Glaring at him, she replied, "*What?* What do you mean?" The book slipped from her hand.

Miles's eyes locked with hers as he moved closer. "I know what's going on . . . I don't know why you stay."

"What are you talking about?"

"Don't pretend," he said. "*Please* don't. I want to help."

"You're talking crazy—acting crazy!" flared Lorna.

"I'm not crazy. I just want to help you somehow."

"Help me?" Lorna laughed sarcastically.

"Yes," Miles said calmly. He reached out to stroke her face again. "You're so beautiful and nice. You don't deserve it. You can't let it go on."

Lorna slapped his hand away. "Who do you think you are—talking to me this way?"

"Someone who—someone who—" Miles stammered as he considered the right words to say. The tension in the air was so strong that it almost choked him.

He tried to take her hand—but she backed away. "Look, Miles," she said gruffly. "From now on, I want you to stay away from me. You obviously have nothing better to do with your time than create some preposterous stories. If my husband found out you were talking to me like this, you'd be in some major trouble."

"I'm not making up any stories," Miles said. "I know . . ."

Her face pale flushed crimson. "You need to mind your own business. You're nothing but trash—filthy white trash from Druryton. You don't belong here."

Swiftly raising her hand, she struck the side of his face, and his glasses flew off and landed on the grass. She picked up her book, then strode across the patio, slamming the patio door behind her.

It took several seconds for him to feel the impact of the blow. The prickling along his cheek quickly turned into a burning sensation. His body shaking, he retrieved his glasses. *I don't understand. How could she have done that? I care about her.* He went back into the house. Flopping down on the bed, he stared at the ceiling, wondering if he could still help her.

* * *

The following week, an unexpected quietness settled upon the Bardells' colonial. The couple's silence alarmed Miles even more. Was Lorna okay? Had her husband struck her so severely that she was bedridden for the time being? Should he just go over there while her husband was at work to find out?

Then, one morning, Miles happened to look out the living-room window and was relieved to see Lorna in her car, backing down her driveway. Now that school was out, he closely watched Lorna's house next door for another week. He saw neither Lorna nor her car return. He suspected that Lorna had finally left her husband. Over and over, he imagined a scene in which Lorna, unable to shed Miles's words, dashed off a I'm-leaving-you note to her husband and took off while Todd was at work.

Miles was so caught up in this fantasy that it almost came as a shock the following Saturday evening when he heard an ambulance rushing down his street.

His heart lurched wildly at the sight of paramedics rolling Lorna down the long driveway on a stretcher. Despite the lights from the ambulance and police car, he couldn't tell how badly she was hurt. An officer was questioning a tall, burly man—*the husband!* He looked composed and tidy in his silk pajamas and robe, as if nothing terrible had happened.

Miles's watery eyes darted up and down the street. He was further astonished that he was the only person staring out the door. If an incident like this had happened in Druryton, not one front porch would be vacant.

This city, Fairfield, troubled Miles. The phoniness of the neighbors, the expensive Venetian blinds and drapery that covered the windows, and the desolate front yards . . . He felt no better off here.

Miles dried his eyes and closed the door. In his bedroom, he pulled out two duffle bags from his closet. After dropping them in front of his dressers, he opened the top drawer. Slowly, he closed it.

He couldn't leave. Not yet.

\* \* \*

Around 2:00 a.m., giving up on sleep, Miles wandered downstairs into the kitchen. He planned to warm a mug of chocolate milk, hoping it would calm his nerves. From the side window, he heard the Bardells' patio door open and shut. Looking out, he saw Todd, illuminated by the moonlight, staggering toward the glass-and-metal patio set. With a bottle of some sort of liquor in his hand, the man collapsed into one of the chairs. After he guzzled down more booze, his head dropped to the table, making a faint *thud*.

Miles's heart began to race. His brow suddenly oozed with sweat. At the counter, Miles opened one of the drawers and pulled out a butcher knife.

*This is my chance—I might not get another. I wasn't there for my sister, but I can be there for my love. I'll make sure he never hurts her again.*

Firmly grasping the handle, he headed outside, crossing from his yard into the Bardells'. Grateful for the darkness, he crouched and crept like a panther toward the patio set, his approach muffled by the almost deafening chirping of crickets.

# GLITZY GARB

*Dedicated to all those who remember
the mid-'80s to early '90s
fashion and music scene . . .*

Glancing out Glitzy Garb's big front window, and noticing he was only across the street, Maggie felt a sudden sense of panic. *Where's the best place to hide?* she pondered, quickly scanning the store. Her heart lurching, she considered backing up a few feet and ducking behind the gold-lacquered display cabinet, or maybe scurrying toward the back and slipping through the purple satin curtains behind the register, or even dropping to her knees and crawling underneath one of the filled clothing racks. Her indecisiveness, unfortunately, cost her valuable time. As her gaze returned to the window, she discovered he was now standing right outside, his neck craned forward and his hawk-like nose almost pressed against the glass. He was glaring in at her with his steely eyes. She knew she had no other choice but to move from the center of the room and turn on the lights.

*What on earth possessed me to come in early today?* Maggie murmured, forcing herself not to visibly shake her head in regret. Thanks to caller ID and the man's hectic work schedule, she had been able to avoid him for over a week.

Unlocking the oval-glassed door to her resale shop, she said, "Good morning, Mr. Sark." In an upbeat voice to cover her fear, she added, "How are you today?"

He didn't respond, only gave her an intimidating glare as he passed. Her eyes nervously twitching, she watched him wander through the store. Scratching the coarse gray hair atop his head, he glanced at the vintage '50s, '60s, and '70s clothing hung on the round chrome racks. There was a sharp contrast between the displayed bright dresses, pants, and shirts and Mr. Sark's own attire—black pants and a black short-sleeved shirt buttoned to the collar, as if he were a church minister or pastor. But he was neither: along with operating a janitorial supplies business, he also owned a few properties in downtown Glenwood.

Mr. Sark pushed aside some polyester blouses resting on a wooden bench, making room for himself before sinking down on it. As if for protection, Maggie went behind the glass front counter.

Standing directly across from him, she smiled and asked, "What are you up to today?" acting as if she were oblivious of what he wanted.

"Ms. Darnell, I didn't come today here to make small talk," he said.

"Yes. I know. You've come for the rent." Maggie fell silent briefly to gather her thoughts. "But—I—I don't have it yet. I know, Mr. Sark, I promised to have the rent by now. You see, business has been really slow. Even though it's early April the weather has been unseasonably warm for northern Ohio. Folks are probably taking advantage of it by doing things other than shopping. Just give me a few more weeks. By then, we'll have some cooler rainy days that'll drive people to the stores."

Mr. Sark's eyebrows shot up. "And what am I supposed to do in the meantime? I, too, have bills to pay."

"*Please*," Maggie pleaded, "be patient for just a little longer." She clenched her hands underneath the register. "Tonight, a woman is coming in to buy several pieces for a production at the Saxony Theatre. She's in charge of providing the actors' wardrobes. I'm sure I'll be able to pay in another day or two, and then I won't be behind. It'll all work out."

"I hope for your sake it does," he said, getting to his feet. "I'll be back in a few days to check on you."

"Thank you."

"But I have to warn you that I'm running out of patience. You can't keep falling behind month after month. Your aunt Loretta never had this problem. If you can't pay the rent on time, then you should look into properties in the area you can afford." With that, he left.

Suddenly feeling very tired, Maggie collapsed into the red velvet chair behind her. She was beginning to wonder if she had made the right decision. Had she only been fooling herself? Could she be successful?

A little over four months ago, her aunt died of a massive stroke at age seventy. When Maggie arrived at Glenwood for the reading of the will, she learned she had been bequeathed all of Aunt Loretta's belongings in the store. (One of her aunt's most trusted friends, the lawyer handling her estate had been put in charge of selling the antique furniture and bric-a-brac from the two-bedroom ranch she had rented for the past twenty years and donating the money to St. Jude Children's Research Hospital, her favorite charity.) Instead of selling the Glitzy Garb's inventory at auction, Maggie took a leave from her fifteen-year career as a legal assistant and decided to run the business herself. Whenever she had visited her aunt, she witnessed firsthand how Loretta's days were filled with the excitement of local actors, musicians, and artists who frequented the store to shop.

Her family in Michigan (where she had lived) thought she was crazy to relocate to Ohio. "You've made some poor decisions in the past—including breaking your engagement with that handsome lawyer," her mother had said in early December, when Maggie called her parents from the store and informed them of her decision to keep Glitzy Garb open. "But this—this has to be the worst. You have no experience in retail." Taking over the phone, her father flared, "You're going to fail—just fall flat on your face!" Bursting into tears, Maggie abruptly hung up. Her parents didn't understand how tired she was of the long hours at the Law Offices of Orelow & Kresney, of the tedious research she did in preparing the case documents and written reports for the two attorneys. It was a welcome relief *not* to spend her work days shackled to a desk and to a computer.

Maggie glanced at the clock above the door. It was just after eleven in the morning. The woman from the theatre said she would stop in later around four or five. What if there were no other customers 'til then? How would Maggie pass her time?

She stood up and walked to the large window where there was a view of the entire block. Across the street were several attached brown-brick buildings of varying heights—a few beauty salons, an Italian restaurant, and a health-food store. Every morning, she told herself she would cross the street to introduce herself to one of the owners, but she never did. Perhaps she feared she might miss a sale even if Glitzy Garb was closed only for a short time. She couldn't afford that happening.

When Maggie took over the business, sales were good for the first month. A steady flow of people who knew her aunt dropped in to express their condolences. They all said what a remarkable person she was. "She had the friendliest smile." "She always knew what we were looking for." "Whenever it was our birthday or any kind of special event, she would call us to wish us well." They went on to talk about Aunt Loretta's eccentric behavior, about how fond she was of emulating stars from classic Hollywood movies. Aunt Loretta donned a variety of wigs and attire to match the clothing and hairstyles of movie stars from her favorite films, and while enacting scenes, she made her customers guess whom she was trying to copy. "It was great fun!" they said. "She was so entertaining . . ." Before these regular customers left the store, they typically bought an item or two. Maggie met so many people her first two weeks in Glenwood, she could only recall a few of their names.

How optimistic she had been about the store!

But business tapered off to the point that now only a few browsers came in each day. No one was actually buying. She hadn't had a single sale in almost three weeks. Besides being behind on the store lease payments, she was almost two months late with the rent on her flat a few blocks away. And it seemed like there was no way of catching up. With her savings account now depleted (about a third of the six thousand lost to breaking the lease on her former apartment), she had a little less than four hundred dollars in her checking. And because of her financial situation, she was forcing herself to be realistic about the future. Before her leave of absence expired at the end of next month, she would have to return to Adrian, Michigan, and her former paralegal position. That thought made her heart sink, like a rock plummeting down a well.

(Although Maggie was barely talking to her parents, she found she could still rely on Gail and Peter, good friends from Adrian, for support. During Maggie's phone conversation last night with Gail, her husband, Peter, overheard his wife responding sympathetically to Maggie's problems. Getting on the phone, he said, "Sorry, Mags, that you're having such a rough time of it. If you *do* move back, you're welcome to stay with us until you find a new place." Holding back tears, Maggie thanked him over and over.)

Despite her store troubles, she enjoyed her life in Glenwood, which was three times the size of Adrian. Even though Glenwood had its rough neighborhoods—small parts of town with vacant and/or deteriorating houses and trash-littered fields—it offered many attractions. After work, she visited art galleries and used bookstores in the area. On weekend evenings, she hung out in local coffee shops and other small venues to hear live music and comedy performances. The musicians and comedians, though not well-known, were talented. The musicians impressed her with how well they sang and played their instruments, and so did the comedians with how their funny skits kept her laughing long after their shows had ended.

Her eyes wandering from the coffeehouses at the end of the block, she focused on a large sunburst locust tree across the street. The tree stood in front of a small parking lot, obscuring it somewhat. In the afternoon, once the high school dismissed for the day, it became a teenage hangout. The same group of kids congregated there from three until five or six. With their dyed spiky hair in a variety of unusual colors—blue, green, purple—and ghoulish makeup, they were an intimidating sight. They reminded her of distorted clowns. "Punkers and goth kids," Aunt Loretta had referred to them on the phone. Maggie had no idea what *goth* meant; so her aunt explained, "It's short for gothic." The punkers and goth kids smoked cigarettes, played CDs with moody-sounding music from a boom box, and sat around on a couple of benches under the tree.

In late December and early January, especially during their two-week Christmas vacation, these teenagers became her best customers. Clad in a variety of black leather jackets and military-style trench coats, they dropped by her store on a daily basis. They often bought outlandish outfits: striped polyester pants with black shirts or blouses, old jeans and bright pullovers with exaggerated collars, oversized dress shirts with wild-patterned ties, black sport coats and formal dresses, along with an assortment of black hats, from berets to derbies to the classic pillbox styles with veils.

By late January, perhaps because the kids had run out of gift and shopping money, their habits changed. They seemed to waste Maggie's time by trying on clothing piece after piece, but not buying anything. At the same time, Maggie started noticing items missing from her aunt's collection: a glittery fabric brooch, a gold lamé scarf, several pairs of '60s black sunglasses. She was certain that they were stealing from her, since the teenagers were her only customers. But there were so many of them, and there was no way she could prove if only one or more of the teens had been stealing.

A week ago, two girls whom Maggie had never seen before came into the store. The first teen had purple shoulder-length hair and wore a long-sleeved white T-shirt with ripped jeans. The other had green and yellow streaks in her long black hair and wore a short black dress. They shook their heads *no* when Maggie asked if they were looking for something in particular. Exploring almost every rack, they spent over an hour in the store. Annoyed, Maggie repeated, "You seem to be looking for something. What can I help you find?" Again, they shook their heads. While Maggie folded some sweaters at the front counter, she observed the purple-haired girl, who was edging toward the front door, put a sparkling see-through blue tank top under her arms.

Maggie acted fast by rushing toward the girl and trying to grab the top away from her. But the teen wouldn't let go. Afraid the garment would be torn, Maggie released her hold on it.

"Lady, what the hell?" the girl said.

"What do you think you're doing?" Maggie demanded. "Are you trying to steal that?" Maggie's own accusatory voice surprised her. It wasn't like her to point a finger at someone unless she was certain that person was guilty.

The girl gazed back at her with narrowed eyes and a creased forehead, as if puzzled.

"What are you talkin' about?" she snapped.

"You're about to leave my store with that top under your arms," she said. "Or are you going to buy it?"

The girl said, "I was . . . but *not* now." With a dramatic wave of her hand, the girl tossed it onto the pink-and-mint-green tiled floor.

The second girl with the streaked-hair finally came towards the door. "Let's get out of here. I'd never buy anything from this bitch. Paranoid freak has got a lot of nerve accusing you of stealing."

"Yeah," the first girl said, "she's a real bitch for sure. She's nothing like the old lady was. This woman is about as friendly as a bull. Now I know why the others want nothing to do with this place anymore."

The door slammed behind them.

Humiliated, Maggie locked the door and didn't reopen until the next morning. In fact, the incident continued to bother Maggie the next day, causing her to cancel her date for the evening with Darrin, a man she had met the previous weekend at a coffee shop. "I don't feel good," she explained on the phone. She asked him to reschedule, but he replied, "Forget it. You'll probably just cancel again at the last minute." Darrin was her type—tall and handsome, with deep brown eyes—even better-looking than the arrogant lawyer to whom she had once been engaged—but Maggie wouldn't have been good company that night. Her hands kept trembling. Unable to relax, she paced the store floor for an hour or more. One thought consumed her mind: once the girls spread the word about what had happened to their friends, her store was as good as dead.

And apparently, Maggie's fear had been realized. Mr. Sark had been the only person to set foot in her store in days.

Shaking her head, to clear it of depressing thoughts, she turned away from the window and returned to the register, where she grabbed a box of old photographs from a shelf hidden beneath the wooden counter. The other day, while rummaging through the store's back room, she had discovered the box under a stack of colorful wool and cashmere sweaters. When she opened it, she was delighted to find photographs of her aunt inside. Maggie had never seen them before. The pictures were black-and-white; many of them had been taken long ago when her aunt was in her late twenties. She wore white dresses; her shoulder-length hair was wavy, her skin doll-like, and her smile mesmerizing. Aunt Loretta had been attractive then and had, in the words of Maggie's mother, "a different man on her arm every weekend." Unfortunately, her aunt's looks hadn't held up over time. In a few of the other pictures, Maggie noticed the creases across the forehead and sagging skin around the eyelids, cheeks, chin, and neck; as well as smiles exposing less-than-perfect teeth. The outlandish blonde wigs she started wearing in middle age only drew attention to the fact that she was growing older. The years of these photos had been penciled on the backs, so she estimated her aunt was in her mid-forties. Determined to remain the center of attention, Aunt Loretta resorted to wearing sequined or low-back satin dresses and beaded hats with veils for a touch of mystery. When her aunt turned fifty, still unmarried, she retired from her job as an assistant editor for a local magazine and opened the store. A decision she never regretted, she claimed. Selling vintage clothing, though it didn't pay as well as her first profession, helped her to earn a decent living in a less stressful environment. Who didn't need costumes for parties or plays? During Halloween, her business usually quadrupled and compensated for the slow periods during the rest of the year. Additionally, her aunt boasted of having great fun attending weekly church rummage and estate sales to stock her store.

As Maggie continued to study the photos, she understood why she had been having problems. Unlike her aunt, she didn't dress the part of a vintage-resale-clothing-store owner. She was still wearing plain blouses and slacks, too conservative for the proprietor of Giltzy Garb. If people were to believe she was an authority on fashion, she had to add authenticity to herself by modeling some of pieces in the store.

Methodically, Maggie searched through the dress racks. She lingered for a little while over a dress with a short pink skirt and a sparkling silver-and-pink checkered top from the late '60s. The color pink always looked good on her, but the dress seemed too flashy. Instead, disappearing behind the satin curtains, she entered the back room to change into a black velvet sleeveless dress that came midway down her thighs. Studying herself in the full-length mirror on the wall, she pinned the sides of her chestnut hair with sparkling silver clips. Turning from side to side, she marveled at how well the clips complemented the dress.

Returning to the counter, Maggie glanced at the clock on the wall. Almost one o'clock. The costumer from the theatre wouldn't arrive for another hour yet. She sank down in the red velvet chair. Since the store was in near-perfect order, Maggie passed the time by leafing through a stack of late '50s and early '60s editions of *Vogue*, *Cosmopolitan*, and *Mademoiselle*.

In an issue of *Mademoiselle*, she became so engrossed in a short story about a woman dealing with a mentally unstable husband that, when the chime above the door rang to let her know a customer was walking in, it took several seconds for her to respond. After carefully folding a corner of the page she was reading, she set it atop the magazine stack on the floor, beside the chair.

"Hi there," Maggie said, standing up and eyeing the tall woman with short dark hair. The woman was browsing through the rack of hound's-tooth jackets and coats. "May I help you?"

"Yes," the woman said, motioning to Maggie with a dramatic gesture. "My name is Sandra. I called you yesterday about looking at your selection of clothes for the play in the works at the Saxony Theatre. It's about three women struggling to keep their romances going and their cosmetics business afloat during the Great Depression. As I said on the phone, I'm in charge of finding appropriate costumes for the actors. What do you have from the 'thirties?"

"Over here, please," Maggie said, copying the patron's exaggerated wave. The woman followed her to the dress rack beside the dressing room. Summoning her aunt's poise, smiling, Maggie held up, then pushed aside hanger after hanger with balloon-sleeved day and evening dresses to show the woman. "They're made of quality cotton or silk," Maggie emphasized, stepping back to give Sandra room to look on her own. "And in good condition—no broken zippers, missing buttons, or unraveling lace."

Maggie pointed to the glass cabinet beside the register where there was a display of gloves, wide-brimmed hats, and fur stoles. "If you want to accessorize the garments, just let me know what else you'd like to see," she said enthusiastically.

After browsing for a while, Sandra said, "Hmmm. I don't know. The prices are a little more than I was prepared to spend. Is there any way I could have a discount?"

"Well," Maggie said, "when we talked over the phone, I gave you an estimate of how much things would cost. You said that would be fine. In fact, you told me that you'd probably be buying quite a few things. I suppose I could do twenty percent off. How many things are you planning to buy?"

Thinking over Maggie's offer, Sandra pursed her lips into a serious expression. "That's really not much of a savings," the woman said. "I was hoping to get half off."

Maggie inhaled deeply, then exhaled slowly to keep her temper under control. Why was this woman being difficult? Was she trying to manipulate Maggie?

"I really can't give you half off," Maggie explained. "Twenty percent is a pretty good savings considering these pieces have already been marked down. After all, they *are* authentic 'thirties garments."

"I'm going to have to pass," the woman sighed. "But thanks for letting me have a look. I suppose making the costumes myself will be the cheapest way. What I've seen today has given me several ideas. Thanks again."

Before Maggie could say anything more, Sandra headed out. Dismayed, Maggie sank back down on the chair behind the register. She cupped her face in her hands and shook her head. There was no redemption for a bad, impulsive decision, she was beginning to believe. How ridiculous to believe she could emulate her aunt! She didn't have what it took to make it in retail. She realized her next step was to advertise a going-out-of-business sale. She had to pay off what was owed on her aunt's lease, which was scheduled for renewal in early June, two months away.

Needing a distraction from her weighty thoughts, she got to her feet and headed towards the front window. Looking out, she noticed the purple-haired girl standing across the street in front of a coffee shop. The teenager was alone. Staring at her, Maggie's anger dissipated like an evaporating steam. Uncertain if she would have another chance, Maggie turned around and grabbed that blue tank top from the rack. With the garment draped across her arm, she crossed the street, approaching the girl.

The girl put her hands on her hips when Maggie halted in front of her. "What do *you* want?" the teen asked peevishly.

"Here," Maggie said, tossing the top across the girl's shoulder. "You can have this. Consider it a token of my apology for wrongly accusing you. Ever since that day, business has been terrible. Bad karma, I suppose."

Clearly speechless, the girl's arms dropped to her sides. Because of the bright mid-afternoon sun glaring down on them, she narrowed her eyes and angled her head to study Maggie's face.

Not knowing what else to say, Maggie turned and retraced her steps back to the store. She picked up a legal pad and pen resting beside the register. Instead of writing on the pad, she began to draft in her head the sale ad she might place in the local newspaper. "Glitzy Garb's Spring Sale Extravaganza," she pondered for the ad title. She considered writing something catchy, like "lowering the temperature of the store for the hot prices," but that sounded too trite. Unfortunately, no other words came to her as her thoughts shifted to her aunt. Would Aunt Loretta approve of this? Of course she wouldn't. Her aunt would have done whatever it took to keep the store open. Guilt washed over her like a wave.

The chime rang above the door as the purple-haired girl walked in cautiously with the sparkling shirt across her arm. Without looking at Maggie, the teen went over to a metal hanging rack in the middle of the store and unhooked the red cashmere cardigan from the '50s. It had pearl buttons and was in perfect shape. The girl brought it to the register. The tag said $25.

"You like sweaters?" Maggie asked, setting down the pad and pen.

"No. It's not for me," the girl said. "I'm buying it for my grandmother. It's her birthday next week. She loves cardigans. She wears them even in the summer. I'd buy her more of them if I had the money." The teen pulled out some folded bills from her pocket and counted out two 20s.

Maggie said, "Well, I have an idea. I could use some help for an upcoming sale. I'd love to pay you, but can't afford it right now. I can, though, have you work towards a sweater you'd like, or some other piece of clothing. Just let me know." If Maggie could get this girl back on her side, perhaps the others would follow. "What's your name?"

"Kendra," the girl said with a slow smile. "Maybe I could stop by tomorrow after school. And maybe I could bring my grandmother with me. She hasn't been in here in quite a while."

"Great!" Maggie said, folding the sweater and carefully putting it inside a gold paper gift bag. "I'm Maggie, by the way," she added, smiling warmly, handing Kendra her change.

Watching the teen leave, Maggie moved the pad and pen to the empty spot on the shelf under the register. She had lost interest in writing the ad, at least for a little while. Instead, her eyes wandered about the store, searching for some glitzy garb that would make a good impression on the girl and whoever else might come into the store tomorrow. Maggie's eyes zeroed in again on that checkered pink-and-silver dress on the middle rack. She walked over to get it.

*Good! Don't be afraid,* Maggie could hear her aunt say in an excited voice.

Aunt Loretta wouldn't give up on Glitzy Garb and neither would she.

# WHILE YOU CAN

On an August afternoon, she sits down on her bed, beside a faded red shoebox of old photos. Reaching into the box, she picks up the one at the top of the pile, a three-by-five taken of her fifteen years ago standing before the sparkling silver doors of A Star is Born, the dance studio in her Upstate New York hometown. Her age at the time only twenty, her eyes then brimming with naïve expectations, her bright smile fueled by the ambition to unveil her talent to the world.

A talent that never made it out of Little Falls . . .

As she brings the snapshot closer to her eyes, the sunlight pouring in from the window blinds her momentarily. Turning away, she adjusts the picture in her hand, holding it back, to avoid the glare. What she sees now accelerates her heart, her breathing, and brings back that beaming smile. It's not *her* face anymore. Rather, it's the image of the young woman living next door.

Instead of short frizzy hair and pale skin marred by car-accident scars, she has transformed into a vision of loveliness—an object of beauty! Her skin has turned smooth and swarthy; her lips have become redder, fuller. Growing rapidly, her hair hangs like flowing curtains down her back. She twists her torso fully into the light so that her wavy tresses, changing from mousy brown to black, can shine brilliantly.

No longer a housewife and mother feeling entrapped by domestic responsibilities, she's now a famous dancer who has suffered a breakdown from all of life's many pressures. She resides in this dull town in order to escape the media and her obsessed fans. When she lived in Manhattan, crowds mobbed her wherever she went. Once fully recovered, she will return to the limelight. It was never her destiny to remain in the shadows.

She is about to rub the photo against her cheek when the sound of footsteps coming down the hall distract her. Her eyes dart to the opening door. A medium-sized figure appears in the doorway—her husband—and he walks with slumped shoulders toward her.

His customary frown, growing deeper by the second, tells her that he wants to talk to her about an important matter but doesn't know how to go about it. He flops down on the edge of the bed, at the opposite end, and she eyes him up and down. Physically speaking, Brian is different from the man she married ten years ago. Having gained thirty pounds, he has settled into middle-age plumpness. Because his hairline has receded into a horseshoe shape around the sides and back of his head, he shaves what's left, preferring complete baldness. Most unsettling, his pronounced crow's-feet jump out at her, as if ready to tear at her eyes. Some days, she can tolerate Brian's embrace, pressing himself against her with his rounded belly and fleshy arms—but mostly he repulses her. They haven't made love in months.

Fearing her fantasy has ended, she gazes at the picture. Her altered image is still there. It stares back at her with such intensity that goose bumps break out along her arms. Shivering, she sets down the photo and picks up the wooden brush from her satin bedspread. Methodically, she runs it through her hair. She could brush her thick tresses for hours without losing interest.

As if determined to force reality, Brian moves closer and begins to speak. She only half hears his word: ". . . this thing with Cindy has been going on . . . ever since we started working together last year . . . but I don't want a divorce . . . because . . . I mean I still love you . . . and the kids . . . I wish I could stop . . . just can't yet. I'm so mixed up . . . Please talk to me . . . say something . . . scream at me if you want."

The words *love* and *divorce* spin around in her head. The name Cindy sounds familiar. His secretary? Another sales rep at the company? But she doesn't want to focus too much on what he's saying. She's not interested. All that matters right now is her hair. Its length, texture, and volume enthrall her.

Brian grabs her brush, tossing it aside. "Are you listening to me?" he demands, his voice firmer than she ever remembers. Roughly, he lifts her chin, looking into her eyes. "I've been trying to talk to you about me and Cindy, but you don't seem to care. You just keep brushing your hair and staring at that picture. It's like you're in a trance or something." He pauses, then asks, as if suddenly noticing, "And why in the hell are you wearing that old leotard?"

Appalled by his harshness, she scoots away and stands up. Dramatically, she uses her hands to fling back her hair, her head held high. Finding his presence unbearable, she runs out of the bedroom, down the stairs, and then out the front door. On the downward-sloping sidewalk, she slows her pace to fast walking. The air is heavy and moist, and the sun's heat blazes down on her despite the hazy sky. Sweat pours out of her forehead, down her cheeks. She wipes it away with the back of her hands.

As she passes her children, five-year-old Calvin and six-year-old Nora, playing across the street, they cry impatiently: "Mommy, we're hungry. Make us a snack before dinner! We want peanut-butter-and-banana sandwiches." To deafen and block their unnerving voices, she covers her ears. Nothing, she tells herself, will stop this process.

At the end of the next block, she shortens her stride, dropping her arms to her side. She has to catch her breath— has to calm her heart rate. Perspiration has now trickled onto her shoulders and the bodice of her leotard. It feels so strange yet exciting to revel in her imaginative powers—to leap into a new destiny. Though her head throbs wildly, she keeps it high. She is young, beautiful, and so happy.

Crossing the street, she sees people standing around in the front yards of their bungalows, playing with kids— people calling, "Hey, Betsy, Betsy, Betsy. . . Why are you dressed that way?" They wave their hands to get her attention, claiming to know her. Their minds are too limited to notice the difference. She must make them understand. So, she stops in the middle of a driveway; and, after taking a bow, she shouts, "I've become a new person! I'm just as free as Rosita—the celebrated dancer who hides out in our little town! Yes, a new person. And you're members of my audience." Using both hands, she gestures for them to come closer.

As Brian pulls up in the family sedan alongside the curb, her sense of euphoria starts to wane. She hears those damn pesky kids screaming in the back. Nevertheless, the show must go on. She walks a bit farther up the driveway, then stops. With shocked faces, her neighbors swarm in, forming a jagged square around her. She bows again, then performs a simple turn and spin, what she first learned in dance class all those years ago. Determined to distract her, hoping to deflate her spirit, Brian won't stop honking the horn, calling her name. She summons her patience to ignore him. Keeping her arms bent and raised level with her chest, eager to show a more complicated dance step, she says, "Enjoy while you can."

# ABOUT THE AUTHOR

A chronicler and dramatizer of the nature of love and human relationships, R. R. Ennis's work has appeared in a variety of local and national publications. Presently, the author is at work on a first novel.

CPSIA information can be obtained
at www.ICGtesting.com
Printed in the USA
BVOW03s0150131117
500065BV00006B/36/P